MORE

THAN

ANYTHING

MORE

THAN

ANYTHING

a love story

Natasha Anders

Montlake
Romance

Published by Montlake Romance, Seattle
www.apub.com

Amazon, the Amazon logo, and Montlake Romance are trademarks of Amazon.com, Inc., or its affiliates.

ISBN-13: 9781542091251
ISBN-10: 154209125X

Cover design by Caroline Teagle Johnson

Printed in the United States of America

In memory of my lovely auntie Vallie

Prologue

"I look like a heifer," Tina Jenson lamented, staring at her reflection in utter dismay. She turned to the side to assess her body in profile. Ugh, why did her butt have to be so huge? Why did her *everything* have to be so huge? She caught Libby's gaze in the mirror.

"You do not. You look like a movie star." The naked admiration mixed with a dash of hero worship glowing in her best friend's eyes made Tina uncomfortable. Libby had the unnerving habit of seeing a version of her that Tina wasn't sure actually existed.

"You're so pretty," Libby said, sounding a little awestruck.

"Do you really think so?" Tina wanted to believe her, but—her eyes flickered back to the mirror—she felt self-conscious with so much of her flesh on display.

"Yes," Libby replied, her voice still tinged with reverence.

Tina smiled in response to the absolute certainty in Libby's voice. Her hypercritical gaze remained glued to her own reflection. Maybe the dress wasn't as tight and short as she thought. It was red; her mother always said that redheads should never wear red. But Tina thought that the deep-ruby color contrasted nicely with her too-pale skin. If Libby's reaction was anything to go by, maybe Tina's instinct hadn't failed her after all.

Libby was so lucky—she was tall, and she had a lean athlete's body. And while the sixteen-year-old often lamented her lack in the boob department, Tina would have given anything to have a body like her best friend's. By comparison, Tina thought she looked like a baby whale. Her boobs were too big, for one thing, and there was definitely nothing athletic about her.

She had tried school netball a few years ago—figuring maybe team sports would be a fun way to get fit and fit in—but that decision had proven to be a colossal failure when none of her reluctant teammates had even acknowledged her presence during the only match she had ever played. She had stood on the court like an idiot, frantically waving her arms to indicate that she was open, while the rest of the team deliberately and maliciously ignored her. Seriously, the girls at her school had been such jerks. Tina, who had graduated from high school just a month ago, was so happy she no longer had to see those awful people on a daily basis.

That was why she and Libby got along so well: they were both social outcasts. One was a "fatty" who didn't fit in with the popular crowd, and the other came from a humble working-class family. And, of course, they had also bonded because they both seriously crushed on the Chapman twins. Tina had a thing for Harrison, and Libby used to follow Greyson around like a lost little puppy. Even though the twins were identical in appearance, their personalities were so distinct that it was pretty easy to differentiate between them. Well, it was for Libby and Tina. Everybody else always got them confused, and it made both girls feel special, knowing they were among the very few people who could tell the guys apart.

"My bum doesn't look too big in this, right?" Tina asked, pensively eyeing the body part in question.

"You have an awesome ass," Libby said, always loyal to a fault.

Not in the least bit comforted by Libby's words, Tina still worried that the dress clung to parts of her that she would much rather have kept hidden. But when they heard cars squealing up the drive seconds later, Tina determinedly set aside her anxiety, and both girls bounced, excited about the evening to come.

"I wish I could go to the party," Libby said, her words accompanied by a sigh.

"Me too." Tina nodded, trying to prevent melancholy from creeping into her voice. "I could use a friend. None of those girls ever talk to me."

"You're going to have a fabulous time. Take tons of pics, and remember every detail; you have to tell me everything later."

"Of course," Tina promised. The twins were celebrating their twentieth birthday today, and they were having a massive party at their huge family home in the affluent suburb of Constantia in Cape Town. Despite living in the same house as the twins, Libby hadn't been invited. She was too young and, because her parents worked for the Chapmans, was never really included in their group's social events. Eighteen-year-old Tina *had* received an invitation, as had her brother Smith, who was the same age as the twins. Tina knew she'd only been invited because the Jenson and Chapman families were close. Harris and Smith were best friends, and Tina had often tagged along with the twins and her brother when she was a kid. That was before the boys had hit puberty and got too cool to hang out with her, of course. Tina knew that she only got invited to the twins' events these days out of obligation.

Still, this was the chance she'd been waiting for, an opportunity to dazzle Harris with her new look. She cast another glance at her too-tight sequined dress and tried not to wince. At least her makeup and hair looked nice. The latter was upswept and elegant, with a few curly tendrils escaping to frame her face. She wore only lip gloss to make her already-pink full lips look moist and inviting and had gone for smoky eyelids to bring attention to her sea-green eyes.

She wanted Harris to see her as more than just his friend's kid sister. Wanted him to see her as a beautiful, sexy woman. After tonight he and Greyson would be going back to school, and Tina would start her gap year. Things would change. What if he met someone in the States? This could be her last chance to make him truly see her. Make him want her. And she was a mass of nerves because she wasn't sure she had done enough. But she had to try. Or he would be lost to her forever.

She smoothed her hands down the front of her short red dress, threw back her shoulders, and gave Libby a final grin before leaving to join the party upstairs.

Oh my God! Libby's not going to believe this! Tina thrilled hours later as she sat up in the rumpled bed, dragging the luxurious Egyptian cotton sheet up over her naked breasts. In fact, Tina could hardly believe it herself. The way Harris had singled her out at the party, how he had danced with her, touched her, looked at her. Like she was the prettiest girl there. He had moved her out to the quiet patio and kissed her.

Her first kiss! It had been everything she'd ever imagined. They had spent half an hour in the dark, kissing, cuddling, touching. Her, Tina Jenson, finally touching beautiful Harrison Chapman, with his perfect body and velvety skin. It had been all her dreams come true and so much more.

She sighed contentedly, staring into the darkness, as she recalled his tongue sliding over her skin and her breasts. Her overly sensitized nipples tightened at the memory. He'd led her into this room, where his touches had become more insistent, more purposeful . . . until she found herself sprawled on the bed naked, Harris hovering above her, positioned between her splayed thighs.

She remembered him asking if she was on birth control, and—feeling like a sophisticated woman of the world—she'd happily told him yes. She'd started on the pill just that morning, wishing for something like this to happen but never dreaming that it actually would.

It had hurt, of course. She had known it would. But he had been gentle and considerate. It was messier and a *lot* quicker than she'd expected, over in less than a minute. But she didn't mind. She knew that next time would be better. She smiled and glanced down into his sleeping face.

He was divine; his big muscular body was dark and powerful against the white bedding. Those broad shoulders looked like they could barely clear a normal doorframe; his sculpted chest and torso, along with his ridged abdomen, made him seem like a young Adonis. He was masculine perfection, and he wanted *her*. She lay back down, cuddling against his side and relishing the amazing warmth and wonderful scent of him. She fell asleep, happier than she could ever recall being before.

Tina didn't know how long she'd slept, but when she woke up, he wasn't there. His side of the bed still retained some of his body heat, so she knew he couldn't have been gone long. She cocked her head, listening for sounds from the bathroom. Nothing. She sat up, pushing her messy hair from her face.

"Harris?"

Silence.

She got out of bed and found her clothing scattered all over the floor. She couldn't find one of her earrings, and both of her shoes were missing. After searching impatiently for a few moments, she gave up on both the earring and her shoes and decided to walk out on her bare feet. She wasn't particularly concerned—she would find them later—but the earrings were a graduation gift from her oldest brother, Conrad, and she would hate to lose one. Maybe Harris would help her search for it. But right now she was eager to see him again.

She left the room; it was quiet upstairs, but she could hear the thumping music downstairs, which meant the party was still going strong. She was confidently walking toward the landing, ready to face the crowds again, when she heard masculine voices and laughter. She had been in this house enough times to know that it was coming from Mr. Chapman's study, which was situated in the room closest to the landing. The man would probably shit the proverbial brick if he knew that any of the partygoers had breached his sanctum. Wanting to keep the twins out of trouble, Tina decided she'd better usher the stray partygoers out of the room before they did any damage.

The door was ajar, and she was about to push it open when she heard her name and paused.

"Man, I can't believe you fucked Tina Jenson," the male voice said with an incredulous laugh. She recognized it as Jonah Spade's voice. She had never liked him; he was a misogynist who treated women like they were disposable. Tina shifted so that she could see into the room and spotted Harris sprawled on his father's leather sofa, one of the older man's expensive Cuban cigars clenched between his even white teeth. He was barefoot and wore only his faded jeans, with his pale-blue shirt unbuttoned, leaving his magnificent chest on display. He didn't say anything in response to Jonah's comment, merely grunting as he lit the cigar.

"Fuck, I don't know if it was worth it, dude. No amount of money could entice me to touch *that* with a ten-foot pole." This gem came from Schaeffer Higgins, another elite asshole. Tina's heart dropped as his words sank in, and her trembling hand lifted to her mouth as the implication hit her.

Her eyes scanned the rest of the room. There were three other guys present. None of them the kind of people she would consider nice. In fact, she wasn't sure why Harris was even with them—they weren't his usual crowd. There was no sign of Smith or Greyson or any of his regular cohorts.

"How did you manage not to puke after fucking that fat freak, Harris? Was it like sticking your dick into a marshmallow?" Jonah asked.

"Soft and gooey, right?" Schaeffer chuckled.

"Soft," Harris said, his voice almost absent as he stared at the lit tip of his cigar. The other guys brayed with laughter, and Tina felt the first scalding tears hit her cheeks.

"Here's your money, bro—you fucking earned it!" One of the guys tossed a note at Harris, and he stared down at it like it was something completely unrecognizable.

"Whaaa . . . ," he began to say, his voice sounding thick and slurred. God, he was completely wasted. How had she not seen that before? He had seemed so lucid earlier. Could he have gotten this drunk since leaving her asleep in the room? She doubted it.

This explained why he had approached her in the first place. She had been so naive and stupid to believe he could have been stone-cold sober and still want *her*. She should have known the entire "romantic" encounter had been too good to be true. The only way Harrison Chapman would ever want Tina Jenson was if he were drunk or high out of his mind.

That seemed about right.

Tina felt used and cheap and so, so humiliated. Her heart shattered into a million pieces, and she mourned the loss of the boy she had idolized. A boy she now knew had never really existed.

The guys bantered back and forth a little longer, all expressing varying degrees of disgust that Harris had had sex with her. Harris himself said very little, his focus still on his cigar. Tina tried to tear herself away, but it felt like her feet were made of lead. She could only stand there punishing herself by listening to their vile garbage. When she realized that they were heading toward the door, she finally forced herself into action and fled, hiding in one of the bedrooms while she listened to them laughingly make their way down the stairs. She waited until she was sure they were all gone and then crept out of the room like a thief.

The study door was wide open. As she once again attempted to pass the room, a slight movement in her peripheral vision snagged her notice. She stopped without thinking, her attention shifting fully to the room, and she was horrified to meet Harris's slightly unfocused gaze. He was still sprawled on the sofa with the cigar caught between his cruelly beautiful lips. Those lips curved upward at the corners when—after a mortifying moment that lacked anything resembling recognition in his gaze—he finally seemed to figure out who he was looking at.

"Heeeeey," he said around the cigar, drawing out the syllable in a way that only confirmed that he was under the influence of something. She hadn't tasted or smelled much alcohol when they had kissed and stuff earlier, so that left some kind of narcotic. Harris had been known to take a puff of something recreational now and then but never enough to impair him this much. And as far as Tina knew, he'd stopped indulging after his eighteenth birthday. All things considered, Harris and Greyson were usually pretty good representatives of clean and healthy living.

Harris pushed himself clumsily to his feet and, after a slight stumble, walked toward her without his usual predatory grace, coming to a standstill directly in front of her. He swayed slightly before lifting his hand and cupping her jaw with casual tenderness, not noticing—or, more likely, not caring—when she flinched away from his touch. He dragged his thumb over her lower lip and kept his eyes intently focused on her mouth.

"Soft." The word was a gravelly purr. His eyelids drooped, and Tina watched, transfixed, as he lifted his other hand to remove the cigar from his mouth before leaning in as if to kiss her.

Uh-uh!

She stepped back just before his mouth descended, and he staggered, wrong-footed by her move.

"C'mon, Tina, let me taste you again," he crooned.

"Why? Do you have more money riding on it?"

He looked mystified by her question, and she made a rude sound in the back of her throat at his show of ignorance. She shoved him, her flattened palms against his hard chest, and he stumbled, reinforcing her belief that he must be on something. She wouldn't have been able to budge him if he were sober. And now she tortured herself by wondering if he'd taken whatever it was *after* he'd made his disgusting bet. Something to help him blur out the reality of touching her and kissing her. "Don't you *ever* come near me again!"

"What the fuck?" He sounded completely outraged by her command, and she swallowed back the hysterical burble of laughter that threatened to escape. It was one of the many bizarre coping mechanisms she'd come up with to make her life a little more bearable. Laughter in place of tears. But if something hurt enough, the laughter would eventually dissolve into tears, so it wasn't a very effective stratagem. "What's your problem? You were keen enough an hour ago."

"That was before," she snapped, and he blinked, looking confused. "Before I realized I was the evening's entertainment. Did you and your buddies have a good laugh at my expense? The pathetic loser who thought she could mean something to someone like you?"

"You're hysterical." He dismissed her in that horribly casual way some guys had when it came to women and their opinions. It pissed her off. She was humiliated, angry, and *very* hurt, and hearing him disparage all that as hysteria pushed her over a precipice she hadn't even recognized was looming right in front of her.

She balled her hand into a fist, hauled back, and completely shocked herself by punching him. He was leaning toward her, which was the only reason she managed to hit her target with such devastating accuracy. Pain shot up through her fingers and reverberated all the way up her arm. Her cry of agony mingled with his, and she couldn't be sure if the crunch she'd felt was his nose or her knuckles. He reeled back and lost his footing entirely, landing on his butt, with his hand cupped protectively over his nose. There was blood. A lot of it. And that—along with the uncharacteristic violence of her action—made her feel sick to her stomach. Her hand throbbed, and she cradled it against her chest, lifting her left hand over her mouth to force back the nausea.

"You broke my nose!" he exclaimed furiously, blood dripping down over his mouth and jaw. Tina gagged at the sight of it and fought valiantly to keep her stomach contents down.

"If I never see you again, it'll be too soon, Harris," she said, her voice quiet. "What you did was despicable, and I . . . I hate you for it."

"Tina." Just her name. She didn't know what to make of it. Especially when he'd said it in that quiet, regretful voice.

She shook her head, her sight blurring as she backed out of the room. He didn't move, merely watching her, blood staining the fabric of his shirt and trousers.

Harris blurrily watched Tina leave—he was having a hard time focusing. He didn't know what was wrong with him. All he knew was that Tina was mad at him; she had shouted at him, hit him. He frowned, the last thought distracting him as he lifted his hand from his nose and stared at the blood on his palm in fascination. He could feel the liquid warmth dripping onto his bare chest.

Why was his shirt undone? Where were his shoes? That's when he remembered . . .

Tina . . . they had made love. He smiled at the memory . . . and then winced when the movement of his lips sent a shaft of pain stabbing through his nose and straight into his brain.

His nose was broken.

Something was wrong. He couldn't quite figure out what. He was hurt. And he was confused, and something had happened. With Tina.

She had looked so beautiful tonight. Her dress had been shiny and pretty, like gift wrapping. He had wanted to unwrap her and keep her as his own.

He *had* unwrapped her. Unwrapped all that pretty perfection.

He blinked. Why was everything so blurry and out of focus? What was wrong with him?

His last thought before he passed out was that Tina was angry with him. And he needed to find her and make things right.

Chapter One

Present Day

In a family filled with overachieving, beautiful people, Tina was the Disappointment. Her parents had often lamented, out loud and right in front of her, how very much Tina's lack of ambition and talent in any field whatsoever distressed them. Tina had come to dread all family functions, because every comment aimed at her tended to start, "Do you know what your problem is, Martine?"

Tonight was a prime example—family dinner—with Tina's perfect siblings and their significant others all present and accounted for. Conrad, the thoracic surgeon, along with his wholesome and thoroughly pleasant and pregnant wife, Kitty. Kyle, the CEO of Jenson Pharmaceuticals, the family company . . . there with his husband, the always impeccably groomed and eminently likable Dumisane Jenson-Sechaba. And, finally, Smith, the youngest of her three older brothers, a disgustingly successful corporate attorney. He was there with his current lady friend, Milla, a chemical engineer.

And then there was Tina, chronically single and working at a library. Part time. One could argue that because of the substantial inheritance she'd received from her paternal grandfather, she didn't really need to work—none of them did—but that would be frowned upon by their parents.

"Jensons earn their lifestyle." The words were practically the family motto. Drilled into them since birth. None of this idle-rich business that so many of their social peers embraced with open arms.

"We're looking to hire a new hospital administrator," Conrad was saying, and Tina tried not to roll her eyes. "You should interview, Martine."

Seriously? She hadn't even finished college. Her brothers often seemed to conveniently forget how unqualified she was to do any of the jobs they kept suggesting she interview for. She frequently wondered if these "lapses" in memory were subtle jabs at her lack of further education.

She sighed and tossed Conrad a glare before shifting her attention back to her chocolate mousse. She attacked it with single-minded focus, relishing the rich taste of the chocolate. So comforting. So familiar.

"Martine." Her parents never called her Tina. With the exception of Smith, none of her family did. "You don't mean to finish that entire dessert, do you?" Her mother's sharp and unwelcome voice intruded into her private chocolate "me time" and jarred Tina out of her happy place.

Her gaze shifted toward the older woman, and she could see how thoroughly repulsed her mother looked at the notion of Tina finishing the substantially sized mousse.

Aaaaaand there it was! As if by clockwork, the *other* disappointment reared its ugly head . . .

Their only daughter wasn't the perfect, svelte, gorgeous creature she should have been. That any child of Mercy and Patrick Jenson had turned out less than physically flawless could only be attributed to the mystery and horror of throwback genetics. Tina was short and overweight with pale, freckled skin and a shock of bright-red hair. Not tall, willowy, blonde, and absolutely gorgeous like her mother, brothers, and father. The cuckoo in the nest. The odd one out.

Physically lacking, intellectually ordinary, and, of course, the maker of huge, embarrassing, reputation-ruining, and life-altering mistakes.

Tina would never, in a million years, live up to family expectations. And she had stopped trying years ago. That didn't mean that these family gatherings didn't bother her, not when she always felt like a complete outsider.

She pushed her mousse aside, and her mother nodded in satisfaction.

"I'll think about the interview," she promised Conrad, intending to do no such thing. But sometimes, pretending compliance was the only way to get them off her back.

"I'll text you the details tomorrow," Conrad said with a warm smile, and Tina returned it with a tight one of her own.

"So Dumi and I have news," Kyle suddenly announced, thankfully diverting the attention from Tina. She cast one last regretful look at her mousse before focusing her attention on her middle brother and his beaming husband. "We've thought about this for a while, and with Dumi now running his IT business remotely and spending more time at home . . . we've decided that it's the perfect time for us to adopt a baby."

There were delighted squeals from everybody, and Tina smiled, genuinely happy for her brother and Dumi despite the hollow, painful thudding of her heart in her chest.

Another baby. Kitty was due in three months, Libby—still Tina's best friend after all these years—was likely to pop at any moment, and now this. She would soon encounter babies in every corner. They'd be inescapable.

The thought made her feel physically ill. She was happy for her brothers, happy for her friend . . . but all those babies. She wasn't sure she was emotionally equipped to be around them. Not yet. Possibly not ever.

She listened to the excited voices ebb and flow around her. Kyle and Dumi had already started the adoption process and were on a waiting list. Possible baby names were being bandied around the table, nursery ideas, schooling . . .

Tina smiled through it all, never venturing an opinion. As always, feeling like a stranger looking in. The disconnect was even more jarring than usual tonight—all she could think about was leaving. Escaping. She didn't belong here. Not with these people, who had so many conditions attached to their love for her.

She wanted out. Away.

Her phone buzzed, and she glanced at the screen and suddenly had the excuse she needed. Even if it wasn't the one she wanted.

"I have to go," she announced abruptly. Her gaze glued to her phone screen. The animated chatter stopped, and all eyes fixed on her. Noticing the abrupt silence, she looked up and realized that everyone was staring at her.

"I'm sorry," she said, holding up her phone. "Libby is in labor. Greyson is still en route from Australia. She needs me."

"Of course," her mother said without hesitation. "You should go."

Appearances above all else. Olivia Chapman was Tina's best friend. But more importantly, she was now wife to the CEO of the Chapman Global Property Group. Daughter-in-law to Tina's parents' closest friends. Even if everybody was still a little horrified that Greyson Chapman had gone and married the Chapman cook's daughter, appearances had to be upheld. If Olivia Chapman was in the process of birthing an heir to the vast Chapman fortune, then of course Tina would have to be there to support her friend. No matter that her parents had never really approved of the friendship when Tina and Libby were kids.

Tina said a hasty goodbye and left. The drive to the hospital was rushed, and she slammed her way into the building a mere ten minutes later. She found the Chapmans and Libby's parents, the Lawsons, very quickly. The two older couples sat in strained silence. Now retired, Stella and Roland Lawson had both worked for the Chapmans for nearly thirty years, as cook and driver, respectively. Their only daughter, Libby, had grown up in the live-in staff's quarters and, despite the four-year age gap, had played with the Chapman twins when they were all children.

The Chapmans had subsidized Libby's education, and she had gone to the same private school as Tina and the twins.

But none of them had ever foreseen Libby and Greyson getting married years down the line. It had shocked even Tina, and Libby had been her best friend since she was fifteen and Libby thirteen.

"Any news?" she asked the room in general, and Mrs. Lawson smiled and shook her head.

"Nothing yet. She's been in there for about five hours already," the lovely older woman said. She and Libby were very similar in appearance: tall, willowy, and graceful, with thick, wavy black hair—the older woman's liberally sprinkled with salt—and beautiful light-brown eyes. Their flawless golden-brown skin a testament to their multiracial ancestry.

"Is Greyson back from Perth yet?" Tina asked.

"His plane will be landing soon," Mr. Lawson volunteered, after another strained silence during which neither Chapman bothered to respond to Tina's question. She smiled at the handsome man—also multiracial, like so many of Cape Town's population—with his gray temples and distinguished demeanor. Tina had always liked Libby's parents; they were warm, welcoming people who had gone out of their way to make Tina feel like part of their family. Of course, her parents would be appalled to know exactly how much time she'd spent with Libby in the private family quarters the Chapmans had allocated to their married cook and driver. But Libby's small, cozy home had felt more like Tina's than the sprawling Jenson family mansion.

"Is Libby alone?" Tina asked, horrified by that thought.

"Harris is with her." Constance Chapman spoke for the first time; she didn't sound completely approving, and in this case, Tina whole-heartedly echoed that sentiment. Why the hell was Harris with her? Why not her mother?

Harris had sent Tina the text from Libby's phone earlier as well. It hadn't seemed that strange at first, but now that she thought about it, she wondered why he was taking point on this. She was considering going in there to relieve him of his birthing-coach duties when the man in question slammed into the room wearing scrubs and a huge grin on his too-damned-handsome face.

"It's a girl," he announced, and Mr. and Mrs. Lawson exclaimed in delight. Even the Chapmans broke into grins, which was unexpected and kind of sweet. Especially when the older couples embraced spontaneously before remembering themselves and going back to their former awkwardness. "Libby's exhausted but fine, and baby girl Chapman will shortly be in the nursery for your viewing pleasure."

The older couples filed out, and Tina had moved to follow when Harris's bulk blocked her way.

"Tina," he said in greeting, his voice terse, all the earlier joviality gone.

"Harrison." She didn't make eye contact, merely attempted to side-step and go around him, but his step was in sync with hers, and they did that awkward little "oops, same direction" shuffle for a couple of seconds before he laughed in exasperation and stopped moving. This time she allowed her eyes to travel up that broad chest, along the strong column of his throat, before darting past that blue-tinged, stubbled jaw, the sensuous mouth and slightly crooked nose. She still vividly remembered the painful crunch of her bones against the cartilage of his nose. She had broken her knuckles breaking that nose . . .

Finally, her eyes met his dark-blue stare, and she was startled to see him doing a similar inspection of her body and face.

"When did you get here?" he asked, his voice hoarse.

"About five minutes ago." Her voice wasn't hoarse, but her throat felt parched.

"You made good time."

"I broke a few speed limits along the way." Why were they having this inane discussion? They rarely indulged in casual conversation.

Then again, they never had the opportunity to talk, not when—despite his best efforts to the contrary—she tried to avoid him like the plague. She could very happily go through her entire life without ever having to speak with him again.

"You look nice," he said, and she blinked at him. Blinked some more and then shook her head blankly.

The *hell* . . . ?

"I think I'll go see Libby now," she said, glad that she probably didn't sound as freaked out as she felt. She sidestepped him, deliberately giving him a wide berth so as to avoid accidentally brushing against him.

"Tina . . ."

She stopped and turned to face him. He looked uncertain, and that was enough to make her pause. She couldn't recall ever seeing him uncertain before.

He offered her a tiny smile. Nothing remotely like his usual cocky grin. "Would you like to grab a coffee with me? After you've visited with Libby."

Would she?

Hell no! Not in a million lifetimes.

"No. Thank you." She kept her voice scrupulously polite, and his smile wavered slightly.

"Right. Next time maybe."

"I doubt it."

His brow furrowed, and he cleared his throat. He looked like he was about to speak again, but Tina beat a hasty retreat. She and Harris Chapman did not do amicable. And they never would.

"Greyson?" Libby's groggy voice called out when Tina pushed her way into her friend's lavish private room. Libby sounded so hopeful, and Tina hated to be the one to dash that hope.

"It's just me," she said apologetically as she stepped fully into the room. Her friend, who had pushed herself up into a half-seated position, lay back down with a despairing little sigh.

"He's on his way," Tina assured her. "His plane just landed."

"I begged him not to leave. I told him the baby was due any day. I think—" She bit off whatever she'd been about to say and shook her head. "It's nothing. It doesn't matter what I think. He's a busy man. I knew that when I married him. Have you seen her yet?"

"I thought I'd pop in and see my bestie first. The baby has her grandparents and uncle fawning over her right now; she doesn't need me."

"She's so beautiful."

"Of course she is—with such disgustingly attractive parents, she was bound to be a looker." Although Tina was living proof that outstanding parental genes didn't always guarantee good looks. She shook her head, disgusted with her private little pity party for one. For the most part, Tina was happy with her appearance—she liked her curly, shoulder-length red hair and her sun-loathing skin with its millions of freckles. It had taken years for her to get to the point of self-acceptance, so to find herself even thinking about these things not just once but twice in the same night was a little disconcerting. Seeing Harris after so long didn't help either. He always reminded her of the dumb, insecure girl she had once been. It was one of the many good reasons she actively avoided the man.

"What will you name her?" Tina asked, determined to shove away her unease after her encounter with Harris. He no longer influenced any part of her life, and he certainly didn't possess the power to hurt her. Not ever again.

"I have a few ideas, but I wanted to discuss them with Greyson first. He's bound to have an opinion." Libby smiled, but the movement of her lips looked stiff and unnatural.

"Of course," Tina said, keeping her voice soft and reassuring. Libby looked fragile, like the slightest harsh word would physically tear her apart. Tina cursed Greyson for his negligence and disinterest. He had never seemed fully onboard with Libby's pregnancy. Had missed every single one of her OB-GYN appointments; Tina had accompanied her friend to those. She had gone shopping for baby things with Libby, had bounced nursery ideas back and forth with her friend. Greyson hadn't been present for any of that.

And worse, when Libby had fallen early in her third trimester and had feared a possible miscarriage, her husband's phone had been off, and he'd been unreachable. True to Chapman form, Greyson was an absolute asshole. What Libby saw in the man was beyond Tina.

"How was family dinner tonight?" Libby asked, and Tina smiled. How like her friend to remember—even after going through labor— that the Jensons had had their bimonthly family dinner. It spoke volumes about the type of person she was. Sweet and caring. A much better friend than Tina deserved.

"Same old same old. Conrad thinks I should interview for the hospital administrator position that just opened up at his clinic . . ." Tina grinned when Libby snorted in amusement at that. "I know, right? Oh, and this just in—the perfect couple are going to adopt the perfect child to complete their perfect life." Another snort from Libby: she clearly knew exactly to whom Tina was referring. "Milla still has a stick shoved up her ass. Smith spent all evening trying to convince me to consider dyeing my hair a 'more serious' color. Auburn maybe."

Libby laughed outright at that.

"Your brothers are buttholes."

"I'm well aware of that," Tina said with a laugh. "Fortunately, I don't have to see them again for another two weeks."

Libby started to respond to that but was interrupted when her parents and in-laws all came streaming into the room. Harris trailed in after them; his hands were shoved into his pockets, and he wore a lazy smile on his sensuous lips.

Right. Time to get out of here. Too much Harrison Chapman in one day could well lead to nightmares.

Tina dropped a kiss on Libby's cheek. "I think it's time to visit Baby Chapman. See you again soon, okay?"

Her friend nodded, and Tina left hastily.

She was halfway down the hall before she became aware of the presence just behind her. The familiar scent of him wafted toward her. He hadn't changed his brand of aftershave since he was twenty. That warm, woodsy fragrance too often wove its way, without prejudice or preference, through her most erotic dreams as well as her most horrific nightmares.

She stopped walking and turned to face him.

"Why are you following me?" she asked on a fierce whisper, and he frowned.

"I'm not. I'm headed to the nursery, same as you."

"You've already been."

"There's no limit on how many times I can see my niece," he pointed out, his voice frustratingly calm. She inhaled sharply and shook her head before turning and resuming her walk. This time he fell into step beside her and shortened his stride to keep pace with her.

Tina ignored him. He didn't push for conversation, and that unsettled her even further.

When she finally got to the nursery, she stopped at the huge viewing area and perused the bassinets of snugly wrapped little bundles.

"Third row from the top, far left." Harris bent down to drop the information directly into her ear, and she jumped when she felt his warm breath on her skin. He was a hair shy of six foot one and had to bend almost in half to get to the five-foot-two Tina's ear. She took a deliberate step to the side, putting as much space between them as she could, before scanning the babies again and focusing on the one he had pointed out. A nurse gently lifted the infant from her bassinet and brought her to the window for Tina to see. The baby was fast asleep, one tiny fist curled up against her chubby cheek while her mouth made little suckling motions.

Tina swallowed past the lump in her throat and felt her eyes burn with tears. She lifted a hand to her chest, trying to still the frantic thudding of her heart.

"Oh my God, she's so beautiful," she whispered, her voice wobbling alarmingly.

"That she is." The deep masculine voice rumbled in agreement, and she jumped again.

Harris.

She couldn't let him see her like this. She couldn't be in his presence when she felt so utterly vulnerable.

"I have to go," she said abruptly, before turning unsteadily and walking away.

"Tina. Hey! Are you okay?" he called after her, concern deepening his voice even further. She ignored him and picked up her pace, her eyes fixed on the elevator, mere steps away. It was her safe haven. An escape from Harrison Chapman's crushing presence. From the memories that being around him evoked. Memories bubbling away much too close to the surface.

The elevator doors slid open before she could even push the button, and she rudely elbowed her way past a couple of exiting doctors and a woman clutching a huge bouquet of flowers. She turned once she was safely inside and leaned against the back of the elevator, her eyes immediately catching Harris's concerned gaze. She couldn't look away, a deer helplessly trapped in the headlights, and she tensed when he took a step in her direction. She breathed a shuddering sigh of relief when the doors slid shut, severing the intense connection between them.

She was shaking uncontrollably, close to hyperventilating, and she wrapped her arms around her torso in an attempt to give herself some comfort. It was a trick she'd learned as a child; her parents weren't big huggers, and her boisterous brothers hadn't been very affectionate either. They had lived to torment and tease their only sister. So Tina had learned to hug herself. The gesture had soothed the lonely little girl she had once been, but the woman she had become found little solace within her own tightly wrapped arms.

Some pain was just too huge to be self-soothed away.

When she finally got home to her neat little one-bedroom flat in Cape Town's picturesque Bantry Bay, she collapsed onto the comfy sofa and stared blindly down at where she knew the stormy ocean was. It was dark, and all she could currently see were the whitecaps of the waves and the lights from cars, streetlamps, and homes.

She had bought this flat five years ago, on her twenty-third birthday, dipping into the inheritance from her granddad. Her parents hadn't approved, of course. They would have preferred she stay with them, where they could monitor her every move, control her comings and goings, and attempt to influence her decisions. Buying this cozy oceanfront flat had been Tina's way of asserting her independence.

She practiced a series of deep-breathing exercises her therapist— back when she had still seen one regularly—had taught her. Fighting back the panic attack that threatened to overwhelm her.

"Don't think about it," she whispered urgently. "Don't. Don't. Don't . . ."

But the memories were there, battering away at her skull, fighting to surface . . . the bet, the awful words, the difficult months that had followed. The heartbreak and disappointment she had suffered for so long after that one moment in time had all but ruined her life and completely shattered her self-esteem. She lifted her feet to the sofa, wrapped her arms around her legs, and buried her face in her knees. Sometimes, it was best to let the memories come. Cathartic almost. Maybe that would be the case this time.

Her phone buzzed, and Tina jumped, still so caught up in the past that it took her a moment to adjust to the present. Her face was wet with tears, and she impatiently scrubbed her palms over her face.

"Get it together, Tina," she muttered. "You're stronger than this."

She looked down at her ringing phone. It was Libby. Tina's brow furrowed as she wondered why her friend was calling so late.

"Hey, Libby?" she answered cautiously.

"Tina? I need you. Please can you come back? It's urgent."

"On my way," Tina promised without a moment's hesitation, already up and heading for the door even as she said the words.

Chapter Two

"He actually *said* that?" Tina asked her distraught friend in disbelief, not quite able to process Libby's words. The younger woman was a mess, her face swollen and wet from all the tears she had shed. Her eyes were bloodshot and red rimmed. A far cry from the exhausted but glowing woman Tina had left just hours ago.

"Yes. I have to get out of here, Tina. You have to help me."

"Of course, but . . ." She shook her head, not sure what to say.

"No buts," Libby interjected angrily. "My husband just told me he doesn't believe that our baby is his. There are no buts here. I'm leaving him."

"That goes without saying," Tina said soothingly. "But I'm not sure you can leave the hospital just yet."

"I can. Both Clara and I are healthy enough to leave."

"Clara?" Tina asked, her eyebrows rising.

"Yes. I've decided to name her Clara." There was a defiant tone in Libby's voice, and Tina knew why. Harris and Greyson had once had a nanny/tutor named Clara. Both of them had absolutely despised the woman. This was Libby's way of sticking it to Greyson.

"It's a pretty name," Tina said truthfully, and Libby sagged back onto the bed, looking exhausted and heartbroken.

"Look, I'll make a deal with you," Tina said quietly, reaching out to take one of Libby's hands into hers. "Spend the night in hospital, and I'll take you anywhere you want to go tomorrow, okay? It's best for both you *and* Clara."

Libby lifted her free hand to cover her eyes and sobbed, tears seeping from beneath her palm and running down the sides of her face, to soak the cushion beneath her head.

"I don't understand why he's being so cruel."

Tina said nothing, merely squeezing Libby's hand comfortingly. Greyson had always been a bit of a cold fish. Harris was the passionate, impetuous one. Greyson was cool, calculating, and always distant. Tina could very easily see him renouncing his own baby if he truly believed he was sterile. What a complete prick. Seriously.

Any other man would probably have double-checked that he was indeed firing blanks before burning his bridges so definitively.

"We'll get you discharged first thing in the morning, okay? It's nearly midnight now anyway, and I'm sure they're going to kick me out soon." The hospital had flexible visiting hours, but Tina was certain that visiting this late was pushing it a bit. "Do you need anything before I leave?"

Libby shook her head, her shoulders shaking with silent sobs.

"Oh, Libby," Tina whispered, her heart breaking for her friend. "I wish I could make this go away, I honestly do. Do you want me to speak with Greyson? See where his head is at?" Tina tended to avoid both Chapman brothers; Greyson was hard to communicate with, unapproachable, and surly, so Tina offering to speak with him was a big deal. And Libby surely knew that. Libby moved her hand from her eyes and met Tina's gaze.

"No. It's fine. Harris has already said he was going to speak with him about this. Against my wishes, I might add. He's trying to fix it. It can't be fixed. I won't forgive Greyson for this."

"Prick," Tina muttered beneath her breath, not sure if she was referencing Greyson or Harris. Not that it mattered. The word applied to both men. "I'll pick you up first thing in the morning, okay? You'll stay with me. Unless . . . I mean, do you want to stay with your parents?"

Libby shook her head, more tears spilling over onto her wet cheeks.

"No. I can't. Their flat was bought and paid for by the Chapmans. I don't want anything to do with that family or their money right now."

"Of course."

"I mean, my parents earned their retirement gifts, and I'm happy for them. But . . . I don't want to feel beholden to the Chapmans. I can take care of myself and my child. I don't need anything the Chapmans have to offer." Libby's voice, strained and nasally with tears, held a firm note of defiance and anger.

"I get it," Tina soothed. "You can stay with me until we figure out the rest, okay?"

"I need Clara's things," Libby suddenly wailed, clearly at the end of her tether.

"Don't worry about that. I'll take care of it," Tina promised grimly.

"Chapman." The curt masculine voice at the other end of the line caused a shudder of something unidentifiable to run down Tina's spine. She sucked in a deep breath before letting it out slowly, in an attempt to compose herself before speaking.

"Harris? It's Tina," she said in her most no-nonsense voice, and the long silence that greeted that proclamation was unnerving.

"It's nearly one in the morning," he finally said, his voice frustratingly neutral. She couldn't gauge his response to this unprecedented call from her.

"I didn't have your number, and Smith took forever to get back to me with it," she explained. "I'm sorry if I woke you."

"You didn't wake me."

"Disturbed you, then," she said, imagining a perfect, beautifully rumpled, and disgruntled bed partner sitting up beside him.

"You didn't disturb me either." His voice was still completely emotionless. "What do you need?"

"Some stuff for the baby," Tina said without further preamble, and there was another long pause.

"Don't get involved, Tina," he warned, his voice taking on a dangerous edge.

"Too late."

"Let them figure it out."

"Libby needs space to do that. Look, she and the baby won't be far. They'll stay with me for a while. I think it's only fair to give her some breathing room. After all, her asshole of a husband just dumped a world of hurt on her."

"Yeah, I know." Something in his voice made her pause: a vulnerability that shocked her. She nearly asked if he was all right but quickly thought better of it. "Look, she can stay with me. I have plenty of space, and she's family."

"No offense, Harris, but staying with a man who looks exactly like the bastard who hurt her won't really help matters."

"She knows we're not the same man," Harris said. Finally she'd provoked an emotion from him; he sounded completely affronted.

"She doesn't even want to stay with her parents because *your* parents paid for their flat. She doesn't want anything to do with the Chapmans right now; just respect that, will you?"

"And yet, she's just given birth to one."

"Not according to your brother."

"It's none of your business," he muttered.

"Libby is like a sister to me, and she's asked me to help her, so that makes it my business. She needs someone in her corner."

"*I'm* in her corner!" His voice was thick with frustration, and Tina felt a surge of spiteful gratification at that response.

"Look, can you help me get the baby's stuff or not? I'd rather not deal directly with Greyson. Not right now. I value my freedom, and if I do to him what I long to do, I'll get locked up for years."

He surprised her with a rusty chuckle in response to her words.

"I know better than most how capable you are of following up on that threat," he said, his voice brimming with dark amusement. It was the first time he'd ever referenced the fact that she'd once broken his nose, and it threw her a bit. She really didn't want to be reminded of that right now. Not so soon after her little wallow down memory lane just hours ago. When she didn't respond to his words, he cleared his throat awkwardly before speaking again, this time all traces of amusement gone from his voice. "Text me a list of what you need. I'll get it for you."

"I need it tonight," she said, and he sighed.

"Fine!"

"I'll text the list soon." She disconnected the call before he could respond and started trembling, bone-deep shivers that seemed to rattle her teeth and shake her to the very core. She wasn't sure she was ready for this, having an infant right there in her space. But her friend needed her, and Tina had to set aside her own neuroses and be there for Libby.

The buzz she'd been dreading came just after three thirty. She didn't know how she would cope with Harris's presence in her small flat. This place was her sanctum, and it was about to be forever sullied by his unwelcome but necessary intrusion. She threw back her shoulders and reluctantly depressed the button on the intercom.

"Yes?" Her voice sounded hoarse and nervous.

"It's me."

She swallowed, tempted to be contrary and ask for clarification, but she knew that would be unnecessarily petty. His voice was unmistakable. She buzzed him in and then cast a quick glance around the pristine flat that she had unnecessarily been scouring from top to bottom for the last two and a half hours.

She swung open her door and nervously waited in the corridor, watching the stairs—there was no elevator—anxiously. It didn't occur to her to go down and meet him, and only when he finally reached the third floor where her flat was did it register that he probably needed help carrying everything.

He was overloaded with bags. He had one slung over each shoulder and one clutched in each hand.

"Are those all baby things?" Tina asked, a little shocked. The list she had sent him after consulting Libby hadn't seemed very long.

"I figured Libby would need some stuff too."

"You went through her clothing?" She didn't know why, but the thought was disturbing.

"Of course not. I made Greyson do it."

He *made* Greyson do it? As far as Tina could tell, nobody *made* Greyson Chapman do anything, not even his twin. So the words were a little unexpected, to say the least.

"And he was okay with that?"

"He knows he has fucked up." Harris shrugged before lifting a hand and gesturing toward her door. "Look, do you mind if I drop these inside? There's more stuff downstairs."

Tina longed to ask for specifics about Greyson, but after a moment's hesitation, she let it go and focused on the rest of his words.

"More?"

"Yeah, the car seat and bassinet and shit."

"Of course," she said, opening the door and stepping aside to allow him entry. He paused just on the other side of the threshold and gave the interior of her flat a quick once-over.

"This is nice. Cozy." By *cozy*, Tina knew that he meant *small*. She knew a man like Harris Chapman would never be caught dead in a place like this under normal circumstances. A flat in Bantry Bay was a luxury few could afford to rent, much less own. But to Harris, Tina knew her flat had to seem extremely small and dingy.

"I like it," she said defensively, and he sent her a wry look before advancing farther into her home to drop the bags on the sofa.

"I do too," he said, and she hated the mellow warmth the sincerity in his voice sent flowing through her.

"I don't care," she said, as much for her sake as his. She couldn't afford to care what Harris thought about any aspect of her life. Not again.

He slanted her an inscrutable look before heading back to the front door.

"I'll get the rest of the stuff."

"Do you need a hand?" she asked reluctantly.

"That would be appreciated."

She followed him mutely and shut the door quietly behind her, mindful of the fact that it was the middle of the night and her neighbors were asleep. She was sure her midnight cleaning spree had already set a few teeth on edge; she didn't want to slip even further out of their good graces by making an unnecessary amount of noise in the echoey stairwell.

She had work in the morning but would probably have to call in sick, because between having to pick up Libby and Clara, getting them settled in, and her complete lack of sleep tonight, she didn't think she'd be able to concentrate on much in the morning.

She was surprised to see the huge 4X4 parked in front of the building. She was so used to seeing Harris in some sleek, racy sports car that it had never occurred to her that he'd show up in something like this. But, of course, it was the practical choice under these circumstances.

"What's wrong?" Harris asked, seeming to notice her hesitation.

"Uh, nothing. I was just a bit taken aback by the car. It's silly, but I was expecting the Maserati."

"I don't have just *one* car, you know," he said in the same way someone else would say, "I don't have just one pair of socks," like it was something completely normal to have two or more cars. Tina understood his world: she came from that same world and visited it frequently, but she'd been living outside of it for long enough to find such innate snobbery grating.

Tina had just *one* car. A perfectly nice Lexus. Like her flat, it hadn't come cheap, but it didn't scream extreme wealth either. Tina didn't deny her background—she wasn't ashamed of it—but she was grounded enough not to think herself above the rest of the population.

She shook herself and gestured toward the car.

"Let's get this over with," she said impatiently, and he sighed roughly before nodding.

"Right." The word was curt, and he opened the back door, bending over the seat and affording Tina an eyeful of his *very* nice butt in the well-worn jeans he was wearing. Damn the man for being so good looking. He had only improved over the last ten years. The surly handsomeness of his teens and early twenties had weathered into rugged gorgeousness that made him look a little more mature than his thirty years. He had grown bigger and broader, the lean athleticism of his youth hardening into a body akin to that of a seasoned street fighter. The slightly off-center nose that she had given him only served to enhance his masculinity into something edgier, almost dangerous.

It was unnerving being alone with him. For more reasons than just their unpleasant history.

Tina knew that, physically, she hadn't changed much at all. The chubbiness of her teens, which her mother still optimistically referred to as puppy fat, hadn't miraculously melted away. Instead she was still carrying the extra weight, especially around her butt and boobs. She had learned to live with that, and, while it had been a long, hard struggle, she had learned to like herself.

But being around Harris again brought back all those old insecurities and self-doubts, and she couldn't wait for her life to go back to normal and for him to once again fade into the background, where he belonged.

He passed her an already-assembled little infant carrier, the handle of which she hooked over the crook of her arm; a large flat, square playpen; and a medium-size box adorned with a picture of a baby happily sitting in some suspended, swinging contraption. Fortunately, both boxes came with handholds, which made them easier to carry.

Jeez, she wondered, how much space was all this stuff going to take? It was a one-bedroom flat, and while she was happy to have Libby, she wasn't sure the place was large enough for two grown women and an infant.

Harris surfaced from the back of his car, burdened with boxes of varying sizes. They were awkwardly shaped, bulky boxes, and carrying them looked like a bit of a juggling act. Tina looked down at the things she was carrying versus the load he had and frowned.

"Give me some of those," she urged, and he threw her a disdainful look before pointing his jaw toward the door.

"Just go," he commanded her in an insufferably bossy voice. She gritted her teeth and led the way back into the building. The stairs seemed longer and steeper than usual, and she did her damnedest to keep her breathing even, not wanting him to see her huffing for breath. She was used to these stairs, used to lugging her shopping up them, and when no one was around to see or judge, she quite happily puffed her way up them. But she'd be damned if she'd allow him to see her winded and carefully measuring each breath as she slogged her way up the sixty stairs to her floor.

She put the swingy-contraption box down and unlocked the door, stepping aside to let him in. He passed her and carefully placed the boxes on the floor. She followed with her own load and placed them with his.

"Thanks for your assistance. I'm sure you want to get some sleep," she said pointedly. He planted his hands on his narrow hips and stared down at the boxes.

"You're going to need help assembling some of this stuff," he said.

"I'll be fine."

"It's nearly four in the morning. I have to be up by six anyway. There's no point going to sleep—I could just help you set everything up so that it's ready for Libby when she gets here."

"I can do it," Tina maintained.

"I don't doubt that, but doing it alone will take much longer. You might not finish in time."

"Don't worry about it. Goodbye, Harris."

"For fuck's sake, Tina!" he suddenly exploded, completely shocking her. "How long are you going to bear this unreasonable grudge against me?"

"I don't think it's unreasonable," she said beneath her breath, and he swore again before running both hands through his thick hair and sucking in an uneven breath.

"It hasn't escaped my notice that you've successfully avoided being alone with me for ten years," he pointed out in a not-quite-level voice. "I've tried so many times, but you've never given me the opportunity to apologize. I was an idiot, Tina. I was a stupid kid, and while this isn't an excuse, someone slipped something in my drink. It impaired my judgment, and I—"

"No! Stop." She held up a shaking hand, her voice louder than she'd intended. But at least it had had the desired effect. It shut him up. "I don't want to talk about this. Not now. Not ever."

"I'm sorry." He ignored her words, forcing his unwanted apology on her. And now it was there, hovering between them like a bad smell, and Tina didn't know what to do about it.

"It makes no difference," she finally said, and his forehead furrowed.

"I never meant to hurt you," he continued doggedly. Tina felt the blood drain from her face in angry reaction to his words.

"Oh my God. The ego on you. Do you think I've been nursing a broken heart all these years? Please just leave. There's really no point in dredging all this up."

"Tina, we were once friends." He sounded almost miserable, and his words forced a bitter laugh from her.

"No. We weren't. I don't know why you would even say that. It's a blatant untruth."

"I don't think it is."

"Why are you bringing all this up again? It's been ten years. Why do you even care?"

"This is the first time since that night that we've been alone together. Not for lack of trying on my part." It was true that over the years, whenever he'd seen her with family or friends, he'd attempted to talk with her, asked her to coffee or lunch. He'd never gone out of his way to contact her, but he'd seized opportunities, usually at her family's functions, when they presented themselves.

Tina had rebuffed all those attempts at communication.

"You've apologized. I'm sure you're happy to get that burden off your conscience. Now maybe you'll stop bothering me," she said.

"Let me help you with this," he insisted, indicating the boxes. Tina sighed, and the short sound was laced with irritation.

"On the condition that you don't bring up all that old crap again," she finally conceded with palpable reluctance.

"Tina—"

"*Ever* again," she elaborated, interrupting him without a qualm.

He huffed impatiently before finally lifting his broad shoulders in a shrug.

"Fine." His voice was surly, but Tina didn't care. It felt like a victory of sorts.

"Would you like a cup of coffee?" she asked when he shrugged out of his denim jacket, tossing it over the back of her sofa, and shoved his hoodie sleeves up to his elbows.

"Please," he said as he lifted a box—the swingy thing that Tina had lugged up the stairs—and scrutinized the images before reaching for his jacket and extracting a utility knife from one of the pockets. He neatly sliced the carton open before removing various plastic-wrapped objects.

Tina left him to it, surreptitiously watching him from her open-plan kitchen as she went about preparing a couple of cups of coffee. Instant. Because she had no intention of making any kind of special effort for him.

She finished the coffee in no time and placed his mug on the table beside where he was kneeling on the floor, softly cursing beneath his breath as he tried to figure out the complicated-looking swing.

Tina picked up a bigger box, a playpen, and reached for his knife where he had left it on the table, and she made short work of opening it up. She read the instructions carefully and grouped the pieces in the order she would need them before starting.

She was making good progress and was wrapped in her own thoughts, effectively ignoring the fact that Harris was just across the room from her, when he spoke unexpectedly.

"I think this stuff was left over from her baby shower. I mean, she had her nursery completely set up already. I think she was going to give these things to charity."

Tina wasn't surprised. Libby's baby shower had been so extravagant that she'd been left with way more gifts than she had needed. Libby had wanted Tina to host the shower and had envisioned something small and intimate . . . but Libby's mother-in-law had insisted on handling the arrangements, and it had turned into a three-ring circus, with women attending whom Libby had barely known.

"It was easier to transport the stuff that was still in the boxes."

"I see," Tina responded, only because a reply seemed required of her. She didn't know why he'd felt the need to tell her this. She didn't particularly care. She just wanted him out of her home as soon as possible.

"These things are going to take up a lot of room in your apartment. It's just one bedroom, right?"

"I don't mind." His observation raised her hackles. It felt accusatory.

"It's going to get crowded pretty quickly," he continued.

"That's not your concern," she said dismissively.

"I could arrange an apartment for Libby—someplace bigger, close to her parents."

"She wouldn't want that."

"You can't speak for her," he protested sullenly, and she gave him her best "dude, please" look.

"I'm pretty sure, in this instance, that I'm perfectly qualified to speak for her. I told you, she won't even stay with her parents because their apartment was a gift from *your* parents. What makes you think she'd be okay staying in a place you've 'arranged'?" She used air quotes for the last word.

"Fair point," he conceded with a grimace. Tina tried very hard to keep the smugness she felt off her face and went back to her task. A few screws later, she sat back proudly and stared at the completed playpen.

"Done," she stated, unable to keep the triumph out of her voice. She pushed the bulky but lightweight piece of furniture aside and picked up the next box. Car seat. It didn't need much, just unboxing. It would have to be affixed in her car before she left to pick up Libby and Clara.

Harris cast her a sulky glare from beneath his fall of black hair, still working on the swing. She could feel him staring at her but chose to ignore the look. She placed the car seat on the sofa behind her before dragging out another box, this one a high chair.

"Don't think she'll be needing this for a good few months yet," she muttered to herself.

"I just grabbed what looked useful," Harris retorted defensively, and she refrained from rolling her eyes. Big man's ego bruised quickly, it seemed.

She shrugged and looked around for something else. There was only the bassinet left, and she unboxed it quickly.

"That one looks complicated—I'll do it," Harris said, glancing up from the swing, which was still in several pieces in front of him.

"Uh . . . you just keep slogging away at that thing, Harris. I've got this," she said in her most patronizing voice, and his dark-blue eyes sparked with something dangerous. He didn't say anything, though, and she snorted disdainfully before unboxing the bassinet. She used the same method as before, arranging all the pieces in the order she thought she might need them, and half an hour later, she very proudly touched the old-school rocking bassinet and watched it swing gently back and forth.

Harris, who was still working on the swing, gave her a quick, disgruntled look before dropping his eyes back to his task. The silence between them over the last half hour had been interrupted only by his increasingly frustrated curses, and Tina, who hated being amused by anything Harrison Chapman said or did, couldn't help being entertained by his irritation at his inability to complete the job at hand.

Tina said nothing, merely got up and began to industriously clean up the packaging scattered around her small flat. Then she moved the stuff she had assembled into the bedroom, which she intended to give up for Libby and Clara.

When she returned ten minutes later, Harris was standing in the middle of the living room—hands in his front jean pockets—glowering at the wobbly-looking swing in front of him and swearing steadily beneath his breath.

"It's not quite right," he acknowledged, without looking up.

"Yeah, I can see that," she said, keeping her voice level, while—for the first time in memory—she wanted to laugh long and loud in this man's presence. "I think you probably needed those as well." She pointed down at a few scattered leftover pins and screws, and he glared down at them before pushing an irritated hand through his hair.

"They didn't belong anywhere. I think they were just extras in case some of the others get lost." He was bullshitting. They both knew that. But he was too stubborn to admit that he'd been defeated by a piece of baby paraphernalia, when Tina had assembled two and a half separate items in the same amount of time it had taken him to (barely) complete one.

Tina didn't say anything in response to his nonsense and instead picked up the leftover odds and ends and set them aside. She would take the swing apart and fix it after he left.

"Well, thanks for your help," she said, barely refraining from layering the last word with the sarcasm just clamoring to creep into her voice. She pasted a polite, impersonal smile on her face and stared at his imperfect yet arrogant nose in an attempt to avoid his eyes.

"I think it's safe to say you didn't need my help after all," he said drily, his deep voice rich with self-directed amusement. The wry self-deprecation surprised her into glancing up and meeting his gaze straight on. "I never was much good with puzzles."

"I remember," she said, her voice husky.

The memory of a fifteen-year-old Harris, impatiently shoving aside a jigsaw puzzle and stating emphatically that it was "boring," floated unbidden into her mind. Tina vividly recalled him claiming that even if it *was* raining, he'd much rather be skateboarding. He had departed without so much as a goodbye, leaving Greyson and thirteen-year-old Tina to complete the puzzle without him.

"Do you?" His voice took on a gruff note, surprise evident in the two words, and Tina was horrified that she'd allowed even that much to slip. She didn't want to remind him of how much she had adored him throughout her teens.

"You were never very patient," she said with a dismissive shrug, her eyes once again drifting south to his nose . . . only this time, she couldn't prevent her gaze from sliding even farther down to his mouth. That wide, beautiful, bow-shaped mouth. Once, long ago, she'd become intimately acquainted with those lips. And she had never really forgotten the taste of them, not even with everything that had happened afterward. It wasn't something she would ever forget. Similar to the way the craving of an addiction stays with you even after you've kicked the habit.

"I'm sure you want to get home," she said pointedly.

"Not particularly. Why don't we get some breakfast?"

"No. Thank you. Please leave." His face tightened, and it once again surprised her into glancing up into his eyes. They held a trace of something very much like hurt. She blinked, and it was gone, to be replaced by . . . nothing.

"I suppose I'll see you around then," he said after a moment, turning to pick up his jacket, knife, and car keys. When he straightened to face her again, he graced her with a perfectly bland smile. "Please tell Libby to call me if she or the baby need anything."

"Clara."

"What?" His straight brows lowered over those deep-set, thickly lashed navy eyes in confusion.

"Libby named the baby Clara."

He absorbed Tina's words for a moment before grinning, his even teeth looking even whiter than usual against the darkness of his stubble. It made him look slightly naughty, and Tina battled to regain her breath. Feeling like she'd just tackled the stairs up to her flat again.

"Good for her," he said. The relish in his voice surprised her, and she tilted her head to stare at him assessingly.

"I thought you hated that name."

"Nah, I hated the evil bitch with the same name who tutored slash tortured Greyson and me for five years, but I have nothing against the name itself. It's pretty. But Greyson is going to hate it."

"Not that he cares," she reminded him, and his face darkened as that beautiful grin slowly faded from his lips.

"Not now. But he will. And when he does, he'll sorely regret his behavior and actions these last few months." His voice was confident but grim.

"And you're happy about that?"

"It's petty, but yeah . . . I'm okay with that. He thinks . . ." He paused, his eyes on her face, but his gaze was turned inward.

"He thinks?" Tina couldn't help prompting, and his eyes snapped back into focus and he winced.

"Shit." He shook his head. There was something close to vulnerability on his face, and it made her curious.

"Harris?"

"Look, don't tell Libby, okay? It'll just upset her more," he said.

"Don't tell her what?"

He sucked in a deep breath between his teeth and shook his head again, and this time she knew she wasn't imagining the vulnerability in his expression. Or the pain in his eyes. He clearly wanted to tell her. If only to share whatever this was with someone else.

"He thinks I'm Clara's father," Harris admitted grimly. His voice cracked a bit on the statement, and Tina gasped in horror. This was so much *worse* than Greyson just accusing Libby of adultery. Accusing her of sleeping with his own brother was seriously twisted. "I told him he was wrong, and I *think* maybe I got through to him . . . but . . ." Another headshake, this one filled with confusion and a little bit of helplessness.

If he were any other man, Tina would have breached the distance between them and . . . *something*. Maybe patted his shoulder or taken his hand. Anything to give him the comfort he so clearly needed.

But he wasn't any other man. He was Harrison Chapman, and she despised him.

"It was bad enough before, but that . . ." She shook her head in disgust. "That's seriously messed up."

"Don't tell Libby, please." It was the *please* that did it. She probably wouldn't have told Libby anyway; her friend had enough on her plate as it was, and this information should come from Greyson or Harris, if it ever needed to come out. Tina was not going to burden her friend with this as well. And that softly voiced, desperate little *please* tacked onto what could have been a command strengthened her resolve.

"She won't hear it from me. She has enough to deal with right now."

"Thank you."

"So polite, Harris," she couldn't help stating, her voice carrying just the gentlest hint of mockery.

"My mama raised me right," he said, his words light but his voice burdened with what sounded like sadness and regret.

Tina chose not to respond. That instance when his upbringing had failed him so completely never far from her mind. She could tell he was thinking about it, too, because he cleared his throat and then shut his eyes for a long moment, as if willing the memory away.

"Take care, Tina." His voice was abrupt, his words final, and he departed seconds later. Leaving her feeling shockingly bereft.

"Are you sure?" Tina asked Libby a month later, watching while her friend breastfed the always-voracious Clara. Libby was running a tender hand absently over the infant's downy-soft black hair. She always seemed to be touching Clara in some way. As if she couldn't help herself. While, to Tina's eternal regret and shame, *she* could barely bring herself to look at the baby. She loved Clara with everything in her, was happy to spoil her from afar, but something inside of her seized up in terror at the thought of actually holding the infant. She knew her behavior confused and hurt Libby, but she couldn't explain it. Not without opening a Pandora's box of shameful and painful, long-held secrets.

Tina had hoped that constant exposure to Clara would help her overcome this one terrible obstacle that was starting to trip her up with much more frequency recently, but instead she found that she was getting worse instead of better. She spent longer hours at work, reorganizing files that were fine, cataloguing a backlog of books that had been lying around for months, updating their electronic lending system. When she got home she was usually completely exhausted, and Libby tried her best to leave her in peace. She knew her friend was starting to feel like a burden, and that was the last thing Tina wanted, but she didn't know how else to make this bearable.

And now, the worst had finally happened: Libby was leaving. And Tina knew it was because her friend felt unwelcome, but she had no idea how to make her understand. And she knew that if she told Libby the truth, it would make her feel even worse and even more determined to move out.

"Libby, I know I've been distant, but work has been full on this last month. I've loved having you and Clara here." Not a lie, not really . . . she did like having them here. She liked watching Libby with her baby. But that was all she wanted to do . . . watch. Not participate.

"I know, Tina," Libby said, her eyes gentle but not quite convinced. "I just want to get away from Cape Town, away from Greyson."

"Has he called? Bothered you?" Tina asked sharply, and Libby smiled, the movement of her lips bittersweet.

"Not at all. Harris calls every day; so do my parents . . ." Libby also visited her parents regularly so they could see their granddaughter often, but she adamantly refused to move in with them, despite their constant pleas that she do so. "And, of course, Constance and Truman have called a few times." Her in-laws weren't the most demonstrative of people and didn't seem quite sure how to respond to the situation between Greyson and Libby, but they were clearly interested in their first grandchild and often sent their chauffeur—Libby's dad's replacement—with gifts for the baby. They had visited only once, and fortunately Tina hadn't been there to witness that awkwardness, but Libby had told her it had been truly horrendous. The only bright spot, apparently, had been the way they had cooed and fussed over Clara.

"I would just feel better," Libby continued, "if there were more distance between us. I hate knowing he's just a few suburbs away."

"So where does this Chris live?"

Libby was considering moving in with an old friend and mentor.

"He lives somewhere on the Garden Route." Tina raised her eyebrows at that bit of information. The Garden Route was a six-hour drive away. A beautiful part of the Western Cape that Tina always enjoyed visiting.

"That's quite a distance," she stated unnecessarily, and Libby nodded regretfully.

"I know, but I think, for now, it's best."

"I could drive you." The offer was out before Tina could think about it, and Libby's face went slack with shock.

"But it's a long drive. Clara and I could fly." Her tone of voice conveyed her reluctance at that thought.

"I suppose it's better than being cooped up in a car all day," Tina agreed.

"Truthfully," Libby said with a grimace, "I'd prefer driving. Even though it's a short flight, I'd rather not fly with her just yet."

"So let me drive! Road trip—we haven't done anything like that for a while!" And never with a baby. Tina wasn't sure it was such a good idea, volunteering to place herself in such close confines with the infant, but maybe this would be the perfect cure for her stupid issues. Total immersion therapy.

"Are you sure?"

"Yep. I haven't tested my car yet. Not really. I've only done these piddling little drives to and from work. Sometimes to my parents' house. This will be fabulous. Let me take you. Please. It's the least I can do."

"You've already done a lot, Tina," Libby reminded her, and Tina waved her hand impatiently.

"You're my friend. My *best* friend. And I love you. 'A lot' is never enough."

Libby graced her with a grateful smile. "Road trip it is, then," Libby said, her voice wobbly and her eyes shining with tears.

Chapter Three

"Oh my God, this town is gorgeous." Tina sighed as they drove into yet another of the many picturesque tiny towns on the Garden Route. This one had a huge sign posted at the entrance of town:

WELCOME TO RIVERSEND
POP 5017

"We *have* to stop here!"

"We're less than forty minutes away from our destination," Libby informed her with an indulgent grin.

"Last stop on our road trip, then," Tina said, her voice cajoling.

Libby laughed. "Fine! Let's have a late lunch somewhere. I need to change my munchkin anyway. I want her fresh and happy when she meets her 'uncle' Chris for the first time."

Tina scanned their surroundings until she spotted a faded neon sign that was switched on, even in the middle of the day: MJ's. The *M* was flickering, and the apostrophe was off. The windows weren't exactly clean, and there were remnants of Christmas decorations still adorning the corners. Clearly someone had attempted to remove them but couldn't be bothered to clear away all the tinsel. Who knew how long it had been there. Somehow Tina doubted it was from last Christmas, which had been four months ago.

"I don't know," Libby said skeptically as she stared at the less-than-impressive exterior of the place.

"Come on; it's an MJ, like me. It's bound to have some hidden charms. Besides, I don't see any other eateries. And I doubt you'd want to take Clara into the pub." Tina eyed the pub, just a few doors away, dubiously. The place looked seedy, but a few locals and tourists were milling around outside. Tina knew there was a huge Saturday rugby test match on at the moment, which could explain the thronging crowd currently populating the pub. Ralphie's—the pub—did have the usual sports-bar paraphernalia on its signage and advertised "big-screen TVs" boldly on its windows.

The huge roar coming from inside the pub affirmed Tina's belief that it was filled to the brim with sports fans.

"Um . . . I think we'll stick with MJ's," Libby said, wrinkling her nose as she clearly drew the same conclusion.

Tina dropped Libby and Clara off in front of the restaurant before driving off to find parking—difficult, when the main road was jam-packed with cars, and the restaurant didn't have any dedicated spaces. She had to drive up the road a ways and find a spot off the main road.

She fed the meter and took a leisurely walk back to the restaurant. It was a glorious autumn day—the pretty little town was close enough to the beach that she could smell the brine in the air and hear the crash of waves in the distance. Occasionally she caught a glimpse of the sparkling blue water just behind the buildings across the street. Riversend was built on a slope, and a lot of the homes were downhill and closer to the water. There were a few larger houses farther up the hill that probably had spectacular, uninterrupted views of the ocean and town.

It was clearly a tourist town, probably busy only in spring, summer, and early autumn, but she loved the appeal of the place. People smiled and nodded at her as she passed them, welcoming and generously warm. She wondered why a place like this, which likely earned most of its money during the peak seasons, had no decent restaurants. Tourists probably stayed here and went out to eat at the nearby larger cities, like Knysna or Plettenberg Bay. Possibly even to Libby's friend Chris's place.

Still, it seemed like wasted potential. A town like this could benefit from a decent restaurant.

She was still ruminating over that when she entered MJ's. The name of the place did give her a childish kick. If she were going to open a diner, she'd probably name it MJ's too. Or possibly TJ's. She considered that, then shook her head. Nah, MJ's definitely sounded better.

She was somewhat surprised by how packed the place was when she entered it. It also had a television blaring in the background. Ralphie's wasn't the only place blasting the rugby today.

The restaurant had the ubiquitous small-town, shabby-diner decor. Red-and-white checkered tablecloths, little oil lanterns on each table. Condiments in wooden holders, with the laminated menus stuck between bottles of ketchup and mustard.

She spotted Libby in the back, close to the kitchen, the farthest distance away from the TV.

"This place is busier than I expected," Tina said as she took her seat. She glanced down at Clara in her baby carrier, which had been placed on a sturdy chair, but thankfully the infant seemed oblivious to the noise. Tina rested her elbows on the table and wrinkled her nose when she realized that the tablecloths were actually plastic. And a bit tacky to the touch. *Ugh.*

A harried-looking server came up to their table and, despite obviously being rushed off her feet, gave them a warm smile.

"Good afternoon—my name's Suzie; I'll be your server today. Would you like anything to drink?"

"Hi, Suzie, just orange juice for me, please," Libby said.

"I'll have a double cappuccino, please," Tina requested.

"I'll have that for you shortly," the woman said with a nod. She left with another smile, and Tina cast her eyes around the place. Really, it had probably been quaint like thirty years ago. Now it was just completely outdated and a little shabby.

"What do you think of this place?" she asked Libby. The other woman, who had been wiping drool from Clara's face, looked up in surprise.

"I mean, it's not the best place I've ever eaten at. Not the worst either. It's just . . . meh. Their menu is super outdated; I doubt it's been changed since 1985. Who still serves prawn cocktails, for God's sake?"

Tina stifled a fond laugh—Libby was such a food snob. To be expected from a trained chef. She glanced around the restaurant again; everybody seemed to be having an awesome time, and they were clearly enjoying both the atmosphere and the food, but they had probably been coming here for years, and it was as familiar to them as their own homes.

"How would you change this menu, if you had the chance?" she asked Libby, and her friend frowned, obviously taken aback by the question. She glanced down at the sticky laminated menu again and shrugged.

"I don't know. You know me—I'd start with the desserts." Of course she would—she was a pastry chef. "But entrees and mains, I don't know. I'd probably minimize and update. There are so many superfluous things on here I shudder thinking what their freezers must look like. I doubt some of these things have been ordered in years, but they'd have to keep the ingredients in stock. Their wastage must be enormous."

Tina nodded, her eyes running over the place again, the people, the menu, and an idea started to percolate in the back of her mind. A new start for her . . . and possibly one for Libby too.

Three Months Later

Harris's phone buzzed, and he dragged it out of his pocket, grateful for the distraction from work. It was a call from Smith Jenson, one of his best friends. The guy usually texted, so Harris answered the call immediately, fearing an emergency.

"Hey, man, I have to bail on our game tonight," Smith said without preamble as soon as the call connected. Harris's eyebrows rose. He and Smith had a standing arrangement to play tennis every Wednesday night after work. The Jenson family had an indoor tennis court on their family estate, and Smith and Harris had been playing there just about every week for the last fifteen years. They were both extremely competitive and almost evenly matched. Harris, having height and weight advantages, had won just a couple of games more.

"Why?" Harris asked. "You scared your lazy, out-of-shape ass can't compete?"

"Please, I was looking forward to watching you wheeze your way around the court trying to keep up with my speedy returns." Smith *was* fast, and—win or lose—Harris was always guaranteed a great workout.

"Shit, I was looking forward to blowing off some steam tonight," Harris muttered.

"What's up? Greyson still being an asshole?" Smith asked sympathetically. He was the only other person—aside from Tina—who knew about Greyson's unfounded and unfair accusations.

"He's being stubborn. He knows he's that baby's father. I know he does. He refuses to admit it, and I doubt he'll ever apologize. I thought maybe he'd come to his senses once he stopped drinking himself into oblivion every night, but he's been sober for nearly three months now, and still nothing! At least I know Libby is doing well—she's happy working for her former mentor. Clara is growing fast, and she's so damned beautiful. My brother is a fool to have so carelessly tossed away the best thing to ever happen to his stodgy ass."

"Yeah, I'm not sure what's going to happen with Libby, bud," Smith said cautiously, and Harris's brow lowered.

"What do you mean?"

"That's why I can't make our game tonight. Tina-related family crisis. *Again!* She didn't tell any of us in time for us to intervene, but she's gone and bought a fucking restaurant. In some dinky town on the Garden Route. And she's enlisted Libby to be her head chef."

Way to go, Tina! was Harris's first thought.

"So, we're having a family meeting tonight, to try and figure out how to spin it when *this* venture goes belly up too. She's never had employees before. People's livelihoods are on the line—the potential PR disaster for the family is fucking catastrophic. Just typical Tina, really. She never thinks things through. What she knows about running a business, much less a restaurant, could fill a thimble."

Harris felt a growl building in his throat, and he gritted his teeth as he continued to listen to his friend bitch and moan about Tina and her past and present failings.

"Why not help her succeed instead of expecting her to fail?" Harris interrupted curtly. He found Smith's catalogue of Tina's supposed character flaws infuriating.

Silence.

"What?" Smith asked after a beat, his voice uncertain, as if he wasn't quite sure what he had just heard.

"You're always expecting her to crash and burn and then criticizing her when she *does* fail. Have you ever fucking *once* tried to offer her support and guidance? You're a business-savvy guy, Kyle runs the family company—either of you could steer her in the right direction. Want to avoid a PR disaster? Man up and be a brother to your little sister. She's been trying for fucking years to find her niche . . . and none of you have lifted a finger to help her."

"She was supposed to go to medical school, you know that." Tina had dropped out of medical school after just six months, which had been shocking, considering her once-burning desire to be an obstetrician.

"And medical school wasn't for her, so she's trying to find something else. I've listened to some variation or the other of this bullshit countless times over the years, Smith. And I'm fed up with it. There's an almost sick glee in your voice when she does flop at something. What the fuck, man?"

"It's not like I *want* her to fail," Smith said defensively.

"You could have fooled me, bro." There was no disguising the derision in his voice. "How the hell do you think she feels every time she has to listen to all of you criticize her every decision?"

"We love her—we want better for her."

"Why don't you just love her?" Harris suggested, the heat going out of his voice. His fingers unconsciously reached for the pendant tucked away beneath his shirt, and he traced its familiar outline through the fabric. "Unconditionally?"

He could hear Smith swallow heavily before clearing his throat.

"I have to . . . uh . . ." Smith stalled, as if gathering his thoughts. "I'll talk to you soon. Okay?"

"Yeah."

They disconnected the call, and Harris swore fiercely beneath his breath. He should probably have gone a little easier on his friend. But after years of minding his own business, thinking it wasn't his place, it was past time he spoke up.

Tina was so damned brave. Never afraid to try new things. He wondered who, if anybody, was advising her. Certainly not her bloody family. Granted, she had a world-class chef in Libby, but Libby unabashedly admitted to having little-to-no business sense. So many startup businesses failed within the first year, and Harris was concerned for Tina. He wanted her to find professional success. Perhaps he was doing her an injustice in simply assuming she'd need help. Tina was a surprising woman, and if anybody could make this work, she could. Still, it always helped to have someone in your corner. Someone to turn to for advice.

He wished Smith would pull his head out of his ass and be there for her. He wished he could be the one to extend an offer of assistance if she needed it, but he knew *that* would go down like a lead balloon.

He sighed and tried to shift his attention back to work, but his concentration was shot. He couldn't focus on the financial report in front of him, his mind constantly drifting to Tina. After half an hour of wasting time googling restaurants in the Garden Route, he still couldn't figure out which one she might have purchased. It would help to know the town's name, of course, but Libby hadn't told him anything about this, and he had no clue where to start looking.

His phone pinged, signaling a text message, and he lifted it absently, expecting to find a message from Smith. Maybe telling him to butt out of Jenson family business.

Instead, he smiled when he saw the name on his phone screen. Libby. She sent him a text every day, never really saying much . . . just telling him they were doing well. The text was usually the highlight of his day, filled with pictures of Clara and Libby in their new life. The baby was growing beautifully. The perfect blend of Libby and Greyson, with golden-brown skin, a shock of dark hair, a rosebud mouth, a tiny and still-undefined button nose, dimples, long, long lashes, and dark-blue eyes. The exact same shade of blue as her father's.

Harris was completely in love with his gorgeous niece, and, as was his habit, since Libby had started sending him these photos, he picked the cutest one and forwarded it to Greyson. He didn't do it out of kindness, more as a "see what you're missing out on because you're such a dickhead?" dig at his stupidly stubborn brother.

Harris and Greyson barely spoke anymore; because of their completely different personalities and interests, they had slowly drifted apart over the years, but Greyson's accusation had been the final straw. It had hurt more than Harris cared to admit. He and Greyson may not have had that much in common, but Harris still loved his brother and would never in a million years have dreamed of accusing him of anything similar. The trust that they'd once had between them was gone, and Harris regretted its loss.

I wish . . .

He shook his head impatiently, inhaling sharply through his nose as the wistful thought entered his head.

No.

Harris didn't do wishes; it was ridiculous and whimsical and completely out of character. He was more of an action man—he didn't waste time dillydallying over wishes and could-have-beens.

He focused on his phone again and flipped through the latest batch of pictures Libby had sent him. A few selfies of her and Clara. Another selfie of Libby with her friend the chef—and ex-model—Christién Roche. He was tempted to send that picture to Greyson as well. Maybe it would prompt his cold-blooded brother to feel a bit of jealousy, knowing his wife was hanging out with a former male model. Libby looked happy and relaxed, and the shadows were disappearing from beneath her eyes. Harris was happy for her; he just hated that she was so far away.

He decided against sending the picture in the end, not entirely sure Greyson would give a damn.

He slid his finger over the screen, and his breath snagged.

Tina.

She was grinning directly into the camera, a big, beautiful smile that Harris would never see in real life. Tina tended to be selfish with her smiles when she found herself in his presence. Her hair was longer than it had been the last time he'd seen her, the gorgeous red mass tied up in a messy ponytail at the top of her head and cascading down over her shoulders. Her usually pale skin looked sun kissed and freckled.

God, she was absolutely beautiful. He had always thought so, and even when she'd been an awkward teen and embarrassingly obvious about her feelings for him, he'd never seen her the same way everyone else had. The extra pounds she carried had never mattered to him and, in his opinion, added to her overall appeal. And though Harris had developed a preference for slender, sporty women over the years, Tina had always pushed his buttons. She looked—and *felt*—soft and plush.

Maybe it was all that gorgeous creamy skin, maybe the fiery hair, perhaps the lush, full lips set in a round face with high cheekbones and snapping green eyes.

He hadn't seen her in months. She had gone to the Garden Route with Libby, and he had always assumed that she was the one looking after Clara while Libby worked. He figured once Libby was settled, Tina would return to her cozy little flat in Bantry Bay. He had *never* imagined that she was thinking of settling there permanently. The thought of her being so far away was shockingly distressing. His hand lifted to absently toy with his pendant again as he considered the ramifications of never seeing her again.

Perhaps that would be better for both of them.

He was still staring at her picture, deep in thought, when the phone in his hand buzzed and Greyson's name and picture popped up on his screen.

Frowning, he glared at the image of his brother, wondering what he wanted. If it was business, the man would have called him on his office number. They rarely exchanged personal calls and messages anymore.

He swiped his finger across the screen and lifted the device to his ear.

"Yeah?"

"I'm bringing them home."

Tina was freaking out. Seriously . . . what the hell had made her think she could do this? She cast her eyes around the interior of her newly renovated, redecorated, and rebranded restaurant and felt a sense of accomplishment and pride mixed with an overwhelming urge to throw up.

MJ's was unrecognizable from the establishment she had first walked into just over three months ago. She had made short work of purchasing the place; she had dropped Libby off at Chris's restaurant three months ago, turned around, and headed straight back to MJ's. Big money talked, and it was just a matter of finding the right price before Tommy Vincent, the owner, had crumbled like wet papier-mâché and sold the business of his granddad—the eponymous MJ. The restaurant had been Tina's less than a month later.

Tina had had a clear vision of how she wanted the place to look and feel. Still family friendly, but with more of a country-cottage feel. Quaint, colorful, and welcoming. She had consulted with Libby every step of the way, Skyping or FaceTiming, once her friend finished her shifts at Chris's restaurant. This project was as much Libby's as it was Tina's.

The menu had been pared down, refined, and would change seasonally to keep things fresh and interesting for their local patrons.

And so here they were, relaunch night. Hours away from opening time, and Tina couldn't quell the butterflies in the pit of her stomach. Seriously, she didn't know why people called them butterflies. Butterflies were pleasant things—these were horrid, disgusting creatures. With talons. Vultures? Maybe she had vultures in the pit of her stomach. Frantically trying to claw their way out and leave her a bloodied mess in the middle of the floor.

She wrinkled her nose. Sometimes her imagination was a bit much.

She pressed the palm of her hand to her stomach and swallowed back a surge of nausea. She wouldn't fail at this. It would be a success. Riversend needed a decent restaurant; the locals deserved this. The tourists demanded it. It made sense.

And even though she had been much too busy to meet people, she was happy here, and she knew that once the dust settled, she would feel at home.

Libby had bought a decrepit house close to the beach. Tina hadn't gotten around to finding anything permanent yet. She was renting a place farther up the hill. While it could do with a paint job, it had a killer view from the front porch, and she was happy enough there for now. And it was in much better condition than Libby's house.

Tina had been trying to get Libby to move in with her until the renovations on her ramshackle beach house were complete, but Libby was stubborn and determined to assert her independence after being reliant on her friends for so many months. Tina couldn't really blame her. Libby had always been fiercely independent. Everybody had been shocked when the other woman had put her career on hold to marry Greyson—it had been so uncharacteristic. Libby had continued to work locally immediately after the small wedding but had taken a break from her demanding career after learning of her pregnancy.

Tina sighed and shook herself mentally: she should be preparing for the daunting evening ahead, not speculating over things that were not her immediate concern.

And, anyway, thoughts of Greyson inevitably led to thoughts of Harris, and that would really send her down a nasty rabbit hole.

Focus, Tina. You have work to do!

"You okay?" Libby asked on her way to the kitchen from the small office she shared with Tina, where Clara was currently cozily ensconced with her young babysitter, Charlie.

"*So* nervous. What if nobody comes?" She couldn't help verbalizing the fears that she had been determined to keep to herself. Libby laughed and veered away from the kitchen to give Tina a huge hug.

"People will come. The place looks gorgeous, the food will be awesome, everything is half-price, the first glass of wine is free. Why wouldn't they come?"

Well, there was the debacle surrounding the banner, for one thing. The huge, gorgeous relaunch banner—along with a few hundred flyers advertising their opening specials—that Tina and Libby had sweated over designing should have arrived yesterday. But somehow Tina had given the distributor the wrong dates. The banner wouldn't be ready for another week. It had been a stupid mistake, and Tina didn't know how she could possibly have gotten something as basic as the date wrong. And the flyers—Tina regretted their loss much more than the banner's. They had been meant for small businesses and windshield wipers and would have been handed out at the community and youth-outreach centers.

It had been a stupid, careless mistake, and Tina felt totally incompetent because of it. She had done this too often in the past. Like the time she had absolutely believed that being a travel agent was the job for her. She had invested a great deal of money in the training course without really considering what it actually involved. But when fantasy had finally met reality and Tina had found herself having to interact with real live, demanding clients on a daily basis, she had discovered an innate lack of anything remotely resembling sales ability in herself. She had started making mistakes: booking the wrong flights or hotels. Not arranging airport transfers. And once—horribly—forgetting to organize airport assistance for a lovely, undemanding elderly lady. The woman had been one of the few nice people Tina had dealt with on the job. The entire venture had been a complete disaster, and her mistake with the old lady had been the last straw. Tina had lasted less than two months before bowing to the inevitable and calling it quits. Yet another "career opportunity" dying a swift and painful death.

That was how it had gone with pretty much every other venture she had attempted. Leaping before looking was her standard operating procedure.

But this was the first time Tina had people depending on her for their actual livelihoods. That was a huge responsibility.

Tina could not—*would not*—make the same mistakes. But it was hard not to fall into the same familiar bad habits. Difficult not to get sucked into that awful downward spiral.

"God, Libby. I'm terrified. I have so many people depending on me. There's so much at stake. I've never done anything like this before. Everything else I've tried have been massive failures. You know that."

"I do not," her friend denied, still so loyal. "I know nothing of the sort. You haven't found something you're passionate about before now. But this is different, Tina. I can see it in the way you look at this place, and I can hear the pride and excitement in your voice when you talk about it."

Tina shook her head and returned Libby's hug before stepping back and giving her friend a concerned once-over. Libby was looking so much better these days. She had lost a lot of weight in the first couple of months after Clara's birth, but she was gaining it back, and, despite the still-lingering sadness in her eyes, she seemed more like her old self.

"And you? Are you okay, Libby?"

"Getting there," Libby confessed, with a strained smile. "This has helped so much, Tina. Thank you."

"Pshaw," Tina scoffed dismissively, blinking back tears as she hugged her taller friend again. "As if I did it for you."

And yet, they both knew a large part of the reason she'd taken this huge step was so that Libby would have someplace to call home as well.

A place where they both belonged.

"Right, enough of this sentimental stuff," Tina said gruffly before checking her watch, just to give herself a moment to regain her composure. "It's T minus fifty-three minutes and twenty-seven seconds to opening time. We need to hustle."

The doors had been open for just over half an hour, and, so far, people had merely trickled in. But—if their awkward shifting on the high-backed, spindle-legged chairs and their whispered conversations were anything to go by—most of the current patrons seemed a little uncomfortable in the newly renovated space.

It was a dismal turnout. Nowhere near the throngs of excited people they had been expecting.

Tina stood at the entrance to the kitchen and reverted to a bad teen habit: lifting her thumb to her mouth and chewing on the nail and cuticle nervously. The vultures in her stomach were out for blood, clawing and scraping at her insides while she tried her best to look unperturbed by all that inner turmoil. If Libby's concerned glances were anything to go by, she was failing miserably.

"Nobody's coming," Tina lamented.

Libby sighed and tugged Tina's hand away from her mouth. "They'll come," she said, her words imbued with a confidence Tina wished she possessed.

Tina wasn't sure what she'd been expecting from her opening night, but it certainly wasn't this. A little more interest maybe, curiosity if nothing else. But this lack of interest felt like a death knell to the business, which was starting to mean so much to her.

"People here are really old fashioned," Thandiwe, a college student home for the midterm break, said. The young woman had worked for MJ's throughout her teens and, according to the former owner, was one of their best servers. She had been invaluable over the last week, helping with the last-minute training of the newer staff members. Unfortunately, she'd be leaving for veterinary school again the following week, and Tina already dreaded the loss. "MJ's has been something of an institution in this town, and maybe they think you've messed with tradition or something?"

"But when I first came here and ate at the place, people were complaining about how the menu never changed and it would be nice to have some variety," Tina lamented.

"Yes, but they've been saying that for years," Thandiwe said with a shrug. "I think they enjoyed complaining about it. But it was familiar, and they loved it. I'm sure people will come. Give it time. It's this or Ralphie's. And everyone knows the food is usually terrible at Ralphie's. Once they've sampled the new menu, they won't know what to do with themselves."

Tina cast another despairing glance around the mostly empty restaurant and fervently hoped Thandiwe's words would prove true. Because just a month of disappointing numbers like these would put her in a hole so deep she wouldn't see daylight for years. Thandiwe excused herself and went to chat with a few of the other servers, who were loitering about, looking bored. After a few words from Thandiwe, they all went scurrying, busying themselves with minor tasks.

Seriously, the woman was a gem.

"You sent notice of the relaunch to the paper, right?" Libby asked, referring to the local paper, the *Riversend Weekly*, which usually circulated on Thursdays. It contained job opportunities, as well as advertisements for local businesses and news about regional events.

"Yes, of course," Tina said, lifting her phone and bringing up her sent-email folder to show Libby the press release she had typed up for the paper. The reporter she had spoken to last week had promised to save a spot for the short announcement. The woman had even sent a reminder four days ago. Tina swiped down her list of recently sent emails but couldn't seem to find the one to the paper.

"I . . ." She frowned, confused. "It has to be here. I sent it on Monday."

"Did you check the paper?" Libby asked, and Tina shook her head.

"I forgot to pick up a copy. I meant to get one, but it completely slipped my mind. But I sent it . . ." She paused, her stomach roiling with dread—the vultures at work again—when she noticed that there was something left in her outbox. She blinked a few times before reluctantly clicking on the outbox.

"Crap," she muttered, feeling queasy as she stared at the unsent message. How could this have happened?

"Tina?" Libby prompted.

"It didn't send. I don't know why it didn't send," Tina said faintly.

"Oh, Tina," Libby exclaimed softly.

"I should have double-checked," Tina said. Hindsight being twenty-twenty, of course. It was a miracle people were actually showing up. She had been swamped the entire week leading up to the relaunch, and instead of creating a proper schedule for all essential tasks, she'd allowed herself to be overwhelmed by the sheer amount of work that needed to be done. Things had started slipping through the cracks. Major things, through huge cracks.

"I'm sorry, Libby. First the banner, and now this."

"It's okay. People are coming in—it could have been worse."

Tina couldn't really see how much worse it could have been. Their entire promotional plan for the relaunch had gone tits up, thanks to her own incompetence. Tina's thumb drifted to her mouth again, and she started gnawing agitatedly at the nail.

The door tinkled, and a couple walked in. They were holding hands and laughing but paused when they realized the place was close to empty.

"Hey. You're open! That's fantastic. Where is everybody?" the woman, pretty in a wholesome way, asked.

"Apparently resistant to change," Libby said, and the woman's eyes swung toward Tina's friend. A smile lit up the other woman's face, transforming her from pretty to beautiful.

"Hello, we haven't officially met. I'm Lia McGregor. You're Clara's mom." She walked toward Libby, tugging the handsome blond man along behind her.

"Olivia Lawson," Libby said with an equally gorgeous smile. "But please call me Libby." She held out her hand, and the other woman took it and shook enthusiastically.

Feeling a bit like the fourth wheel on a tricycle, Tina kept an awkward smiled pasted on her face. She guessed Libby knew the other woman from Clara's day care. Typical. Libby had moved to Riversend just a couple of weeks ago after purchasing her decrepit house on the beach and already knew loads more people than Tina did. Libby was like the sun: people were just naturally drawn to her warmth.

"Really lovely to officially meet you," the other woman, Lia, said. She gestured to the lean, good-looking man standing beside her. "This is my fiancé, Sam Brand."

"Nice to meet you," the man said, also taking Libby's hand. Tina thought she detected an English accent—hard to tell with just a few words—and he had a wicked, sexy smile.

"This is the restaurant's new owner, Martine Jenson. But everybody calls her Tina," Libby said.

Oh *good*, acknowledgment at last. She thought Libby was going to gush over her new buddy all day. Okay, maybe Tina was being a little uncharitable. But she was already tense after everything that had gone wrong, and it was making her bitchy. Still, at least the couple was here and supporting the restaurant tonight, and Tina was immensely grateful for that. She tried to disguise her edgy impatience behind a warm smile and reached out to shake Lia's, and then Sam's, hands.

"Ooh. You're an MJ too? That's perfect," Lia enthused. "Well, I've been excited about this new MJ's, and I called my sister when we saw your doors were open. I know she and her husband will be along soon. She's a little slow these days. Super pregnant. I know quite a few other people who said they were keen on trying the new MJ's. Don't worry: as soon as people see you're open, this place will be filled to the brim very quickly."

The evening was disappointing.

Nothing like the huge success Tina had been fantasizing about for months. She felt like curling up into a ball and crying her eyes out but kept a smile plastered to her face while she thanked her staff for their hard work and praised them for their excellent service that evening. It was the least she could do, considering how badly she had let them all down tonight.

The people who *had* come to the relaunch had left with smiles on their faces and full bellies. They had enthusiastically promised to encourage everybody else to come to "the New MJ's." In fact, so many people had referred to the restaurant as "the New MJ's" that Tina caustically wondered if she should include it on all her signage. She feared that the moniker would stick and thus doom the restaurant to a—probably short—lifetime of otherness.

She didn't want it to be referred to as "new"; she wanted them to think of it as MJ's, the beloved institution that they had supported for three decades. But, after tonight, that might well prove to be an exceptionally tall order.

Lia McGregor had called her family and all her friends, urging them to come out and support MJ's, and they, in turn, had called *their* friends. By the end of the night they had managed to scrape together a respectable number of patrons. Not exactly a capacity crowd, but half-full was better than they'd hoped for at the start of the evening.

Tina was exhausted, and Libby, who had kept a tight ship in the kitchen all evening, looked absolutely destroyed. After Tina's post-dinner-service pep talk, Libby had retreated to the kitchen to oversee the cleanup, and Tina had gratefully made her way to the small back office.

Only when she entered the office did she remember that Clara and her babysitter, Charlie Carlisle, were still in there.

The pretty teen looked up from her e-book and smiled.

"Hi. How did it go?"

"Less than ideal," Tina admitted, squeezing her palm around the nape of her neck. God, she could sleep for a week. She picked her reading glasses up from the cluttered surface of her desk and put them on before sinking into her desk chair, grateful to finally get off her feet after hours of standing.

"I'm sorry to hear that," Charlie was saying. "I'm sure it'll get better. My family was here; my sister-in-law, Daff, texted me rave reviews about the food and the atmosphere."

"Daff's your sister-in-law?" Tina asked distractedly, more in an effort to keep the conversation going than out of real interest—she wanted to get to her accounts and see how great the damage was. Daff was Lia McGregor's oldest sister. The woman was at the huge and uncomfortable stage of her pregnancy. She was married to Spencer, an intimidatingly large, good-looking guy. It was hard to imagine this petite slip of a girl having a brother that size. The girl was biracial, so the familial relationship wasn't immediately apparent, but upon closer inspection Charlie did have her brother's gorgeous green eyes, appealing dimples, and shy smile.

"Uh-huh," Charlie replied. "Also, Mrs. Chapman sent me some dinner and dessert earlier, and it was all so much better than the old MJ's food. As soon as people hear about how awesome the food is, they'll be lining up down the street."

"I hope so," Tina muttered, her eyes burning and her head pounding as she stared at the bright computer screen. She had a migraine coming on, she just knew it. She wasn't sure she could do the accounts tonight. Not with any accuracy, but delaying the task would only add to her tension.

She had put most of her rapidly dwindling inheritance into this business. She would have very little left if it went bust. She felt a surge of nausea as anxiety set in and practiced the breathing techniques that had helped her through so many of her past panic attacks.

She tried to get her rapid heartbeat under control, keeping her breathing measured. In through the nose, out through the mouth. Everything would be fine. It had to be fine. She was vaguely aware of Charlie still chatting away while she packed up her stuff. Tina made affirmative little noises but kept her gaze glued to the screen in front of her, hoping the teen would think she was distracted by work.

Libby entered the office, and she and Charlie started chatting. Tina couldn't hear what they were saying above the heavy, thundering beat of her heart and tried to swallow back the nausea as the tips of her fingers started to tingle, the unpleasant sensation of pins and needles racing down her arms from shoulders to fingertips. Her arms felt heavy and unresponsive.

Oh God! Please. Not now.

Libby didn't know about Tina's panic attacks, and she couldn't succumb to one now. Not here, while there were still staff members about. It would undermine everything she was trying to achieve; it would strip her employees of any confidence they might have in her as a leader.

The thought made her heartbeat surge even more, and her steady breathing began to falter.

Stop this! It's nothing. It's nothing. You can get it under control.
GET YOURSELF TOGETHER, MARTINE!

The inner scream snapped her back to a semblance of normalcy. It didn't often work, but this time it managed to drag her back from the precipice. The deafening beat of her heart started to recede, and she managed to catch bits and pieces of Libby's conversation with Charlie. The girl was leaving.

"Sweet dreams, Clara. See you soon. Night, Mrs. Chapman. See you, Tina," she called warmly as she left the room. Unable to speak yet, Tina raised her hand—grateful that she managed to move the heavy limb with so little effort—and waved.

"She's sweet," Tina said, forcing her thick tongue to move and grateful when the words came out sounding normal. She tugged her glasses off and pinched the bridge of her nose tiredly, hoping to ward off the migraine blossoming behind her eyes just a little longer. "God, I'm knackered."

"Me too." Libby sounded exhausted as she sank into the chair opposite Tina's. "How did we do?"

"Just about broke even tonight," Tina lied; she had no clue how they had done. She would take everything home and look through it later, after she'd knocked back a few painkillers and taken a long, relaxing bath. She was pretty certain they were in the red at the moment.

"It'll get better," Libby said, and Tina nodded, forcing a smile.

"It has to."

"Tina." Libby's voice was soft and hesitant. "How much did you spend on this place? Renovations and rebranding included?"

She hadn't asked before, and Tina wondered if the worry she was feeling was obvious. She smiled again, hoping to convince Libby of her sincerity. God knows, she didn't want to transfer her anxiety onto her friend. Libby had more than enough going on right now.

"My inheritance more than covered it," she said, trying to inject a certain amount of blasé into her voice. "It's fine. It's just . . ."

"Just what?" Libby prompted, and Tina struggled to find the right words.

"This is the first thing I've done—the first meaningful thing—and my parents are just waiting for me to fail. I know it. They think that I'm a total waste of space. Their flighty daughter, who could never hold down a job, trying to run a restaurant. Without any qualifications whatsoever. And, after the way I messed up with the banner and the ad . . . I'm starting to think they're right."

"Stop it," Libby snapped, and the fierceness in her voice surprised Tina somewhat, drawing her out of her funk.

"What?" she asked blankly.

"Stop allowing what your parents think of you to influence the way you think about yourself. You can do this, Tina. We both can."

Tina scrubbed her hands over her face and allowed herself one more deep sigh before lifting her gaze to Libby's again.

"Yeah, maybe I can get another ad in the paper. That's assuming they ever want to do business with me again. But if the townspeople really are as stubbornly loyal to the old MJ's as Thandiwe thinks, then I'm not sure what it'll take to lure them back."

"Look, it's only the first night. They have to drive thirty minutes to get to another halfway decent, affordable family restaurant. Or leave their kids at home and go to Ralphie's for limp fish and chips or stale burgers. Soon, more than anything else, desperation for a good night out will have them coming back. Besides, a lot of them don't even know we're open, so we may be putting out fires that don't even exist."

"Maybe." Tina nodded, unconvinced.

"Definitely. And Daff said she'd help us with some marketing." Apparently Daffodil Carlisle—young Charlie's sister-in-law—was the marketing and promotions manager for her husband's three huge sporting-goods stores and had promised to work up a marketing strategy for MJ's while she was on maternity leave. Tina wasn't sure her husband was too thrilled about her offering to work while she was supposed to be resting, but the woman had complained of being bored at home while "waiting for the baby to drop."

"It seems like a lot to expect from a total stranger," Tina said, allowing her skepticism to creep into her voice.

"I don't know about you, but after five minutes with those sisters, I felt like I'd known them for years."

Of course she did. That's how Libby was: she took everybody at face value and liked and trusted them until they gave her reason not to. For the most part, her instincts were spot on. After those grim high school years when she and Tina had been each other's only friends, Libby had blossomed into something of a social butterfly. She was well liked by most people. People who weren't snobs or assholes who judged her because her parents were honest and hardworking.

"Yeah, they're pretty nice," Tina said cautiously—she tended to reserve judgment. They had all seemed quite genuinely warm, but Tina didn't make friends easily. She tended to keep people at a distance until she knew them well enough to decide if she could trust them. And more often than not, her decision went against trusting them. As a result, she didn't have many friends.

"More than nice," Libby insisted, and Tina nodded to appease the woman she considered her only true friend.

"Come on, let's go home and get to bed. We have another long day tomorrow," Libby said, and Tina nodded again. She powered down her laptop and tucked it under her arm. She dreaded it, but she knew she would have to look at those numbers tonight.

Tina did a quick walk around the restaurant before locking up for the night. The staff had done an amazing job of cleaning up and resetting for tomorrow's brunch-into-lunch service. The place was absolutely beautiful, and Tina had received a slew of compliments about the new decor tonight. It had boosted her pride in her achievements.

She traced a loving finger over the surface of one of the gleaming round wooden tables before turning to where Libby was waiting by the front door.

After another futile attempt to persuade Libby to stay with her until her friend's home renovations were complete, she bade the other woman good night, and once they were both safely in their cars, which they had parked a few meters down the road from the restaurant, they headed off in opposite directions.

Chapter Four

It was a short drive through the quiet streets before she reached her quaint little rented place. She sat—her hands at ten and two on the steering wheel—in the warm, dark interior of her car, allowing the silence and peace of the moment to wash over her. She was reluctant to go into her flat. She hadn't unpacked much yet, and, with the exception of a few items of clothing, most of her personal things were still in boxes. The place was chaotic and not conducive to relaxation.

She dropped her forehead to the steering wheel—between her hands—and sighed. Her head was starting to pound, and she wasn't entirely sure she could get to the accounts tonight. Perhaps she could give them a miss. It wasn't entirely responsible, but right now ignorance was the option she preferred. Never mind the pervasive dread that not knowing created.

A sharp rap on the driver's window made her shriek in fright, and her head snapped up and whipped around to stare out at what she was sure would be a masked thug with a gun. She blinked repeatedly when the image that met her eyes didn't at all gel with expectation. How strange—her headaches had never resulted in hallucinations before.

The man standing beside her car made an impatient circular gesture with his hand, obviously wanting her to lower her window, but she could do nothing but stare at him blankly.

"*Tina!*" The muffled sound of his voice through the glass snapped her out of her weird funk, and she jumped before depressing the button to open the window.

"Harris?" She could hear the disbelief in her voice. There was no reason on earth for him to be here right now. What the hell was going on? "How did you get in here?"

Perhaps that was not the most relevant of questions, but it was the only one that came to mind. She lived in a house that had been split down the middle to make two flats. The house had one access gate, and because the place next door was unoccupied, Tina was the only one—aside from the landlord—with access to the property.

"The landlord gave me a remote control."

"Why are you here?" That was more like it: relevant and concise. Feeling a bit discombobulated by the exchange, she opened the car door and stepped out, hoping that standing up would make her feel less disadvantaged. A mistaken belief, as it turned out, since he towered over her as always. She should have known better.

"I came with Greyson. He's here for Libby. I wanted to make certain he didn't say or do anything stupid."

"Where is he now?" She had so many other questions, but that one seemed the most pressing right now.

"Waiting for her. At her house."

"Waiting to ambush her, you mean?" Kind of what Harris had just done to Tina. "And you're *here*? You're failing at your self-appointed task already." He shoved his hands into his jean pockets before shrugging uncomfortably.

"I thought I'd let them have privacy for this first meeting."

"He shouldn't have come. Libby isn't going to be happy about this, and she definitely won't want to hear anything he has to say."

"I know that."

"Why are you here, Harris?"

"I told you, I wanted—"

"I mean *here* specifically," she interrupted, impatience making her words curt. "At my house."

"Well, for one, you're the only other person I know in this town."

She raised her eyebrows at that, and he offered her another awkward shrug.

"I'm exhausted," she said. "I don't have the time or inclination to entertain you."

"I also figured it would take a while for Greyson to win Libby back—"

"Try never," she corrected with a snort, and his lips lifted at the corners.

"I don't much fancy his chances either, but he won't leave until it sinks in that this is probably a lost cause. So, I figured I'd need accommodation."

When he didn't elaborate, she huffed. He was seriously testing her patience. Showing up without any warning, when she was feeling emotionally and physically drained, was just beyond bearing. She wanted him gone *right now*, and she needed to call Libby to find out how she was coping with the emotional shit storm that Greyson had probably just landed at her doorstep.

"You should leave—I'm knackered and not in the mood to deal with this insanity right now."

"I'm trying to tell you that I rented the place next to yours," he snapped, his patience clearly wearing thin, and Tina felt her jaw drop as she stared at him uncomprehendingly.

What?

"I don't . . . what do you mean?" she stuttered, not sure she had heard him properly. *Praying* she hadn't heard him properly.

"I reckoned it would take some time for Greyson to admit defeat, and I'd need a place to stay in the meantime, so I rented this place."

Was he serious? What the hell?

The notion of Harris living in the other half of the split house was so completely outlandish that Tina could do nothing but stare at his tall figure for a long moment while her mind tried to process his words.

"That's ridiculous!" she said, hoping he could hear the contempt in her delayed response.

"It's the only place available for short-term rental," he said.

"You won't be here that long. You should have rented a room from the motel."

"I tried. They're full. There are few other options in this tiny town—just a limited number of guesthouses and boutique hotels. All full, before you ask," he added hastily when she opened her mouth to ask him why he wasn't staying at one of those places. "I rented this place for three months—the shortest lease term available—but that doesn't mean I'll be staying here for that long."

"And you couldn't find any other rentals?" she asked dubiously. It seemed unlikely that there would be absolutely no vacancies anywhere. It was the middle of July: not exactly peak tourism season.

"I told you I couldn't. Apparently, there's a cheese festival the next town over, and everything is fully booked this weekend."

Of course, the cheese festival. One of the reasons Tina had chosen this as her opening weekend—she'd hoped that the out-of-town visitors would boost business. But tourists couldn't very well eat at an establishment they didn't even know existed. That thought just made the entire disaster of a night feel much worse.

"And you knew I was renting the place next door?"

"No."

She tilted her head as she considered that short, curt response. He looked pissed off. Harris was always at his most honest when he was angry.

"Big coincidence." She still couldn't keep the disbelief from her voice, and he made a fierce gesture with his hands, obviously frustrated with her.

"I thought so too," he said through gritted teeth. "Hard though this may be for you to believe, Tina, my world does not revolve around you. I have my reasons for being here, and those reasons have next to nothing to do with you."

Ouch. Like she needed that pointed out to her. But she supposed the slight was largely her fault. She *had* been responding to all his comments with blatant suspicion and disbelief. Still, she hated being put in her place by Harrison Chapman; it felt unjust. She should have him on the back foot, not vice versa.

"The landlord told me that my neighbor was the new owner of the local eatery, and I put two and two together."

"How can you and Greyson both just up and leave work like this?"

"We can run the company from anywhere—just need a laptop and a phone, really. And a dedicated team of people who are amazing at their jobs."

"Nice work if you can get it," she groused, thinking of the dismal evening she'd just had.

"How was the relaunch?" he asked, seeming to read her mind.

"Why do you know so much about what I've been up to?" she asked, irritated that he seemed so up to speed on her comings and goings.

"Smith and Libby."

Of course. Tina was a little annoyed with the other woman for divulging so much of her private business to Harris, but at the same time she knew her friend didn't have any reason not to. Libby likely wanted her conversations with Harris to remain neutral and Greyson-free. It was inevitable she would keep her chats with him limited to Clara, Tina, and work. Of course, Libby knew Tina and Harris didn't get along, but she didn't know the extent of it. Some wounds were too painful to discuss.

"Also, Greyson," Harris admitted, and Tina's eyes widened. Now that was more than a little unexpected.

"What?"

"He's been keeping tabs on Libby."

"Oh my God, she's going to be furious." Tina gasped. "*I'm* furious!"

"I was too," Harris said while Tina surveyed his strong, handsome features pensively. The only source of light came from the porch, and it highlighted the stark angles and planes of his face dramatically, casting shadows and giving him a vaguely sinister look.

"Are you still . . ." She paused and thought for a second before attempting to reframe the question. "Does he still think . . ."

"Does he still think I'm Clara's father?" Harris completed the question for her, and she grimaced.

"Yeah."

"I don't know," Harris admitted, his voice soft yet brittle at the same time. "We haven't spoken about it again. We don't really speak about anything much these days. I don't think he believes his own accusations anymore. But who knows what the fuck is going on in his screwed-up head?"

They were silent for a moment, each wrapped up in his or her own thoughts.

"It's been a long day. I have to get some sleep," Tina said, breaking the increasingly strained silence.

"You didn't answer my question," he said, his voice taking on a gruff note. "About the relaunch."

"It was fine. We had a good turnout."

"That's fantastic, Tina." The gruffness in his voice increased. "I'm happy for you."

"Thanks. I have to go."

"Of course. Good night." He stepped aside, allowing her access to her well-lit porch.

"Night," she muttered as she fumbled in her bag for her house keys. Thankfully they were in a side pocket, and she didn't have to search for too long. She let herself into the house, shutting the door without looking back.

The thought of Harris living next door, separated from her by nothing but a thin wall, was disturbing, to say the least. She hoped he kept a low profile, but somehow she doubted he would. He didn't do low profile.

She groaned before dropping her large bag on the floor and leaning back against the front door, wrapping her arms around her torso in an attempt to calm herself and stave off panic. This was going to be a nightmare. She only hoped Libby and Greyson sorted out their shit sooner rather than later.

God! *Libby.*

She stooped to pick up her bag again and grabbed her phone from the outside pocket. She hoped her friend was okay. If Tina had reacted like this to Harris's arrival, then who knew what Libby's response would be to finding Greyson on her doorstep.

She tapped the call button and lifted the phone to her ear.

"Hello?"

Crap. Libby sounded subdued—not a good sign. "Be warned," she said urgently, even though she knew the warning came too late. "The Twisted Twins are in town! Harris just showed up at my door."

Harris valiantly refrained from slamming the front door behind him. He didn't want Tina to know exactly how disturbed he had been by her cold reception. Although, seriously, what had he expected? Of course she wouldn't be thrilled to see him. She never was. He glared at the shabby furniture in the place for a long moment, not sure what his next move should be. He needed to get to bed, but then he would have to change the linens. Everything was dusty and looked like it hadn't really been cleaned since the last occupant had left.

There were dishes in the sink, for God's sake. He seriously doubted that this place had passed any rental agency's basic health and safety regulations. Which probably explained why the owner was handling all the negotiations himself. He wondered if Tina's place had been this bad. And for some reason the thought of her living in such squalor made him want to break something.

He swallowed back his anger and started going through cupboards and cabinets, hoping to find reasonably clean bedsheets. He was going to have to purchase some stuff at the closest home store in the morning. He finally found some yellowed sheets that looked cleaner than the rest but smelled musty.

"Shit," he muttered beneath his breath as he proceeded to strip the bed in the master bedroom. "What the fuck are you even doing here, Harris?"

He knew Greyson resented his interference. He hadn't been too thrilled to find Harris already seated on the company chopper when he had boarded. And he had glowered at Harris during the entire short flight over. Then—while they were picking up their waiting rental cars—Harris had attempted to warn his brother to proceed with caution. And Greyson had ignored him.

Harris wasn't sure Libby would feel any more charitable toward him than Greyson did. And he already knew where the hell he stood with Tina. He should just cut his losses and get back to his life. But no, here he was, interfering where he wasn't welcome.

Once he'd covered the bed, he stood back and surveyed his work.

Housekeeping—more specifically bed making—was definitely not his forte. The sheets weren't fitted, and he had done a sloppy job of tucking them beneath the mattress. He ran his hands over the mattress and sheet in an attempt to smooth out the wrinkles, but it didn't seem to help. He was standing and glaring down at the bed, hands on hips, when his phone vibrated in his back pocket.

He fished the madly buzzing thing out and glanced down at the screen absently.

Greyson. Not a text, a phone call. Again.

He swiped his thumb across the screen, bed forgotten for the moment, and lifted the device to his ear.

"Yeah?"

"There are no vacant hotels, motels, or guesthouses in this fucking town," his brother growled by way of greeting, and Harris stifled a grin.

"Libby didn't welcome you back with open arms, then?" he asked unnecessarily, and the silence that met his question was answer enough. "What did you think was going to happen, Greyson?"

More silence.

Harris shook his head in frustration. "I rented a flat; it has two bedrooms. You can have the spare room if you want. But the place is small, so you're going to have to resign yourself to seeing more of me than you'd probably like."

Another lengthy silence, finally broken by a long sigh.

"Where?"

"This place is a hovel," Greyson said matter-of-factly after striding through the front door like he owned the place.

"Yeah, well, you don't get to be choosy," Harris retorted calmly. "The smaller room is yours. There may be some clean bedsheets in the linen closet in the hallway."

"I'd hardly call this a hallway," Greyson responded, eyeing the narrow passage leading from the open-plan living and dining quarters to the (shared) bathroom and bedrooms in the back.

"Make yourself comfortable—I'm off to bed." Harris turned to leave, but his name falling from his brother's lips without any inflection made him pause.

"Why did you come?" Greyson asked, his voice coldly curious.

"Libby. She seems happy here. Settled. You're going to destroy that happiness if you insist on—"

"It's really none of your business," Greyson interrupted frigidly, and Harris huffed an impatient sigh.

"You know that's not true. Contrary to what you may believe, Libby is like a sister to me. I care about her well-being."

"I'm your brother; you should care more about mine."

Harris laughed outright at that claim and shook his head. He couldn't believe Greyson had uttered those words with a straight face.

"Yeah? I think you lost the privilege of being called brother when you accused me of fucking your wife and fathering your child."

"I'm reconsidering my opinion," Greyson said, his voice and demeanor stiff and uncomfortable.

"Big of you. So I can expect an apology soon, then?" Harris didn't know why he had asked that.

"Is that what you want, Harris? An apology? Will that fix everything? Make it all right again?"

Harris paused and considered his brother's words before shaking his head.

"I don't know. But it's a step in the right direction." He watched Greyson's gaze turn inward as he considered Harris's words. When it looked like nothing more would be forthcoming from the man, Harris shook his head again, impatient with himself for thinking his emotionless automaton of a brother would ever really apologize, and strode toward his bedroom. This time Greyson didn't call him back.

Tina woke feeling completely out of sorts the following morning. The little sleep she had managed to get had been restless and plagued by nightmares. A sensation of undefined dread roiled around in the pit of her stomach. The vultures were back, their movements subtle enough to only gently remind her of their presence.

She lay staring at the stains on the wall opposite her bed. The room hadn't been painted in possibly ever, and what had once been an already terrible shade of green had faded to something that closely resembled baby puke. And then there were the stains. Possible water damage? She hoped so. Anything else would be . . . disturbing.

Well, at least she had thoroughly cleaned the house and moved in her own furniture from her place in Bantry Bay, so the house looked and felt very cozy, despite the unpacked boxes and less-than-ideal walls. She still missed her pretty little flat, which she had leased out to a young couple.

She sat up and groaned when she caught sight of her laptop casually flung onto the armchair beside her bed. Harris's appearance, combined with her massive headache—which thankfully had not developed into a migraine—had thrown her so completely last night that she hadn't even looked at her accounts. Now the daunting task lay ahead of her, coiled like a serpent ready to sink its venomous fangs into her vulnerable flesh. *Ugh!*

She was being fanciful and dramatic with her vultures and serpents. What the hell was wrong with her?

Tina tossed off the deliciously warm and thick comforter. The cold and wet mid-July winter climate definitely called for comforters and fleecy pajamas. She slipped into her comfy fuzzy slippers, dragged on a thick, fluffy robe, and padded into the kitchen to pour a huge mug of coffee from the timed machine.

She inhaled the rich aroma appreciatively before heading out to her porch. This was her favorite part of the day. Just after dawn, the air was fresh and had an icy bite to it, but everything was bathed in the warm orange glow of the recently risen sun. It looked like it would be one of the crisp, clear winter mornings she loved so much.

She sat down on the rickety, cushioned porch swing and shifted her feet beneath her butt as she watched the sun bathe the ocean and sky with fire. In this perfect moment, she could forget all her troubles and just *be*.

"Hey."

Her peace shattered in an instant. The precious morning ritual destroyed by an unmistakable, husky male voice that she absolutely loathed.

Crap!

She shut her eyes for a long moment, hoping he'd take the hint and just leave, but instead she heard the wooden boards on their shared porch creak as he came closer. She had never known Harris to be an early riser. And never in a million years had she expected to see him out here at sunrise on a Saturday morning. Even if it was a fairly late winter sunrise. She bit back a groan and opened her eyes to meet his gaze. He looked uncertain and way too good for an unshaven guy in sweats . . . damn him!

He was also clutching a mug, and he tentatively crossed the distance between his front door and hers. He seemed to be waiting for her to say something. But she kept her mouth shut and merely tracked his movements with her unblinking gaze, hoping he'd turn around and head back into his house. But he seemed to take her silence as approval and sank down on the other end of the rickety swing.

Tina held her breath, waiting for the ancient thing to give beneath their combined weight, but it groaned and held. Sturdier than it looked.

"Sleep well?" he asked softly.

She didn't reply, merely stared at him. Fighting to keep her expression neutral, not at all sure how to respond to this intrusion.

"I didn't sleep very well. My mattress has lumps," he said, keeping his voice conversational as he sprawled with his legs spread and his free arm resting along the back of the swing. His hand was uncomfortably close to her shoulder. He was taking up more than his fair share of *her* swing. His hard thigh brushing against her toes.

He sighed appreciatively, his eyes on the horizon. "This is an amazing view. It almost makes up for the less-than-ideal living conditions."

She bit her tongue, and the impulse to tartly inform him that he could leave if it was so awful. She took a sip of her coffee instead, shifting her attention back to the view.

"First thing on my agenda this morning: getting a new mattress," he said, still sounding way too damned chatty in the face of her silence. "Any idea if I can buy one in town?"

She contemplated the black liquid in her mug glumly, stubbornly refusing to leave until she had finished it. While at the same time just wanting to get up and escape his overwhelming presence.

"You can keep ignoring me; it won't stop me from talking to you." The words were said in the same conversational tone of voice he'd been using all along, and for a moment they didn't sink in. When they did, she turned her head and lifted her eyes to his face. She was startled to find him staring straight at her. His gaze warm and tender. The expression so at odds with those haughty cheekbones, stubbornly jutting jaw, and cruel mouth.

The movement of her head brought her face within touching distance of his fingertips, and she flinched—nearly spilling her coffee—when he opened his hand, breaching the short distance to stroke her cheek with the back of his forefinger.

"Easy," he said in response to her startled reaction to his gentle touch, his voice soothing.

"Don't touch me," she whispered, her voice carrying no conviction at all, and he smiled, the expression inexplicably tinged with sadness.

"I'm sorry," he murmured, his hand retreating and settling on the back of the seat again.

"I prefer to spend this time of the morning alone," she said, her voice sounding high and defensive. "It's my . . . my ritual."

"I understand," he said, his voice soft, but he made no move to leave, and she watched him in mute frustration. "I'll bear that in mind.

But I'm here now and I'm having my coffee. I'll just sit here. I won't bother you anymore."

Didn't he understand that his mere *presence* bothered her? But telling him that would reveal too much, and she clamped her lips shut before fixing her eyes on the ocean again. She felt tense and horribly out of sorts. Her morning in tatters.

He drank from his mug, exhaling softly with every second sip. It should have irritated her but didn't. And that baffled her.

He smelled good, all warm and musky male, and he was sitting so close she could feel his body heat. It was nice and acted as a comforting buffer against the cold air. Tina hated that she was enjoying his warmth. She didn't want to appreciate anything about this man.

The silence stretched on, oddly comfortable as she listened to him sip and sigh his way through his coffee. Five minutes passed without another word between them, the sun climbing steadily in the blush-tinged sky, promising a beautiful day ahead.

"Maybe Knysna," she murmured, breaking the silence, and she felt his gaze turn to her profile. He didn't prompt her, just waited patiently for her to continue. She took another fortifying sip of her now-cold coffee before adding, "For the mattress. I think Knysna's your best bet."

"Yeah? Thanks, I'll drive out that way later."

A movement on his left caught her attention, and her gaze shifted to his front door, where *Greyson* stepped onto the porch.

She leaped to her feet and glared at the man furiously.

"What the hell are *you* doing here?" she asked angrily before shifting her gaze to Harris. "What's he doing here?"

"He needed a place to stay," Harris said levelly.

"Good morning, Martine," Greyson said coolly—like her family, he always called her by her full name. Pompous ass.

"And you're letting him stay with *you?*" Tina asked incredulously, ignoring the other man. "After everything he's accused you of? After what he did to Libby and Clara?"

Greyson went rigid, but she continued to ignore him, her glare fixed on Harris's face.

"He's my brother," Harris muttered defensively. "You can't hold that against me, Tina."

"Trust me—that's the *least* of the things that I hold against you, Harris," she promised him acidly, and he pushed to his feet to tower above her.

"For God's sake—" he began, but she held up a hand and, still pointedly ignoring Greyson, swept through her front door, slamming it behind her with a satisfying bang.

She was so dumb, allowing herself to briefly soften toward him. So the silence between them had been comfortable and companionable—so what? It didn't mean they were friends, didn't mean they could ever be more than what they were. And seriously, how could he let Greyson stay with him? If the man had no place to stay, then maybe he'd leave sooner, maybe they'd *both* leave sooner. That would be best all round.

She didn't know what either man hoped to achieve here . . . but the longer they stuck around, the more likely this entire situation would end in heartbreak for Libby. And Tina.

She had to acknowledge that she wasn't as immune to Harris as she'd like to be. He'd been her first and only lover. And while the experience had been less than ideal, it had still meant something. She had once considered him important enough to allow him that privilege, and while she would never—*could* never—feel that level of infatuation toward him again, the anger, hatred, and residual desire she felt for him could result in some confusing and complicated emotions.

One of the many reasons she'd avoided him so determinedly in the past.

She blinked back angry tears, not sure why she felt like crying. It was stupid . . . *she* was stupid. She had bigger concerns right now than Harrison Chapman and his irritating brother, but still it was very hard to keep unhappy memories at bay when he was living right next door. Technically in the same house as her.

When she got to her bedroom, her laptop caught her eye, and a surge of nausea hit her as the vultures returned with a vengeance. She was pressing one hand to her stomach and the other to the dresser as she doubled over when a massive wave of panic nearly sent her to her knees.

Breathe.

She focused on that. In through the nose, out through the mouth. Slow and steady. Until she forced the nausea back.

She would have to face up to her responsibility eventually, would have to crunch those numbers and see how deep in the hole she was. Logic told her that one night could not have sunk her business completely. Not yet. But more of the same . . . and it wouldn't last. Not a year, maybe not even six months.

More nausea.

In: nose. Out: mouth. Calm down.

She could do this. She had overcome worse . . . so much worse in her lifetime. This was a piece of cake.

She just wished it didn't mean so much.

After a quick trip to Knysna to buy a new bed, bedding, and a state-of-the-art microwave, Harris decided to stop at MJ's for lunch. His first impression was overwhelmingly positive. The place was welcoming and cozy and reminded him of Tina's lovely flat in Bantry Bay. But, after his initial surge of pride at what she had accomplished, he sat down and surveyed the sparse lunchtime crowd. He accepted the menu from a cheerful server whose discreet name tag identified her as Suzie and continued to sweep his eyes around the place. There were about ten people scattered around the empty room. Some sat in pairs, and a few were alone and tapping away on laptops or with their eyes glued to their phones.

It was lunchtime on a Saturday, the day after what should have been an exciting relaunch. There were opening-weekend specials available and a free bottomless nonalcoholic beverage offered with each meal. Suzie asked if she could get him a drink, and he ordered a glass of their house red.

"Did you work for the previous owner?" he asked before she could leave to fulfill his order.

"Yes," the woman responded. "I've been working here for about three years."

"And is this your normal Saturday lunchtime crowd?"

Suzie cast a glance around the room, and her smile faded slightly.

"No. We're usually run off our feet on Saturdays. People haven't welcomed the change as much as we were hoping they would."

"How was your opening night?"

The woman looked uncomfortable and shrugged. Recognizing that she might feel gossiping would be disloyal, he told a slight untruth to set her mind at ease. "I'm a friend of Tina's." Well, he had been. Once. "And Libby's brother-in-law." At least that part was true. For now.

She still looked uncertain, but her smile took on a bit more warmth.

"Opening night wasn't great. We had less than half of our usual Friday-night crowd."

Shit. That was disheartening to hear.

"Uh. Is Libby in the kitchen? I just arrived in town and haven't had a chance to see her yet."

"Yes. Would you like me to get her for you?"

"Would it be all right if I surprised her?" Suzie hesitated, and Harris dazzled her with his best smile. "I'll tell her it was my idea."

"I suppose it wouldn't do any harm. Why don't you go and say hello while I get your wine?"

"Thanks, Suzie. You're a star." The woman blushed when he winked at her, and he got up and headed toward the silver double doors leading into the kitchen.

Libby had her back to the door, but her tall, slender figure was instantly recognizable. He smiled affectionately as he watched her issue brisk commands to her subordinates. They all hastened to do her bidding, comfortable with her natural leadership. She was completely in her element, and Harris loved watching her like this. So confident and self-possessed . . . the complete opposite of the heartbroken woman she had been the last time he had seen her.

She turned unexpectedly and froze when she caught sight of him, her face reflecting her shock at finding him in her domain. His smile faded and he cleared his throat, uncertain of his welcome.

"Hey, Bug. I've missed you."

Tina had briefly spoken with Libby earlier about her friend's after-work encounter with Greyson Chapman, but Libby hadn't been very forthcoming. She merely said that she had told him to leave. The lack of information, as well as the cold tone in Libby's voice, had disturbed Tina, but she hadn't pushed, afraid that probing too much might hurt or upset Libby even further.

Besides, Tina had other things to worry about, like the fact that it was another disappointing service. Tina—coward that she was—had retreated to her office rather than witness another dismal turnout. Charlie was there, but the teen was doing homework, and other than occasionally checking on the peacefully sleeping Clara, she was wholly absorbed with that task.

Tina was grateful to be left alone. She had her laptop opened on the desk in front of her but was checking her emails, surfing the internet, doing everything she could to avoid the bookkeeping. She told herself she would have a clearer idea after the lunch service anyway. There was no point in doing it now.

She was only delaying the inevitable, she knew that . . . but playing solitaire and opening junk mail was a vastly more appealing alternative right now.

The office door swung inward, and a laughing Libby entered the small room with Harris directly behind her. The tiny space immediately felt claustrophobic and airless after Harris shifted his six-foot-plus bulk through the door.

Libby's smile faded when she spotted Tina, and her perfectly shaped, full lips formed an O of surprise.

"Tina, I thought you'd be on the floor," she said blankly, and Tina cleared her throat awkwardly. She should be out there, ensuring that things were running smoothly, but quite frankly she felt superfluous and a little out of her element. Thandiwe and Ricardo, their service manager—or maître d', as Libby preferred to call him—had things well in hand, and what could possibly go wrong when they had only a handful of patrons?

She had fled to avoid feeling like a failure and, worse, appearing incompetent and foolish in front of the staff.

"I had to do some accounting. And I'm drafting an email to the newspaper," she said softly, angling the screen of her laptop downward so that they wouldn't see that she had cat memes up on the screen.

She *had* intended to send an email to the newspaper to apologize and attempt to explain the mix-up. But she couldn't think of a way to word the message without seeming like an unprofessional idiot. She would have to bite the bullet eventually; they needed to maintain a friendly relationship with the paper for advertising purposes. But Tina rationalized that it was Saturday, and they would probably only see the email on Monday anyway. So why not send it on Monday?

"Harris wanted to say hi to Clara," Libby informed her, and Tina forced the corners of her lips up into what she hoped was a semblance of a smile. Harris was watching her closely, his hands shoved into his trouser pockets. He looked less casual this afternoon, dressed in charcoal-gray suit pants and white dress shirt, with the collar undone and the sleeves rolled up his strong forearms to his elbows. Still not full work regalia, but not as casual as the jeans and T-shirt of the night before. Or the sweats of that morning.

"That's nice," Tina said, her voice faint. Charlie was watching them all curiously, and Libby made quick introductions. Harris tore his unfathomable gaze from Tina's face long enough to smile down at the petite teen, and then he had eyes only for Clara. His face softened dramatically as he stared down at her.

"God, she's gorgeous. The pictures didn't do her justice. She's bigger than I was expecting." He sounded awed and choked up. His hands left his pockets and reached for the sleeping baby before he paused, looking uncharacteristically uncertain.

"Can I . . . is it okay if I hold her?"

"Of course it is, Harris," Libby murmured gently as she reached down and lifted the sleeping infant from her bassinet. She carefully transferred Clara into Harris's strong, waiting arms, and he eagerly cradled the tiny body close to his chest, instinctively rocking as he held her close.

Tina kept her eyes on his face, the love and tenderness she saw there bringing scalding tears to her eyes, and she swallowed painfully as she watched him coo tender little nothings into Clara's ear. He nuzzled the soft hair on the baby's temple and kissed her cheek.

Tina's hands balled into fists beneath the desk, and her short nails cut into the soft flesh of her palms. She welcomed the physical pain, since it detracted from the envy that burned like acid in her gut. How easy it was for him to hold Clara and how at home he seemed with a baby in his arms. It left a bitter ache in her heart, one that she loathed herself for feeling. She shouldn't care. Not anymore.

When he dropped another kiss on Clara's forehead, Tina surged to her feet clumsily, nearly knocking the desk chair over.

"I have to get back to work," she said, her voice wobbling embarrassingly. She had to get out of this room before she humiliated herself even further.

"We'll be out of your hair in—"

"I'll see you later, Libby," she said, interrupting her friend's words rudely. She hurried from the room with very little grace or dignity and, instead of going back to the restaurant, made a beeline for the ladies' room.

Thankfully it was empty, and she went straight to one of the basins and braced her hands on the countertop, employing her breathing tactics for the second time that day. She had to stop reacting to him like this, had to stop allowing his very presence to unsettle her so much.

But seeing him with Clara, watching him cuddle and cradle her. It had been too much. The tears snuck up on her. One second she was staring at her face in the mirror, and the next she could barely see her reflection because of the blistering tears seeping down her cheeks.

"Come on, Tina," she implored her blurry likeness. "This is stupid. It was a lifetime ago."

"Tina?"

Oh God.

She shut her eyes and scrubbed at her cheeks in an attempt to get rid of the tears, but she knew that her pale, blotchy complexion and red-rimmed, swollen eyes would give her away in an instant.

Did give her away in an instant.

She lifted her eyes to meet Harris's in the mirror. He looked concerned. Of course he looked concerned. She was crying like an idiot.

"This is the ladies' room," she said inanely, possibly the stupidest thing she had said to him to date.

"I know that," he said, his lips kicking up at the corners.

"You shouldn't be in here."

"I know that too. In fact, I feel like I should be taking notes and pictures for all male kind. This isn't at all what I was expecting."

He ventured farther into the room, deliberately releasing her eyes and giving her an opportunity to gather herself, while he allowed his gaze to roam around the space. Tina gratefully yanked up some tissues from the box on the countertop and dabbed at her wet face before swiping at her nose. She could do nothing to disguise the bloodshot eyes and unattractive red splotches on her otherwise pale skin. She was an ugly crier . . . a redhead's curse.

"What were you expecting?" she asked, more for the sake of keeping the conversation neutral than anything else.

"I don't know . . . candy floss machines, perfumes, hand creams. Girlie stuff. It looks like the men's bathroom, only without the urinals."

"This can't be the first time you've ventured into a ladies' room," Tina said, still desperate to keep the conversation from veering into more personal terrain. Her voice sounded uneven and thick with tears. He finally allowed his eyes to drift back to hers, meeting and holding her gaze in the mirror.

"Believe it or not, it actually is," he admitted and cautiously moved a step closer to her, reminding her of the way a man would approach a skittish wild animal. Which was fair enough, since she felt pretty damned skittish right now. He very, *very* slowly inched his way forward until he was standing directly behind her, so close that she could feel his every breath stirring her hair.

But he did not touch her.

"Why did you follow me in here?" she asked.

"You seemed upset. I was concerned."

"About me?"

"Who else?"

"You have no right to be concerned."

"And yet I am."

She had no response to that. His words confused her, disconcerted her.

"I wish you hadn't come here."

"The ladies' room or the town?"

"Both."

He sighed deeply, and the movement caused his chest to brush against her back. She shuddered, disturbed by his extreme proximity. Disturbed and excited.

"I came here for Libby," he said, his voice lacking conviction.

"Did you?"

"And for you. We have unfinished business."

Chapter Five

"No, we don't," Tina denied. His breathing seemed to be getting heavier. It sounded uneven, jaggedly sawing in and out of his lungs.

"Turn around." The words were whispered, and she watched as his eyes closed helplessly while he buried his nose in her hair.

"No."

"Tina." Her name sounded like a prayer on his lips. "Please."

"I can't." She didn't know what was happening. It unsettled her. This was not something that should be happening. Ever. This *awareness*. This need to turn and step into his arms. It was undermining *years* of progress.

His hands lifted, hesitated—hovering in midair for a timeless moment, during which they both stopped breathing—and then settled on her upper arms. Lightly shackling her in his hold.

She was wearing a sexy black short-sleeved wiggle dress that celebrated her voluptuous curves . . . and his strong hands left scalding imprints on her flesh.

They both froze at the skin-on-skin contact before Tina shuddered in reaction and Harris groaned.

"I'd forgotten how soft you are," he whispered, his voice taut, and Tina stiffened at that word.

Soft.

It brought back so many terrible memories. She shouldn't allow this. Shouldn't be duped by him again. But when his hands stroked down the length of her arms, to her wrists, and then down to her hands, where his fingers entwined with hers, she was completely powerless to resist him. She craved his touch more than she had ever imagined possible.

His eyes still held hers captive, and she swallowed painfully.

"Why were you crying?" he asked on a whisper, and she shook her head as her eyes flooded again.

"It's been a stressful twenty-four hours. B-business hasn't been ideal . . ."

She was stuttering on the half truth when one of his hands released her fingers to palm the side of her neck, his large thumb stroking the sensitive underside of her jaw. She made a soft sound, somewhere between a mewl and a groan. His front was pressed fully to her back by now, and she could feel the unmistakable swell of his arousal in the small of her back. It was shocking and intimate and completely surreal.

"I'm sorry," he said, directly into her ear, his hot breath fanning against the temple.

"You shouldn't be touching me," she said, her voice lacking resolve.

"I like touching you," he replied, and she shuddered.

"Let me go," she said, her words a weak command. He immediately complied, leaving her feeling inexplicably bereft. He stepped away from her, and she felt distinctly wobbly without the warmth and support of his big, hard body.

She dropped her palms to the countertop in an effort to brace herself and lifted her eyes to meet his in the mirror. His pupils were dilated, he had a bright flush riding the crest of his sharp cheekbones, and his fists were clenched at his sides. He looked none too steady himself.

"I don't like seeing you cry." Tina nearly laughed out loud at his words. Ironic, when she had shed so many past tears because of him. "Would you let me help you? With the business, I mean."

Every atom in Tina's body rejected that idea, and she was shaking her head vehemently before he'd even completed the question.

"I don't want your help," she said, and his face tightened in annoyance.

"Why not?"

"Because this is my responsibility, and if this place succeeds after I accepted help from you, everybody would assume it was because of your involvement. It wouldn't ever be *my* success."

"That's ridiculous." But his denial sounded unconvincing, and she knew he could see the truth in her words.

"Nobody believes I can do this, Harris."

"Libby does. *I* do."

The latter part of his statement stunned her, and she turned around to search his eyes for any hint of deceit . . . but he held her gaze, the belief he'd just spoken of shining in his eyes like a beacon.

"Why?" she asked bluntly. "I've been a total fuckup for most of my life. Not even I believe that I can do this. So why would you?"

"You haven't been a fuckup."

She made an impatient scoffing sound and dropped her eyes down his body to the erection still straining at his zipper.

"Are you saying these things because you want to get into my pants? And what the hell is up with that, anyway? Haven't you gotten that fat-girl fetish out of your system yet?"

He glared at her, the tenderness that had been shining in his eyes just moments before replaced by brittle defensiveness. "You know I think you're gorgeous, so don't give me that bullshit," he said, his voice low and rough.

She raised her eyebrows. *Gorgeous* was it? "I'm sorry, but my self-esteem took a bruising ten years ago when you and your asshole buddies made the sick bet that you wouldn't be able to . . . what was it? Oh yes, 'fuck the fat freak,' right?"

He winced.

"Damn it, Tina. I've apologized for that. You accepted my apology."

"You hurt me, you asshole. You did more damage than you could ever comprehend. I *want* to forgive you. I want to forget about it because I can't keep looking back on that as the defining moment of my life. The moment that ruined my entire future."

"I know you were young and that what I did, what was said, hurt you. And I've hated myself for it . . . but I do think you're being over-dramatic, Tina. It was a stupid mistake, and I know it must have stung for a long time, but it shouldn't have, *couldn't* have, defined your life. You can't blame me for every fucking bad decision you've made since then. You have to take ownership for some of it."

She stared at him, her eyes burning with unshed tears as she recalled that night, then the days and months that followed it, and the terrible years after that. Her inability to pick herself up after the consequences of that moment had ruined her life and turned her into an anxiety-riddled wreck of a woman. She'd had ambitions—her ultimate goal, before Harris had so casually ripped out her heart and destroyed her future, had been to become an obstetrician. Now she could barely look at babies, much less deliver them.

"I take ownership of the fact that I stupidly thought my crush on you was something more than that and that I allowed myself to be seduced by you, but—"

She was interrupted when the door to the ladies' room swung inward and a couple of giggling teenagers strolled in. They both stopped dead at the sight of Harris, and one of them squealed in horror.

"Sorry," he muttered. He slanted Tina a look that promised her that their conversation wasn't close to done yet before excusing himself to brush by the two girls and exit the restroom. The pretty teens turned their speculative stares on Tina, and she offered them a tight, apologetic smile before vacating the room as well.

She strode blindly back to her office. Clara was crying—screeching, to be more precise—and Charlie was calmly attempting to soothe the distraught infant, cradling her and trying to get her to suckle on the rubber teat of a full bottle of milk. The baby screwed up her face and turned her head away from the offering. The wall of sound that met her ratcheted Tina's anxiety up to the ceiling, and she stood glued to the floor for a moment, not sure what to do.

"She's fussy," Charlie said with an unperturbed smile, and Tina envied the girl her natural poise with the baby. "Not a fan of the bottle."

Libby was attempting to gradually wean Clara from the breast. A necessity, since the infant was now in day care for four hours every weekday. But the plan was to keep the baby in the office in the evenings and on weekends, because Libby wanted to breastfeed her at night. The bottle was in case of emergencies. And Clara clearly wasn't interested in it right now.

"I—" Tina swallowed past the dry lump in her throat, feeling overwhelmed by just *everything*: Harris, the business, the screeching baby, and the memories that were threatening to claw their way back to the surface. "I can't. I can't . . ."

Luckily the words were soft, distressed little pants that Charlie—whose focus was on Clara—didn't hear. Tina turned and walked back out. She was vaguely aware of somebody—possibly Ricardo—trying to speak with her, but she kept going, walking until she was outside.

The sunshine that had been promised that morning had been replaced by black clouds that threatened to spill a deluge of rain at any moment. The icy wind had picked up and was gusting around her legs and under the skirt of her tight dress. She had left her coat behind, and the cold cut through her like a knife; the short sleeves that had seemed appropriate for the weather this morning were now working against her. She was shivering violently, and she folded her arms over her chest and bent her head to protect her face from the frigid wind as she walked toward her car.

She didn't remember much of the short drive at all and blinked in surprise when she looked up and realized that she was home.

She stumbled out of her car and into the house and methodically removed her clothing, one item at a time, from the front door to her bedroom. Shoes, dress, bra, stockings, panties . . . she shed them all and reveled in the brutal cold against her vulnerable naked flesh.

She crawled into her unmade bed and lay curled up—holding herself tightly—while she shivered beneath the comforter. And once there, naked and alone, she allowed herself to unravel completely.

The noise that emerged from the dark, deep, ruined part of herself was raw and agonizing and shattering.

Tina was broken. She had been for a very long time, and she was beyond repair.

Harris was taking a leisurely drive home after finally having his—pretty damned delicious—lunch at MJ's. The food was good, the atmosphere was great, and the prices were reasonable. There was really no reason—beyond the Riversend citizens' irrational stubbornness—for the restaurant not to succeed. Tina just needed some good PR and marketing, and the place would take off.

Their exchange in the ladies' restroom had been disturbing, and he definitely wanted to continue that discussion. He hated that she still resented him for his behavior ten years ago and should have known better than to press her on it. In all honesty, expecting his half-assed apology to be enough had been a bit optimistic, to say the least. But he wasn't sure what else to say or do. He genuinely regretted his stupidity but had no idea how to make her believe that.

He wasn't even sure he should push it. Perhaps it would be best to leave it alone. They could continue on as they had been doing for the last ten years.

Only . . . he didn't want that.

He wanted her to forgive him, and yes, he wanted to "get into her pants" again, as she had so crudely put it. It was self-serving and selfish . . . but he wanted to fucking rock her world like he had failed to do ten years ago. Maybe part of it was ego—he had been drunk and doped and had put up a pretty dismal performance that first time—but a larger part of it was a fascination with Tina that he had never really gotten over.

He drove his car through the gates leading up to the house and frowned when he saw Tina's Lexus parked out front. He was surprised to see it there. He hadn't seen her leave MJ's. The restaurant was only half-way through lunch service, and while business was slow, it had picked up a bit while he had been there.

He got out of his car and stared at hers for a while, seriously contemplating knocking on her front door to continue their discussion. He was taking a step in that direction when the front door of his flat swung open, and Greyson stepped out onto the patio looking . . . well, his brother looked fucking rough.

Shit. Greyson had gone a little off the rails after Libby had left, and, while the man had tried to keep it hidden, Harris knew his brother had been hitting the bottle hard for a few weeks.

Harris had been on the verge of intervening when Greyson had stopped cold, coming in to the office early every day and leaving late, working himself to the bone, and not touching a drop of alcohol (as far as Harris knew) from then till now. He had never let on that he was aware of Greyson's concerning behavior, but he had kept a close eye on matters, going so far as to have his brother's equally worried household staff report any potential problems to Harris and Harris alone. Fortunately, the other man had managed to cling to his icy self-control, and the lapse—so uncharacteristic for Greyson—had been a mere blip on the radar.

But now, seeing his usually impeccably groomed brother sporting stubble and disheveled hair, dressed in . . . what the hell was that? Sweats? Jesus . . . he hadn't even known Greyson owned sweats. His brother worked out in shorts and T-shirts. And even then, Mr. Cold as Ice barely broke a sweat. Seeing Greyson like this, Harris worried that the man may have dipped into the bottle of cheap wine Harris had spotted in one of the kitchen cabinets.

"Greyson," he said cautiously as he climbed the patio steps and walked toward his brother, who stood staring at him through bleary eyes. "You okay?"

He came to a standstill directly in front of his twin. They were exactly the same height, but the fact that Harris wore shoes and Greyson was barefoot gave the former a fraction of an advantage.

"Where have you been?" Greyson asked, sounding groggy. Harris didn't smell any alcohol on the man's breath and knew his brother must have just woken up. Also uncharacteristic . . . as far as Harris knew, Greyson hadn't taken an afternoon nap since kindergarten.

"To Knysna for a new mattress, and then to the restaurant . . . to see Libby and Clara." He watched Greyson closely for his reaction. But only by the slightest tightening around his eyes did the guy betray that the news disturbed him.

"There's no food in the house," Greyson pointed out after a lengthy pause, and Harris raised his eyebrows.

"So go and get some groceries."

Greyson stared at him as if he'd spoken in a foreign language, and Harris fought back a grin. He wasn't sure his brother had ever set foot in an actual grocery store in his entire life. Harris liked to cook and often went out to buy his own produce. Greyson's housekeeper did the shopping for him.

"Maybe later," Greyson prevaricated and turned to head back into the house. Harris followed, eyeing his brother closely.

"Greyson, are you wearing my clothes?" he finally asked, disbelief rife in his voice. Not even when they were kids had Greyson ever borrowed Harris's clothing. The brothers had always had vastly different tastes. Harris liked to bum around in whatever was most comfortable, usually jeans or sweats, when he wasn't forced to wear a suit to the office, while Greyson always wore neatly pressed chinos and dress shirts as casual wear. Harris couldn't recall ever seeing the other man in jeans and doubted his brother even owned a pair.

Seeing his twin looking less than impeccable and then realizing that he was wearing Harris's own sweats was a double whammy that left Harris feeling a little speechless.

Greyson looked down at the navy-blue sweatpants and matching hoodie as if only now realizing that he was wearing them and then shrugged, the movement of his shoulders looking listless and disinterested.

"It was the closest thing available. I haven't unpacked my bag yet."

Harris's eyebrows shot up.

The ever-organized, professional traveler Greyson Chapman hadn't unpacked yet.

Well . . . hell.

"You look like crap," Harris said, forcing the sympathy from his voice. He didn't want to feel sorry for Greyson. The idiot was getting his just deserts . . . still . . . he looked miserable. And pathetic. It was hard not to feel sympathetic.

"Fantastic. Nice to know I look like I feel," Greyson said drily, and Harris gaped at him, a little shocked by the self-deprecating humor he heard in his twin's voice. He couldn't recall the last time he'd heard anything similar from Greyson, and he couldn't quite hide his astonished reaction.

"What?" Greyson asked, swiping self-consciously at his nose. "What's wrong?"

"Nothing. I just thought you'd completely lost the ability to laugh at yourself, is all."

"Yeah, well, when your only options are laugh or—" He stopped abruptly, and Harris silently completed the sentence for him.

Cry?

Greyson cleared his throat uncomfortably and glared hard at the floor between his feet.

"Anyway," he continued awkwardly, "when your options are shit, it's best to choose the path of least resistance."

"So what are your plans, Greyson? What do you intend to do here?"

"I don't know," Greyson admitted, and Harris was astounded by the naked honesty in his voice. Greyson always knew what to do, and even when he didn't, he soon worked it out. "I'm taking some time to figure it out."

"And taking time out means slouching around here, wearing my sweats all day?"

"They're surprisingly comfortable," Greyson admitted, his lips lifting in a half grin, inviting Harris to smile with him. But Harris wasn't quite ready to laugh with his brother yet, and he averted his eyes.

"There's a sporting-goods store in town—I'm sure you'll find something similar there," he offered before looking back up to gauge Greyson's reaction. The small smile had faded from the other man's lips, and he looked . . . *shit*.

He looked miserable.

Harris didn't want to hurt Greyson; God knows there had been way too many ill feelings and misunderstandings flying around since before Clara's birth. But a large part of him *wanted* to punish Greyson. Especially since nothing had been resolved between them yet.

"Yeah? Maybe I'll go and check that out."

"I have a few emails to take care of," Harris muttered. "If you're going out, don't forget to get some groceries. We need everything. The basics, from toilet paper to milk and sugar . . . and get a couple of steaks, will you? I'm thinking of throwing something on the grill later."

"Sure, I'll take care of it," Greyson said, and Harris nodded before striding to his tiny room. He genuinely needed to send emails and get some work done, but it was also a convenient excuse to avoid Greyson's company.

He sank down onto his lumpy bed and sighed dismally. Seeing Libby happy and settled and also finally getting to spend time with his adorable niece had made his decision to come here worth it. But he didn't know what to do about Tina, and he definitely wasn't sure that being here would in any way improve his relationship with Greyson.

He shoved both hands through his hair and swore shakily. Like Greyson, he usually knew what to do in most situations, but this entire fucked-up mess was confusing and had him doubting his every decision.

It was dark.

Tina blinked, disoriented and terrified by the absolute blackness of her surroundings. She was curled up in bed.

Naked. Freezing.

She sat up and wrapped her arms around her body in an attempt to both self-soothe and warm up. The gesture did neither.

She felt around for her phone, finding the device under her pillow. The screen lit up, flooding her immediate surroundings with light, and she sucked in a relieved breath, only then realizing that she had been breathing in shallow, panicked pants.

She swore when she saw the time. After seven—dinner service would have started already. There were dozens of missed calls and messages on her phone. Most of them from Libby; some from Ricardo, the restaurant's service manager; and one missed call from her mother.

"Crap!" she swore, frantically punching the call button on Libby's number. Her friend replied almost immediately.

"Tina? What the hell? Are you okay? Where are you?"

"Hey, Libby. I'm so sorry. I came home to do some work and I fell asleep. My phone died, so I got none of your messages until now."

"Charlie told me you left when Clara wouldn't stop crying."

Tina winced, remembering her complete meltdown earlier. Triggered by the fraught encounter with Harris in the ladies' room and culminating with the baby's crying.

"I needed to . . . I'm sorry. I needed to concentrate."

There was an extended moment of silence from Libby, during which Tina could hear pots and pans clamoring in the background and raised voices as the kitchen staff communicated back and forth.

"I'm sorry I left," she said, once it became clear that Libby wasn't going to say anything. "I'll be right over. God, this is so . . ." She couldn't bring herself to utter the word *unprofessional* and instead let the sentence die.

"I'll see you soon." Libby's voice sounded distant. Cold. And Tina bit back a sob. She knew she must have offended Libby by implying that she couldn't concentrate with Clara in the office, but it had been the most convenient excuse for her appalling lack of professionalism today.

"Fifteen minutes," she promised, leaping out of bed. She wasn't sure her friend had heard her words, though, because the call had been dropped. Or Libby had hung up on her.

She entered the restaurant exactly fifteen minutes later and stopped for a moment as she blinked at the scene that met her eyes. It was a good crowd. Their best yet. Still not at capacity, but nearly three-quarters of the tables were filled.

Ricardo looked relieved to see her and came bustling over to her.

"Miss Jenson, hey, I've been trying to reach you. We don't have enough napkins. We ran out halfway through our lunch service, and I had to send one of the busboys out for paper serviettes. With the other napkins in the laundry, I—"

"Ricardo." She halted the nervous torrent of words with a raised hand, and the man stuttered to a halt. "I'll call the company on Monday to find out what went wrong with our order. We should have had more than enough to last the week. In the meantime, keep using the paper, and well done on finding a solution so quickly."

He looked relieved and nodded, offering her a small smile.

"Did everything else go smoothly?"

"Pretty much," he said. "Our lunchtime crowd grew a bit after you left."

"Fantastic. I'm sorry I didn't get back to you earlier. My phone died." He looked surprised by that but nodded, accepting her explanation. "I'll just check in on the kitchen, and then I'll be in my office if you need me."

She headed straight to the kitchen and found Libby bent over a countertop, putting the finishing touches on a dark-chocolate mousse. She watched as her friend dotted some raspberry coulis around the mousse and garnished the dessert with a sprig of mint and more raspberries before calling for service.

"Libby," she said quietly before the woman could move on to another task, and Libby's head snapped up. Her expression cooled when she saw who had called her, and Tina tried not to let that look hurt her. She couldn't blame Libby. She had abandoned everybody in the middle of a service and then tried to blame it on her best friend's crying, innocent baby.

"I'm sorry about—"

Libby held up an authoritative finger, effectively shutting Tina up.

"Agnes!" she called, and her sous chef stepped forward. "I'm stepping out for a moment—take over."

"Yes, Chef," Agnes responded, practically genuflecting when Libby strode past her and headed toward the back doors. Tina had no choice but to follow. The back doors opened up into a narrow, well-lit alley. A couple of busboys were loitering out back sneaking a smoke, and they both started and put out their cigarettes when the two women stepped into the alley. They apologized and hastened back inside.

Tina knew they couldn't give a damn about her, but they were appropriately terrified of her friend, who was a sweetheart in her everyday life but a no-nonsense authoritarian in the kitchen.

"I'm sorry about earlier." Tina completed her apology once they were alone, and Libby folded her arms over her chest and stared at Tina for a long moment.

"Having Clara in the office is clearly not working," she said, ignoring Tina's apology. "I'm trying to find another solution."

"No. Libby . . . that's not necessary. I just—"

"Tina, it's not fair that you have to work with a crying baby in your space."

"And it's not fair that you have to move your infant daughter to a place where you won't be close to her. We can make this work. It's only day two. We'll all get used to the arrangement."

"Like you got used to having us stay with you that first month?"

Tina's mouth fell open as she tried to figure out how to respond to that incredibly perceptive question.

"I . . ."

"It's obvious you're not too fond of babies, Tina. And that's okay . . . but I'd rather have Clara around people who love her and enjoy her."

That hurt so much it stole the breath right out of Tina's lungs.

"I do love her," she whispered, horrified that Libby would for a moment think that she didn't. Libby didn't look convinced, and Tina swallowed past the massive lump in her throat.

"It's not just Clara. It's all babies, Libby. I can't be around them."

"What happened to you?" Libby's question didn't sound concerned so much as accusatory. "You wanted to be an obstetrician, for God's sake. And now you can't even stand to *look* at my baby."

Tina hadn't realized that Libby had noticed that, and it made her feel sick to her stomach that Libby knew. And that her friend had completely misunderstood her reaction to Clara.

"I *do* love her. She's beautiful."

"It's okay, Tina," Libby said dismissively, when it so clearly was *not* okay. "I'll work something out."

She turned and walked away before Tina could fully formulate a response.

Tina wrapped her arms around her midriff and swallowed down a sob. God, this was supposed to be their exciting new start. Everything was supposed to get better, but . . . instead, nothing was going right, and Tina's life looked like it would never get better.

That night, in bed after a long and stressful evening at the restaurant, Tina fell into a restless sleep, and for the first time in months, she had the recurring nightmare that had plagued her for nine years.

She was happy. So happy. The baby in her arms felt warm and perfect. Tina felt bathed in light and love, and everything in her world was finally wonderful again.

Sunshine. Warmth. Laughter. Love.

And so much happiness.

She held the baby close. She would never let him go. He belonged in her arms, and she loved having him there.

She looked down and he smiled at her. A beautiful smile. She shivered when the sun slid behind a cloud and looked up. The cloud was massive. Pitch black and stretching from one end of the horizon to the other, it covered the sun and left everything cold and dark and miserable.

She instinctively held the baby close, but her arms were empty . . .

He was nowhere to be found. She looked around for him. But he had vanished. It was getting darker, making it impossible to see. She called out to him.

But there was nothing. No sound at all. As if the black cloud had muffled all noise. She called him again . . . but even her voice had gone. She screamed until her throat felt lacerated, but there was never any sound.

Harris woke with a start. What the hell *was* that? It sounded like an animal in pain. He tilted his head, not sure if he had dreamed the noise, when it came again, louder than before.

"Fuck!" He leaped out of bed and slammed out of his room. The kitchen light was on, but there was no sign of Greyson.

The scream came again, and he made a panicked sound in the back of his throat as he fumbled with the front door locks before yanking it open and running the short distance to Tina's place.

He banged on her door and yelled her name, but she didn't respond, just screamed again. It sounded like she was being murdered in there, and it made him frantic. Without giving his actions any thought, he slammed his shoulder into the door—it didn't budge, and he was left with a bruised shoulder for his trouble. He pounded his fist against the wood again before going around the side of her house and checking windows. The living room window was slightly ajar. He pushed it open even farther and climbed through. He then stumbled around in the dark, slamming into furniture as he felt his way to the kitchen counter.

It was easier to navigate from there. The place had the same layout as his, only with a shitload more furniture, and he seemed to hit every piece on his way to where he knew the larger bedroom should be.

She wasn't screaming anymore, but she was crying. Painful, devastated sobs that broke his heart. He cursed himself for not bringing his phone—the flashlight would have been handy—but he eventually made his way to her door, opened it, and stepped into her bedroom. Her bed, like his, was pushed directly against their shared wall, which explained why he had heard her cries so clearly. She had a night-light: a tiny little globe plugged directly into a wall socket. One of those he knew parents used for scared children. There was a pretty little ocean scene in the globe, and it cast a restful blue reflection onto the wall.

He was grateful for the small light because it helped him find his bearings very quickly. Tina was on her back and tangled up in her bedsheets, moving restlessly, her face drenched in tears as she cried in her sleep.

Harris made a rough sound in the back of his throat and sat down on the edge of her bed and tentatively stroked his hand up and down her arm.

"Hush now, sweetheart," he murmured. "You're safe. I'm here."

She was trembling violently, and he was tempted to curl up next to her and wrap his arms around her shaking body, but he wasn't sure how she'd respond to that once she woke up. It was bad enough he'd broken into her house and made his way into her bedroom. The best he could do was waken her as gently as he could and try to keep her calm and comforted.

"Tina, wake up, sweetheart. Come on. It's just a dream."

She sighed, the sound filled with so much sadness it just about killed Harris. Her beautiful face was swollen and blotchy with tears.

"Tina . . . ," he tried again, and this time her forehead scrunched slightly before, with another long, sad sigh, she opened her eyes and looked straight at him.

"Harris?"

"You had a nightmare," he whispered, and her face crumpled as she burst into tears. Horrified and not sure what to do, he intensified his stroking of her arm. "It's okay, sweetheart. It's fine."

"No, it's not," she denied in a thick voice. "It can never be fine. Oh *Harris*." She sat up and launched herself against his chest. For one shocked moment, Harris just stared down at her bright-red head before closing his arms around her wildly trembling body.

"It's okay, it's okay . . ." He kept repeating the inane phrase and dropped kisses to the top of her head, stroking a comforting hand up and down her back, while another—less *good*—part of himself loved the feel of her soft body pressed up against his.

"It's not okay," she said again, lifting her head to look at him, and Harris sucked in his breath at the expression on her face. "Please. *Please*, Harris. Make it okay. Make me forget."

She lifted her hand to his face, cupping his jaw, while her thumb brushed over his lower lip in an unmistakably seductive motion. There was no doubting what she meant . . . what she wanted . . . and Harris, immediately and painfully erect though he was, wasn't at all sure he should take her up on the offer he saw shining in her beautiful, tear-drenched green gaze.

"Tina . . . I can't do that. You're not . . ." The rest of what he'd been about to say was muffled when she moved her hand round to the back of his head, entangled her fingers in his hair, and pulled his head down until he was close enough for her to place her lips on his.

The kiss was soft and chaste at first. Innocent and inexperienced, but then her mouth moved against his, her tongue licked at the seam of his lips, and absolutely all bets were off.

He groaned, and one of his hands swept up her back and palmed her nape beneath her fiery mane of hair. His own tongue took over, showing her exactly what she should do and how she should do it. She proved to be an apt pupil, and soon they were dueling back and forth, tongues parrying and thrusting in an endless game of one-upmanship.

His other hand tunneled beneath her cotton pajama top until it found skin, and they both shuddered at the contact. His hand stroked up her front until it reached one of her breasts. He groaned when he cupped her. She was bigger than he was used to, and he loved the weight and feel of her in his palm. Her nipple was burning into the flesh of his palm, hard and hot. His thumb found the coal-hot nub and strummed it expertly. She arched into his touch, and he bit back a groan at her ardent response. God, he loved this . . . she was so responsive.

He shoved the top up, wanting to see and then taste her for himself. He reluctantly lifted his lips from hers and gently moved her until she was flat on her back and he was kneeling between her soft, pale thighs. That was when he made the welcome discovery that she wasn't wearing any pajama bottoms, just a pair of skimpy cotton bikini panties.

He said a reverent little prayer at the sight of her near nudity.

"Oh my *God*, you're so beautiful."

Their new position allowed him better access to her chest, and once they were both comfortable, he tasted and explored her beautiful breasts at his leisure. Licking, suckling, plucking, stroking, he fucking loved it.

Tina was making gorgeous little mewling sounds, and it made him harder than steel to hear her soft gasps and squeals. She was so sexy it was killing him. He wasn't wearing much, just his boxer briefs, and he could feel the scalding heat of her through the thin fabric of his briefs and her skimpy cotton panties. He needed more intimate contact and lowered his hips until his straining hardness was grinding up against her damp furrow. She was incredibly wet, and soon her slickness, combined with his own, soaked through the flimsy material of their underwear.

But it wasn't enough. He wanted more, she *needed* more, and they pushed and ground against each other, a disturbing—almost violent—urgency in their movements.

He had unbuttoned her top and was feasting on her full, soft breasts while pushing against her core. She had her hands buried in his hair, pulling almost painfully as she urged him to do more, to suck and bite and grind.

He reached down between their bodies, his aching cock feeling constricted within the confines of his briefs. He was too hard and too swollen, and he needed release in more than one way. He shoved his underwear down past his hips, all the way down, until he had kicked them off. He heaved a shuddering sigh of relief after he had freed himself and got straight back to business.

His hand burrowed down the front of her panties and found the straining nerve-filled button demanding his attention, and she tensed at his touch, her breath catching as one tentative stroke sent her tumbling into an orgasm.

A little stunned by her responsiveness, Harris kept stroking until the tension left her body completely, on a soft sigh. For someone who made so many raunchy little sounds when she was turned on, she was surprisingly quiet when she came. Just that one long, contented release of breath.

His fingers dipped farther down, finding her tight, slick channel and plunging inside. She immediately tensed again, and he watched her face closely. Her eyes were glassy, unseeing, her beautiful, soft mouth open as she strained against him. Her full breasts shook with each shuddering breath she took, the high, tight raspberry tips looking painfully distended. She was a sight to behold, and it made him want to immediately replace fingers with cock and make long, hard, satisfying love with her.

He dragged her panties off, meaning to do just that. He fisted himself and was poised to shove into her welcoming warmth when he swore viciously.

Tina, still coming down after her amazing orgasm, didn't immediately register Harris's abrupt shift in mood. When he swore again, she blinked and focused on his strained face hovering above hers. His eyes looked fierce, lips swollen and face flushed.

"What?" she asked, her voice sounding thick and sluggish even to her own ears.

"I don't have a condom." He groaned, and she shut her eyes for a brief moment, reality starting to creep into their surreal little bubble. "Are you on the pill?"

The question felt like a bucket of ice-cold water being tossed over her fevered body, and she went still.

Déjà vu all over again.

Chapter Six

"No." This time her voice was like ice, and she shoved both hands against his hard, sweat-slick chest. "Get off me. Please."

"I can get one from next door, just give me a second to—"

"No," she interrupted sharply. "This was a mistake, Harris."

He swore, his body quivering and tense above her as he fought for control.

"Right," he said, his voice low and terse. *"Right."*

He rolled off her to sprawl out on the cramped double bed beside her, while she sat up, her wild mane of hair falling forward into her face. He took up most of the space as he glared up at the ceiling, his rampant, throbbing penis arching angrily up over his abdomen.

Despite her twenty-eight years, she hadn't seen too many penises in her lifetime. In fact, Harris's was the only one she had any experience with, and ten years ago she hadn't seen very much of it. Now she tried hard to keep her curious gaze averted, but she couldn't stop herself from sneaking glances. It looked angry, swollen, and *huge*. Of course, she had nothing to compare it with. It could be perfectly average, but she didn't have much frame of reference, so by default it was the biggest penis she'd ever seen.

She bit back a groan at her rambling thoughts. She tended to focus on boring minutiae, since it kept the mind from dwelling on more disturbing thoughts. Yet another one of her coping mechanisms.

Not that his penis was boring . . . it totally wasn't. It was fascinating and—

"Stop staring at my dick," he suddenly grumbled, interrupting her crazy train of thought, and she flushed bright red, knowing that the current color of her skin was clashing horribly with her hair. "You're making matters worse."

"I'm sorry," she said sincerely. "I'm sorry I left you like . . . like *that*, but you know it would be a mistake to have sex."

"Right now, I'm finding it hard to agree with that sentiment," he said emphatically, and she wrinkled her nose.

"Maybe if you covered it up or something?" she suggested, hoping he would tuck it out of sight. "It's very distracting."

"This is a weird fucking conversation," he suddenly said with an amused snort, reaching behind his head for a pillow and thankfully— *disappointingly?*—covering his groin with it.

"Thank you," she mumbled. He snorted again and turned his head on the remaining pillow to stare at her. Tina self-consciously dragged the two sides of her top together, buttoning it up hastily.

"You okay?" he asked, his voice curt and gravelly.

"Yes," she said with a small nod and pushed her hair out of her face, meeting his gaze full on, hoping to convince him of her sincerity.

"You had a nightmare," he said. "It looked bad. What did you dream about?"

"I don't remember," she lied. He held her gaze for a moment before chewing on the inside of his cheek.

"You scared me," he admitted. "It sounded like you were being attacked."

"I'm sorry." She didn't know what else to say.

He exhaled, the sound long and weary, before sitting up. He crossed his long, powerful legs and repositioned the pillow over his lap. His chest, which had seemed to be the pinnacle of masculine perfection ten years ago, now looked even more massive and hewn from rock. The sight of him sitting almost completely naked on her bed didn't feel entirely real, and part of her wondered if she was still dreaming.

"How did you get into my house?" The thought hadn't occurred to her before. Now she found herself wondering how the hell he had managed to get into her bedroom with the front and back doors locked.

"The living room window was open," he said, his brow lowering in displeasure. "You should be more careful with security, Tina. You could have been burgled, or murdered in your sleep. Check all windows and doors next time."

"Lesson learned," she said pointedly.

His lips lifted in an unrepentant grin. "You were screaming bloody murder—nothing would have kept me out. In fact, I tried to break down the door before it occurred to me to have a quick look around the house."

"Break down the door?" she repeated, appalled. "It's solid oak. You could have broken your arm."

"More like bruised my ego," he said wryly, wincing as he massaged and squeezed his left bicep. Tina gasped and reached over to switch on her bedside lamp to get a better look at the massive bruise forming there.

"You idiot," she chastised, barely curbing the impulse to punch him on the same bruised shoulder. "What were you thinking?"

"I was thinking that you were screaming, and I would have moved mountains to get to you."

"Oh." She wasn't entirely sure what else to say about that. His smile took on a hint of sadness, and he hesitantly reached out to cup the side of her face in one of his large palms.

"I wish you wouldn't hate me." The words were soft and wistful. Tina placed a hand over his and shook her head helplessly.

"I don't hate you, Harris. Not really. I just . . . it's very hard for me to be around you. It brings back too many heartbreaking memories."

"I can't remember exactly what was said that night, but I remember the gist of it, and I do know that I would never intentionally have hurt you, Tina. I honestly liked you . . . I liked everything about you. But before seeing you that night, I lacked the courage to approach you."

"You weren't exactly lacking in self-esteem, Harris," she said, removing her hand from his. "I find it hard to believe that you needed *courage* to approach me."

"You were my best friend's sister. We grew up together—you were smart and funny and sweet. Approaching you with any kind of sexual intent could *never* be casual, and I was a foolish twenty-year-old. Anything more than casual sex was a terrifying prospect. I wasn't ready for anything serious."

"So you used a *bet* to bolster your courage?"

"I don't remember even agreeing to the fucking bet." She scoffed at those words, and he shook his head helplessly, lowering his hand from her face and dropping it to the pillow on his lap. Sincerity shone from his eyes. "I know you don't believe me. I wouldn't believe me either. But it's the truth. I remember seeing you—you looked so beautiful in that little red dress—and I recall thinking that I didn't care what Smith thought, what anybody thought. I wanted to be with you. Jonah handed me a drink as I led you to the patio . . . I drank it because I wanted him out of my face. I wanted to concentrate on only you. But everything after we danced and kissed is a blur. I can recollect only snippets of what followed. I know I was as excited as a fourteen-year-old with his first crush. And that, combined with everything else, made me fumble like a fucking amateur. I barely even remember the act. I woke up and you were naked next to me, and I was devastated because I knew I'd fucked up what should have been a great experience for both of us.

"I don't know how I wound up in my dad's study; there are frag-ments of Jonah and Schaeffer and the rest of those assholes throwing money at me. I can't tell you exactly what was said . . . just words, a few jumbled sentences. But the shit I remember . . ." He shook his head, his voice sounding absolutely wretched. "It was bad, and—*fuck*—it kills me to know you overheard all of that. When you confronted me afterward, I didn't initially know why you were so angry. I clearly remember you hitting me. But I was so confused and disoriented. I think I passed out shortly afterward. But when I woke up and pieced everything together the next morning, I was gutted when I understood what had happened and what you must have overheard."

"This is all a bit much, Harris. I can't . . . I don't . . ." She shook her head, not sure how she felt about this confession. Not sure she had ever wanted to know all of this. It didn't change the end result: the impact it had had on her life and on her self-worth and her plans for university and a career.

"I wanted you to know that not everything about that night was a lie," he said, and she swallowed audibly.

"How could you have liked me? When everybody else made fun of me for being a fat, awkward carrot head?" She didn't know why she had asked that question; she didn't want to revert back to the insecure teen that she had once been. Always so self-conscious about her hair and her body and her freckles.

"You have the most amazing hair. It fascinates me; it's like fire. I always imagined touching it would scald my flesh . . . it was a turn-on. And you had—*have*—amazing tits, and don't get me started on that gorgeous ass of yours. And over the years you've only grown more stun-ning. Those tight damned dresses you wear have been a form of personal torment for way too long. You have no idea how often I was left hot and bothered and hard after seeing you at some function or the other."

He was referring to the wiggle—or pencil—dresses she had discov-ered after deciding to embrace rather than disguise her curves. She loved those dresses: they made her feel sexy and seductive, showcasing her full breasts and rounded hips and butt while emphasizing her indented waist. They showed off her figure to its advantage.

Still, she was having a hard time believing that Harris had harbored some secret crush on her all these years. It seemed completely improbable, given the very many women with whom he'd kept company between then and now. Then again, he wasn't exactly professing to undying love, merely abiding lust. Two completely different animals.

She wasn't sure how to respond to these revelations, not sure what he expected from her. This entire experience felt crazy and more than a little surreal, with both of them sitting practically naked on her bed and her body still buzzing after the orgasm he had given her.

She slid out of bed and stood up on shaky legs, trying to ignore the way his eyes flared as they took in her naked thighs. The pajama top barely covered her butt, and she was acutely aware of the fact that she wasn't wearing underwear.

"You should go," she said and tried not to be affected by the shock and disappointment on his face at her abrupt dismissal.

"Uh . . . yes. Right." He set the pillow aside and got up. An involuntary glance down confirmed that he was still in a state of semiarousal, and she fought back a blush at the sight. He found and dragged on his underwear, and she quickly averted her gaze to the messy bed. When she sensed he was covered again, she reluctantly lifted her gaze to his face and then to his somber eyes.

"Are you sure you're okay?" he asked.

"Yes. Thank you for caring."

"Of course." He looked troubled, like he wanted to say something more.

"I'll see you around," she said pointedly.

"Yeah," he agreed gruffly before, *finally*, turning toward the bedroom door. "Close the living room window." The last was tossed over his shoulder as he walked toward the front door. "And lock the door behind me."

"Okay," she said distractedly, following close behind him. Her eyes feasting on his tanned back, so broad and beautiful, tapering down to a narrow waist and a gorgeous, firm butt, leading into perfectly sculpted thighs. God, he was absolutely stunning. She was tempted to throw caution to the wind and tell him to go get those damned condoms. But years of restraint and animosity toward him curbed that impulse.

Instead she watched him unlock her front door and pause for a long moment before turning the handle and leaving. She locked the door and leaned back against it with a soft, helpless huff of air.

"Oh my God," she whispered, running her fingers through her tumbled mass of curls. "What the hell?"

With everything else going on in her life right now, Harris's revelation was definitely a complication she could do without.

MJ's was closed on Sundays, a fact that Tina greatly appreciated after her night of restless tossing and turning. She hadn't managed to get a wink of sleep after Harris had left, her brain unable to switch off and her body too wired to relax. She got up at dawn and, after pouring her habitual cup of coffee, padded out onto the porch to watch the sun rise.

She stopped dead when she found Harris already sitting on the porch steps. She contemplated heading back inside, but she didn't want to miss out on her morning ritual. She needed it after the night she had just had. With a resigned sigh, she sat down on the swing and watched the horizon brighten. It was an overcast morning, cold and gray, with heavy storm clouds darkening the sky.

Instead of the spectacular light show of the day before, the gunmetal-gray clouds took on a sullen orange hue, beautiful but menacing. She wrapped her robe tighter around her body in an attempt to ward off the cold and continued to rock back and forth silently, her eyes constantly dropping to the back of Harris's dark head. The wind was affectionately flirting with the spiky strands of his messy short hair, restlessly lifting and ruffling the silky black stuff. He kept his gaze fixed on the horizon, but she knew that he was aware of her presence. His shoulders had tensed when he heard the swing creak beneath her weight.

"Aren't you cold?" she asked, reluctantly breaking the silence. He was wearing dark-blue sweats, sneakers, and a hooded black windbreaker but didn't have on gloves or a hat. Tina was protected from the wind sitting farther back on the porch, while he was exposed to the elements.

"It's not too bad," he said, turning so that his profile was to her. He had a mug of something in his hand, and as she watched he took a sip and then sighed. The sound almost made her smile.

"It's going to rain," she said, her eyes tracking back to the horizon.

"Yes." There was another long silence, surprisingly companionable, while they both sipped their coffee.

"Greyson didn't come home last night," Harris offered, and Tina's eyebrows shot up in surprise.

"What? Do you know where he is?"

"I was concerned—he hasn't been himself recently, so I messaged him, and he said . . ." He stopped and shook his head in disbelief before lifting his gaze to hers. "He says he's with Libby."

"With Libby?" Tina repeated blankly. "I have a hard time believing that."

She was reaching for the phone, tucked away in her robe pocket, intending to message her friend to find out what was going on, when the memory of her last strained conversation with Libby stilled her hand. She didn't think the other woman wanted to hear from her just now.

"I did too . . . until he said he had slept on the couch."

"That's still more than I would ever have believed possible."

"I know," he said with a baffled shrug. He took another sip of coffee, and instead of sighing this time, he wrinkled his nose. "This tastes like shit. I forgot to buy a decent coffee maker yesterday."

"Did you manage to get a mattress?" She could have kicked herself for asking, but he had a way of drawing her in, of making it impossible to ignore him.

"Yeah, but they can't deliver until Tuesday, so I have another couple of lumpy nights ahead of me. I'm going to need a chiropractor after this."

She took a sip of coffee to disguise her smile at his disgruntlement. He was kind of endearing when he was grumpy.

"Help yourself to some of my coffee," she offered before she could stop herself. But then couldn't regret the impulsive invitation when he gifted her with a boyish smile.

"Seriously? God, you're a lifesaver. Thanks, Bean." He leaped up before she could rescind the offer—not that she would have—and strode into her house without pause.

She rolled her eyes at the nickname; he hadn't called her that in years. When they were kids, he'd taken to calling Libby "Bug," short—he claimed—for "Lovebug." Tina, in the meantime, had been saddled with the much less affectionate "Bean." She had never known where the nickname stemmed from, since he'd always remained closemouthed about why he called her that. Tina had always assumed it was a shortened version of "Jelly Bean" . . . and, being way too paranoid about things as a teen, had reached the conclusion that it was because every part of her body wobbled like jelly when she so much as breathed.

She snorted as she thought about the self-conscious, silly girl she had been. When she looked at pics of her as a teen, always slouching, or hiding behind a piece of furniture or someone else, she felt overwhelmingly sad. She hadn't even been that overweight—she'd been on the slightly heavier side of average—but because of the importance everybody else had put on how her body should look, she had hated herself and the fact that she wasn't perfect and petite.

She shook off the melancholy and stared into her mug. When Harris returned moments later with a fresh cup of steaming coffee, she waited until he sat down again before she broached the question.

"Why 'Bean'?"

His eyebrows slammed together in surprise. "What?"

"Where did that nickname come from? I always assumed it was short for jelly bean, because of my weight." He was in the process of taking a sip of his coffee when she revealed that long-held belief, and he choked on his drink.

"Shit," he swore in self-disgust, dragging a sleeve over his chin to mop up some of the spilled coffee. "Why the fuck did you think that? I never gave you reason to think that, did I?"

She lifted her shoulders awkwardly, her red face betraying her embarrassment. He swore again.

"Jesus, the damage we do to ourselves and others when we're dumb kids is just—" He stopped abruptly and glanced skyward as if seeking strength, but what he got was a face full of water as the heavens opened up. "Fuuuuck!"

He jumped up and ducked beneath the porch roof as a massive amount of water sheeted from the angry sky. He said something, but the thunderous rain clamoring down onto the tin roof drowned his voice out. Tina shook her head and cupped her hand around her ear to indicate that she couldn't hear him.

He glared at her and very determinedly made his way to the swing and sat down next to her.

"It wasn't short for *jelly bean*," he yelled directly into her ear, and she winced at the volume. He toned it down a bit before adding, "I thought you were cute as a bean."

She jerked back her head to stare at him in surprise.

"What the hell does that even mean?" she asked, and it was his turn to look surprised.

"You know, like the saying?"

"That's cute as a *button*, Harris." Her voice was dry as a bone, and his brows lowered even farther—he looked completely flummoxed.

"It's not. *Is* it?"

"Are you being serious right now?" she asked, her voice brimming with laughter, because she could see that he was.

"You know English was never my best subject."

"Yeah, I'm always shocked when you manage to string two coherent sentences together," she said sardonically, and he shot her a moody glare, which just amused her more.

"I hated those things. Similes. 'Poor as a vicar . . .'"

"Church mouse."

"'Strong as a bear . . .'"

"Ox," she corrected again, a burble of laughter escaping with the word.

"'Bear' could work," he said, his voice sulky, and she smiled.

"It could," she agreed generously. "But I'm not too sure about 'cute as a bean,' though."

"So . . . all these years I should have been calling you Button?" He wrinkled his nose. "I don't like it. I prefer Bean."

They shared a smile, the first genuine one in more than ten years, before she lowered her eyes self-consciously and he cleared his throat. He took a sip from his coffee and sighed again; this time the sound was long and appreciative and ended on a slight groan.

"This is some great coffee, Tina," he said, and she risked a quick glance at his handsome profile.

"Glad you like it."

"Think it's going to rain all day?"

"Looks like it."

"What are your plans?"

She circled the rim of her coffee mug with her forefinger as she pondered her response.

"Probably do my bookkeeping. I've been procrastinating. It wasn't exactly the opening weekend I was hoping for. I don't think the numbers are going to be that great." It was more than she'd wanted to reveal, but admitting it was remarkably liberating. It felt like a weight had been lifted off her shoulders.

"The place looks great—it has an amazing atmosphere and an appealing menu. There's no reason for the locals not to come flocking back."

"I'm so scared that they won't," she whispered, her voice alive with fear and insecurity. She felt her breathing escalate at the thought of what that would mean for her business and fought to keep the ever-present panic at bay.

She looked terrified.

Harris clenched his fists in a desperate attempt not to touch her. He wanted to help her, wanted to make this better, but he knew his offer would be rejected again, and it frustrated him. He hated that she would not let him help her resolve this . . . but he also understood her need to go it alone. Her need to prove to herself and everybody else that she could make a success of this venture.

She had her eyes fixed on her mug, while her finger continued to endlessly, almost compulsively, circle the rim. He ran his gaze over her profile: that pale, freckled skin, so pretty and smooth; her long, dark, sweeping lashes, which contrasted so strikingly with her sea-green eyes; that cute little button nose; her round and soft cheekbones and jaw; and a full, lush rose-pink mouth. And when you added in that mass of flame-red curls, so soft and luxurious . . .

She was fucking perfect. And he ached for her.

Last night had been unexpected and so damned wonderful. To taste her, touch her, to have that memory seared into his brain without alcohol distorting and blurring it, was *beyond* priceless.

It had nearly killed him to stop and then to leave her. He would have given anything to stay with her. Even if it meant just holding her. *Even . . . ?* God, he would have *loved* to just hold her all night.

He wrestled his errant thoughts back under control and focused on her last, shockingly honest, statement.

"They *will* come back, Tina. Your marketing will have to be on point, though. I know you don't want my help, but I could write up a few pointers for start-up businesses—"

"I have someone to help me with that," she interrupted tersely, clearly annoyed by his suggestion, and he swallowed back the rest of his words. Talking to her was always an exercise in restraint and frustration.

"Right. Okay. Of course you do."

"Aren't you here to ensure your brother doesn't hurt Libby again?" she asked, finally lifting her fierce gaze to his. "He spent last night with her, and you have no idea why. You're doing a really crappy job, Harris."

"Libby asked me not to interfere."

"She did?"

He was surprised that she wasn't aware of that fact, since she and Libby usually discussed everything. "Yesterday, when I came to the restaurant."

"Oh."

"She didn't tell you?"

"She must not have had the time." Tina was hedging. Harris knew her well enough to recognize that she was being furtive as hell right now. "Well, if Libby doesn't need your help keeping Greyson off her back, then you should probably head home to Cape Town. I'm sure you need to get back to work."

"I haven't been away that long, and I told you before, I can work from here. And I'm not ready to go yet. I like it here."

There was such rampant and offended disbelief in her glare that he very nearly grinned—she was cute when she was outraged.

"You do *not* like it here. Your mattress is lumpy, and your coffee maker sucks. And you have to share your space with *Greyson*."

"I admit, the latter is challenging, but he's been different." Honesty compelled him to add, "Part of the reason I want to stay is because I'm concerned about him."

"Concerned? Why?"

"He fell apart after Libby left, Tina. I've never seen him like that before. And he hasn't been the same since. He was wearing my *sweats* yesterday, for Christ's sake." Tina's jaw went slack at that revelation. "I'm worried he won't be able to pick up the pieces once he understands that Libby really is done with him."

"He accused you of sleeping with his wife," Tina reminded him.

"Yeah, and part of me will probably never forgive him for that, but he's still my brother, and he's . . . I don't know . . . I think he's lost. I want to be here to help him find his way back."

She stared at him for a while before finally shaking herself and getting up.

"It's freezing out here. I'm heading inside."

He opened his mouth to thank her, once again, for the coffee, but she was inside with the front door shut before he could get a word out.

He sat on the swing a short while longer, gazing out at the relentless rain, before heaving a deep, despondent sigh and levering himself up. He turned to look at her front door, every cell in his body desperate to knock on that door, invite himself in, and spend more time with her. But he knew he wouldn't be welcome.

He bit back a frustrated groan and trudged back into his miserable excuse for a house. It looked worse than ever in the gloomy daylight. Greyson had bought groceries yesterday: a random assortment of food and cleaning products. He had placed the perishables in the refrigerator and had left everything else—still bagged—on the kitchen counters, probably expecting the nonexistent household staff to put everything away.

Harris had left it alone yesterday, hoping his brother would take the hint and unpack the bags, but then Greyson had disappeared overnight without bothering to set the kitchen to rights. Harris shook his head, shucked his windbreaker, and rolled up his sleeves, ready to tackle the unappealing job.

Unlike Greyson, Harris didn't keep a permanent household staff; instead he employed a twice-weekly cleaning service and was quite comfortable cleaning up after himself when he had to. He didn't enjoy it; he merely considered it a necessary evil.

The task served to keep his body and mind mostly occupied for the next few hours. He was contentedly scrubbing down kitchen cabinets when Greyson walked in. The other man stopped dead just inside the front door and gaped at Harris, who was staring back at Greyson with what, he was sure, was an identical gobsmacked expression on his face.

"What the hell are you wearing?" Harris exclaimed, stunned by Greyson's uncharacteristic appearance.

"Is that an *apron*?" Greyson asked simultaneously, referring to the old pinafore apron Harris had donned before starting the cleanup. He had found it in one of the kitchen drawers. It was a ridiculously frilly, disgustingly stained thing, and it had made his skin crawl to put it on. But the alternative—getting years of grime and gross all over his clothing—had been much worse. He was aware that he probably looked ridiculous.

But Greyson had him beat when it came to surprising wardrobe choices. He was wearing jeans. *Jeans*, for God's sake! With sneakers and a long-sleeved light-gray hoodie. He looked quite unlike himself. If not for the conservatively cut, side-parted, slicked-back hair, he could have passed for Harris.

"Were you trying to fool Libby into thinking you were me?" The suspicious—*ridiculous*—question was out before Harris knew it, and Greyson gave him the mocking laugh he deserved.

"Libby didn't fall for that when we were kids, and she for damned sure wouldn't fall for it now," Greyson stated unnecessarily. "I'm not here to play games, Harris."

"I'm sorry. It was a dumb question." His apology hung between them, both men acutely aware of how easily he had uttered the words, when Greyson—who had committed a far greater sin against Harris— still hadn't articulated a single word of contrition.

They stood staring at each other uneasily for a moment before Harris pointed the sponge he was holding at Greyson's brand-spanking- new pair of blue jeans.

Distressed blue jeans. His usually conservatively styled, ultrastaid, clean-cut brother was wearing faded blue jeans with rips at the knees and a shallower tear on one of his thighs.

"Why are you dressed like that?" he asked, and Greyson actually flushed before lifting his shoulders in an awkward gesture that was completely unfamiliar to Harris. Greyson was never awkward.

"I bought new clothes yesterday. I thought I'd help Libby fix some stuff in her house."

"Fix some stuff?" Harris repeated. "What stuff?"

"There are plumbing issues . . . things that need painting. General handyman stuff."

"Greyson, you're a lot of things, but last time I checked, *handyman* wasn't one of them. Did Libby agree to this?"

"Kind of. She has her hands full with the restaurant and the—the baby . . ." A fleeting look of longing crossed Greyson's face before it was tamped down and replaced by the familiar stoic facade he normally wore.

"Greyson, you can't just *insert* yourself into her life. It won't end well." Harris was well aware of the irony in his statement, since it was exactly what he was doing with Tina. He would do well to follow his own advice.

"Libby . . ." Greyson's voice went husky, and he cleared his throat before continuing. "She let me hold Clara last night, Harris."

To Harris's knowledge, it was the first time Greyson had ever held his daughter, and if the awed expression on the man's face was anything to go by, it had been life altering and game changing for his brother.

"Shit," he swore beneath his breath, pretty sure this wasn't going to end well for anybody.

"Greyson, I hope to hell you know what you're doing. And I'm not just talking about the fucking plumbing."

His brother's face closed up.

"I'm not staying, I just came round for my tools."

"Tools? What tools?"

"I bought a toolbox yesterday."

Jesus. The world was going nuts. Greyson disappeared into his room and returned shortly carrying a huge, heavy red toolbox. One that appeared to have the bells and whistles a professional handyman would have wet dreams about.

Harris hoped to hell his less-than-handy brother didn't hurt himself trying to impress Libby.

"Uh . . . don't save any dinner for me. I probably won't be back in time."

"I never had any intention of cooking for you, bro." Harris felt obligated to set his delusional twin straight.

"Regardless," Greyson said, and Harris barely refrained from rolling his eyes at the word. No matter how he was dressed, Greyson always sounded like he had a stick up his ass. "I'll see you later."

He left without a backward glance, and Harris swore beneath his breath, still staring at the door through which his brother had exited. It swung inward while he watched, and Harris tensed, expecting to see

Greyson again, but the wind completely left his sails when Tina stepped over the threshold.

She was comfortably dressed in black leggings and a long shell-pink loose top that tragically hid her sexy curves. Her long bouncy hair was tied up in a messy ponytail, and her skin was naked of any cosmetics, making her look like a teenager. She turned to face him, and her eyes widened comically when she saw the apron.

"That look suits you," she said tartly, and he grinned, ridiculously happy to see her. She darted a furtive glance around the open-plan living room and kitchen before dropping her voice almost conspiratorially. "Was it my imagination, or was that Greyson? In jeans and a *hoodie?*"

"Definitely not your imagination," he said, and she covered her mouth with her hand, her eyes huge in her face. "Apparently he intends to be Libby's handyman. Have you spoken with her yet?"

"Uh . . . no. I've been busy. Have you?" He wasn't sure he believed her. She and Libby always had time to chat with each other. Something was definitely up.

"No. I didn't want to contact her while Greyson was there." And his mind had been fully occupied with thoughts of the woman standing in front of him. Tina was right: he was a fucking terrible self-appointed guardian to Libby.

"Anyway . . . I just wanted to find out what was up with Greyson's new look," she said, suddenly self-conscious again. "I should get home."

"Stay." He knew she probably wouldn't but couldn't stop himself from issuing the invitation anyway. Shockingly, she hesitated, her hand on the doorknob and her body half-turned away from him. "I'm cooking a couple of steaks and baked potatoes for lunch. I'd very much like it if you'd join me. Please?"

"I shouldn't," she said, sounding torn, which gave him hope.

"Why not?"

She tilted her head back and stared at the ceiling.

"Oh God, *so* many reasons," she said on a humorless laugh.

"How about I give you one *great* reason to stay?" he asked, and her shoulders slumped in defeat before she turned her head to look at him, curiosity gleaming in her green gaze.

"What?"

"My baked potatoes will change your life." He was watching closely enough to see the smile flicker to life in her eyes, making them wrinkle at the corners, before it jumped to her mouth, tilting her lips up at the corners.

"Don't make promises you can't keep, Harris. I take my baked potatoes very seriously," she warned. And Harris lifted his right hand—still clutching the sponge—to his heart.

"I swear on my great-aunt Elsie's life, Tina." His words surprised a delightful little laugh from her.

"You forget I was at your great-aunt Elsie's funeral fifteen years ago, Harris."

"Well, on her soul, then. Trust me," he cajoled.

She shouldn't, she knew she shouldn't . . . but he looked so damned appealing in that frilly pinafore, with bright-yellow rubber gloves on his hands and that wet sponge clutched to his chest. She couldn't resist; she would have to have a heart of stone to have resisted.

"Fine," she relented, and his smile widened into a huge grin, one that showcased the shallow dimple in his left cheek. "Should I come back later? After you're done with whatever you're doing over there?"

He glanced down at himself with a sheepish smile.

"I've been cleaning the kitchen. It was left in a pretty awful condition. I couldn't cook in here the way it was before. I'm nearly done. Why don't you grab a couple of glasses and pour us some wine?"

"It's not even midday yet," she pointed out, vaguely scandalized at the prospect of drinking alcohol so early in the day.

"It's a rainy Sunday morning—nearly afternoon—we've both had busy mornings . . . who's going to begrudge us a drink before midday?"

She pursed her lips as she reflected over his words. It *was* nearly noon, and after another morning of procrastination, she could definitely do with a drink.

"Where are the glasses?"

"Good girl, Bean," he murmured approvingly.

Cute as a bean. The memory of his—frankly ridiculous—confession gave her warm fuzzies, and she hid her fond smile at the nickname that she had resented so much when she was a teen. He opened a cabinet above the sink, and she went onto her tiptoes to reach for a couple of gleaming—obviously recently cleaned—wineglasses from the second-lowest shelf. She could barely reach and looked over her shoulder for some help, only to find Harris staring at her butt with an appreciative, almost dreamy smile on his face. Recognizing that her long top had pulled up to reveal her bum and thighs in the tight leggings, she flushed and quickly grabbed the glasses.

She turned around quickly, keeping her butt against the sink, and was weirdly satisfied to see the look of disappointment in his eyes when the little peepshow ended.

"Wine?" she asked, and he almost visibly shook himself.

"There's a bottle of red wine in the cabinet under the sink," he said, his voice brusque, and Tina huffed an impatient breath when she realized she'd have to turn around and bend over to access the cabinet.

Biting the bullet—and okay, some part of her was really enjoying this strange, sexy game—she turned and opened the cabinet, aware of his eyes once again glued to her ass. She rooted around the cabinet but couldn't find the wine.

"It's not in here," she said, and there was a long silence before he cleared his throat.

"My bad . . . it's on the countertop next to the shitty coffee maker."

Seriously?

She turned around to take him to task for his obvious little ploy, but he looked flushed and sweaty and *very* uncomfortable. He was turned on. That much was obvious. He could barely stand upright.

Oh *my*. The knowledge of his condition made her feel outrageously smug and extremely powerful. She gave him her best cat-that-got-the-cream grin before sauntering her way past him to the coffee maker. Loving it when he groaned in reaction to the extra little wiggle she'd put into her walk.

Luckily the wine had a screw top, because she sincerely doubted there was a corkscrew in this kitchen. The flat was in much worse condition than hers had been. Hers had been unfurnished, because she had wanted to move her own things in, but this place was cluttered with unnecessary junk, and she wondered if the landlord had just moved stuff from her flat into this one.

"This place is a hoarder's paradise," she said while pouring the wine.

"I know. I took it sight unseen. Not the way I normally do business, but beggars can't be choosers."

The Chapman name was almost synonymous with property development, and Harris's family had built and sold homes and residential estates for generations, so this was most definitely not the type of place one would expect to find the Chapman brothers staying. Especially not the current CEO and CFO of the company.

Harris had always been the more down to earth of the brothers, and she wondered how Greyson was finding this unexpected foray into penury.

"Greyson must hate it here."

"Well, he hasn't really been around that much . . . but he didn't have anything good to say about the place."

"Well, in his defense, there really is nothing *good* to say about it," Tina said, and Harris, who was scrubbing the kitchen cabinet again, chuckled. "And Libby's house isn't that much better. If he intends to be her handyman, he'd better be prepared to fix toilets, sinks, and possibly the wiring."

"I hope to God he doesn't electrocute himself."

"Maybe he intends to call in the professionals?" Tina's voice raised in question, and she took a swallow of her wine before crossing the short distance to Harris and placing his glass on the counter beside him.

"Thanks," he muttered, giving the cabinets a wipe with a dry cloth before setting it aside and tugging off the gloves. Tina's nose wrinkled when the unpleasant smell of the warm rubber on his hands wafted up to her nostrils. Thankfully he turned away to wash and dry his hands before turning back to pick up his glass and take a thirsty sip.

"He bought a *toolbox*, Tina," he continued after his drink. "I'm pretty sure he's trying to prove something to her."

"His sheer incompetence at anything resembling physical labor?" Tina asked incredulously, and Harris grinned. He was smiling a lot, and it did crazy, fluttering things to her stomach. The vultures, for the moment, had been replaced by genuine butterflies, and their wings were soft and pleasant.

"He may surprise us," Harris said, but his grin belied his words; he obviously thought his brother was going to crash and burn. "I don't want to talk about them anymore."

The statement surprised her and made her immediately uneasy. The butterflies fled and the vultures returned. She didn't want to talk about anything else; discussing the other couple was safe and easy. Delving into any other conversational territory could very soon become sticky and uncomfortable.

"I'd rather know how you'd like your steak cooked?" he elaborated, and Tina breathed a soft sigh of relief. Well . . . that wasn't too bad.

"Um . . . medium rare." She retreated to one of the mismatched tall stools at the breakfast bar and clambered up onto it. It wobbled but thankfully held her weight, despite its less-than-stable appearance. She watched him competently move around the kitchen, cleaning and washing the spuds before readying them to go into the oven. He hummed softly beneath his breath as he worked. The tune was very familiar, but because his humming was so off key, she couldn't quite place it. The title hovered on the edge of her brain.

"Ugh, what *is* the name of that song? It's driving me crazy!"

He looked up, startled. "What song?"

"The one you're humming."

"I'm not sure. Wait . . ." He hummed again and then breathed a few lyrics in a falsetto voice that reduced Tina to stitches. He repeated the same two words over and over again. And the words, combined with the seriously off-key tune, were definitely familiar to her.

He shook his head before saying, "I'm not sure what that song's called—hey, stop laughing. I know for a fact your singing voice isn't much better." His offended observation just made her laugh harder. "Do you know the song title?"

"It's . . ." She gasped for breath, then broke down into gales of laughter again when she glanced up into his expectant face. She folded her arms on the countertop and dropped her head for a moment as she tried to bring her giggles under control. Once the laughter abated, she lifted her gaze to his smiling eyes—he didn't really look offended at all, just gently amused. "I'm sorry. It's not your singing . . . okay, it kind of is. But I think I found it funnier that you were asking for the song's title when you k-kept . . ." She inhaled deeply when it felt like the laughter was threatening again. "Kept singing it in that godawful voice."

"What do you mean?"

"The song's called 'No One,' Harris. By Alicia Keys."

"Oh." He twisted his face into a sheepish grimace before chuckling, the sound deep and masculine. "That makes sense. I like that song."

She did too. In fact . . .

"We danced to that song. On my twentieth birthday," he said, his voice quietly reminiscent. She nodded, surprised that he remembered the song, considering the state he had been in that night.

"I know." Danced. And then kissed. Her very first kiss. The song had come to mean so much more to her, but she determinedly tamped down those particular memories.

Amusement fled, and they exchanged an uncomfortable look before both averted their eyes. Silence descended, their troubled history once again asserting itself between them. Tina nervously drummed her fingers on the Formica countertop.

"Tina." His voice sounded anguished. "If I could do it all over again . . ."

She stopped tapping and lifted her hand to prevent him from saying anything further.

"Let's *not* go into this again, Harris." She watched him screw his eyes shut as he battled with what looked like some pretty powerful emotions.

"*Fuck.*" The word was soft and fierce and sounded like a prayer.

"Why don't we . . ." She paused as she considered the words she was about to utter. No matter which way she phrased them, they would seem like an olive branch. And she wasn't sure if she wanted to extend one yet. Or ever. Still, she was in his—temporary—home, about to break bread with him, so to speak, and maybe, for her emotional health, it would be best. "Why don't we set this aside? For today at least."

She watched his throat move as he swallowed and then shifted her gaze to his navy-blue eyes, which were alight with gratitude.

"I'd like that," he said gruffly, offering her the tiniest of smiles.

Tina heaved a relieved sigh, feeling lighter than she had in months. Possibly years.

"Good. Now, how about you get those steaks on? I'm starving."

Chapter Seven

"Oh my *God*, that was amazing," Tina raved an hour later, leaning back in her chair with a contented groan. "Where did you learn to cook like that?"

The last hour had been surprisingly stress-free. Once they'd made the mutual decision to leave the past alone, they'd relaxed into a companionable rhythm. Harris had cooked, Tina had kept the glasses filled, and they had chatted about nonsensically safe topics, like the weather, sports—both enjoyed watching cricket and tennis—and television shows. Harris didn't have time to watch much, so he'd been asking her to fill him in on current shows he'd heard about but had never watched.

When she'd refused to spoil *Game of Thrones* for him, he'd laughed at her and told her the only way he'd ever watch the show was if she watched it with him. She'd agreed without thinking. So nightly *Thrones* viewings were now going to be a thing, and Tina wasn't sure how she felt about that.

Maybe she could wriggle her way out of it at some point, but for now, she was just really enjoying his company.

"I learned the basics of cooking from Auntie Stella," Harris said. "Libby wasn't the only one paying attention when she cooked, you know?"

Natasha Anders

Tina's jaw dropped at the information. "Auntie Stella," as Harris—and *only* Harris—called her, was Libby's mother. Not even Tina—who had spent a lot of time during her formative years with Libby and her family—had ever felt comfortable enough to call her friend's parents anything other than Mr. and Mrs. Lawson. But Harris had called them Auntie Stella and Uncle Roland as a sign of familiarity and respect. Tina wasn't sure what—if anything—Greyson called them. She couldn't recall the other man ever addressing them directly.

"I didn't think cooking interested you?"

"It doesn't, not as much as it did Libby, but I watched and I asked questions and I learned. I enjoy cooking my own meals. What about you?"

"Me? I hate cooking. I cook because I have to. And I'm not particularly good at it." She laughed bitterly. "I'm not particularly good at anything."

"So no passion for food, then?"

"Beyond my obvious love of eating it?" she asked with an amused snort, brushing her hands down her "childbearing" hips . . . which had the unanticipated effect of making his breathing a lot heavier as his eyes followed the movement of her hands.

"I like that you love your food," he said, his voice taking on an added dimension of gravel, and she tilted her head as she watched him assessingly, trying to figure out if he actually meant that.

"I exercise regularly, you know?" she said. Wanting him to know that there was more to her than the obvious and resenting the inexplicable desire to tell him this about her.

"Okay?" He looked baffled by her non sequitur, and Tina cleared her throat awkwardly, committed to this pointless cause now.

"People always assume that if you're overweight, you have to be a lazy, unhealthy person who doesn't take care of yourself."

"I never assumed that. You glow with good health," he said sincerely before his eyes went flat and his voice went cold. "I'd appreciate it if you didn't lump me in with these other 'people,' though."

"It's hard not to, Harris," she said, her voice low, her eyes somber, and even though the topic was taboo for the day, they both knew she was thinking of a time he'd allowed what his peers thought to rule his actions.

He nodded regretfully. "I know."

"I'm sorry."

"Jesus, don't apologize, Tina! You have nothing to apologize for. Ever."

She did, though. A secret so huge it was starting to drive a wedge even between her and her best friend.

"So . . . ," he said with determined cheer, pushing himself away from the tiny excuse of a dining table and leaping to his feet, "what do we do now?"

"The dishes?"

"Nah. Those can wait. Let's check out the town. I haven't really been anywhere yet, just drove through it to Knysna yesterday."

"I don't think there's much to see," she said doubtfully, also getting up.

"Nonsense, there's the beach . . ."

"It's pouring," she pointed out.

"We could just drive by? And after that, we could go to the pub."

"It won't be open today. Apparently, this town is super traditional, very family oriented. People go to church and have big Sunday lunches, followed by afternoon naps. That's why the restaurant is closed today— it wouldn't be economically viable to open on Sundays. And I know for a fact that the liquor license doesn't permit the selling of alcohol today. So no pub."

"That's a fucking bummer," he said, sounding so disgusted that she couldn't stop herself from laughing.

"Let's go for a drive anyway." His restlessness was almost palpable. "We could go and check out that cheese festival."

"That's half an hour away," she pointed out, and he shrugged.

"You got anywhere else to be today?"

She thought about her laptop, sitting unopened on her kitchen table. She had spent most of the morning finally unpacking those boxes, finding a productive way to dodge the accounting. She had finished just as Greyson had left in those jeans, and now she had no more procrastination boxes to unpack. Decision made. She was definitely *not* in the mood for being a responsible adult today. She shook her head recklessly in answer to Harris's question.

"Great. Grab a coat and meet me on the porch in three minutes."

She grinned, abruptly excited about this unplanned excursion. She'd been living in Riversend for over a month and hadn't done anything but travel between MJ's and this house. She hadn't met anyone beyond her staff, and there was a certain formality between her and the people she employed. The prospect of going out and just being *normal* for an afternoon was unexpectedly appealing.

"Make it five minutes—I have to do something first," she said, and he nodded with a happy smile.

Tina made her way home, and—determinedly keeping her eyes away from her laptop—she pulled off her slouchy long top en route to her bedroom. She replaced the top with a fuzzy cream sweater and dragged on her black peplum leather biker jacket over it. Back in the open-plan living area, she picked up her phone, which she had left forgotten on her kitchen counter in her rush to head next door and ask Harris about Greyson's jeans earlier. She checked it, and her stomach sank when she saw that there were no messages from Libby.

A couple from Smith and another missed call from her mother, but nothing else.

She sighed and with a few sweeps of her thumb had Libby's number up on her screen. Her finger hovered over the call button before she swore and swiped to hide her friend's contact page. Instead she went to her messages and sent Libby a quick text. It felt safer—if a little more cowardly—than talking.

I'm so sorry about yesterday. I want to tell you about it. I want to explain. I do love Clara so much. But it's really hard for me to talk about.

She sent the message before she could reconsider and then watched her screen anxiously. It remained unread. A glance at Libby's details told her that her friend hadn't been online in more than two hours.

Well, that was . . . interesting. She sent another message: I hope you're making him unclog drains and plunge toilets. I love you. Chat later.

She put her phone on silent before tucking it into her jacket pocket. She dragged on her favorite high-heel, knee-length black leather boots; a fluffy ice-blue scarf with matching gloves; and an adorable matching tasseled aviator hat. She grabbed her huge purse on the way out.

Harris was waiting for her on the porch, looking mouthwateringly gorgeous. He had changed out of his sweats and was wearing distressed denim jeans, a red-and-black plaid shirt, and a faded denim jacket with a fur collar, along with leather gloves and a slouchy black beanie.

His eyes were returning her frank appraisal, a bemused smile flirting with his lips.

"You look stunning," he said, his voice filled with genuine warmth and appreciation, and she grinned.

"You don't look too bad yourself."

"Good enough to ravish?" he asked hopefully, and she giggled.

"Shut up." She dismissed him lightheartedly with a casual flick of her hand and then descended the porch steps, with him following close behind.

The rain had slowed to an annoying drizzle, and Tina stopped at the bottom of the steps, her eyes darting between her Lexus and his gigantic 4X4. It was such a masculine vehicle. She hated getting into those: her legs were too short, and she always hopped around inelegantly on one foot while gracelessly trying to drag herself up into the passenger seat.

She didn't foresee it being any different trying to clamber into Harris's beast of a vehicle.

"Why don't we take my car?" she suggested, and he opened his mouth as if to argue before shutting again and nonchalantly lifting and dropping his shoulders.

"No skin off my nose. You know the area better."

She didn't know why, but she'd expected some manly debate about how he should drive. His easy acquiescence reminded her how laid back Harris could be about ceding control to others . . . well, not so much *others*. Usually Greyson. Harris had always been happy to sit back and let his brother—older by a mere five minutes—take the lead. Greyson liked to control most situations, and Harris was quite content to let him. But he could also be very vocal when a decision was made that he didn't agree with.

It was a fascinating insight into his personality, and Tina considered it while they climbed into her car and dragged on their seat belts. She wondered if his willingness to let Greyson lead was less about Harris and more about the fact that his brother was a compulsive control freak. It was Harris's way of keeping Greyson happy.

Which was kind of sweet, actually.

And all complete speculation on her part, of course.

"You look so serious," he said, his eyes on her profile, and she turned to meet his deep-blue gaze.

"I was surprised you let me drive, is all."

His brow furrowed at her words.

"What? Did you think I was going to go all alpha asshole on you and demand we go in my big manly truck?" She could hear the laughter bubbling away just beneath the surface of his question.

"Well . . . yes."

"I'm not that guy."

"I'm beginning to get that, yes. Greyson is." She tacked on the last bit offhandedly and watched him closely for his reaction. The smile faded from his eyes.

"Greyson likes to be in control of everything," he said quietly, confirming Tina's previous suspicions. "His life, his home, his emotions. This whole situation with Libby and Clara has him spinning very far out of his comfort zone. I suspect—at some point—he's going to go full asshole until he realizes that it won't get him anywhere with Libby. I'm hoping he recognizes that he's going to have to change a lot about himself if he wants to win her back."

"I don't think he can change himself. Or win her back," Tina said, and Harris shook his head.

"Before yesterday, I would have agreed with you. But . . . he's over there right now. Wearing ripped jeans and a hoodie. Probably fixing toilets. And she's letting him. I'm not so sure anymore."

He reached over and tugged a strand of hair out of her collar. His hand lingered, and his thumb very gently brushed across her jawline.

"Why are we talking about them again?"

"Habit?"

"Time to form new habits," he said, his thumb still lightly grazing her skin, and Tina's breath snagged in her chest.

"Such as?" The question was embarrassingly breathless, and his lips kicked up at the corners while his palm moved to cup the side of her neck, and his thumb lazily stroked the sensitive skin of her throat.

"Give me some time. I'm sure I'll be able to come up with something," he murmured, his eyes following the movement of his thumb.

"We should get going." Her voice emerged on a squeak, and, to her eternal regret, he removed his hand and nodded.

"Right. Cheese. Let's get to it!"

"These are some passionate turophiles," Harris stated bemusedly beneath his breath an hour and a half later. They were observing the cheese-carving competition. Harris had his arms folded over his broad chest as he attentively contemplated the group of focused cheese carvers.

"Don't you mean turophiliacs?" she asked, and he rolled his eyes at her. Harris had been using the word *turophile* as often as possible in the hour since he'd first seen it in the festival pamphlet. He was like a kid with a new toy, and Tina thought it was endearing.

"Hush, and let me enjoy this. I don't often learn fun new words. It's all accrued expenses, assessed values, and capital gains or losses in my world. Boring as hell." He went back to watching the cheese carvers. Tina was tickled by how genuinely diverting he seemed to find this entire experience. He stopped at most stalls, asking questions and sampling so many different cheeses that Tina felt sick just watching him. She wasn't lactose intolerant, but she was pretty sure she was developing an allergy just from being around this much dairy.

"The guy over there, with the beard? Wearing the orange beanie and the pride scarf?" he said, pointing with his jaw, and Tina glanced over at a slight young man with overlong hair and full beard.

"What about him?"

"He's seriously talented. He's carving a tiny version of Michelangelo's *David*. It's pretty good. He should win."

"I don't know, Harris," Tina mused. "The flower child with the daisy-chain crown and the bell-bottoms over there is doing a pretty great job of re-creating SpongeBob CheesePants. I think she has a real shot."

"No way!"

"I mean, at least he's actually yellow. *David* is going to look jaundiced!"

"Care to place a friendly wager on that?" he asked without thinking, and she raised her eyebrows pointedly.

"Seriously, Harris? A *bet*?" Clearly comprehending how insensitive that suggestion must have seemed, he flushed and had the grace to look shamefaced. Tina allowed him to dangle uncomfortably for another long moment before letting him off the hook with a chuckle. "Ten bucks says SpongeBob takes it!"

"You're on!" he said with a relieved smile, and they shook on it.

"This might take a while. Should we get some drinks and come back later?"

"Yeah, there's a lot more to see."

"Not really," she said with a laugh. "We've been to the World of Cheese tent"—which had been filled with dozens of stalls representing different countries and showcasing cheeses from different regions within said countries. Harris had spent an inordinate amount of time sampling his way through France. "And you participated in the cheese wheel–rolling competition."

"That beefy asshole with the arms the size of my thighs cheated," he grumbled. "He pushed me! I was winning."

"Harris," she said patiently, for what felt like the thousandth time. "I was watching. You tripped."

He sported a now-muddied pair of jeans and a bruised ego because of that little stumble. And he had finished dead last.

"I felt his hand on my back," he said, looking outraged.

"Yes, you did, when he stopped to help you up. It was pretty impressive that he still went on to win after that."

"I'm not discussing this any further," he said decisively.

"Oh God, I hope not," she replied fervently. The cheese-roll race had been pretty tame compared to one she had seen on YouTube a few years ago. No steep hills and no spectacular tumbles. Harris had been one of the few participants to actually fall down the gentle incline. And despite his grumbling about it now, he'd been a pretty good sport about the whole thing. He had been laughing like a kid after that tumble, despite the muddy conditions after the rain.

"Anyway, I wanted to try the camembert ice cream," he said, and she made a gagging face.

"I don't care what you say—cheese ice cream sounds disgusting, and I refuse to try it."

"You can watch me try it," he said generously, and she slanted him an unimpressed side-glance. She followed him to the stall, which had an improbably long queue. Who knew so many people were into cheese ice cream?

Yuck.

He hooked a casual arm around her shoulders as they made painstakingly slow progress down the line. Tina nearly shrugged out of his hold until she realized that he had done it unthinkingly, and if she moved away from him, she'd be making a big deal out of something he didn't seem to consider particularly significant.

He made wry observations about the people around them directly into her ear, causing her to laugh often. She was enjoying his company. She had never—not even when they were kids—*truly* enjoyed his company. As a girl, she had been too nervous around him, and after his twentieth birthday, she had spent most of her adulthood avoiding this very situation. But she now found that being the sole focus of his overwhelmingly charming personality was a heady experience. And the thrill of it was giddying. She felt special and interesting and like the most beautiful woman in the world.

And part of her hated it. Because it was a lie.

Still, she shoved aside her reservations and told herself to enjoy this for what it was. An ephemeral moment in their tumultuous relationship. Likely never to be repeated.

So, she allowed the cheeky, off-color comments, the sweet smiles, and the constant touching. *So* much touching. His elbow was crooked around her neck, and his hand dangled down to just above her breasts. He caressed her face a lot, played with her hair, and she was 100 percent certain his lips had brushed against her temple on several occasions.

The butterflies were going crazy, and she was trying very hard to get them under control, but they refused to be tamed. She had no option but to let them soar, and she relaxed against Harris's side, sliding a timorous arm around his waist.

When they finally got to the ice-cream stand, Harris gleefully ordered his camembert ice cream in a waffle cone. Tina watched him queasily as he consumed his treat with relish while they strolled from stand to stand.

"This is quite good, Bean. You sure you don't want a lick?" He ran his tongue down the side of the creamy-looking treat, trying to tempt her . . . but the only thing Tina found herself tempted by was the tip of his tongue as it delicately and expertly created grooves in the soft ice cream.

She resisted the urge to fan herself, suddenly feeling incredibly hot and flushed on this cold gray day.

"Uh, I'm good, thank you," she said, aware of how obviously red her face must be. He looked up at her—his attention previously focused on his ice cream—and his expression froze when he seemed to recognize her reaction for what it was. His eyes sparked.

"You sure?" he asked, his voice dropping several decibels. He kept his slumberous gaze on her as he deliberately swirled his tongue around the top of the round scoop of ice cream. Tina's nipples tightened into painfully hard points while her mind spun with images of Harris twirling his tongue—still cold from the ice cream—that exact same way around her breasts.

"Tina?" His soft voice drew her attention away from her outrageous thoughts. She focused on her surroundings again and saw that they had come to a standstill behind the cheesecake stall. Her back was pressed against the damp plywood material of the temporary stall, and he was standing in front of her, shielding her from the crowd.

"Yes?" she asked, her voice trembling and unsure.

"Fair warning . . . I'm going to kiss you now." He didn't wait for her response. Tossing the remainder of his ice cream into a nearby dustbin, he cupped her jaw in both hands and lowered his cold mouth to hers.

She sighed and parted her lips, melting into his kiss in much the same way the ice cream had melted beneath his tongue. She could taste the savory creaminess of the camembert on his lips and welcomed his tongue deeper into her mouth as she eagerly explored the appealing flavor.

He moaned, the sound soft and desperate as he happily feasted on her mouth. The only other points of contact between them were his hands on her face, and Tina, whose hands had been fisted into the lapels of his jacket, found herself wanting more than that. She smoothed her hands down the front of his shirt and then burrowed beneath the sides of his jacket, coming to rest at his waist. That still wasn't enough, and she circled around to his back and pulled him closer until their fronts were pressed together. Her breasts to his torso, his crotch to her stomach. So close, and there was no mistaking his reaction to their embrace. She felt him, hot and hard and throbbing through the layers of their clothing, and wished for those layers to disappear.

She loved this: loved the feel of him, the taste of him, the scent of him . . . the absolute masculine appeal of him. And if the soft little curses and the desperation seeping into his embrace were any indications, he loved it too.

He jerked his head up unexpectedly, and she went up onto her toes, her mouth following his lips, but he moved his head back.

"God. Jesus!" He sounded shaky and groaned when he looked down into her face. "Stop looking at me like that, Tina."

"Like what?" she asked, startled by the unfamiliar thickness of her voice.

"Like you want to tear my clothes off." The words made her blink sleepily as reality slowly seeped its way back into her consciousness.

They were in a public place.

"Oh my God! Did anyone see?" she asked, horrified. His thumbs brushed across her cheekbones before he dropped his hands and shook his head. He stepped back, putting some space between their bodies. She didn't need to look down to know that he was still aroused, but he stood close enough to her for his condition to not be immediately evident to anyone else.

"Not really. And it doesn't matter if they did," he said. "Nobody knows us here."

He spoke too soon . . .

Chapter Eight

"*Tina?* Martine Jenson?" An unfamiliar voice called from their left, and they both turned their heads to stare at the couple standing hand in hand just a few meters away from them. The woman was smiling warmly; the man looked vaguely bored.

"Who the fuck are *they*?" he asked beneath his breath.

Tina, smiling at the couple, replied from between clenched teeth, "People from Riversend—just smile and be nice."

She stepped away from him and placed herself deliberately in front of him. Just in case he was still sporting that massive erection.

"Oh, hello. Lia and Sam, right?"

"Yes! Oh my goodness, how lovely to run into you here. Isn't it, Sam?"

"Yeah. Lovely," Sam repeated, sounding not one bit sincere, and Tina bit back a grin.

They stood awkwardly for a moment before Lia's eyes shifted speculatively to Harris.

"Hello. I'm Lia McGregor; this is my fiancé, Sam."

"Harrison Chapman," Harris said, stepping forward with his hand outstretched. Lia shook it enthusiastically. "Great to meet some of Tina's friends. I'm her . . . ." He floundered, obviously not quite sure where he fit into her life.

"Harris is Libby's brother-in-law," Tina supplied and was surprised when he sent her a glare.

"I'm *also* an old family friend of Tina's," he added, somewhat unnecessarily, in Tina's opinion. He turned his attention to Lia's fiancé, and the two men shook hands firmly.

"Sam Brand," the other man said in his curt English accent, and Harris tilted his head as he assessed the shorter man.

"Security, right?"

Sam Brand's lips quirked, his piercing blue eyes assessing Harris right back.

"Property development, right?"

Lia and Tina both rolled their eyes simultaneously, and the moment of feminine camaraderie surprised a laugh out of Tina. She rarely had moments like these with anyone other than Libby, and it made her look at the other woman in a different light. Maybe she wasn't too bad after all.

"We saw you earlier," Lia said to Harris, surprising Tina. "We didn't know you were with Tina, though."

"Yeah, saw your spectacular face-plant during the cheese-rolling thing," Sam said with a grin.

"He was pushed." Tina leaped to his defense with a vehemence that startled both Harris and her. Tina's face went bright red when he sent her a quizzical look, arching his brows in surprise.

"Was he?" Sam Brand asked mildly. "Bummer."

The two men exchanged meaningful glances, and Tina knew they were having a moment of male humor at her expense.

Ugh. See if she ever defended Harris again.

She'd blatantly lied to protect his ego. Harris was more than a little touched by that. He watched her self-consciously converse with the other woman and felt his heart swell in his chest. It was an unfamiliar emotion. His heart didn't swell; it didn't melt, bleed, break, or sink. It barely raced when it came to the opposite sex. It always plodded along at its normal pace, doing what it was meant to do, and doing it pretty damned well, if his last medical checkup was any indication.

His heart didn't *do* romance. Relationships were ruled by body and brain.

But this was Tina, and exceptions would *always* be made when it came to Tina.

Consequently, his heart swelled, and it filled his chest cavity with warmth and—he tilted his head as he examined this other wholly unfamiliar sensation blending so well with the warmth—*joy*.

Joy, a barely remembered sensation. The last time he had felt it was when they'd been dancing to that Alicia Keys song so many years ago. In that instant of lucidity before everything had gone to hell, he had known that he'd never been as content as in that moment when he'd held her in his arms.

He averted his eyes to the man standing in front of him and grinned sheepishly when he realized that the guy had been talking.

"I'm sorry. I didn't catch that," he said, loud enough for only Brand to hear.

"No worries, mate," the man said with a smile, his penetrating eyes missing nothing. Harris knew the man owned one of the most renowned international security companies in the world. He worked with politicians, royalty, and A-list celebrities. A little over a year ago he had been injured saving some pop star, and enough media outlets had reported on the incident to make the guy memorable.

"So, security, huh? Must be interesting," he said, and Brand nodded.

"It has its moments," the man said, reaching into his back pocket for his wallet. He withdrew a card and handed it over.

Harris stared at the plain white card. It simply stated in bold black, slightly raised lettering:

BRAND EXECUTIVE PROTECTION SERVICES
SAMUEL BRAND
CEO

His contact details were on the flip side.

Harris acknowledged receipt of the card with a tilt of his head and tucked it into his breast pocket.

"Cheers," he thanked the man. "I don't have any of mine."

"I'll find your number when I need it," Brand said, and Lia, tuning into their conversation, sighed.

"Gosh, Sam, do you have any idea how ominous you sound sometimes?" she asked exasperatedly, and Brand turned his attention to her.

"Do I?" He looked and sounded so genuinely startled by her question that Harris laughed.

"Dial back the intensity a notch, and you'll be fine," Harris advised, and the other man smiled.

"I'm in the process of moving down here; my company will be based out of Cape Town. Chapman Global Property Group needs a new security company. Call me about that sometime."

His cockiness startled a laugh out of Harris.

"Seriously, Sam?" Lia sounded both embarrassed and amused. Tina was watching everyone with a small, awkward smile on her face.

Harris abruptly recognized that he had never really seen Tina with any friends other than Libby. She didn't mingle. She never had. Even when they were kids—he now recognized—she had always been on the outside looking in. He found the thought disturbing. She needed more people in her life.

The other woman went back to valiantly attempting to converse with Tina and got only one-word replies in response. Tina had closed up tighter than a clam. He didn't know what to make of this behavior. He hadn't been with her outside of their social circle enough to see her around strangers before.

"We're having a baby shower for my sister next Sunday. I do hope you'll come," Lia said, and Tina's face froze.

"I don't think your sister would like that. I-I mean, I'm a s-stranger," she stuttered, clearly thrown by the unexpected invitation.

"Nonsense, she'd love it if you came. And Libby, too, of course."

"I-I . . ." Her eyes drifted to Harris's, and he could see the quiet desperation in them. He nodded before smiling urbanely at Lia.

"Of course she'll be there," he interjected smoothly. "I know you're worried about our date next week, Tina. But don't worry. I'm more than happy to take a rain check on that so you can attend the party."

Her jaw dropped, and the desperation in her gaze sharpened into daggers. Her look promised definite retribution, but she forced a smile to her lips and nodded.

"Lovely," she said through clenched teeth. "Thanks for letting me off the hook, Harris. I'd love to attend, Lia. If you're sure Daff won't mind?"

"Of course not." Lia stepped forward and hugged Tina, who went completely rigid in the other woman's arms.

"Yeah, she's a hugger," Brand said in an aside to Harris, who swallowed a laugh at that. "I keep telling her not everyone is into the PDA, but she's fucking adorably incorrigible."

"So nice meeting you, Mr. Chapman," Lia said after releasing Tina, who fled to Harris's side like a traumatized hare.

"Charmed, I'm sure," Harris said with a smile. He and Brand exchanged another handshake and a couple of curt nods.

The shorter man's eyes drifted to Tina, who stared back at him like a doe in the headlights.

"Don't worry," he said with a grin. "I'm not going to hug you. Nice seeing you again."

"Same," she squeaked from somewhere over Harris's shoulder.

The other couple sauntered away, their hands closing the distance between them once more.

Harris felt a thump on his shoulder and grinned before turning to face Tina, who was glaring at him furiously.

"Don't *ever* speak for me again! How could you do that?"

"You were practically begging me for help," he retorted indignantly.

"I wanted you to help me get out of it. Not . . . not *that*. Whatever that was."

"Come on, Tina, what harm will it do? She seemed nice."

"*Too* nice," Tina muttered balefully. "Who the hell hugs a stranger like that?"

"Okay, that was weird, but she has a bit of a Sugar Plum Fairy thing going on. I think she's sweet."

"*Too* sweet," Tina said, her brow lowering into a glare. "She keeps talking to me like we've been friends for years. I barely know her."

"She's friendly."

"*Too*—"

"Friendly, I know," Harris completed with a laugh. "And maybe she *is*, but people are generally friendly. They're not all awful."

She stared at him mutely, clearly not agreeing with that sentiment, and he heaved a heavy sigh.

"Let's go and see who won the cheese-carving competition," he suggested, and she nodded, still not saying a word.

They turned around, and Harris contemplated reaching for her hand the way Brand had reached for Lia's. He was on the verge of doing so when she spoke again.

"Don't do that again, Harris. I can speak for myself. Don't do good, or whatever that was, on my behalf. My life is fine the way it is."

Only it wasn't. He knew it wasn't. He didn't say anything in response to that and shoved his hands into his jacket pockets to resist the temptation of reaching for her again.

Tina was laughing as she parked the car outside the house an hour later. Harris was complaining about the results of the cheese-carving competition. To her amusement, he'd been grumbling about it on and off during the entire drive. He had been even more invested in the contest than Tina had realized.

"Bart Simpson," Harris muttered as he unclipped his seat belt. They had both been disgruntled when neither SpongeBob nor *David* had even placed in the top three. Instead Bart Simpson had taken the prize, followed by a daffodil and a smiling emoji. A round yellow face with a smile and eyes carved into it. It had required the bare minimum of work.

"And don't get me started on that emoji," he continued to complain, practically reading her mind.

"It was carved by a ten-year-old, Harris," she reminded him, trying not to laugh again.

"It ruined the integrity of the competition."

"I mean, it was more of an honorary mention than an actual placing," she said, and he muttered something unrepeatable.

They got out of the car, and Tina immediately noticed that Greyson's rented sedan was back.

"Looks like your brother is home," she said, and Harris's gaze fell on the car as well.

"Looks that way."

Once they reached the top of the stairs, they went silent and stood staring at each other for a moment.

"Should I . . . ?" he began, jerking his thumb toward her front door.

"No."

"Of course," he replied hastily.

"Good night, Harris."

"Yeah. Good night."

She was aware of him watching her broodily as she reached for her keys and unlocked her door.

"Tina?"

"Yes?" She turned to face him, and the corners of his lips lifted in a solemn smile.

"I really enjoyed today."

"I did too. Thank you."

"I hope—" He stopped abruptly and glared at the wood between his feet as he seemed to search for the right words. "I don't want to go back to the way it was before."

She didn't know what to say in response to that and remained silent. He lifted his eyes to glare at her from beneath that messy shock of black hair.

"Good night, Harris." It was all she could give him right now.

Monday's brunch-into-lunch service was busier than Tina had anticipated, and while she was dying to speak with Libby, her friend—beyond a brief "good morning" earlier—had been too rushed off her feet to spare much time for her. Tina felt lost in her own restaurant. The staff and Libby were so efficient that she felt superfluous. They didn't really need her for anything.

The duties she had expected to perform, like staff coordination, keeping track of inventories, and overseeing food preparation and service, were all very efficiently handled by Libby and Ricardo. Which left Tina to wander around, making uncomfortable small talk with some of the patrons. She soon gathered that—aside from handling their finances, paying the staff, and managing the marketing and PR—this was to be one of her main functions. She was the eponymous MJ, the "friendly" face of the business. And it was yet another aspect of the job she found herself completely unsuited for. She had briefly entertained the crazy notion of hiring someone to be Martine Jenson, but it was too late for that now. Everybody knew she was *the* MJ.

The thought of making cheerful small talk with strangers every day was enough to make her nearly break out in hives. She could feel her skin prickling at the very idea, her breath hitching in that awful stop-start manner that warned of an impending anxiety attack.

But it was a fleeting moment that she managed with barely a hitch. She wasn't sure if she should be proud of the efficient way she'd fended off the incipient attack or saddened that she'd experienced so many of them in the past that she could handle the milder ones like a pro now.

She settled on satisfaction. She was happy that she'd managed to keep it together, especially after Saturday's meltdown. Her victories were so few and far between that she'd take them where she could.

Still, it didn't solve her immediate dilemma of being the unofficially official spokesperson for the restaurant. But she'd figure it out eventually.

She had to.

She was still making stilted small talk when the door opened and Greyson and Harris walked in. She ignored Harris for the moment in favor of glaring at Greyson, who strode in like he owned the place. Looking much more like his arrogant self in a three-piece Armani suit. *Three piece!* Like he needed the formality of a vest in Riversend. His hair was slicked back urbanely and side parted. He looked like he'd just stepped off the cover of *GQ* magazine.

"Martine," he said smoothly when he saw her, and her glare intensified. He didn't smile at her—then again, he rarely smiled—but soberly tilted his head in greeting.

Tina nodded at the elderly lady with whom she had been having a very uncomfortable chat and excused herself. She tried not to notice the relief in the woman's faded gray eyes.

She clamped her hand onto Greyson's strong forearm and led him away.

"Try not to kill him, Tina," Harris advised calmly, and she shot him a glare over her shoulder before plastering a fake smile to her lips for the benefit of the other patrons as she practically dragged the tall man toward her office.

"I'll just stay here and order for us," Harris called from behind them, and Tina ignored him.

"What do you want, Greyson?" she asked, turning to face him, hands planted on hips, once they were in the privacy of the office.

"Lunch. But I suppose we're doing this instead," he said, his voice even and revealing little emotion. Tina was struck by how very different he was from Harris. Greyson was on permanent lockdown, whereas his brother smiled often and wasn't afraid to show emotion, good or bad. In fact, Tina doubted the man actually *had* emotions.

"What the hell are you doing here?" she asked on a furious whisper.

"I'm here for Olivia." He swallowed, the first sign of anything resembling uncertainty she'd ever seen from him, before adding, "And Clara."

"You don't deserve them."

She suddenly noticed that his left hand was bandaged and was about to ask him about it when he spoke again. And sent all other thoughts fleeing from her mind.

"And you don't have the right to an opinion in this matter, Martine. It's between my wife and I."

Oh no, he did *not*! Tina clenched her fists and fixed a deathly glare on him. It was time to set this bastard straight once and for all.

Harris had briefly considered intervening but in the end decided that Greyson was a big boy. He could take care of himself. Besides, Tina needed to have this conversation with him, and far be it from Harris to deprive her of that. He was perusing the menu, trying to figure out what he was in the mood for, when he heard Libby's voice coming from behind him.

"Harris? I heard you were here . . . with a look-alike." She cast her eyes around the room. "Where is he?"

"He was accosted by a pissed-off little redhead and dragged away into the back office," Harris supplied and watched his friend bristle quite magnificently. Even her hair seemed to stand on end.

"She has *no* right," Libby practically growled before turning to stomp off in the direction Tina and Greyson had gone, but Harris jumped up and grabbed her hand to stop her.

"Sit with me for a moment, Bug," he invited quietly, and she tried to tug her hand out of his. But his grip was gentle and unrelenting. "C'mon, Libby, sit. Please."

The wind seemed to leave her sails, and her shoulders slumped before she turned and plonked herself into a chair at his table. Harris joined her and smiled at her.

"Maybe he should hear what Tina has to say," Harris suggested, and Libby shook her head.

"*I* don't even know what Tina has to say. She has been so weird since we've moved here. She hasn't been honest about how this place is doing, I know that. She's been borderline bitchy to the nicest people. She went home in the middle of the brunch service on Saturday." She shook her head in disgust at that. "Ostensibly to work. Because apparently she can't work around a crying baby. She can barely look at a *non*crying baby, by the way. She has been *awful*, and part of me wishes I'd never agreed to run this business with her. I'm not sure our friendship can survive it. And now *this*? She has no right to interfere in my marriage."

"What marriage?" He silenced her with the question, and Libby sucked in a shuddering breath and wiped at her eyes. But she couldn't keep the tears at bay, and they seeped slowly down her cheeks.

"Forget about what Greyson and Tina are talking about for a moment and answer me this. How many friends do you have?"

She looked baffled by his question and shrugged helplessly.

"I don't know . . . a few."

"And since coming here? Have you made any new ones?"

"Yes, of course."

"Of course," he repeated with a warm smile. "It's easy for you: you're sweet and warm and genuine, and people are drawn to you."

She shook her head, looking perplexed, and shrugged.

"Maybe."

"Tina has *one* friend, Libby. You." She stared at him in shock. Her eyes filled with regret and then defiance.

"Well, that's her own fault. She could have more if she wasn't so distrustful of everybody she met."

"People haven't given her much reason to trust them in the past, Bug. You know that."

"I've been through the same experiences—I overcame them."

"Your experiences haven't been the same," Harris murmured, thinking of that damned bet. "You had supportive parents; you had *me*. You had Tina. And once you went to university, you had so many new experiences, made new friends. Tina only ever had you."

"You don't even like Tina. I don't understand why you're talking like this," she murmured, swiping her hand across her eyes again.

"I like Tina. I've always liked her. But *I'm* the reason she and I could never be friends and never got along. If she hasn't told you about it, then I can't. But whatever caused this rift between you, it's making her"—he paused, his hand reaching up to find his pendant through his shirt as he considered his next words—"sad. It's making her so sad. And I have to tell you, I'm finding it . . . *difficult* to see her sad."

His words made Libby pause, and she tilted her head to eye him thoughtfully for a moment. She sighed in frustration.

"She won't even *look* at Clara, Harris. Won't pick her up. I don't think she's ever touched her. I don't want Clara around someone who hates kids."

"Tina doesn't hate kids." Harris thought back to that night in the hospital, the absolute love and delight on Tina's face when she had first laid eyes on Clara. "She adores Clara."

"One of the reasons I moved up here was because, while we were staying with her, she went to great lengths to avoid coming home until very late at night. She never offered to hold Clara or bathe her or any of the other normal things people want to do when they're around babies. My God, your *mother* spent half an hour cooing inane little nothings to Clara when she and your father dropped in for a visit. And you know how she is."

Harris was having a really hard time reconciling her words with the image of Tina staring yearningly through the glass when the nurse had lifted Clara.

"I don't know what's going on, but there has to be a reason for her behavior, Libby. Talk to her."

Libby's gaze softened.

"I will, Harris. Of course I will. She's my best friend, and I do want to figure this out . . . but it's hard. I'm so much more protective of Clara than I ever dreamt I would be. I can't bear the thought of her being exposed to such negativity. She was born into rejection. I don't want her to experience any more of that."

"I understand," Harris said quietly, and she cleared her throat.

"Thanks for talking me off the friend-murdering ledge," she said with a half smile. "But I still want to get in there and tell her to back the hell off. Gently, of course." This last added when he had opened his mouth to caution her to do just that.

He smiled and nodded, got up when she got up, and watched her slender back as she walked toward the office in that brisk, no-nonsense way of hers.

"Tina." Libby's quiet voice came from the doorway, and Tina looked up from the dazed-looking Greyson, who had sat down on the sofa roughly halfway through her tirade. Well, not sat so much as dropped, his knees seeming to have given in. He'd spent the rest of the time sitting there with his forearms resting on his spread thighs and his hands dangling between his knees, just gazing at the carpeted floor, while she continued to rant at him like a fishwife. In hindsight, maybe she had been a little *too* honest with him.

"That's enough," Libby continued without heat, and Greyson's head snapped up at the sound of her voice. Tina was stunned to see his eyes gleaming with moisture, and for a second she wasn't sure how to react.

Greyson leaped gracelessly to his feet, but Libby kept her focus on Tina. She didn't look angry; she looked emotional and teary, and Tina wondered how much she had overheard.

"Would you mind leaving us, please?" Libby asked, and Tina nodded, her reflexes feeling off, her legs leaden. She looked at Greyson again, feeling strangely compelled to apologize to him. But his eyes were glued to Libby's face, and Tina wasn't sure he would hear anything she said right now.

She finally reached the door, and as she passed Libby, her friend grabbed her hand and squeezed.

"We'll talk later, okay?" Libby said, and a strangled sob burst from Tina's lips before she could stop it.

"I'd like that," she said thickly, her eyes burning with unshed tears. Libby gave her hand one final squeeze and allowed her to pass. Tina shut the door on the way out and stared at it for a long moment before slowly making her way back toward the restaurant. The lunchtime "crowd" had thinned, and she spotted Harris immediately; he was seated at the same table as last time, his head down as he checked his phone.

She walked toward him on wobbly legs and sank down across from him. He lifted his head and smiled when he saw her. The smile was quickly replaced by concern.

"You're white as a cloud."

"Sheet," she corrected, and he rolled his eyes.

"It still works. Anyway, you're pale. Are you okay?"

"I think maybe I was . . . I was too mean to Greyson."

His eyebrows darted up to his hairline.

"I don't think anybody in the history of the world has ever used that combination of words in that order before. At least not in relation to my brother. Nobody. Like ever."

"Don't be silly, I'm serious."

"Me too. What did you say to him?"

"He told me—*me*—that I didn't have a right to an opinion on his relationship with Libby." She shook her head, still galled by the nerve of him. Harris snorted in amusement.

"What an idiot. I assume you set him straight?"

"Oh yes. So many missed doctors' appointments to catch him up on. Falls, miscarriage fears. Baby falling. Baby getting sick. Baby's first smile . . . I was there. He wasn't. How dare he say I don't have the right to an opinion?"

"He's a moron, but I'm sure he knows better now."

"I feel bad. He looked shell shocked."

"Good," Harris said, his voice filled with relish.

"I think maybe he was crying. At least a little."

"Nah. Greyson doesn't cry."

"Do you?"

"Of course. But only ever a single man tear, which usually slides stoically down my lean cheek."

She laughed and chucked a paper napkin at him. The gesture reminded her that she needed to sort out the napkin shortage. But she couldn't get anything done with Greyson and Libby in her office. Which meant she was free for lunch.

"Did you order yet?" she asked.

"I was about to. Are you joining me?"

"I think so. Ranting at your brother does work up quite an appetite."

He laughed, and Tina liked that she'd caused that genuinely happy sound.

"Sorry I couldn't join you for coffee this morning," Harris said after they had placed their orders. "I had an early-morning conference call."

Tina bit back a laugh at his nerve. He knew she barely tolerated his company in the mornings, so he had some cheek apologizing for not interrupting her blessed solitude that morning. Although, if she was being completely honest, Tina had kind of, maybe, in just the tiniest of ways, missed him that morning.

She had been a little disappointed not to find him already waiting for her, but she had fully expected him to join her later, and when he didn't, she had felt more than a little deflated. Still, she would never admit as much to him.

"You don't have to explain. I mean, it's not like I noticed," she lied without a single qualm.

"Well," he said, the glint in his eyes telling her he didn't believe her lie at all, "I thought I'd tell you anyway."

Thankfully Suzie chose that moment to bring their food—seafood pasta for her and ostrich medallions with cranberry jus and roasted vegetables for him—offering enough distraction for Tina to organically shift the subject to something else.

They talked about nonsensical things while they ate their lunch. Libby and Greyson exited the office together ten minutes after Tina had left them. Libby, to Tina's relief, looked none the worse for wear and headed straight back to the kitchen with a wave to Harris and Tina and not another word to her estranged husband.

Greyson stopped by their table. He was pale but had himself under rigid control.

"I'm headed back to the house," he said, avoiding Tina's gaze and keeping his eyes on Harris.

"You're not having lunch?" Harris asked, concern in his voice, and Greyson shook his head.

"I'll grab something at the house."

"Have some lunch with us, Greyson," Harris said, insisting.

"I'm not that hungry."

"Well, do you want the car?" Harris asked, reaching into his pocket for his car keys.

"That's fine. I'll walk."

"Looks like it's going to rain again."

"Harris, I'm fine!" It was the closest Tina had ever seen him get to losing his patience. "I have to get some work done. I'll be watching Clara at Olivia's place while she's working tonight."

The revelation had both Tina and Harris gawking at him in disbelief.

"What?" Harris asked, his voice urgent. "Greyson, you know nothing about babies!"

"I'm sure I'll be fine," Greyson said, his usual arrogance coming to the fore, and Tina choked on her pasta and then suffered a coughing fit, violent enough to cause both men to stare at her in alarm. Her eyes streaming with tears, she chugged down some water before finally getting herself under some control.

"Jesus, Tina!" Harris's voice trembled with shock. "Are you okay?"

"I'm fine, no thanks to you guys! I could have been choking, and neither of you even *considered* doing the Heimlich maneuver."

Harris had the nerve to smile, and she narrowed her eyes at him, all but daring him to say something flippant. He must have recognized the warning in her eyes and held his hands up in surrender.

"You weren't clutching your throat and gasping for air. I assumed you had things under control."

Tina clicked her tongue in dismissive disgust before refocusing her attention on Greyson, who was staring longingly at the door. He took a hesitant step in that direction.

"Uh-uh! Hold up, mister! What do you mean, you're watching Clara tonight?" she asked, and he threw his eyes up to the ceiling before bringing his grim focus back on her.

Cold.

Well, it looked like Greyson was back to his usual frigid self, then.

"Exactly what I said."

"That's ridiculous—she needs to be close by so that Libby can breastfeed her."

"She said something about a mixture of breast milk and formula."

"God, give me strength," Tina muttered beneath her breath. She met Harris's concerned gaze. "Excuse me."

"Of course."

Tina hurried into the kitchen, where Libby was delicately piping meringue onto lemon tartlets.

"Libby, I need to have that chat with you right now," Tina stated in her most authoritative voice, and Libby's focus shifted from her task to Tina. She looked set to argue, but her shoulders slumped when Tina tacked a fervent "please" onto the end of her demand.

"Agnes, take over, please," she instructed her eager second, and Agnes stepped in seamlessly. Libby's kitchen was nothing if not a well-oiled machine.

Libby followed Tina into the office, and Tina sat down behind her desk to stare at her friend. She felt mentally and emotionally spent, and it wasn't even one in the afternoon yet. She scrubbed her hands over her face, trying to think of what to say.

"Please don't allow my shortcomings to affect the way you raise your child, Libby," she finally said, and Libby sank into the chair opposite hers. The other woman's brown eyes were probing and intent.

"What do you mean?"

"Ignoring for a moment that you're letting Greyson watch Clara tonight, I'm talking about the fact that you wanted to continue partially breastfeeding her until she was six months old, and now you'll be pumping milk so that she can be fed off-site. That wasn't our arrangement. The deal was she would be in the office during dinner service so that you could feed her whenever possible."

"Tina . . . I can't overlook the fact that you're uncomfortable around her. I know she's just an infant, but babies can pick up on stuff like that. She's so tiny—I don't want her to fret over things she can't possibly understand. That I, quite frankly, don't understand myself."

Tina swallowed audibly, trying to lubricate her parched throat, while fighting desperately to keep her breathing manageable and her panic on lockdown. She wrapped her arms tightly around herself, hoping the gesture would help her keep it together for what was to come.

"I-I . . ." She swallowed again. Her eyes felt dry and scratchy, and she fought hard to keep the incipient tears at bay. "I want to be different. I love Clara. But . . ."

She shut her eyes. It needed to be said. In order to preserve this friendship that meant the world to her, she needed to let her friend in. And finally reveal her most private pain and her darkest secret.

"I once had a baby," she whispered, the words scraping across her throat as they clawed their way out. She heard Libby gasp and opened her eyes to meet her friend's shocked gaze. Her breathing was fast and shallow, and she fought to keep the dizziness at bay as she forced the rest of it out. The unvarnished, irrevocable, soul-destroying truth. "He died."

Chapter Nine

Greyson had ultimately allowed himself to be coerced into having lunch while Harris ate dessert and kept him company. They watched Tina and Libby march back toward the office, and Harris saw the concerned and curious gazes of their staff as they, too, observed the grim pair. It had certainly been an eventful afternoon so far.

If nothing else, a lot of the patrons would return in hopes of witnessing the staff's continued personal drama. They'd be getting dinner *and* a show.

"How did you manage to talk her into letting you babysit?" Harris asked, and Greyson lifted his broad shoulders before dropping them heavily.

"I didn't. This was all her. Olivia's already let me hold her and change her nappy. And yesterday . . ." Greyson's lips tilted in a reminiscent smile. "She allowed me to rock her to sleep."

"Why?" Harris asked, genuinely puzzled by the concessions Libby was making. She had moved hundreds of kilometers just to get away from Greyson; Harris couldn't imagine her relenting to his demands so easily.

Greyson looked troubled. "She says she wants me to have a fair shot at a relationship with Clara. But maybe she wants me to know exactly what I'm missing out on before she yanks the rug out from beneath my feet."

"And what happens if, or when, she yanks that rug out from under you?"

"I fall down and I lose. *Everything.*"

"You won't fight her?"

Greyson pushed the pasta listlessly around his plate and shook his head in reply to Harris's question.

"What's going on with you and Martine?" Greyson asked unexpectedly, deliberately changing the subject while nailing Harris with his piercing stare. The forthright question was so unexpected that Harris wasn't sure how to respond to it.

"I don't know what you mean," he prevaricated.

"Bullshit. You picked the house right next to hers for a reason."

"There were no other places available," Harris said uncomfortably.

"More bullshit. I know for a fact that the vet's family is leasing out that little house on the edge of town."

"I didn't know about that one. Besides, I don't see what relevance this has to anything."

"It's all right to be up in my business, but you don't like having the tables turned, do you?" Greyson sneered, and Harris tossed down his napkin, feeling hunted and more than a little exposed.

"There are no tables to turn."

"I know you slept with Martine ten years ago, Harris. I heard about that fucking bet. You're lucky those assholes weren't dumb enough to say anything to Smith, or I doubt you'd still have your balls."

Harris felt sick to his stomach at the revelation that his brother knew his most shameful secret. Although, in retrospect, he didn't know why it had never before occurred to him that Greyson might be aware of what had happened.

"That is . . . it was—"

"Despicable," Greyson spat, and Harris's hands curled into fists on top of the table.

"No more despicable than, say, renouncing my own child."

"*Fuck* you, Harris!" Greyson growled through clenched teeth. His second f-bomb in less than five minutes. He was definitely pissed off. He rarely used any profanity stronger than *shit*.

"No, fuck *you*, Greyson!" Harris retorted. "Don't you dare compare what you did to Libby with something that happened ten years ago. Something that I've regretted and tried to remedy every day since."

"Do you think you're the only one with regrets, Harris? The only one allowed to fix his fucking reprehensible mistakes? *Don't* ruin this for me! She's my daughter. I want . . . I need to do this. Don't talk Olivia out of letting me babysit." Greyson's voice was frantic, his eyes—ice cold and distant just moments before—burning like coals and lit with desperation.

"The thing . . . ," Harris said after a long, tense moment, "with Tina. I hate myself for that."

"I can relate," Greyson said with a grim smile.

"But for the first time in years, she's actually talking with me again. Laughing with me. Smiling at me. I came here because I wanted to be sure you wouldn't hurt Libby again . . . but I also came because I knew Tina would be here."

Greyson nodded. "You may think I'm a self-centered, unobservant asshole, Harrison. But I'm not entirely oblivious. I see the way you look at her. The way you've always looked at her."

"I'm pretty sure some part of her will always despise me. She over-heard some stuff that night. About the bet. That's why she hates me."

Greyson winced sympathetically.

"Why the hell did you make that bet?" Greyson asked, and Harris laughed, the sound filled with bitter self-recrimination.

"That's just it . . . I didn't. I don't recall making the bet. I remember dancing with her and kissing her. After that, everything's hazy. I know

Jonah and his buddies said some fucked-up shit that I later discovered Tina had overheard. I think Jonah handed me a spiked drink just before my dance with Tina. It's the only thing that makes sense."

"I never liked Jonah Spade," Greyson said distastefully. "Always an asshole."

"Yeah. I saw him at a restaurant the other day," Harris said, then grinned. "He has a comb-over."

"No shit?" Greyson said, his own smile surfacing. "Remember he always carried that comb around with him?"

"The gold-plated thing? Yeah. He was so proud of that retro pompadour. Kept running that tacky comb through it."

"Wonder if he still has that comb?" Greyson mused drily.

"He would be getting some real use out of it now," Harris said, his voice quavering.

Their eyes met, and they both started laughing. The moment of shared amusement so rare and so priceless that they both stopped chuckling simultaneously as they acknowledged the break in the habitual and long-standing tension between them.

They grinned at each other again, and this time there was a cautious diffidence in their smiles.

Greyson cleared his throat and dabbed at his mouth with his napkin. "I knew almost as soon as I said it that it was ridiculous, Harris," he admitted after a moment, his voice weighted in sadness, shame, and regret.

Harris knew to what he was referring but needed him to verbalize it. It was the only way to begin: if not healing, then patching the ever-expanding rift between them.

"What do you mean?"

"I didn't want to believe, even as I was saying it, that you were the baby's father. And I regretted it the moment the words were out. I was angry and you were there, taking her side. Always her friend and confidante, while she never told me anything. *Libby* and Harris, with your in-jokes and games and fun. Dull, tedious Greyson would never get the joke, so why bother including him? That's how it looked from the outside. And I was *always* on the outside. I thought, maybe after I married her, things would change. *I* would be her best friend. I should have been her best friend. She's *my* wife, but I can't laugh with her the way you can."

"Jesus," Harris muttered. "I'm so—"

"No. This is *my* apology, Harris. Don't take it from me. I just wanted you to understand the place that indictment came from." He squeezed the nape of his neck and darted a self-conscious glance around the nearly empty room. "I was jealous of the relationship you had with my wife, and while I knew it was strictly platonic, it was still more meaningful than the one I had with her. That was my fault, not yours. And I'm so sorry, so goddamned sorry. That accusation, those words, will always be out there now. I can't take them back . . . but I can tell you that I regret them so damned much."

"Greyson . . ."

Harris's words were trailing off when Libby exited the office and made a beeline for their table. She looked pale and upset and avoided Harris's gaze as she focused on Greyson.

"Uh, Greyson. About tonight." Greyson stood up abruptly, panic flaring in his eyes as he obviously feared she was going to cancel their arrangement. "I need you to come here. I'd prefer to have Clara close by."

"You're not canceling?" Greyson asked, heaving a relieved breath, and Libby's pretty brow furrowed.

"No. Just a change in venue, that's all."

Greyson gave her a grateful smile. "No problem. I'll be here just before six." He sat back down.

"Thank you." She turned away from the table, still avoiding Harris's eyes, and his stomach sank.

She knew. After all these years, Tina had finally told her about the bet.

Natasha Anders

"Where's Tina?" he asked quietly, and her eyes darted to his face before flitting away again. As if it hurt her to look at him.

"Leave her alone," Libby said, her voice cold. "She needs a moment."

"Libby . . . ," he began miserably, and she finally looked at him. Her beautiful eyes were alive with anger, sadness, disappointment, and, most crushing of all, absolute revulsion.

"Don't talk to me right now, Harris," she said. Her voice strained. "I can't deal with you right now."

She turned and swept back into the kitchen.

"Shit." Harris's eyes tracked to the back, where the office door was hidden from view. He willed Tina to step out—he wanted to see for himself if she was okay. A long moment passed without any sign that she would be exiting the office, and he'd placed his palms flat on the table, intending to push himself up, when Greyson's quiet voice intruded.

"No."

"But . . ." His voice trailed off. He couldn't find the words to justify going into that office and checking on her. He had no right. He kept his anguished gaze focused in the direction of her office for another minute before shaking his head and tossing a few bills on the table.

"I'm walking back to the house," he murmured, dropping his car keys onto the heap of bills. "I'll see you later."

He strode out before Greyson could say a word of protest.

It was a blustery day, and as he walked up Main Road toward his ramshackle rented property, he tried hard not to think of Tina. The sweet, trusting girl she had been and the unhappy, wary woman she had become. He knew she blamed him for everything that had gone wrong in her life . . . and while he acknowledged the role he had played, like he had told her before, he couldn't be held responsible for ten years of bad decisions. Tina had to accept culpability for her own choices.

176

Naturally, it was convenient to blame Harris for every awful thing that had ever happened to her, but they'd had sex, *once*, ten years ago. And maybe the immediate fallout had been harsh and painful, but he didn't understand how it could have shaped the rest of her life.

She had disappeared for a while after that night, at first actively avoiding him by not coming out with her family when they attended Chapman family functions, and not even visiting Libby. Then she'd gone away to Scotland for her gap year.

He'd followed her on social media, but she hadn't posted any pictures—strange for someone who was enjoying her first independent trip abroad. He'd questioned Libby about Tina's whereabouts, and she had been equally clueless. Saying she only received the occasional text message. He had even tried to ask Smith about her, but the other guy had shrugged off his questions. The lack of information had been bizarre, but, while he'd had the resources, Harris had known it wasn't his place to pry and had left her alone, focusing on his own life and studies instead. He'd moved on, met other women, traveled, and enjoyed his early twenties with reckless abandon.

When Tina had returned from her mysterious gap year, Harris had been shocked by the change in her the first time he saw her. Such haunting sadness in her eyes—she'd lost some weight and had a fragile appearance. She didn't speak unless spoken to and didn't make eye contact with anyone.

Harris had tried to talk with her, but she made it very plain she wasn't interested in anything he had to say to her.

She'd started college, her aim to go into medicine, then dropped out less than a year later. She tried random jobs, none of which stuck, and always seemed aimless and disinterested in doing much with her life. Her family had, at first, made excuses for her, but as the months and then years wore on, they made it quite clear that they were disappointed in her. And soon every time any of them referred to her in conversation, it was generally to say something negative. She had become the family failure, and they had no qualms about disassociating themselves from her bad decisions.

She's lost yet another job? Oh, typical Tina, really. That girl can't do anything right.

It had been hard to witness, and Harris had always felt a measure of guilt over it. Wondering if some of it was because of what had happened between them all those years ago, while simultaneously admiring her willingness to always try something new. But he'd beaten himself up over it for way too long, and while he wanted a new start with Tina, she had to let go of this long-standing resentment first.

And he wasn't sure that would ever be possible. Libby had stared at him earlier like he was a monster. And if Tina could still paint him in such a negative light after the day they had spent together yesterday, then he hadn't made any progress with her at all. She really did still hate him. Despite his apologies and attempted explanations.

He stared at the structure in front of him and dimly registered that he was home. He wasn't sure how long he had stood staring at the house without even recognizing that he'd reached his destination. He trudged up the porch stairs and glumly made his way into the house.

He cast his eyes around the place. Despite the cleaning he had done yesterday, it still looked dingy and dirty.

Harris walked to his room on leaden feet and dragged out his duffel bag. Somewhere between the restaurant and the house, he'd made the decision to leave. Libby didn't need him; that much was clear. She had a handle on Greyson and didn't need Harris to run interference for her. Greyson didn't need him either; he seemed better every time Harris spoke with him. He thought back to the lighthearted moment he had shared with his brother earlier. He wished he'd have time to explore that camaraderie even further and hoped that by the time Greyson returned home, they could continue where they'd left off.

And Tina . . . his hands stilled in the act of folding a T-shirt. He would never be to Tina what she was to him. It was time he accepted that and moved on with his life.

So this was him . . . moving on.

Tina felt dead inside. Everything was numb, and some part of her dumbly registered that it was probably for the best. She would likely be curled up in a ball right now if she could actually feel anything. She had harnessed every single coping mechanism in her arsenal to tell Libby about her baby without falling apart completely. She had never spoken of him to anyone. And even while talking about him to the woman who was like a sister to her, she had still been unable to actually say his name.

Libby had listened in shock, then horror, and finally with tears streaming down her face as Tina recounted the bare bones of her tale. No overly emotional explanations. Just the cold, hard facts. It was only when Libby asked for the details that Tina had found herself stumbling. Straying from the specifics into the traumatic emotions associated with that period of her life had been hard for her.

Admitting that Harris had been her baby's father had been even harder. Libby had stared at Tina like she'd never seen her before, the betrayal the woman felt that her *best* friend could have kept such a momentous secret from her for so long evident in her eyes. The look of wounded shock had only deepened when Tina had refused to delve into the details of her one night with Harris. For some unfathomable reason, she wanted to protect Harris from the disgust she knew Libby would feel if she mentioned the bet.

Predictably, Libby—this time out of concern for Tina—wanted to continue her original arrangement with Greyson. She had only relented after Tina insisted that having Clara around helped her immensely, even if she couldn't actually bring herself to physically interact with the baby. Yet.

But Libby had insisted Tina take that evening's service off. And Tina, too emotionally exhausted to argue, had gratefully accepted the suggestion.

She dragged herself up off her office couch and gathered up her belongings, desperate to get home.

"What are you doing?"

The sound of Tina's voice coming from behind him in his home startled Harris into dropping his bag. He whirled around to face her; the movement was jerky and abrupt and made her jump in fright.

He stared at her in disbelief, quite sure his mouth must have fallen open in absolute shock. He had not expected to see her again. Certainly not standing just outside his bedroom door.

"Harris?" she prompted, and he blinked, not sure what she wanted. "What are you doing?"

"I-I . . ." He tossed a look over his shoulder at the bag he had zipped up just seconds ago, and the visual cue helped. "Packing. I was packing. Why are you here?"

"You're packing?"

Was that dismay in her voice? Disappointment in her eyes? What the fuck?

"Yes. I've decided to leave tomorrow."

"Why?"

"I think I may have overstayed my welcome," he said, his voice embarrassingly rough with emotion. "Why are you here?"

She held up a hand, and in it she had . . .

"Microwave popcorn?"

"Well, I have the evening off, and I don't want to spend it alone, so I thought we could get started on that *Game of Thrones* binge we discussed yesterday."

"You want to spend time here? With *me*?" he asked, knowing he sounded dumb as a bag of potatoes but wanting complete clarification on the matter.

She cast a glance around his room and then over her shoulder at the grubby living space. She wrinkled her nose and pursed her lips, looking like she'd smelled something putrid.

"Frankly? I'd really rather we spent the time at my place. My furniture is comfier. And cleaner. And my TV is much better than whatever that relic is in your living room."

"I thought you were pissed off with me."

His words seemed to surprise her—her eyes widened, and she tilted her head quizzically.

"Why? We had a relatively nice lunch together." Yes, they'd had a very amicable meal together before she'd gone off with Libby to tell her all about Harris's shameful past transgressions.

"I thought . . . well, Libby was angry with me, and I figured it was because you told her about the bet, and I thought if all of that got dredged up again, then you were probably back to hating me."

He watched as she sucked her lush bottom lip into her mouth, the expression on her pale and strained face looking regretful.

"I had to . . ." She paused as she gathered her thoughts. "I needed to explain certain quirks in my behavior to Libby, and in doing so . . . part of my history with you had to be revealed. She knows we slept together, that one time. She doesn't know anything of what happened immediately after that less-than-momentous occasion."

He grimaced at her bluntness.

"Way to remind a guy of his worst hour," he muttered.

"Or *minute*, as it were," she corrected primly, surprising a rusty chuckle out of him. Against all odds, she seemed completely relaxed with him. And it confused Harris. Libby had been very cold toward him. If Tina really hadn't told her about the bet, then what could have prompted such an extreme reaction? Surely, she couldn't be this inordinately angry about a onetime ill-advised sexual encounter between two adults?

It made him wonder what Tina wasn't telling him. Because he was sure there was something else going on here. And now Libby knew whatever it was, while Harris remained—once again—lost in the dark.

"So these, uh . . . behavioral quirks . . ." He prodded gently, not wanting to spoil the mood but needing to know more about what was going on with her. "They're my fault?"

"They're the result of various life-altering experiences. Our encounter—for want of a better word—happened to be one of those experiences."

"I'm sorry."

She didn't acknowledge the apology, just held up the popcorn again. "So? You interested?"

"Definitely!"

Three hours—and a *lot* of nudity, violence, and profanity—later, Harris called for an intermission. The show was good, but *damn* it was messed up.

"My brain needs a break," he insisted, and Tina laughed. "This is some heavy shit, man. Let's watch the news instead. It's bound to be lighter viewing than what we spent the last three hours watching."

"You're being dramatic," she said, still laughing. "You were completely riveted."

"Well, I didn't say I hated it. Just needed a break. Are you hungry?"

Tina, who had been curled up on the comfortable easy chair, unfurled her legs from beneath her butt and stretched luxuriously.

"I could eat."

"I'm thinking takeout?"

She laughed again. "It's like you've forgotten that there are only two eateries in town. Well, one and a half: I don't think Ralphie's serves anything other than basic pub food. Stuff like fish and chips or burgers and fries."

"Well, I've heard the newly reopened MJ's has fantastic food," he said with a wicked grin. He was sprawled out on her sofa, his feet dangling over one arm and his head resting comfortably on the other. Her chair was at the end by his feet, so he could see her without straining his neck.

"We don't have a take-out system in place."

"You should get on that, *soon*. It's a great way for the dumb assholes who are too stubborn to come into the restaurant to at least sample the food."

"I suppose we could arrange a small take-out menu," she said thoughtfully. "Pizzas and pastas, maybe. But I'd have to look into carry-away containers first."

"You have doggie-bag containers, don't you? Use those in the meantime."

"I'll think about it."

"Well, I'm going to call and place an order."

"The staff won't accept telephonic orders."

"They will if *you* call," he said with a sly grin. "It's a good way to do a test run. Call in, order, and pick up. See how it goes."

She lifted her thumb to her mouth and gnawed at the nail. Harris watched her ruminate over his suggestion, obviously wondering if looking into the idea could be considered breaking her self-imposed rule of not accepting his help or advice.

"Fine," she finally decided, reaching for her phone. "What are you in the mood for? And don't expect me to pick it up. I'm off duty. If I go into the restaurant, it'll be like work. I'll do my boss thing and fuss. Not that they need me. They're perfectly fine without me."

He wondered if she knew how wistful she sounded.

"You're the boss—none of them would have work without you," he pointed out gently.

"Yeah, well . . . for what *that's* worth." Something in the way she said it made him pause. But he didn't comment, wanting to ponder over it for a while longer.

"I'll have whatever you're having," he eventually said, in response to her original question. "Tell them I'll be around to pick it up in ten minutes."

The food wasn't done by the time he got there, so he popped into the back office to see how Greyson was coping with his babysitting duties.

As it turned out, the answer to that question was not very well. At all.

Harris stood in the doorway, his eyes wide and his jaw slack as he watched, completely unnoticed, as Greyson paced up and down the tiny office. His shirtsleeves were rolled up, the top button of his shirt undone, and he had a towel thrown over one shoulder. The towel seemed to serve no purpose at all, since it was the other shoulder that was covered in spit-up.

In his arms he held his squirming, screaming, clearly unhappy nearly five-month-old daughter. He was attempting to rock her, but her tiny body was tense, and she refused to be soothed.

"What the hell?"

Greyson didn't hear him. His desperate eyes were fixed on Clara's angry face, and he was pleading with her to stop crying.

"It's okay, darling. It's all right. Don't cry. Please don't cry. Daddy's here."

"Greyson!" Harris raised his voice, and his brother's eyes flew up to meet his. It seemed to take him a second to register Harris's presence.

"Harris! Oh, thank God you're here." Greyson's voice was urgent, with naked relief in his eyes. Harris had never seen his suave brother this harried before, not even during those dark days immediately after Libby had left. And that was saying a lot. "She won't stop crying. I think she's sick. Do you think she's sick?"

Harris stepped forward and took Clara from Greyson, cradling her in the crook of his arm and resting the back of his hand on her forehead.

"She doesn't feel feverish." Clara stopped screeching, one plump fist crept into her mouth, and she suckled, her big eyes fixed on Harris's face.

"Oh my *God*, she hates me." The comically dramatic exclamation from Greyson would have made Harris laugh if his poor brother didn't look genuinely gutted by the possibility.

"She doesn't hate you," Harris dismissed calmly. "You were tense and panicking. She probably picked up on that."

"I can't do this. You have to help me." This time Harris *did* laugh. "No way. You seemed confident you could handle this. So handle it. Libby is literally a stone's throw away if you need her. You'll manage."

"No. Damn it. She'll never let me near Clara again if she thinks I can't cope."

"Greyson, you're able to run a multimillion-dollar organization without blinking an eyelid—you can handle one tiny female."

"No, I can't!" His voice was frantic. "You know I can't. She fucking up and left me before I had a chance to even recognize what an idiot I was. She defies handling."

"I . . . uh . . . I meant the baby," Harris pointed out, very determinedly keeping his grin at bay. It was really hilarious seeing Greyson *this* frazzled.

"Oh."

"Now, take your daughter. I have a date to get back to. Call Libby if you run into trouble; she won't think less of you. It'll show that you're more concerned for Clara than you are about your ego."

He dropped a kiss on his sweetly cooing niece's soft head and gently placed her back into her father's less-than-capable arms. The crying started up again as he was leaving the office.

"Harris!" Greyson's voice was sharp and fraught, and Harris just chuckled as he gently shut the door behind him.

Chapter Ten

"Lamb shanks braised in red wine and served on a bed of creamy mashed potatoes for milady's gastronomic pleasure," Harris said as he placed the foam containers on the kitchen table with a flourish.

"Awesome! I'm starving."

"Got any wine?"

"In the cabinet above the fridge. Glasses in the cupboard next to that one. I'll get the plates."

They bustled around efficiently and a mere few minutes later were seated at the kitchen table, staring down at their delicious-looking meal in anticipation.

"My mother would have a heart attack if she were to see us having a meal at the kitchen table," Harris said with a chuckle. Tina laughed.

"My mother would, too, but most of her horror would be reserved for the portion size. 'Don't tell me you're going to eat *all* of that, Martine!'"

Harris shuddered.

"God, you sound just *like* her! Never do that again!"

"I would hope I sound just like her—I've heard that phrase enough times in my life to parrot it with absolute ease."

Harris shook his head in disgust.

"Fuck that! Dig in," he said with relish. Tina grinned and happily obliged. While they ate, Harris told her about Greyson's babysitting woes. He had her in stitches by the time they got to the part where Greyson had pleaded with him to stay. He paused in his story, just to watch her laugh.

She was absolutely gorgeous. Then again, she was always gorgeous, but the radiance that shone through when she laughed was fucking blinding.

Her amusement faded as she became aware of his intense stare.

"What?" she asked. "Do I have something stuck between my teeth?"

She lifted a knife and bared her straight pearly whites to check. She ran a tongue over her teeth, making little sucking sounds as she probed behind them.

"Did I get it?"

"No . . . I mean. There's nothing in your teeth."

"Why are you staring, then? Oh God! My nose?" She lifted her hand to cup her palm over her nose, and he chuckled.

"Your nose is clean as a syringe."

"What? Seriously, you're doing that deliberately, right?" she asked incredulously, and his brow lowered as he tried to figure out what she meant.

"What do you mean?"

"A syringe? *Syringe?* That's the weirdest one yet. You know it's *whistle!*"

"Why would it be whistle? That's fucking gross. Think of the spit in a whistle. A syringe *has* to be completely hygienic. I can't think of anything cleaner."

Well, she couldn't fault his logic.

"Is English even your first language?" she muttered, looking completely put out with him, and he laughed.

"So why were you staring at me?" she asked moodily, and he felt a little self-conscious about admitting the truth, sure she would shut him down the moment he said it.

"I was just appreciating how pretty you are."

Her expression froze, and she stared at him unblinkingly. It was unnerving—he wasn't even sure she was breathing.

"You shouldn't say things like that."

"Why not? It's true."

"There are some people who would argue with you."

"Why should I, or more importantly *you*, give a fuck about what those people think? You're beautiful. You've always been beautiful."

Her face went an unbecoming shade of red. It was cute how unflattering a blush was on her pale complexion. It didn't detract from her beauty but added to her charm.

"*I* don't care what they think." The emphasis on the personal pronoun told him that she still believed *Harris* cared what they thought. Of course she did. Nothing he said would ever dissuade her from thinking that. "I haven't cared in years."

He said nothing, not prepared to argue the point with her. Not when they were having such a great evening. If he was leaving tomorrow, then he wanted this to be a good memory. One that could—if not replace—somewhat diminish the memory of that terrible night ten years ago.

"Any dessert?" he asked, deliberately changing the subject.

"Dessert? Mister, you must not know whose house this is. Of course there's dessert," she said, her voice light. She seemed as keen as he to just let any contentious matter fall by the wayside.

He watched as she jumped up and practically skipped to the fridge. She was wearing another pair of those ass-hugging leggings he so enjoyed; these were electric blue and were combined with a loose, slouchy orange top. The color clashed horribly with her hair, and she clearly didn't care. The top kept sliding off one smooth, rounded, *naked* shoulder, and he'd found himself speculating throughout the evening about what she could possibly be wearing under it. No bra strap didn't automatically mean no bra, but he could—and *did*—fantasize about that exact possibility.

How easy it would be to slip his hand under that top and find her breast. His head would follow his hand, and he'd happily lose himself under that roomy garment, exploring every charm she had to offer.

He shuddered, fighting to bring his raging hormones under control. She was bent at the waist as she rummaged around in her fridge, and he had a perfect view of her round, firm butt. God, he wanted to cup that ass, caress it, stroke it, *bite* it . . .

He easily imagined getting up from the table, walking up to her, lining himself up behind her, reaching out with his trembling hands, and . . .

"Harris?"

Jesus!

He blinked, coming out of his erotic daze, and stared into her wide eyes for a long uncomprehending moment. She was speaking, and he couldn't quite make sense of the words. All he could think of was pulling down those leggings and easing into her warm, welcoming femininity from behind.

"*Harris*, snap out of it!" She was repeatedly clicking her fingers in front of his eyes, and he lifted his hand to gently push hers out of his face.

"Stop that," he remonstrated mildly.

"Where did you go?" she asked curiously, sitting down across from him.

"No place you'd be interested in going. Not with me." Well, that came out sounding a lot more bitter than he'd intended. "I thought you were getting dessert."

She cast her eyes pointedly down to the table, and he frowned when he saw the bowl of delicious-looking chocolate mousse placed in front of him. He hadn't even noticed her putting it there. Okay, so he'd been a little more preoccupied than he'd realized.

"Thanks," he said, picking up a spoon and sampling the rich dessert. The creamy chocolate melted in his mouth, and he moaned involuntarily as angels danced on his tongue. He felt his cheeks heat at his embarrassing overreaction to the treat. "This is great. Did you make it?"

"Hah! Nice one, Harris. You know I couldn't do something like this if my life depended on it. Libby made it, of course."

"Of course," he parroted dumbly. He should have recognized it as one of Libby's desserts; she always added the tiniest hint of orange to her chocolate mousse.

"So . . . ," she said after they'd both plowed their way silently through half their desserts. "Try me."

God, I'd love to! Harris thought irreverently.

"What do you mean?" was the question he verbalized instead.

"You said I wouldn't be interested in whatever it was you were daydreaming about. Remember how I told you not to speak for me yesterday? The same applies to thinking for me." She licked the back of her spoon, and he bit back a pained groan. She was going to be the death of him. "So tell me what that was about."

Tina watched his already-dark eyes go almost black, and suddenly she knew what he'd been thinking about, *fantasizing* about, earlier. How could she not, when he was staring at her with such naked intent? She nearly told him she'd changed her mind, that she didn't want to know, but then he spoke . . . his voice hoarse, his words curt and matter-of-fact.

"I was picturing us. Making love."

Making love. His choice of words was shockingly romantic. She would have expected something earthier from him. His terse expression and his rigidly controlled voice certainly did not convey an ounce of romance. Instead they spoke of a raw and lusty urgency. A drive to do something wholly elemental. And that—more than his words—was what resonated with Tina. That urgency . . . that fundamental craving to claim and be claimed.

She carefully set her spoon aside, pushed her dessert bowl away, and folded her hands primly, one above the other, on the table in front of her.

"I don't want to make love, Harris," she said, her words brutally frank. "Not with you. But I do . . ." She faltered before taking in a deep, fortifying breath and continuing with renewed determination. "I *do* want to fuck."

Harris felt the impact of her words like a fist to his solar plexus. The breath left his body in an instant, leaving him dazed and disoriented.

It was only when he started feeling lightheaded that he realized he had stopped breathing completely. He gulped in huge lungsful of air in an attempt to compensate, but it wasn't doing much to reset his equilibrium. She had wrong-footed him, and she continued to keep him off balance by getting up and crossing the very short distance between them to straddle his lap.

And there went his breath again. He felt like a giddy old lady, his head was spinning so damned much. His body seemed to know what to do with the warm lapful of femininity even while his mind still reeled. His hands dropped to that sweet bottom he'd just been admiring, cupping the soft, curvy mounds in an attempt to keep her steady.

Her arms had wrapped around his neck, her hands were buried in his hair, and her face was within inches of his. His eyes dropped to her mouth, now within kissing—and *licking*—distance, but he couldn't bridge that distance, not when this seemed much too good to be true. He kept wondering what the catch was. But while he attempted to examine this wonderful gift from every angle, she lost patience and dropped her closed mouth onto his.

The kiss was chaste, sweet, and completely innocent, and it possessed more seductive power than any other kiss he'd ever experienced.

His mouth opened beneath hers, his lips coaxing hers to do the same. She happily complied, and he groaned as his tongue explored the hot, decadent temptation of her mouth. His hands left her butt and grabbed fistfuls of the thick mass of hair that fell down around her shoulders and tugged her head gently back to allow for greater access to her mouth and her neck.

He grew increasingly hard beneath her softness, and she moaned when she felt him starting to push insistently up against her, returning the favor by happily grinding herself up against him.

"Tell me you have condoms," she demanded, and he shuddered, hardly able to believe that they were really going to do this.

"Back pocket," he said curtly, embarrassed by the gravel in his thick voice. He sounded like a caveman. He was an accomplished lover; the overeager, premature boy she had encountered ten years ago had never made a reappearance.

But with her mouth on his, her hands twisted in his hair, and her heat grinding eagerly and urgently against him . . . he found himself precipitously close to coming in his trousers.

Shit!

"Sweetheart," he muttered, yanking his mouth away from hers. What she lacked in experience, she certainly made up for in enthusiasm. He could tell she wasn't entirely sure what she was doing, but hell, she was hitting *all* of his buttons. She pouted when he refused to give her his mouth again, her brows lowering in a sulky glare when it became clear he wanted to say something. "I need you to get off me, Bean."

"I don't want to."

"Ah, sweetheart, I don't want you to either . . . but I promise, I'll make it worth your while."

"How?"

"I can tell you," he said slowly, before deliberately bringing his hands down from her hair to her breasts, which he cupped through her top, his thumbs finding her nipples with unerring accuracy through the fabric.

"Or I can show you."

She gasped and twitched, and he groaned. Fuck it, he was going to come if he didn't get her off his lap immediately.

Fortunately, it become clear that she would rather be shown than told when she leaped off his lap and watched him expectantly, her breath coming in excited gasps. Harris got up slowly, too hard to move without a great deal of care.

"What are you going to show me?" she asked breathlessly, and he grinned.

"You made me miss dessert," he said, his voice still sounding like rocks being dragged over boulders. "So, I'm going to have to eat something equally sweet as compensation."

She swayed slightly when his meaning sank in.

"Oh my God, yes, please. I've always wanted someone to do that to me." Her honesty was refreshing and a huge turn-on. He grinned, grabbed her hand, and dragged her into the bedroom.

He had her stripped—gratified to find no bra beneath that top—and on her back in seconds. He stared at her glorious nudity for a moment, while Handel's "Hallelujah" chorus exploded into song in his head. Thank God for comfortable, slouchy clothing. Easy on and easy off. His jeans were going to take more effort, especially since he had to work around the erection pushing against the button fly. He dragged his T-shirt off, and she made an appreciative sound before her hands reached up to explore his chest.

He shuddered at the first tentative caress and then groaned when her soft hands found his nipples.

"Wait. Stop . . . Tina," he implored, and she glared up at him.

"Stop telling me to stop doing the fun stuff."

"The fun stuff will make this end sooner than either of us would like," he said, and she looked put out by his response.

"Again?"

He choked back a laugh at her plaintive cry.

"Just let me do my thing."

"Well, less talking and more doing, then!"

He chuckled, loving this bossy streak, and then bent to suckle one of her perfect breasts.

"Oh."

Her soft, surprised gasp made his heart soar. The heart that only ever soared and dipped and fluttered and swelled for her.

She went quiet, her breathing escalating as she arched her back with each strong pull from his mouth. He gave her other nipple similar treatment before happily kissing and suckling and licking his way down her soft, sweet curves, over the gentle mound of her stomach, stopping for a moment to explore her shallow belly button, before continuing to the beautifully maintained triangle of fiery curls that so gorgeously ornamented her femininity.

He used his thumbs to open her plump, pretty pinkness up to his gaze and stared for a reverent moment before taking his first hungry taste of her.

The helpless sound that emerged from her throat was deeply sexy, and Harris reached down with one hand to adjust himself, unbuttoning his fly clumsily in an attempt to relieve some of the pressure.

He continued to feast on Tina's lush sweetness, adoring the unique taste and creamy texture of her.

He suckled her clit in the same way he had done her nipples, and it drove her wild—she cried out and bucked whenever he did that—so he used it sparingly, wanting to make this last for her. For them both.

She was begging now. *"Please, please, please, please!"* And he reached down again, this time to stroke himself.

"Do you want to come, baby?" he asked thickly. And she made an incoherent sound of assent. "I'll make you come."

Her fingers were twisted in his hair, pulling with more force than he thought she recognized. But he didn't care . . . all he cared about was her pleasure. All he wanted was to feel her explode on his tongue.

He closed his mouth over that hard little clit and applied a small amount of suction. He held her on the brink for the longest moment before flicking her with his tongue and then pulling her more deeply into his mouth. Suckling hard enough to send her tumbling into orgasm.

She squeaked, an honest-to-God little squeak, and then moaned, the sound low and long. He squeezed his forefinger and thumb around his cock, where head met shaft, in an attempt to stave off his climax. A successful attempt. By the time she'd stopped thrusting against his tongue, he had himself back under some semblance of control again.

Tina sank slowly back down to earth, like a feather floating leisurely on the faintest of breezes. Harris was very, *very* good with his tongue. She had always expected to feel embarrassed by cunnilingus. But there had been no time for self-consciousness, and his every sound, word, and look had been so ridiculously flattering it had been hard to be embarrassed. It had helped that he'd clearly been extremely turned on by what he was doing.

He repositioned himself, kneeling between her widely spread thighs, his ripped chest bare. She feasted her eyes on all that magnificence, the hard abs leading down to that Adonis belt, the fly of his jeans open enough to reveal the plum-size, angry-red glans of his penis.

"I want that," she said, pointing to his crotch with a shaky forefinger. "I want it in my mouth, I want to taste it the way you just tasted me."

He swore vehemently beneath his breath and lifted his intense gaze to hers.

"I'll hold you to that, sweetheart. But later, okay? Right now, I want to make love with you."

"I told you I don't want to make love," she reminded him, and he squeezed his eyes shut, visibly trembling as he fought to remain in control.

"I know. I'll do the other thing instead." He got off her, standing beside the bed, his fevered gaze glued to her body, while he toed off his sneakers. He dug around in his back pocket and produced a condom. He slotted the foil package between his even white teeth before using his hands to push his jeans past his narrow hips down to his feet and half tripping as he stepped out of them.

His eyes tracked down to the spot between her still-spread thighs, where she felt wet, heavy, and swollen, and—instead of following her natural inclination to squeeze her thighs together—she spread them farther apart. And, feeling particularly daring, reached down to stroke herself for him. The swollen knot of her clit pulsed against her finger-tips, and she moaned in response to the sensitivity, her own gaze moving down his body to where his hand was clutched around the head of his shaft. His knuckles whitened as his grip strengthened.

He swore softly beneath his breath and removed the condom from between his lips with his free hand. He was forced to let go of his rigid length, which arched up to visibly throb against his abdomen, the tip slick with moisture.

He fumbled a bit before finally smoothing the latex down his shaft, and he eagerly climbed between her thighs again. He claimed her mouth in a hot, demanding kiss and reached down to move her hand out of the way before he took over the task.

"Please," she begged, her orgasm building with each flick of his finger. "Please, Harris."

"Okay. It's okay," he soothed, easing two of his fingers into her narrow channel, testing her readiness, but she was more than ready to move on to something bigger and harder.

"More," she urged, pushing greedily against his hand, lost in sensation, loving the weight of him on top of her, the hardness of him between her thighs. Her hands moved to his tight buttocks, and her fingers dug into his tautness as she tried to pull him toward her.

His fingers left her, and she looked down between their bodies, watching keenly as he wrapped his hand around his straining erection and fed it into her waiting body.

"Oh!" she moaned, lifting her pelvis to ease his entry, while her knees shifted to his hips.

He was gentle. Much gentler than she wanted, needed, or expected. He eased into her, filling her to the brim, hijacking her senses, claiming every inch of her body and mind with that one long, slow stroke.

"Tina." Her name was a reverential prayer on his lips, filled with longing and tenderness. He remained still inside of her for an endless moment, his breath snagged in his throat, while hers caught and released in desperate, ragged pants.

"Harris, more!" Always more. He moved, withdrawing in that same gentle motion, before filling her again. His gentle thrusting was unbearable, and she wasn't sure how much longer she could stand it. She didn't want this tenderness. She wanted . . . *"More!"*

She was so goddamned perfect. Her beautiful, strained face, flushed and dewy with arousal. Her lips were swollen from their kisses, her nipples puckered and demanding attention. Every inch of her was soft and needed to be stroked and caressed and loved.

But she wanted to be fucked. Harrison was an expert at fucking—he'd fucked many beautiful women in his time.

But fucking entailed sex without emotion, and that wasn't what he wanted to do now. Harris, who could not contain his affection for this woman, or his joy at being with her, did not feel capable of leaving emotion out of the act. Not when every touch, every kiss, every stroke of his hands and his cock paid homage to the reverence he felt when he looked at her.

When she once again begged for more, he gave her more. With his mouth, with his tongue, and then with his hands on her breasts. She gasped, and he caught the sound in his mouth, savoring it. He moved his hands down to her thighs and farther down to hook beneath her knees and lift her higher, allowing for deeper penetration.

His groan matched hers when she clenched around him. And his thrusts shortened with the changing angle. He didn't know how much longer he could last and reached down to stroke her straining clit with his thumb.

She shuddered and cried out. Her orgasm sneaking up on both of them. The strength of her internal convulsions made him lose rhythm, and he finally gave her the *more* she'd been begging for. He slammed into her as his own climax hit him like a freight train.

His breath caught while he fought desperately to regain his control, wanting it to last longer, but when she clenched around him again, he was lost, and he groaned as he emptied himself into her tight heat.

"Oh God." The words sounded like a prayer of thanks. Possibly *were* a prayer of thanks. Harris wasn't a religious man, but this felt like heaven to him.

His bones melted, and after a few more lazy thrusts, he reluctantly left her welcoming warmth. He hurriedly dispensed of the condom, knotting it and placing it carefully aside, to be chucked out later. He slid his pendant to the side, so that it wasn't in the way, before dragging her into his arms and holding her close. He loved how comfortable she felt in his hold and wanted to keep her there forever.

Her head was on his chest, and her fingers idly traced whorls around his nipples. He contained his moan and stroked one of his own hands up and down the length of her back, the other toying with her hair, which was spread all around them like a cloak of flames. She was curved voluptuously against him, one knee bent with her leg draped over his thigh. Her pale, creamy skin and bright-red hair bringing the timeless beauty of a Rubenesque painting to mind.

"Guess I'm going to have to stop thinking of you as 'Hasty'—done in thirty seconds—Harris now."

Her dry comment surprised a shout of laughter from him.

"Not cool, Bean," he chastised, unable to keep the affectionate warmth out of his voice.

Tina snuggled close, feeling like a contented cat. If she could purr, she would; instead she settled for sighing blissfully. His fingers gently combed through her tangled mass of hair, the movement soothing and hypnotic, lulling her into a dreamlike state. She couldn't remember feeling this relaxed in years.

"Every inch of you is perfect," he said, sounding flatteringly awestruck. "This fucking hair. God. I could lose myself in this hair."

"You're not too bad yourself," she teased, her fingers idly stroking down the ridged plane of his abdomen, causing his muscles to jump in reaction. She lifted her head lazily to look at him. "You're ticklish."

The sleepy contentment disappeared from his face, to be replaced by alarm.

"No. I'm not." She prodded an experimental finger lightly between his ribs, and he jerked in reaction.

"You totally are," she said, her lips parting in a grin of delighted discovery. Another poke produced another jump, and he eyed her warily.

"Don't . . . ," he warned, and she laughed. He looked hilariously terrified.

"Oh. I won't," she promised, settling back down and resting her head on his hard chest again. She waited until he'd relaxed completely before continuing. "Not until you least expect it."

"Tina." He tried to sound mad, but she could tell he enjoyed her teasing and smiled before giving in to temptation and dropping a kiss on the taut masculine nipple situated so conveniently close to her mouth. She followed it up with a scrape of her teeth, and he groaned in helpless reaction. She felt his immediate response swelling against her leg and smiled smugly, loving how easily she could influence that big masculine body.

"So . . . what now?" he asked cautiously, and she flattened her palm against one firm pec and rested her chin on the top of her hand to stare up into his handsome face. He tried—and failed—to look nonchalant, but she could see the tension in his expression.

"Now? I'm ready for a catnap," she said with a fake yawn that became very real as soon as she opened her mouth. She felt abruptly exhausted. "Just a little rest before round two."

"Round two?" he asked eagerly, and she giggled.

"Yep. I was promised a little snack, remember? Something to keep my mouth busy." The lazy, half-mast erection that had been growing beneath her leg went rock hard in seconds, and he swore vehemently under his breath as her meaning became clear. She moved her hand down—not sure where all this brazenness was coming from, but enjoying it immensely—and clamped her fingers around his straining length. She gave him a leisurely stroke, followed by a reassuring pat. "Later, okay. I just need to sleep for a bit."

Harris watched her eyes drift shut and felt her go limp in his arms as sleep claimed her almost immediately. He felt envious of the ease with which she'd drifted off, leaving him hard and aching and desperate to know what the new parameters—if any—of their relationship were. He thought of the bag he had packed earlier and couldn't imagine leaving now. Not after this. Not without her.

His mind and his emotions were in turmoil. But at the forefront was a sentiment as rare as the joy that had so recently made a reappearance in his life. He explored this new, fledgling emotion from all angles, poking and prodding at it, not sure if it had a place in his ever-changing relationship with Tina. But no matter how much he tried to suppress it, tried to tell himself that he was a fool for feeling this way . . . the exuberant, uncontainable *hope* would not disappear.

He hoped this meant she'd forgiven him. He hoped it was the beginning of something more. He hoped she cared for him even a fraction as much as he cared for her.

He hoped. And it terrified him.

Tina jerked in her sleep, and the movement dragged Harris out of his own restless slumber.

"Wha—?"

The half-formed, sleepy question died on his lips when she jerked again and whimpered in her sleep. He sat up and rubbed his eyes drowsily. The room was pitch black. He had turned off the bedside lamp before dozing off earlier, and he was fumbling around looking for the switch when she screamed. A shrill *"No!"* that set his heart galloping.

"Nonononononoooo!" He couldn't find the fucking light switch and reached for her writhing body instead.

"Tina! *Tina!* It's okay. It's okay. It's a dream."

She shrieked, the sound loud, piercing, and terrifying. His eyes filled with helpless tears as he tried and failed to soothe her. Eventually he simply wrapped his arms around her and held her while she shook helplessly in his hold. He made soft, crooning noises, hoping she'd be comforted by them. Wanting her to know he was close by and there for her.

Every breath caught in her chest on a sob, her face wet against his chest, while she cried as if her heart were breaking.

"Tina, sweetheart, please. Wake up. It's a dream. It's just a dream."

She gasped sharply and went rigid in his arms.

"Harris?" Her voice was reedy. Her arms wrapped around his waist, and she hugged him close. He thought she would relax now that she was awake and knew he was with her; instead her breathing grew shallow, coming in rapid pants.

"Tina?"

"Dark. Too dark," she gasped. She was breathing so fast, he worried she would hyperventilate and pass out.

He recalled the night-light she'd had on when he had come in here a couple of nights ago and could have kicked himself for turning the bedside lamp off and engulfing the room in complete darkness. He swore and once again fumbled for the lamp switch, thankfully finding it this time and flooding the room with light. She inhaled a huge gulping breath of air, and he grabbed her face and planted a relieved kiss on her lips.

They simultaneously became aware of the pounding on the front door, and Harris swore again as he reluctantly extricated himself from her clinging arms.

"No. Please . . . stay."

"It's Greyson. You don't know how bloodcurdling your screams are, Tina. He probably thinks I'm murdering you in here. Just give me a moment, okay? I'll be right back." He searched for his boxer briefs and found them entangled in his jeans. He dragged them on and rushed to the door, where Greyson was still banging and shouting. He sounded alarmed. Thank God they had no other neighbors in close proximity.

He unlocked the door, and it flew open. Greyson stormed in, looking wild and ready to do battle. His hair was messy and sticking up on one side, and he had a sleep crease on one of his cheeks. He wore pajama bottoms and nothing else. Which was still better than Harris, who was practically nude.

"Is Tina okay?" Greyson asked urgently.

"She's fine. She had a nightmare." Harris kept his voice pitched low so that Tina wouldn't hear him. "She had one Saturday night too.

I think it's the same one." He couldn't keep the concern from creeping into his voice, and Greyson's gaze sharpened as he took in Harris's clothing, or lack thereof.

"I'm guessing this isn't a friendly neighborly visit," he said, folding his arms over his chest while his mouth tilted up sardonically on one side. That smug, know-it-all grin irritated the living hell out of Harris.

"That's none of your concern," he said, sounding as stuffy as Greyson usually did.

"You're sure Tina's okay?" his twin asked again, and Harris nodded. "Jesus, I won't be forgetting the sound of those screams anytime soon. They were spine chilling."

"I know," Harris said grimly. He needed to have a talk with Tina.

"Right. I'll leave you to it. Good night." He opened the front door and shuddered dramatically. "God, it's freezing!"

He threw his shoulders back as he braced himself and stepped out into the cold, wet night, dashing back home on his bare feet. Harris shut and locked the door behind the other man and, after getting a glass of water from the kitchen sink, he padded back to Tina's bedroom.

She had dragged on a T-shirt and looked a lot more composed, which he was grateful for, even though he silently lamented the fact that her defenses were firmly back in place. He knew he'd get little to no information about the nightmare from her now.

He sat down on the edge of the bed beside her and handed her the water. She took a thirsty gulp before rewarding him with a smile.

"Thank you." He said nothing in response to that, instead reaching over to smooth a few stray curls out of her damp face.

"Better?" he asked after she'd drained the glass. She nodded, and he took the glass from her to place it on the bedside table.

"I'm sorry," she murmured, keeping her eyes downcast.

"You have nothing to be sorry for," he said, his voice gruff with emotion. "But—"

She lifted her eyes to meet his concerned gaze. "Don't ask, Harris," she said, her voice firm. "I'm not prepared to discuss it."

"Then it's the same nightmare," he said matter-of-factly.

"I could go for months without having one. It's been a while since I've had two so close together."

"Am I the trigger?" The question was hard to ask, because he wasn't sure he could handle the answer, but he needed to know.

The pause before she replied was significant and telling. And it just about killed him.

"Sometimes," she admitted, and he successfully smothered the urge to mutter something vile. Depressed by the fact that while he had been entertaining thoughts of more with her, hope for a future . . . he *sometimes* triggered nightmares that made her scream in absolute terror. How the hell was he supposed to live with that demoralizing fact?

"Can you tell me what it's about?"

"No. I told you, I'm not prepared to discuss it."

"Tina—"

"Harris," she interrupted impatiently. "Drop it or leave. On second thought . . . just leave. Please."

"What if you have another nightmare?"

"I won't."

"Tina. About us—"

"Not the time, Harris." Her words were delivered in a no-nonsense tone of voice that brooked no argument.

"I've changed my mind about leaving tomorrow." The words were out before he'd even realized he'd made the decision, and she had a moment's hesitation before gracing him with the tiniest of smiles.

"Good."

He felt an overwhelming sense of relief, and he exhaled on a slow, shuddering sigh. And there it was again, irrepressible and steadfast.

Hope.

He didn't trust himself to speak; instead he nodded and pushed himself up, gathering his clothes and dragging them on quickly and efficiently. When he was done, he captured her eyes with his determined gaze.

"Try to get some sleep."

"I will."

"Do you need anything else?" he asked, and her eyes flickered and dropped to his crotch. The dip in her gaze was so fast that, if he hadn't been watching her closely, he would have missed it. But it had happened, and it fed his ever-increasing hope. He felt it expanding in his chest, warming him from the inside out.

"N-no. Thank you."

She folded her arms over her chest, giving off some unmistakable "keep away" vibes, and he made an animalistic sound in the back of his throat—shocking himself in the process—before deliberately ignoring the defensive body language and closing the distance between them. He bent and dropped a hard kiss on her mouth.

"We'll talk tomorrow." Even Harris wasn't sure if his words were a promise or a threat.

Chapter Eleven

He was sitting on the porch steps—coffee mug in hand—waiting for her the following morning, and Tina fought to keep her expression neutral. Difficult, when all she wanted to do was grin like an idiot. She hadn't felt capable of dealing with his presence immediately after her nightmare, but that didn't mean she never wanted to see him again. Not after everything *else* that had happened last night.

"Morning," he said in greeting, his eyes uncertain and his voice lacking that usual cocky confidence.

"Hey. There's fresh coffee in the pot if you're interested," she offered insouciantly and was rewarded with an eager smile.

"Fantastic," he enthused, tossing the contents of his mug to the grass below the porch before leaping agilely to his feet. He was in and out of the house, with a freshly filled mug, in thirty seconds. Instead of heading back to the step, he sat down next to her and placed his arm behind her shoulders along the back of the swing.

Tina didn't say a word, snuggling to his side and dropping her head on his shoulder with a soft, contented little sigh. God, he smelled divine. She buried her nose in his neck, allowing the earthy masculine scent, reminiscent of green forests, sandalwood, and expensive leather, to envelop her entirely.

He tensed for a microsecond before he relaxed and dropped his arm over her shoulders. His fingers inevitably found her hair—he did seem to love toying with her hair—and idly wound their way through some of the fine curls that had escaped her ponytail.

They said nothing for a long time. Harris sipped and sighed as he drank his coffee, and Tina found herself comforted by the now-familiar sounds of enjoyment he made. She kept her eyes on the horizon—clear for the first time in days—and allowed herself to believe, just for one perfect moment, that this evanescent *thing* between them was sustainable.

"Pretty," Harris said quietly as they watched the sun put on a spectacular show of light and color for them.

"Yes," Tina agreed, not feeling particularly chatty this morning.

"It's going to be a nice day," he continued.

"Yes." It did look like it would be a good day: mild temperature, with not a cloud on the horizon. There was no trace—other than the wonderful fresh, wet smell of grass and glittering drops of moisture on the leaves and plants—of yesterday's rain.

"Tina—"

Sensing that he was about to steer the conversation in an unwanted direction, Tina pushed to her feet. "I have to get ready for work," she said, and he scowled, not bothering to hide his disappointment and frustration from her.

"You can't evade the subject forever," he said.

"I sure as hell can give it my best go," she said flippantly, then instantly regretted her attempt at humor when she saw the muted anger in his eyes. She shut her eyes and drew in a deep, shuddering breath. "I'm sorry. I'm not great at talking about stuff."

"I'm not either, but I think . . . if we want this to work. We have to make exceptions."

"Harris, there's too much *history* between us for this to be anything other than what it is right now."

"And what exactly is it?"

"Sex."

"I don't agree."

"That's your prerogative, but if you're expecting much more from me, you're setting yourself up for disappointment. I have to get ready. I'll see you later." She half turned to walk away, but he stopped her.

"Wait. Tina . . ."

She looked back at him, and he surprised her by slanting a completely roguish grin at her. "What?"

"Gimme a kiss?" His voice was so ridiculously, and boyishly, hopeful that Tina was helpless to do anything but comply. She made her way back to the swing, and he watched her with predatory intent. Her lips parted in an unconsciously seductive smile, and she bent at the waist to drop a completely chaste kiss on his waiting mouth.

He growled, obviously unhappy with the dry little peck, palmed the back of her head beneath her high ponytail, and deepened the kiss. Tina's knees turned to jelly when his tongue deftly slipped into her mouth, and she gasped when it drew hers out for a quick bout of thrust and parry before he ended the kiss without warning.

Tina wobbled before righting herself almost immediately. She stood upright and smoothed her damp palms down her pajama-covered thighs.

"Remember that when you think of me," he said, his smile filled with lazy confidence. "That . . . and *this*." He cupped his straining erection through the thick fabric of his jeans, and she unconsciously licked her lips before lifting her eyes back up to his. He was still smiling. Arrogant bastard.

"Definitely," she responded, her voice hoarse with desire. "And *you* remember you still owe me a taste of that."

The smug smile disappeared from his face and leaped to hers. She waggled her fingers at him and walked away.

"You have a visitor, boss," Ricardo announced after interrupting Tina's solitaire session halfway through their afternoon service. After a half an hour of schmoozing random patrons that morning, Tina had retreated to her office. She had opened her laptop, brought up her daily sales reports, and taken one quick panicked look at the numbers before minimizing the accounting program and opening up her card game instead. She'd played about seven games back-to-back before Ricardo's interruption.

She had never gotten around to contacting the paper again either. She had all but convinced herself that it was probably too late to apologize now.

"Oh?" she asked, lifting her eyes and fully expecting to see Harris standing behind Ricardo. Instead it was a vaguely familiar woman, whom she couldn't immediately place. It was only when Ricardo shifted to one side and she saw the woman's huge belly that Tina recognized her as Daffodil Carlisle.

"Hey," the woman said with a quick smile. "I should probably have called and made an appointment—I know you're likely busy. But I was seriously bored out of my gourd at home, so I hopped into the car and popped over. I wanted to show you what I've been working on."

Ricardo, clearly figuring he was no longer needed, left without further word, and the pregnant woman waddled into Tina's office and sat down across from her, dumping her satchel unceremoniously onto the other chair.

"Sorry. Just give me a sec to catch my breath. This baby is heavy as hell. I swear, he's probably going to be as huge as his dad someday."

"It's a boy?" Tina asked, for lack of anything else to say, really.

"Damned if I know," the other woman said with an indifferent shrug. "It better be. A girl the size of my husband would be a little unfortunate."

The irreverence surprised a laugh out of Tina. Earth mother Daffodil Carlisle was *not*.

"Anyway, I've been thinking about what we could do to promote the—"

"Wait, hold on." Tina held up both hands to stop her, and the other woman gave her an impatient look but stopped talking. "I'm sorry. We should have discussed this before. I wasn't expecting you to just up and run with it like this. Look, Mrs. Carlisle . . . I really appreciate this. I do. But I don't think I can accept your help."

"Why the hell not?" the other woman asked, her brow furrowed and impatience still gleaming in her gray eyes. "And Jesus, call me Daff. Mrs. Carlisle sounds like some fuddy-duddy old bird in slouchy gray support stockings."

Tina choked back a laugh. She was starting to really like this woman. She was completely different from her huggy, overly sweet sister, and Tina appreciated her frankness.

"I don't think I can afford your services."

"Damned straight you can't afford my services, not the way this business is clearly struggling. I know it's early days and everything, but *damn*, woman, this place is emptier than a church on a Saturday night out there. Luckily for you, I'm not charging you for my services."

Like Tina needed even more affirmation of how terribly the restaurant was doing. Clearly, *everybody* could see how badly she was botching up this business. Even perfect strangers. It was disheartening to hear all her worst fears about MJ's being verbalized so frankly. And having the woman offer her services for free was absolutely humiliating. Did the situation look dire enough to outsiders to actually warrant charity?

"I can't accept that," Tina said, inserting an entire glacier's worth of ice into her voice. Wanting this woman to know exactly how insulted she was by even the *suggestion* of charity. Daff responded to her affront by rolling her eyes.

"Okay, get your panties out of that twist. I had your friend pegged as the easily offended one, not you. I'm not charging you, because *you're* the one doing *me* the favor. Do you have any idea how mind-numbingly boring it is to sit at home every day waiting for this baby to pop? Spencer won't let me lift a finger at home, and for some dumb reason he seems to think using one's brain is overtaxing as well. I *need* this. Or I'll go stir crazy.

"Besides, I think this will be fun. It really won't require too much work from me at all. You've already done such a fantastic job with the place. It looks amazing, and the food is wonderful. MJ's now has the potential to be a drawing card to tourists and out-of-towners as well as locals. And that would be great for the entire town. It just needs a few tweaks."

Tina considered Daff's words for a moment, and the defensive tension slowly drained from her. Hearing praise from someone as impartial, blunt, and honest as Daffodil Carlisle felt . . . well, it felt amazing, actually. It felt like validation, like she was doing *something* right. Like her instincts about the place may not have been as terrible as she had started to believe they were.

She had failed at so very many things since her baby's death—it had become her norm. She had allowed herself to start each new job or project with the assumption of failure looming over her. And her family's low expectations had only reinforced that lack of self-belief. But maybe MJ's really was her chance to move forward. Her opportunity to finally—after so many years of failing at so many things—allow herself to succeed.

Not wanting to seem too eager, she gave Daff a long, measuring stare before resting her elbows on the desk and steepling her fingers. She hoped she looked as cool and businesslike as the guys who did the same in the movies.

"Okay," she said, relenting. "Show me what you've got."

Half an hour later, Tina couldn't keep the excited smile off her face. Daffodil Carlisle looked a little peaked but extremely satisfied with herself. Her smugness was completely justified. She had outlined a comprehensive social media marketing strategy and partnership ideas with a few of the local businesses, including her husband's Riversend store and an upmarket clothing boutique she had worked for in the past. Daff's community-outreach ideas were also phenomenal; it would mean more work, but she had suggested donating pastries to some of the local charities, as well as the youth center her husband ran. She had even proposed catering the city council's next few meetings free of charge. "Give a little to get a lot," was her motto, and Tina could not find a single flaw in that strategy. Gaining favor with the leaders would go a long way in a small town like Riversend.

"This is *really* great, Daff," Tina enthused, and Daff smiled smugly. "I don't know why I didn't think of some of these things myself."

"This is why I demand my husband pay me the big bucks," she said with a grin. "I know my stuff."

"I can't let you do this without some compensation," Tina said again.

"Free meals for the hubby, Charlie, and me for a year. We're the ones scoring."

"Done." Tina stretched her hand out across the desk, and Daff shook it firmly.

"I want to get started on this right away," Daff said. "I'm due in just a few weeks, and I won't have as much time to dedicate to this project after the baby gets here. I'd like to get the ball rolling, start a Facebook page; I know someone who can set up a website, and I'll do the newsletter every month. We can showcase things like seasonal specials, new menu items, staff news, and so on. I know a journalist with the local paper; we can do a spread on the restaurant and everything it has to offer.

"But here's the thing: I can only do so much, Tina. You and Libby, you're the driving force behind the brand. This is a close-knit community, and MJ's has long been the social hub of the town. People consider you an outsider, and it didn't help that there was absolutely no promotion of the relaunch and no attempt to engage the locals whatsoever. Not even an ad in the paper. It offended folks. They think you don't care about MJ's or how much it means to the town."

Tina winced at that bit of honesty. Her botched PR attempts coming back to haunt her.

"I was in here earlier, watching you walk around aimlessly, chatting with a few people here and there. It was so half-assed and insincere it would have been better if you hadn't even bothered. You didn't even notice me, did you?" Tina shook her head, incredibly embarrassed that her terrible people skills had been witnessed by this woman.

"Look, I'm the last person to talk about interpersonal skills. I'm the worst. I always say the wrong thing at the stupidest time. And apparently, I rub people up the wrong way. I'm better behind the scenes. Play to your strengths. Promote your chef. She's likable—" *Ouch!* Daff really didn't pull her punches. She must have noticed Tina's wince, because she grimaced. "Shit. See? I told you. I *suck*. I tend to speak my mind without really considering the consequences. I don't mean you're not likable, of course. You're clearly shy and a little more reserved than Libby, but other people won't pick up on the shyness. They'll just assume you're standoffish. People like to think the worst of others. Human nature and all that."

"I can never think of the right thing to say," Tina admitted beneath her breath. "At least you say *something*, even if it's the wrong thing. I clam up."

Tina couldn't believe she'd just admitted as much to the other woman. She was never that frank with strangers. But something about the woman's candidness really appealed to Tina and made her want to confide in her.

"So don't put yourself in that situation. Unless you're completely comfortable, it's better to not attempt speaking with the customers. Let your manager deal with that; let your chef and your staff smile and play nice. People know when you find it a chore to speak with them. And it puts them the hell off. You can't stay in hiding forever, of course—at some point people will want to meet you and speak with you. But for now, while we're building this brand, we can work something out. Give you a mystique that will get people curious about you. The more intrigued they are, the more likely they are to come to the restaurant to try and figure you out."

"I don't think I'm comfortable with people trying to figure me out." She had enough people trying to figure her out: her family was always lamenting about how they didn't understand her, and Libby wanted to know more about the baby she had loved and lost.

And Harris . . . it terrified her how little he knew. The thought of him learning more was untenable, and yet she didn't know how much longer she could keep the truth from him.

And now this. All Tina had wanted was to finally accomplish something she could be proud of. This restaurant—with her name on the sign—had been her best shot. And if she didn't properly market it, the place was going to sink without a trace. It had been naive of her to think MJ's would succeed simply because the brick-and-mortar establishment had been standing for thirty years. Tina had thought she was giving the town what they wanted and that she would easily inherit the existing clientele.

She didn't want to fail at this; she may have gone into it half-cocked, with some vague idea of helping Libby out . . . but the more time she spent here, in this town, with these people, the more important it became to her to succeed.

Tina now saw that she had been self-sabotaging. Same as she had done since losing her baby. Going into a venture without a solid plan in mind and then failing spectacularly when things got too difficult. If she wasn't careful, MJ's would become yet another disaster to stick into her thick scrapbook of failures. And she didn't want that. She wanted to be good at something.

She wanted to be good at *this*.

Purchasing the restaurant may have started off as yet another impulsive decision, but it was coming to mean so much more to her. Tina had stubbornly believed she could do this without help. But that was always her fatal flaw. Keeping everyone who cared about her at arm's length. Never asking for—or accepting—assistance, always so sure that "maybe this time" she could make it on her own. She had never felt able to ask her family for help, not when they had made it so clear to her how little faith they had in her ever accomplishing anything noteworthy. But she now recognized that—if she wanted this restaurant to succeed—she would have to set that pride aside.

Her talk with Libby about the baby had opened Tina's eyes to the fact that she had other family. She had a *sister* who believed in her, who loved her, and who cared about what happened to her. And Libby wasn't the only one. This woman, Daffodil Carlisle, a relative stranger, believed in Tina and MJ's enough to approach her with these ideas. And there were others.

There was Harris . . . she would be lying to herself if she didn't admit that he cared about her. That he had for a long time.

For the first time in years, Tina could see that she was not alone. She had never been alone. She just hadn't believed in herself enough to see the faith people like Libby had in her.

This plan, so concisely worded and neatly outlined in flowcharts and timelines, was her best shot at finally succeeding at something. Daff, with her swollen belly, her frank talk, and her unflinching regard, was tossing her a lifeline, and Tina would be foolish not to grab it with both hands.

"Tell me when we start."

Daff smiled approvingly and folded her hands over her belly. "Right now."

Harris went to MJ's for lunch. The place was half-empty, and he shook his head at the poor turnout.

The now-familiar Suzie came to take his order.

"Hey, Suzie," he said. "Is Tina around?"

"She's in a meeting," the older woman said, and Harris's eyebrows rose. Tina hadn't mentioned the fact that she had a meeting today.

Then again, why would she? She didn't have to tell him a damned thing. He was just a booty call.

"Right," he said and flashed her a quick smile before requesting a cup of coffee. He dragged out his phone when the woman left and half-heartedly returned a few emails. Aside from an existing embezzlement problem in Perth, Australia, which was being handled, there was nothing that demanded his immediate attention.

"Harris, have you spoken with Greyson today?"

"*Goddamnit!* Don't sneak up on me like that," Harris chastised, clutching his chest like a maiden aunt and frowning at his sister-in-law, who sat across the table from him. His heart was going a mile a minute. She had come out of nowhere.

"Stop being such an old woman," she said with a dismissive wave. "When last did you see Greyson?"

"Do I look like his fucking social secretary?" he snapped, irritated.

"Don't test me, Harris. I'm already seriously peed off with you."

"Why?"

"You *know* why," she said, and he felt his temper rising. He hardly ever lost his temper with Libby, but she was pushing all the wrong buttons today.

"No, please do elaborate!"

"Okay. You slept with Tina. It didn't end well. You knew she had a serious crush on you when we were kids, and you took advantage of that."

"You don't have the first fucking clue what you're talking about."

"Don't you dare use that language with me, Harrison Chapman! There were repercussions. Did you even care about what happened after you slept with her and then just dropped her?"

"I didn't drop her!" He knew he sounded defensive, but fuck it, he felt defensive. Libby was attacking without provocation. Taking sides when she had only heard Tina's story. Treating him like he was a monster, when she had no idea. No real clue how things had been for him. "She wouldn't speak to me. I tried. And then she left. For a whole year, and after that, she still wouldn't speak with me. For ten fucking years I've been trying to fix things. I've been trying to make it right . . . and she wouldn't—she *won't*—let me."

"Why *should* she, Harris?" Libby asked, her voice quietening while her beautiful eyes shone with tears. "She's broken. I didn't even know how broken until I spoke with her yesterday." She swiped angrily at her tears before shaking her head and pinning him beneath her accusatory stare. "She's so broken. And *you're* the one who broke her."

You're the one who broke her.

The words reverberated through Harris's head for the rest of the day. He had finished his coffee, after Libby had stormed off in a huff, and had left without ordering lunch. Because it was a fairly mild day, he had walked to MJ's and was now taking a long, meandering walk back. The town was really quite quaint. He hadn't taken the time to appreciate that before. He couldn't quite appreciate it now either, not with Libby's censure ringing in his ears.

Something else was going on, something beyond the bet. Something Tina had told Libby but had refused to tell Harris. And the resentment was chewing through his gut like acid. How was he supposed to make things better when she persisted in keeping secrets from him? It was beyond frustrating and—

A strident car horn jolted him from his thoughts, and he was shocked to realize that he'd attempted to cross the road without bothering to check for traffic. He was standing in front of a big, old-timey powder-blue Cadillac.

"Moron! Watch where you're walking!" the driver, an elderly lady with white hair, thick, hairy white eyebrows, and a nasty attitude, shouted at him. She wound down her window and flipped him the bird before driving off at a snail's pace.

"If she *had* hit you, I doubt the impact would even have left a bruise," an amused voice coming from one of the storefronts called. A behemoth of a man, dressed in sweats, was standing at the entrance to the sporting-goods store, his arms folded across his huge chest. "She couldn't have been going more than fifteen kilometers an hour."

"Should she even be driving?" Harris asked, a little bemused by both his encounter with the little old lady and with this huge enigmatic-looking guy.

"Probably not. Our only traffic cop will pull her over later and escort her back to the retirement home. She comes out for a drive once a month—people usually know to stay out of her way."

"Well, some of us aren't familiar with your small-town quirks," Harris snapped, abruptly annoyed with everyone and everything in this fucking place.

"Hmm? Well, maybe I'm just an ignorant country guy," the big fellow said slowly, "but even I know not to walk straight into traffic. Anyone else but our quirky Mattie, and you'd be in the hospital."

Fair point.

"I'm sorry—I was being an asshole," Harris said, closing the distance between them and offering his hand. "Harrison Chapman."

The man eyed his hand for a second before reaching out and giving Harris a firm handshake. None of the macho bullshit he sometimes got from big guys who squeezed that extra bit tighter to assert their dominance.

"Spencer Carlisle."

Harris eyed the sign above the man's head. "Ah. Of Carlisle Sporting Solutions, I presume?"

"Hmm."

"Good to meet you."

"Likewise." He stepped back and folded his arms over his chest again.

"Well, see you around, I guess," Harris said awkwardly, feeling dismissed. This town was full of truly weird people.

"You play football?"

What?

"A little," Harris offered warily, and Spencer Carlisle nodded.

"Good. We need extra players. Be there on Saturday night, after seven. Sports field." Concise. He didn't waste words, this one. "Already told your brother."

Of *course*, he knew Harris had a brother. People in this town seemed to know everything. He wondered what Greyson's response to the invitation had been.

Spencer stepped back into his store without waiting for Harris's answer. Which was great, because Harris wasn't exactly sure what his reply would have been.

At least the encounter had managed to *briefly* take his mind off his problems with Tina. As he walked home, paying closer attention to his surroundings, he tried to figure out how to get her to trust him with her secrets.

Secrets he wasn't sure he wanted to know.

It wasn't as bad as she'd been expecting. It wasn't great, but it wasn't truly awful either. Bolstered by Daffodil Carlisle's visit, Tina had finally managed to garner enough courage to look at her accounts.

She had staved off a mild panic attack when she had calculated how much Daff's marketing strategy would cost to implement, but compared to the alternative, it was well worth the risk. She felt lighter: a huge weight had been lifted from her shoulders, and she was hopeful for the first time since they'd opened.

God, had it *really* only been five days? It felt like forever ago. So much had happened between then and now. Not just with the restaurant, but with Harris.

Her phone beeped, and she checked it automatically. Another message from Smith. He had texted every day since Friday, and she hadn't bothered to respond to him. Now, cloaking herself in the residual courage from her earlier decision to do her overdue accounting, she picked up the phone and called her brother.

He answered almost immediately.

"Tina?"

"Hi, Smith."

"I wasn't expecting you to call," he said. Damn, why did it always have to be so awkward between them?

"Would you prefer me to hang up?"

"Don't be ridiculous. I was just expecting a text, that's all."

"I can do that if one-on-one communication makes you uncomfortable."

"Jeez, why are you being so weird?" he grumbled. "I wanted to know how the restaurant business was treating you."

"I had a crap opening weekend," she said, her voice challenging. Waiting for him to launch into the usual passive-aggressive diatribe that always made her feel like a total failure.

"I-I'm sorry. If you need help or advice, please let me know. Okay?"

Her jaw dropped, practically all the way to the floor. Well, this was new. "Wait? No 'Jesus, Tina. Why do you always go into these things half-cocked?'" She lowered her voice in a terrible imitation of his. "Or 'God, Tina, do you ever do any market research?' or—"

"Enough," he interrupted, his voice strained. "It's already been brought to my attention that I've been a shitty and unsupportive brother."

"It *has*?" Who would have had the nerve to tell any member of her family that they were shitty? "Brought to your attention by whom?"

"Harris," Smith admitted, the word sounding torn from him, as if it physically hurt him to say the name. "And he was right."

"Harris?" she repeated blankly. "Why would Harris tell you that?"

"I think the real question is why should he *have* to tell me that? You're my little sister. The only one I have. I should have been helping, supporting . . . instead I—all of us—made you feel small."

"And useless. And stupid," she felt compelled to add, and the silence on the other end of the line screamed for so long that for a second she thought the call had disconnected, until he cleared his throat.

"You're none of those things," he said.

"Yep. Especially not small," she quipped bitterly. Maybe she should be a little less bitchy and just accept his apology, but, yeah . . . she was feeling a bit petty today. "Just ask Mother."

"Fuck. Tina, I'm sorry." He sounded so miserable she did her own mental swearing. It wasn't as much fun as she'd thought it would be to let him flounder, so—after the briefest moment of hesitation—she let him off the hook.

"You can't apologize for all of them, Smith, and you're not responsible for what the rest of them have said or how they made me feel."

"But I am responsible for not protecting you from them. For allowing everybody—including me—to make you feel inadequate."

Tina toyed with her pen, spinning it endlessly round on her desk.

"Smith, did you know?" She asked the question she'd never been brave enough to ask before.

"Know? Know what?" His blank question was all the information she needed, but she answered his question nonetheless.

"When they sent me away to Scotland? For my so-called gap year? I was pregnant."

"Oh Christ, Tina. I didn't know that."

"It kind of messed me up a bit."

Her brother was quiet again—another long silence—but this time she knew he was there; she could hear his ragged breathing as he fought to bring whatever he was feeling under control.

"The baby?" he finally asked. "You gave it up?"

Tina swallowed dryly. Saying the words out loud never got easier. "He died."

Her brother swore again, his voice hoarse with raw emotion.

"I'm so sorry, Tina. I should have been there to support you. I should have been a better brother."

She didn't respond to that; there was nothing to say . . . because he was right: he *should* have been a better brother. But she should have been a better sister too. She could have brought his failings as a big brother to his notice, or . . . she could have reached out and told him she needed him. Needed his help and love and support. He would have given her that love and support. She could see that now.

"The father?" he asked suddenly, his voice filled with menace.

"He was never in the picture."

"He was in the picture long enough to conceive a kid."

"Drop it—it's ancient history."

"It's not ancient history to me," he pointed out, his voice hoarse with suppressed anger.

"I know, and maybe I shouldn't have told you."

"You *should* have told me! You should have told me ten years ago!"

"I thought you knew. I thought Conrad and Kyle knew too. I thought you were ashamed of me."

"Fuck." His voice broke on the word, and he sounded helpless and sad and angry all at the same time. "You were a kid. You should have had support and love. You shouldn't have been carted off to another country to face all of that alone. Mom and Dad have a shitload of explaining to do!"

"Leave it, Smith. You'll just rake it all up again. I've moved on."

Mostly.

"I want to help," he said decisively, thankfully changing the subject. "With the restaurant. Let me help."

"Thank you for offering. I-I *think* I've got it under control now. I have a marketing plan in motion. But if I need help, I'll let you know. I think this one is going to succeed, Smith. I really do."

"We don't have much time," Tina said. She had rushed over to Harris's place after her phone call with Smith. Eager to see Harris after learning about how he had stood up for her against her brother. And desperate to reward him for his unexpectedly sweet gesture.

Harris looked up from his laptop, visibly shocked to find her standing at the entrance to his room. She stepped inside and shut the door, leaning back against it and toeing off her pumps in the process.

"What are you—" He stopped in midsentence when she surged toward where he was sitting on the side of his bed and grabbed the laptop from his grasp in clumsy haste. She set it on the side table before placing her hands on his shoulders and pushing him back. He offered no resistance, his eyes curious as he lay on the bed with his knees bent and his feet still planted on the floor.

She grinned at him, pulled the tight skirt of her dress up to her thighs, flashing the front of her lacy blue panties, before she straddled him, her knees planted on the bed on either side of his thighs. His T-shirt rode up, revealing his hard abs and the slight sprinkling of hair trailing down from his belly button to disappear into the waistband of his jeans. *So sexy.*

She fumbled with the belt buckle and then clumsily went to work on the button fly of his jeans. Tina wasn't too adept at undressing a man, but what she lacked in expertise, she hoped she made up for in enthusiasm.

His breath caught when she slid her hand into the now-open fly of his pants and then released on a long, slow groan when she curled her fingers around the hardening column through the cotton fabric of his briefs. She loved the feel of him stiffening and growing in both length and girth beneath her grip. It was a wholly new experience for her, and she squeezed appreciatively, eliciting another involuntary groan from him.

She peeled his underwear back slowly, revealing—inch by impressive inch—his masculine beauty to her eager eyes. She tried to tug his trousers and briefs down but was frustrated when she could barely move the heavy denim fabric.

"A little help, please," she said, deciding to enlist Harris's aid, and he lifted his hips without protest, surging up between her thighs, the head of his penis coming within touching distance of her mound. She shimmied out of the way, not wanting that contact yet. She needed to maintain control of this encounter. She had a clear idea of how she wanted it to go; unsolicited touching and rubbing and suckling and grinding from Harris would mess up that plan.

She got up and dragged off his jeans, tugging them to his hips, and gazed at his nude male part in wonder and a fair amount of appreciation. It was throbbing, and the glans—so close to his belly button—was an angry red and shiny with moisture. The shaft itself was thick and lightly veined and nearly as long as her forearm.

She eagerly clambered back onto the bed and knelt next to him, her knees pushing against his waist. She slipped one hand under his shirt and rested it on his perfectly defined chest and placed the other on one of his hard thighs, inches away from his member.

"I like your penis," she said conversationally, and he choked before covering his face with one of his large hands. Only his sexy mouth was visible, and that had a slight tilt at the corners. "Because of my lack of experience with them, I couldn't figure out if yours was quite big or just really average."

His lips thinned for a moment, and he spread his fingers to peer at her from between them.

"And? What did you decide?" he asked, his voice taking on that gravelly note that she only heard when he was sexually aroused.

"I think it's perfect."

His fingers closed again, and he gifted her with the smallest of smiles.

"I think *you're* perfect."

"Nobody's perfect," she said absentmindedly, taking hold of his shaft and measuring his girth between forefinger and thumb before closing her fist and pumping up and down his length. He bucked, startling her.

"You *are* perfect," he maintained, his voice strained. "Perfect for me."

"Stop saying silly things," she criticized mildly, leaning over to drop a kiss on his lips. "And let me concentrate. I told you we don't have much time. And I want to enjoy this."

God, Harris fucking adored this woman. He didn't know if this was a feeling that had been there all along, or if it had developed recently. All he knew was that it felt like it had always been a part of him. This naked adoration that vied for space with the joy and hope that had taken up residence in his expanding heart.

She kissed him again, her hand lazily stroking his aching cock, and he started to tell her that the condoms were in the bedside drawer when she lowered her head to his chest, trailing her lips over the T-shirt that had been shoved up to just below his pecs. She nibbled at his nipples through the thin cotton. When had his damned nipples become so sensitive, anyway? They felt like they had a direct line to his throbbing dick, and he was about to urge her to draw one into her mouth when she moved on. Leaving him frustrated and feeling like his skin was too tight for his body.

His hand dropped from his eyes, and he pushed himself to his elbows to watch her every move intently. Wanting to know what she was up to. Her lips trailed lightly and quickly over his torso, her loose hair blanketing his chest in the process. The sight of all that bright hair covering him was as huge a turn-on as the lips that were trailing down the center of his chest, all the way to his belly button. He was left wondering what her endgame was when her tongue came out and licked the trail from his belly button down toward his—

"Oh God! Tina . . . *fuck!*" His back bowed when her curious lips finally reached the head of his cock and delicately drew it into her mouth. The suction ended, and he nearly wept when she lifted her head and gave him a delightful smile of discovery.

"Salty," she observed before lowering her head to go to work again. She nibbled, licked, sucked . . . God, could she suck. And she wriggled in excitement as she fed more of his cock into her waiting mouth, feasting like she'd been deprived of sustenance for months. She found a rhythm very quickly—it was sweet and untutored and mind blowing in its sensuality.

One of his hands could no longer resist the allure of her hair, and his fingers wove through, and then fisted in, her curls. His other hand crept beneath the tight skirt that was still hitched up over the creamy thighs, and he delved into the warmth between those soft thighs, seeking and finding the dampness he had known would be there. His fingers burrowed beneath her sodden lacy panties, and his thumb found her swollen clit almost immediately. She wriggled in appreciation, spreading her thighs as far as her skirt would allow, and he happily used the extra space to put his other fingers to work, plunging three of them into her grasping, hot, slick channel.

She squealed around his cock and enthusiastically rode his thrusting hand while increasing the suction on his length. Harris's breath was gusting in and out of his chest; he couldn't concentrate on anything other than what her mouth was doing and where his fingers were playing. He didn't want to come. Not until she did. But because she was clearly a complete novice at blow jobs, she didn't know to tease and titillate—she full on went for it. Demanding his orgasm with relentless suction that overstimulated him nearly to the point of pain.

He tried to stop it, but he couldn't find the breath to tell her to slow down; instead all he could produce were inarticulate, frantic sounds. Her hand fisted around the base of his cock, adding another dimension to the pleasure pain that was driving him relentlessly toward his climax.

By now his fingers were plunging into her as he desperately tried to make her come before he did. But it was a lost cause. She swirled her tongue around the bottom edge of his corona, and he was gone.

"*Tina.*" Protest? Plea? Prayer? He did not know. But it was the only word he could utter before his entire body convulsed and he lost control, spilling into her eager mouth. She cried out, the force of his orgasm taking her by surprise, and for a second she hesitated before continuing to suckle. Her mouth gentling around his jerking shaft. After one last suctioning pull, she reluctantly lifted her head. She gave him a smug grin, wiping her lips with the back of her hand.

He carefully used the fist in her hair to tug her head up and brought her to him for a hungry kiss. He could taste himself on her lips, and it was more erotic than he could ever have imagined.

She made a muffled sound against his lips and *finally* clenched around his still-thrusting fingers and came. Beautifully. Her head flying back to reveal the arch of her throat, her mouth opening on a soundless scream. The tightening of her sheath around his fingers was almost painful, but he fucking loved it. Against all odds—considering his mind-blowing orgasm of just a few minutes ago—he was semihard watching this fully clothed, wantonly disheveled, gorgeous creature come on his fingers.

She collapsed on the bed beside him and snuggled against his side. He wrapped an arm around her shoulders and held her close, burying his nose in her fragrant hair. Apples . . . her hair smelled like freshly sliced green apples. It was appealing. Like everything else about her.

"That was nice," she said sleepily. Her hand had crept under his T-shirt, and her fingers were toying with the pendant he always wore beneath his clothes. He tensed. The damned thing was such a part of his identity that he hardly gave it much thought anymore, and he knew she hadn't noticed it before now. She had fallen asleep soon after their bout last night. And then after the nightmare everything had gone to shit. But now, the more she fiddled with it, the more he sensed her interest growing.

She lifted her head and pushed his shirt up. But he flattened his hand against hers, effectively stopping the movement.

"What is that?" she asked, her voice alive with curiosity.

"Nothing."

"I didn't know you wore a necklace."

"Pendant," he corrected stiffly, and she rolled her eyes.

"Potato, potahto," she said dismissively.

"I never got that. Nobody ever says *potahto*."

"You're dissembling. What is it? Show me."

Shit.

He sighed and tugged on the corded black leather strap, dragging the pendant out from beneath his T-shirt. She flipped over onto her stomach, draping one arm over his chest and lifting the pendant with her other hand. She peered at it closely, looking baffled.

"What *is* it?" she asked, circling the thick, heavy silver hoop round and round on her finger. He knew the instant she recognized it and flushed when she lifted her shocked gaze to his.

"It's an earring. *My* earring." He'd had it welded shut and smoothed out so that the little hinge closure would no longer open—it was practically seamless now. But yes, it was her earring. And he'd been wearing it like a sentimental fool for more than ten years. He didn't even know why. He should have returned it to her. Or thrown it out . . . but he'd found it in his bed the day after that awful night and couldn't bring himself to part with it.

Her initials were engraved on the inside . . . another reason he should have returned it to her, and yet it had felt like an even better reason to keep it.

"What is this?" she asked in horror. "Some kind of trophy? A reminder of your conquest?"

Goddamnit! Of course she would think that.

"Nah, I have bedposts to notch for that," he retorted scathingly, getting off the bed and dragging his jeans up, buttoning and belting efficiently before angrily straightening his T-shirt and—keeping his eyes focused on hers—deliberately, and somewhat defiantly, dropping his pendant down the neck of his shirt again.

"Give it to me," she demanded, leaping from the bed and holding her hand out.

"No. It's mine."

"It's not yours. Oh my God. It has my initials engraved into it. It's mine and I want it back."

"Do you still have the other one?"

"What does that matter? You can't have it."

"Jesus, this is fucking childish!"

"You stole it!"

"*You* lost it!"

"It wasn't lost. You've had it all this time. That's theft."

"Why do you want it?"

"What does that matter?"

"*Why?*"

"Why?" she repeated furiously, folding her arms over her chest and looking more pissed off than Harris had ever seen her before. "*Why?* So that you can't have it! That's why."

The words stung. Well, not the words, but the absolute loathing behind them. It more than stung—it burned. Like acid. He swallowed and tried to formulate a response, but she wasn't quite done scalding him with her vitriol yet.

"You don't get to have a fond keepsake of the worst night of my life, Harris. You just don't!" Her face was red with anger, her hair bristling like a fiery halo around her head. She looked fierce, furious, and completely devastated, and Harris had no defense against that.

He scrubbed his hands over his face and stared up at the ceiling for a moment before tugging the pendant out and yanking it up over his head. Two steps between them, but it felt like a thousand miles as he crossed the distance. He dropped the pendant into her waiting hand and gently folded her fingers around it.

He lifted her hand and kissed her closed fist before brushing past her and leaving the room.

Tina's breath caught in her throat, and she felt a lump form and solidify there, making it painful to swallow. Her fist was clenched around the silver hoop, which still retained his body heat. Why had he kept this? All these years he had been wearing it around his neck, close to his heart. She didn't understand. *Was* it a trophy? Somehow she doubted that; maybe she would have thought that before, but those kinds of accusations no longer rang true after the last few days spent in his company. Harris simply wasn't the cold and callous man she had once believed him to be.

He was caring, considerate, and genuinely interested in her well-being. He had stood up for her against her brother, one of his best friends. She *liked* spending time with him, and she felt certain that he felt the same way.

Her gaze moved unseeingly around the stark bedroom. He had left the comforts of his lush lifestyle to come to this town and live in this awful house to provide support for his friend as well as keep a concerned eye on the brother who had slighted him so terribly. A callous man would not do that. She unclenched her fingers and stared down at her earring . . . Harris's pendant. Slightly larger than a woman's wedding ring, it could no longer function as an earring. Not with the hinge welded shut. The hoop was completely smooth on the outside with only the curlicued MJ on the inside. He had looped a simple leather strap through it. Anyone looking at it would have no idea that it had once been an earring.

She sighed, her heart like lead in her chest, and dropped the pendant on the bedside table.

She exited the room and carefully shut the door behind her.

"What the hell is going on?"

The deep voice made her jump, and she turned to face Greyson, who was seated on the threadbare sofa with a thick book facedown on his chest.

"Oh my *God!*" Tina squeaked, her hand fluttering to her chest. "How long have you been sitting there?"

"If you're wondering whether I heard you and my brother having sex, the answer is . . . kind of. The argument that followed was a lot louder, hence unmissable. Then he storms out of here and drives off without a word. Like I asked before, what the hell?"

"You shouldn't eavesdrop."

"I live here. If you want privacy, move your liaisons next door . . . although that's not much better. The walls are paper thin."

Tina peered at the book on his chest, and her eyebrows flew to her hairline when she recognized it for what it was.

"That's a baby book," she pointed out.

"I know," he responded drily.

"Why do you have it?"

"Because I'd rather not continue being a shitty father."

Not sure how to respond to that, Tina stared at him for a moment before slumping, not in the mood to spar with Greyson.

"I have to go. Tell Harris . . ." She paused. There really was nothing to say, and she shrugged helplessly.

"Martine, for what it's worth . . . ," Greyson began, and she lifted her eyes to meet his solemn gaze. "My brother would never intentionally do anything to hurt you. Not ten years ago and not now. That ridiculous bet was so out of character that it makes me question the circumstances surrounding it."

"You knew about the bet?" she asked miserably, fresh humiliation washing over her, nearly crushing her beneath its weight.

"Only after the fact. Jonah Spade spoke of it to me precisely once, and to my knowledge he has never, and will never, speak of it again." Greyson looked so threatening in that moment that Tina actually gulped. "He was also ostracized from our group immediately after that."

"Does Smith know?" she asked, terrified of what the answer would be, and when she looked up, she was shocked to find a look of tenderness in Greyson's usually enigmatic gaze.

"Of course he doesn't, Tina." It was the first time *ever* that she had heard him use the shortened version of her name. His voice warm and so compassionate she had a hard time keeping her tears at bay. "I can guarantee Jonah Spade and his cohorts would all have been permanently injured if Smith ever got wind of it. And, quite frankly, even though Harris sometimes annoys the hell out of me, he's still my brother, and I dread to think what Smith would have done to Harris if he ever found out. It was selfish of me, but that's one of the reasons I quashed any and all potential rumors."

Even at twenty, Greyson Chapman had been a formidably resourceful man. He had only gotten more dangerous over the years. Which was why it was so bizarre to see him still clutching that baby book to his chest.

Before she could think about it too closely, Tina crossed the living room and bent down to drop a kiss on Greyson's cheek. He looked completely disconcerted by the unsolicited show of affection and blinked at her in shock before flushing like a schoolboy.

"Thank you, Greyson," she said and left before he could utter another word.

Chapter Twelve

He should go home. Harris had lost count of how often that thought had crossed his mind over the course of the week. Now it was Saturday, and he was standing in the middle of a sports field, freezing his balls off because he'd been dumb enough to allow Spencer Carlisle of Carlisle Sporting Solutions to kit him out in football gear for the big match. Oldies versus young'uns, or something like that. A group of thirtysomethings playing a group of teens from the youth-outreach program, all in the name of charity.

The best thing that could be said about this game was that Tina was here. MJ's was one of the sponsors of the event and was providing refreshments for the spectators and halftime snacks for the players.

She was sitting in the stands with Spencer's hugely pregnant wife, whom Harris had met in passing earlier. The woman was the genius who was helping Tina with her marketing. Harris had seen flyers advertising the restaurant all over town, a flattering review in the paper yesterday, and a lot of hype around MJ's sponsorship for tonight's event. People were paying attention, and it was showing; whenever Harris had dropped into the restaurant this week, there had been more asses in seats than during those first few days. He was happy for Tina; he knew she had to be relieved. Even though he couldn't be sure.

They hadn't spoken since their argument on Tuesday.

He'd returned home from his frustrated drive to Plettenberg Bay and back again to find the pendant on his side table. He had slipped it into the drawer and hadn't worn it since. He kept thinking of her referring to it as a keepsake of the worst night of her life, and the thought of having it touch his skin after that made him feel physically ill.

"Hey, Harrison Chapman! Focus up." Harris lifted his head. Spencer's brother, team captain Mason—in town for the weekend so that his wife could attend Daff's baby shower—was giving him a million instructions, and Harris tried to keep up, but his mind and his heart just weren't in it.

"Don't embarrass me."

The cool voice, coming from beside him, finally succeeded in provoking some kind of reaction from Harris.

"Shut up, Greyson," he seethed. "I'm a better player than you'll ever be."

"Doubtful."

"You've always been terrible at sports."

"We'll see about that." The twins had never been competitive—they were much too different for that. But with those words, the proverbial gauntlet had been flung down for the first time in their lives, and Harris felt a surge of adrenaline at the prospect of wiping the floor with his arrogant brother.

"Oh my God, they suck," Daff said with way too much glee in her voice as they watched the older team get soundly trounced by the teens. "Spence should stick to rugby or cricket . . . football is *not* his sport."

"Sam's not too bad," Lia said loyally and then winced when an extremely talented sixteen-year-old stole the ball away from her fiancé and went on to score seconds later. It was the younger team's third goal. In the fifteenth minute of the first half.

"God, I wish I could drink," Daff said, her voice filled with yearning. "This is going to be a long night."

Tina only half listened to the sisters bantering back and forth; her eyes kept tracking back to Harris. He was magnificent. He wore a pair of shorts that ended just above his knees and a roomy team jersey. His loose-limbed, rangy body was perfect. On a field full of beautiful men, one of whom was his identical twin, Harrison Chapman was by far the best-looking man out there.

She missed him. In the week since he'd shown up on her doorstep, he'd entrenched himself so completely into her life that not having coffee with him in the mornings started her day off wrong. What the heck was that even about? How could she miss him after only three mornings? How could she regret no longer binge-watching *Game of Thrones* with him when they had done that only once? How could she yearn for his presence in her bed when she had only shared it with him that one night?

She was being ridiculous. She knew that. Ten years of anger and antipathy toward the man, and she found herself longing for him after just five days of—she wasn't even sure what to make of those five days. Everything had just been *different* between her and Harris.

It wasn't logical . . . it made no sense, but emotions rarely did.

She just wanted to move past whatever *this* was and carry on with her life. Her life that would not, and never could, include Harrison Chapman.

"Oh, thank God," Daisy—youngest sister to Daff and Lia—breathed seconds before everybody in the stands applauded. Tina blinked and watched as the group of men all thumped Greyson on his back. He didn't look too pleased with all the overly familiar physical contact, but he accepted it without protest.

"What happened?" Tina asked, even though it was self-evident.

"Dishy Twin Number One scored a goal," Daff said.

"But only because Dishy Twin Number Two passed him that zinger," Daisy elaborated.

"Well, at least it won't be a complete washout," Lia said. "I don't think I'd be able to deal with Sam's sulking if that were to happen."

It was the first vaguely negative thing Tina had ever heard Lia say, and she stared at the other woman in surprise. Lia laughed when she noticed her expression.

"That Englishman can be a total baby." She laughed. "Sick, injured, or slighted, and suddenly he's like a bear with a sore paw. I wouldn't wish that on my worst enemy."

"They're all like that." Daff chuckled. "Guys, I mean."

"Do you think so?" Tina asked before she could stop herself.

"Yeah, I mean, you know that," Daff said with a laugh. "You and DT Two—you guys have a thing, right?"

Tina went bright red and shook her head, unable to bring herself to verbalize the negative response to that question.

"Jeez, Daff, that's none of your business," Lia rebuked mildly, and Daff rolled her eyes.

"Anybody can see it. You're with DT Two, and Libby is having all kinds of drama with DT One. They had a huge argument right on Main Road yesterday."

They did?

That was news to Tina. Libby wasn't here tonight because she was overseeing dinner service. Ever since Tina had finally opened up and been honest with Libby last week, their friendship had been back on an even keel. Tina still had only minimal exposure to Clara, but Libby was no longer resentful of that. Her babysitting arrangement with Greyson seemed to be going well, and even though Libby continued to keep her husband at a distance, she no longer tried to curb his access to Clara.

Why would they have been arguing? In public?

By the end of the match, at least a dozen people had approached Tina to compliment her on the cupcakes MJ's had provided, and the Chapman twins had scored an additional two goals for their team. One each. Taking the older team's final tally up to three, against the younger team's six.

"At least the suckage wasn't too bad," Daff said with a grin after the final whistle signaled the end of the match. "But God, without the Dishy Twins, that would have been pretty grim."

"And Spence wants to make this a monthly event? I don't think I'd be able to live with Sam's premanstrual tension before each game."

Tina choked on her chocolate cupcake, coughed, and then laughed. Lia was pretty funny for such a sweet do-gooder.

"So we'll see you and Libby at the shower tomorrow, right?" Daff asked while her sisters left the stands to go comfort their men. Daff just waved at Spencer, who blew her a kiss. She rolled her eyes, but Tina could see she was pleased by the gesture.

"I wasn't sure it was okay. I mean, your sister just invited us, and you barely know us."

"Yeah, Lia is one of those weird idealistic people who thinks everybody should love everybody and we should all just get along," Daff said fondly.

"Libby has similar tendencies. Not as bad as your sister, though. I mean . . ." Tina lowered her voice confidentially before whispering, "She *hugged* me."

Daff made a derisive sound in the back of her throat, but her smile was affectionate.

"Sam and I have been trying to break her of some of her more cringey tendencies, but I think we'd both be gutted if she actually listened to us. Lia's just . . . Lia."

"She's very sweet," Tina offered.

"*Too* sweet." Daff's unwitting repetition of Tina's own words made her chuckle again. She really liked this woman. And that was practically unheard of for Tina.

"We'll be there," Tina promised, suddenly excited by the prospect.

"So are you going to ignore that poor man all night, or do you intend to throw him a bone?" Daff asked; the shift in topic startled Tina into following the other woman's pointed stare and looking straight into the very gaze she'd been avoiding all evening.

Daff got up—her husband appearing as if by magic to escort her down the stands—leaving Tina still staring at Harris, who couldn't seem to tear his own eyes away. His hand went to his chest, in a gesture she had always noticed but never really registered before now. Suddenly she knew what he'd been seeking all those other times: that contentious pendant.

She wondered if he was wearing it now . . . and found herself unable to decide how she felt about the possibility. She deliberately remained seated on the wooden bleachers, and he took that as the assent that it was and slowly, almost reluctantly, made his way toward her.

He moved with such sexy masculine self-assurance that he quite stole her breath away, and Tina found herself absolutely riveted by his devastating grace.

"Thanks for the snacks," he said inanely once he'd finally reached her. He sat down next to her, maintaining a polite distance between their shoulders. His hands were loosely clasped between his knees. She could feel the heat coming off him in waves and smelled the clean, healthy sweat of exertion, mixed with that delicious forest scent he always wore, and it reminded her of the last time they'd been together. Reminded her of Harris coming helplessly in her mouth. He had smelled this way, been this hot . . .

She swallowed convulsively as she remembered the salty, musky taste of him. And mentally shook herself. She was being ridiculous. That was just sex . . . *this* was reality. This awful, awkward silence between them.

"You're welcome," she finally responded and then found herself at a loss. Not sure what else to say. She finally settled on "Good game."

"Yeah, if you call being humiliated by a bunch of kids *good*," he said with a wry twist of his lips.

"From what I understand, those kids needed the victory more than your fragile male egos did," she said, and he smiled.

"That's the only thing making it tolerable."

"You and Greyson were pretty good."

"He was better," Harris said with a frown. "I'll never hear the end of it."

"Really?" Greyson had never struck her as the competitive sort.

"I think he's been hanging out with Spencer Carlisle too much."

"He has? They don't seem to have anything in common at all."

"I think Greyson likes no longer being the quietest person in the room. I mean, that Spencer guy rarely speaks."

"I heard Greyson and Libby had an argument in public."

"Are we back to talking about those two?" Harris asked gently. "I think we have plenty more to discuss than them, don't you?"

"It's safe," she admitted miserably.

"I know. But we have to talk, Tina."

"About?"

"How about the fact that I don't want to leave town but I feel I should? Or the fact that I know there are things you haven't told me? Things that make it difficult, if not impossible, for us to ever have the kind of relationship that I want."

"What kind of relationship is that?" she asked, her voice embarrassingly weak and thready. She shouldn't have asked. Not when she wasn't prepared to hear his reply.

"Do you really want to know?" he asked, and she shook her head.

"I'm not sure. I honestly don't think there's a future for us beyond what we've already had. And that was a *lot* more than I was prepared to give."

"Why can't we have a future, Tina?" His voice was teeming with frustration and anger. He couldn't possibly understand. And that was *her* fault. She should tell him the truth. But the prospect of talking about it was daunting and had the power to make her breathing quicken and her heart rate accelerate.

He was still speaking, the anger in his voice giving way to anguish. "Because of some dumb thing I did when I was a kid? I know I hurt you. I know it's left indelible scars, but I can only say I'm sorry in so many ways. At some point, you're going to have to forgive me."

"I'm so sorry, Harris," she whispered, her voice breaking. She could forgive him. She *had* forgiven him, but forgiveness wasn't the problem. He reminded her of everything terrible that had happened in her life, and she didn't think she could ever be around him without those painful memories constantly haunting her. And that wouldn't be fair to either of them. Better to make a clean break of it.

She squeezed her eyes shut in a futile effort to prevent her tears from escaping. But they spilled anyway, and her breath whooshed out on a shuddering sob.

"It would be impossi—"

She opened her eyes, trying to find a way to explain why it could never work, but it was hard to find the words to make him understand when she would be omitting so much of the truth. But she needn't have bothered—he was walking away. The lithe grace of before replaced by a stiff, contained stride that only accentuated how very much he was hurting.

Greyson said something to him as he reached the field, and when Harris ignored him, the other man grabbed his elbow in an attempt to stop him. Tina gasped when Harris shrugged out of his brother's hold and shoved him violently. Greyson stumbled back but let Harris go, his eyes instead tracking up to the bleachers where Tina still sat with one of her hands helplessly clasped over her mouth and tears streaming down her face.

"Olivia and I have a sort of date," Greyson shocked Harris by saying the following afternoon. The two men had barely spoken all day, the atmosphere becoming strained after Harris had shoved Greyson without provocation the previous evening. Harris had spent the day packing, *again*.

It was time to go home. He had urgent business that could no longer wait. The situation in Perth, which had seemed almost resolved just a week ago, had blown up when more parties were discovered to be involved in the embezzlement scheme that he and Greyson had uncovered five months ago. He would probably have to fly to Australia soon. Which would serve as a welcome distraction.

"A what?" Harris asked, not sure if he had understood his brother clearly.

"A date. She asked if we could have dinner tonight, after the baby shower thing. But her regular babysitter has an exam tomorrow, and we need a sitter for Clara. I was wondering if you wouldn't mind?"

"Not that I mind babysitting, but wouldn't Tina be the obvious choice?" Harris asked, and Greyson shook his head.

"Well, that's the thing. Libby wants both you *and* Tina to watch Clara."

"Why?"

Harris fought the surge of ridiculous hope from rekindling. That was quite enough of that. His previously strong heart could no longer take the constant upheaval of being around Tina.

"Not a clue."

More secrets. Of course.

Greyson's eyes shone with muted happiness and excitement, and Harris found himself unable to disappoint the guy. He hadn't *ever* seen that expression on his brother's face before. If there was a chance Libby and Greyson could salvage something from this entire mess, then Harris was happy to babysit. With Tina. Not that looking after his niece would ever be a chore. He hadn't spent enough time with her, and he was looking forward to it. Especially since he'd be leaving soon. He was just a little concerned about being around Tina. He wasn't sure what more there was to say.

"Sure, I'll be happy to help out."

"Thank you," Greyson said with a grin. An honest-to-God *grin*. Greyson never grinned; in fact, he rarely showed his teeth when he smiled. A grin was unprecedented.

"Yeah, man, anytime," Harris said honestly.

"You've packed again, I see," Greyson said stiltedly, and Harris nodded.

"I'm flying out to Australia on Wednesday. I should have gone in March," he said pointedly, a reference to the fact that Greyson had used the Perth incident as an excuse to avoid the last stage of Libby's pregnancy and had missed Clara's birth as a result. It had always been Harris's responsibility, but his brother had pulled rank. Greyson averted his eyes and nodded.

"Yes." His voice was quiet and filled with regret, and when he brought his gaze back to Harris's, it too shone with remorse.

"So what time tonight?" Harris asked, trying to lighten the atmosphere a bit.

"Seven? At Tina's place."

"That's cool. Where are you taking Libby?"

"There's this restaurant on Leisure Isle. Right on the lagoon. Spencer told me about it. Quite romantic, apparently. Great food, so my little food snob won't have much to complain about in that department." Harris's jaw dropped at the affectionate possessive pronoun, but he managed to pick it back up before Greyson noticed. His brother was still talking about the restaurant and the table he'd reserved; he was like a dizzy teen, drunk on his first crush. It was both alarming and kind of endearing to witness.

Endearing was not a term he'd ever thought to associate with Greyson, and he couldn't quite believe it had come to mind now. But he couldn't be anything other than happy for Greyson. He hoped, for his brother's sake, that the guy did not screw up again.

Tina wasn't sure why she had agreed to this, but she had been so damned grateful that Libby had trusted her enough to look after Clara that she didn't even care if it was only under supervision, so to speak. As a result, Tina had felt incapable of nitpicking about Libby's choice of babysitting partner. She and Harris were adults; they would deal.

Now, as she watched Harris and Greyson set up Clara's crib, and while she listened to Libby go over her list of "dos and don'ts," Tina found herself feeling absolutely terrified. What was she thinking? She couldn't do this. She could *not* do this.

She was on the verge of telling Libby that she had changed her mind when Harris picked the contentedly gurgling Clara up from her baby seat and gently rocked her back and forth. And the words froze in her throat.

"Tina? *Tina?*" Libby prompted, and Tina jumped, her eyes darting back to her friend's concerned face. "Are you sure you're okay to do this?"

"I'm fine."

"I know this is a huge step for you. And maybe adding Harris into the mix is a bit insensitive. Considering . . . *everything*. But I had no one else to ask, and I knew you'd feel overwhelmed looking after her by yourself. I know I could have asked Harris to do it alone, but . . ."

"Libby." Tina reached out and grabbed her friend's hand. "It's okay. I know why you asked Harris to help. And you were right to do so. We'll be fine. Are *you* sure? About tonight?"

Libby, who had told Tina that she was going to present Greyson with divorce papers tonight, nodded somberly.

"It's inevitable," she said quietly so that the men could not overhear them. Her eyes shone with unshed tears. "He knows it too."

Tina drew her in for a fierce hug.

"It'll all work out, Libby. I promise."

Tina fell apart. The second Clara started crying, she fell completely apart. Up until that point she'd been okay. Making stilted, painstakingly polite conversation with Harris and watching from a respectable distance while he cleaned and changed Clara. Tina didn't once offer to hold the baby, and while she sensed Harris's confusion, he thankfully didn't comment on her strange behavior.

But then Clara started crying, and Harris, who was in the kitchen warming her bottle, looked over his shoulder at Tina.

"Pick her up, will you? She's hungry and cranky. I'm just going to get her bottle warmed, and then I'll feed her."

Tina froze. Caught halfway between the kitchen and Clara's baby seat. Her eyes were trained on the baby's screwed-up face as she started crying louder and more passionately, and Tina could not bring her feet to move.

"*Tina!*" Harris called, clearly irritated. "Pick her up."

Tina shook her head.

"Can't," she whispered under her breath.

"What?" he snapped, tossing the towel over his shoulder as he tested the milk temperature on the inside of his wrist. He winced and opened the cold-water faucet, holding the bottle beneath it.

When Clara's crying didn't subside, Harris looked up, annoyed that Tina could just continue to let her wail like that. Tina stood in the middle of the living room. She had her arms wrapped around her torso as she rocked back and forth, staring at the crying baby yearningly, as if she wished it were Clara she were rocking. While looking wholly incapable of actually moving to pick the infant up.

"Jesus, Tina," he said, not entirely sure what was going on here. "How can you stand to hear her cry like this and not want to help? Please, just hold her."

"I can't," she said on a gasp. "I can't hold her."

"It won't be for long," he said, using his most reasonable tone of voice. "I just have to cool the milk down. It'll only take a couple of minutes."

"Is she sick?" Tina asked, her eyes riveted on Clara's face. "You should call a doctor. Please, call a doctor. Ask Libby to come back."

"She's not sick, she's hungry. That's all."

"How can you be sure?" she asked frantically. "How can you know that? Babies get sick. They die. Call the doctor."

"She's fine. She's not even running a fever," he reassured her. He was fast losing patience with her. "You committed to watch her tonight— what the hell did you think that entailed?"

She was starting to hyperventilate. *Fuck!* What the hell?

"Tina? Shit. Calm down." He stepped away from the sink, bottle forgotten, as his concern for Tina took precedence over even Clara's angry cries. He placed a tentative hand on her back. "Come on, sweetheart, follow my lead: in . . . slowly . . ." She attempted to follow his breathing, clearly familiar with the technique. "Good girl. Now out. Through the mouth. That's right."

His soothing tone was starting to calm Clara down as well, and the baby's shrieks were dwindling to sad, hiccupping snuffles.

"I'm sorry," Tina was saying, repeating the words over and over again. "I'm sorry. I'm so sorry. I want to help. I want to. But I can't. I can't, please don't ask me to. I can't."

"It's okay, sweetheart," he reassured her, confused and alarmed and so damned terrified to ask her *why* she couldn't help. "I won't ask you to. I promise. She's better now, see? I'll give her a bottle. I think she's exhausted herself."

Tina let out a heartbroken sob as her tear-drenched eyes took in the no-longer-crying, but still fussing, infant.

"She's not sick?" she asked again, still rocking back and forth.

"No. She's fine," he repeated, keeping his voice gentle even though he was screaming inside. Helpless to do anything to make this better for her, when he had no idea where it was coming from.

Tina knew how she must look, how she must sound. And she knew she owed him an explanation.

"Better now?" he asked quietly, and she nodded, sucking in a deep, cleansing breath as she attempted to return to normalcy. He gave her an intense, probing stare before striding to Clara's baby seat and checking on the fretful infant. Tina watched him enviously; he was so adept at that, so good with the baby. She owed him more than an explanation: she owed him the truth.

He returned to the kitchen sink, picking the bottle up again and darting the occasional wary glance to where Tina still stood, her feet seemingly glued to the living room floor.

"I had a baby." The words came tumbling out, louder than she'd anticipated, and Clara, who had been blessedly quiet, started crying again. Tina cringed at the sound, but she continued. Determinedly avoiding Harris's eyes. "I had a baby, and he died. He died . . . and I can't stand the thought . . . I can't hold . . . I can't. I can't. Please. I can't. I want to. I wish . . ." She shook her head, knowing she was making no sense, hating how crazy and illogical she must sound. But she couldn't find her words, couldn't control her emotions, and—when she found the courage to sneak a glance at him—she hated the look of complete shock on Harris's pale face as he stared at her in horror and dismay.

Clara's cries were building, and Tina clapped her hands over her ears in an attempt to block the sound out. She couldn't stop shaking—her teeth felt like they were rattling around in her skull, and she could do little to disguise violent trembling. Harris seemed to snap out of his reverie and walked to the baby seat to lift Clara and soothingly rock her. He passed Tina again on his way back to the kitchen and removed the baby's bottle from the counter where he had left it. He tested the temperature on the back of his hand, the one cradling Clara, before transferring the rubber nipple to her eager mouth.

Tina wiped her wet face with the backs of her hands and turned away from him. She was desperate to escape and retreated to her bedroom, excruciatingly aware of his eyes on her back as she fled.

The knock on the door—when it came half an hour later—was quiet. She had been expecting it, but it still made her flinch. She hadn't locked the door, knowing that to do so would only delay the inevitable, and—even though she didn't call for him to enter—the sound of the handle turning didn't surprise her.

She was curled up on her bed, her back to the door, and couldn't see him as he entered the room. She felt the bed depress behind her and tensed even further, bracing herself for what was to come.

She expected angry demands, furious questions . . . but what she got was a gentle hand on her back and a quiet, achingly tender voice with a simple invitation. "Please. Won't you tell me what happened?"

"I got pregnant," she said, after a long, fraught silence as she debated what to tell him and how much. "I had a boy. A beautiful baby boy. I named him Fletcher. He was perfect. I had him for nearly two months.

My parents had sent me to my aunt in Edinburgh, and they were all trying to pressure me into giving him up. They kept reminding me of my future, of college. But I refused to give him up. I knew it would be hard, but I fully intended to keep my baby *and* go to medical school when he was older. He was mine, my perfect boy, and I loved him."

His hand never paused in its gentle stroking of her back, and it encouraged her to reveal more. Secrets, long held, pouring from her in a soft, halting voice.

"My pregnancy was difficult, complicated. I was young and stupid, and I didn't take care of myself the way I should have. He was born two weeks early . . . there were complications, and they were on the verge of performing a C-section. But after a long labor, he was born naturally. He was so small and needed respiratory support. I was terrified I would lose him, but he was such a fighter. After he gained another half a kilogram and his lungs strengthened, they allowed me to take him home.

"He was fine. He was healthy. And he grew like a weed. He knew me, knew my voice. The day before he died . . . I swear, he smiled." The sweet memory made *her* smile. Her aunt—a mean-spirited woman who had made no secret of the fact that she resented having Tina and Fletcher in her home—had dismissed the movement of his mouth as gas, but Tina had known it was a smile. A perfect, precious smile. "He died for no reason. Of nothing. Sudden infant death syndrome, they said. How is that an explanation? How does that tell me why my baby died?"

She turned over to face him, scooting up until she sat with her back against the headboard. Harris's eyes were stark, his face strained and pale.

"He looked like you, you know?" she whispered, and this time he flinched, his face going from pale to ashen.

He had known it was coming, of course, known since the moment she'd confessed to once having a baby. It explained why she'd held on to her hatred of him for so long. It explained why, even though she'd allowed him to touch her and love her, she had continued to keep him at a distance.

He had known it was coming, and yet her words still felt like a punch to the gut.

No. To the scrotum.

The burst of pain was indescribable and crippling and *nothing* compared to the agony he could see in her eyes, on her face; hear in her voice; and sense in the very still way she held herself.

"You were on the pill," he heard himself saying, his voice sounding lifeless and the words making him cringe. It felt like exactly the wrong thing to say right now. Like an accusation.

"I was a stupid, naive girl who thought that going on the pill just hours before a sexual encounter would somehow magically prevent pregnancy," she said, her words bitter and self-deprecating.

She had been eighteen, young, and inexperienced; Harris should have worn a condom; he should have protected her from the painful consequences. But he hadn't exactly been himself. He was shocked that he'd even thought to ask her about protection. It was a wonder he'd been able to perform at all. Truth be told—the state he'd been in—he very much doubted he would have managed to maintain an erection with anyone other than Tina. He had been wanting to get into her panties for months and—despite that—still managed to cheapen what should have been a special moment for her with that fucking unremembered bet. His worst, and fastest, sexual performance ever, and it had resulted in a pregnancy. Had resulted in a baby. A *son* . . . who had looked like him. He swallowed down an anguished sob at the thought.

"I'm sorry," he whispered. The most inadequate two words in the English language. No matter how heartfelt, they were nowhere near enough to express his absolute remorse and anguish at the pain he had caused her. At the incomparable loss they had both experienced.

"I felt like I was the only one who cared about him. Who cared that he had once lived and then died."

"I care," he said fiercely, his voice harsh with the strength of his emotions.

"That means a lot. Thank you," she said, and he nearly swore. How could she thank *him*? The selfish, arrogant prick who had ruined her life in a single night? Her gratitude killed him because he didn't fucking deserve it. Not one bit.

He swiped a hand over his face, barely able to meet her eyes. His beautiful Tina, whom he had so utterly and irrevocably fallen in love with. How could he ever expect her to forgive him for this? To love him even a little?

"I've been having some difficulty," she continued unbidden, and he locked his gaze on hers once more, "being around babies. I know it's stupid . . . and makes no sense. I love babies. I love Clara. But I can't hold her. I'm *terrified* of holding her. And I so desperately want to."

"Have you . . ." His voice failed him, cracking and fading before he could complete the sentence. He cleared his throat and tried again. "Did you see someone? After?"

She nodded, her fingers restlessly toying with the drawstring on her hoodie.

"For a little while. The hospital arranged a social worker; she was very kind." The words damn near killed him. Who else had been kind to her during that time? The parents who had tried to force her to give the baby up? Her brothers, who had never displayed one iota of patience with her in the entire time that Harris had known them? *He* should have been there. He should have known. But at the same time, the young, irresponsible fool he had been would have been ill equipped to deal with such an overwhelmingly adult situation.

"What about a therapist?" he asked, keeping his voice gentle, not wanting to spook her when she was in such a fragile emotional state.

"Not immediately. After I returned home and found myself unable to continue with medical school, I saw someone for a little while. I was having panic attacks and night terrors. The therapist taught me a few breathing techniques, coping mechanisms. I recovered physically and—eventually—emotionally."

Emotionally? When she couldn't so much as hold a baby? That wasn't a recovery; that was a festering wound. He didn't argue. She had been staring at the wall somewhere beyond his left shoulder and suddenly shifted her gaze to meet his. Those wide green eyes still drenched in tears and red rimmed. She wasn't a pretty crier, yet somehow the raw, honest emotion made her even more beautiful to him.

"Would you . . ." Her fingers curled into the string of the hoodie. So tightly they went white where it pushed into her flesh. "Would you like to see a picture of him? Of Fletcher?"

God.

The half-hopeful, half-terrified note in her voice precisely echoed what he was feeling after that question. He wanted to see a picture, *needed* to see it, but he wasn't sure he was emotionally fortified to deal with the pain he knew was just waiting to be unleashed once he did see it.

"Yes, please." He kept his voice firm, not allowing a single ounce of hesitation or uncertainty to creep into those two words. She wanted to share their son with him. He needed to let her do that.

She untwisted her fingers from the drawstring, and they went pink as blood rushed back into them. She reached for her phone, swiping the screen while she spoke. The rush of nervous words barely registering with Harris as he watched her hands anxiously.

"I took so many pictures of him during the short time I had him," she was saying. "I printed all of them—they're in a photo album in the living room. But I also keep them in a folder on my phone. I'm terrified of losing them. Then I'd have nothing left of him. Of my beautiful little Fletcher."

She stopped swiping and stared down at her screen for a long moment before inhaling deeply and holding the device out to him. Harris stared at her hand for an equally long moment, terrified of looking. But at the same time equally terrified of not seeing. Harris knew that if he waited too long, she'd change her mind and snatch her phone back. He slowly and reluctantly reached out to take the phone from her and flipped it around. He shut his eyes and held his breath for a long moment before exhaling once he opened his eyes again.

He stared at the image on the screen for what seemed like hours and felt a piece of his heart break off, lost forever. The damage was irreparable, the loss irreplaceable. And Harris knew that nothing in his life would ever be the same again.

His son.

Fletcher.

A tiny little human with a full head of black hair, an angry old-man face, wearing nothing but a nappy and socks that looked a couple of sizes too large for his minute feet.

"He looks so small," he whispered shakily.

"He was just slightly longer than a ruler," she said, her voice low as well. "He weighed under two kilograms at birth, but he picked up weight really quickly. He was close to six kilograms by the time he . . . when I lost him."

Slightly longer than a ruler. Just a bit bigger than a rugby ball. Harris would have been able to cradle him one handed, right in the crook of his arm. He flipped slowly through the pictures: some of just Fletcher, the rest selfies of a glowing Tina and the baby. God, how young she looked. A mother at nineteen. While Harris had been off at university—screwing around indiscriminately, drinking, partying . . . not a fucking care in the world—Tina had been dealing with *this*. All alone.

Jesus. No amount of "I'm sorrys" would ever make up for this.

The photos became a blur, and he blinked rapidly in an effort to clear his eyes. Only when he felt moisture trickle down his cheek did he recognize the blurriness for what it was.

Her hand, soft and so gentle, reached out to cup his cheek and thumb away the wetness. He tilted his head into the cradling hand, accepting the comforting gesture even while he didn't fucking deserve it.

Harris felt the sob welling up in his throat and tried to swallow it back down, but it escaped anyway.

"I'm sorry," he muttered, trying to maintain his composure. But it was a losing battle, and another sob rose up and escaped. She made a soft crooning sound, and she cupped his other cheek, drawing his head down until his forehead was buried in the sweetly scented cove of her neck.

"I'm sorry," he said again, apologizing because he had no right to accept this solace from her. No right to expect it when she'd been so alone for so long, with no one to offer her the same. But he was nothing if not selfish, and his arms curled around her waist while another involuntary sob escaped, followed by another and yet another. He wept on her shoulder, mourning the loss of the son he had never known, *would* never know, except through the memories his mother had so lovingly chronicled in two-dimensional pictures. Images that would never tell Harris how his son had smelled or how it would have felt to cradle him in his arms. They couldn't detail his sounds—the gurgles and sighs and baby snuffles—or the faces he had made when he was sad or sleepy or contented.

Harris wept inconsolably for both the loss of his child and the loss of the dream he had nurtured that maybe *someday* he and Tina could have more.

"I'm sorry, I should have told you," she said into his hair, her voice filled with heartbreak and regret, and he lifted his face to look at her. He knew he probably looked like shit, his eyes swollen, face wet, and nose streaming. But he didn't care. He needed her to know that she had nothing to regret. That this was all him.

"How could you have? For all intents and purposes, the prick who got you pregnant did it on a bet. That dickhead didn't deserve your explanations then, and he doesn't deserve your regret or your apologies now."

"You were young."

"You were *younger*," he reminded her bitterly. "I should have known better. I should have *been* better . . . but I'd wanted you for so long. It's no excuse, but . . ." He sighed, his voice tapering off.

He pushed himself away from her and got up.

"Clara?" she asked.

"She's asleep."

"Tina," he began, then stopped. Not sure what he'd been about to say.

"Yes?"

"I should have been better," he repeated, having no clue what he meant by that, and yet her eyes softened, as if *she* knew exactly what he meant. "I'm trying to be better," he continued. "But how can I be? When the asshole I once was has already irretrievably fucked everything up?"

"I wish you could have seen him, Harris. He was so beautiful, and I loved him so much," she said, her voice soft and heartbroken, and his eyes flooded with tears.

"I think . . . ," he whispered, then raised his voice and spoke more decisively. "No. I *know* I would have loved him, too, Tina."

She made a soft, anguished sound and buried her face in her hands.

Harris desperately wanted to hold her, but that was a privilege reserved for a better man than he was or ever could be.

"Why don't you try to get some sleep?" he suggested. "I'll take care of Clara."

She lifted her face and met his eyes before shaking her head determinedly.

"No. Libby trusted me to be able to do this. I have to try."

He smiled, feeling an overwhelming sense of love and pride at her determination.

Brave. So fucking brave. He'd always known it, but he'd never truly understood the extent of that bravery. Until now.

Chapter Thirteen

"Take your time," he said. He felt brittle inside, completely shattered, but if Tina could be brave, so could he. So *should* he. "I'll get some tea on."

He hastily turned away, desperate to get out of the room and away from her. It physically hurt to be in her presence without touching her, and he needed to take a moment to find a way to cope with the devastating impact of the blow he had just been dealt. The double loss of Tina and their baby was massive and crippling, and Harris was amazed he could still stand beneath the weight of despair that threatened to crush him.

After a quick check on the peacefully sleeping infant in the living room, he dashed into the bathroom to rinse his face with ice-cold water. He braced his hands on the basin and stared at his reflection in the mirror blankly; his gaze turned inward as he flipped through the mental images of Tina with Fletcher.

He would have had a nine-year-old son if the baby had lived. He knew she would eventually have told him about the baby, and he wondered how he would have reacted to the news. Harris had really liked Tina, and he would have tried to do right by her. But he was honest enough to admit to himself that—because of his youth—he probably would have resented the burden of responsibility that impending father-hood would have placed on him. Yet, despite that youthful resentment, he would have loved that kid. Harris knew that much. He would have adored him.

"What a fucking mess you've made," he told his reflection, his voice colored black with bitterness. "What a colossal fucking mess."

When she crept out of the room five minutes later, it was to find Clara asleep in the living room and Harris nowhere in sight. There was no sign of the promised tea. She knew he couldn't have gone far, probably to the bathroom, or maybe next door for something that she didn't have in her pantry.

Clara made a little sound, and Tina froze before tiptoeing over to the portable crib, where Harris must have laid the baby down before coming to check on Tina. She leaned over and sighed in quiet relief when she saw that Clara's eyes were still closed.

Her eyes lovingly traced over the plump curve of the baby's cheek, and she wished she could find the courage to run her finger over that sweet, soft skin. Clara's lips made a cute sucking little motion, and Tina smiled. Fletcher had often done the same thing in his sleep. The baby's plump fist crept into her mouth, and she suckled lazily.

Clara's eyes opened unexpectedly, and she pinned Tina with her wide eyes. The dark blue—so very like her father's—a startling contrast against her golden-brown skin. She frowned, then blinked, and her plump lower lip popped out in a sulky pout just moments before her face screwed up.

Tina looked around wildly for Harris, who had *not* miraculously reappeared while she'd been gazing at the baby. Clara gasped, making the tiny warning sounds that babies made to let you know that they were *not* happy and they were going to show you exactly how unhappy they were unless you did something about it fast.

"Oh no . . . ," Tina pleaded. "No no no, sweetheart. Don't cry."

But Clara didn't want words—she wanted action—and before Tina could overthink it, she reached down and carefully lifted the baby into her arms. She gently cradled Clara's warm, comforting weight to her chest.

She rocked the baby soothingly and started singing, the words soft at first and the tune familiar. A song she had sung often to lull Fletcher to sleep.

"No One," by Alicia Keys.

She dropped her cheek to the top of the baby's soft head, still swaying slowly from side to side. Clara clutched at, and then caught, one of Tina's curls in her fist, and Tina laughed through the tears that were clogging up her throat and sinuses.

The baby smelled warm and clean and powdery. The scent poignantly familiar. But instead of the unbearable loss she'd have felt before at the prospect of merely *holding* a baby, all she felt now was love. Love for this beautiful baby and love for the child she had lost. The recollection of holding his warm, sturdy little body had been buried beneath the other memories. Awful memories of picking him up and finding him cold and heavy and unmoving.

The other, more precious memories of holding him, loving him, inhaling his sweet baby scent, all of that came flooding back now, thanks to Clara.

She sensed a movement to her left, and she lifted her blurry eyes to stare at Harris, who was watching her warily from just outside the bathroom door.

"Tina?" he asked hesitantly, and she smiled at him.

"Shh, she's falling asleep again," she told him quietly, and his eyes dropped to where Clara was contentedly nuzzling against her chest, chubby fist in mouth, on the verge of dozing off.

"You okay?"

"I used to sing that song to him," she confessed. "When he wouldn't sleep."

She watched Harris's throat work as he swallowed convulsively.

"She has his eyes, you know?"

"What?" His voice was sharp as his gaze dropped to the sleeping baby.

"Clara's eyes are the same shade of blue that Fletcher's were," she said, her voice thick with tears. "I never noticed that before. And he had the birthmark too."

"The *C*?" he asked, his own voice sounding gruff.

"Yes. On his thigh."

"Of course he had it," he said softly. And she nodded. It was practically a Chapman brand. He cleared his throat abruptly before heading to the kitchen to put the kettle on. He turned to watch her while he waited for it to boil.

"Do you want me to take her?" he asked, his voice curt, and she shook her head, sitting carefully down onto the sofa behind her.

"We're fine." In fact, she wasn't sure she ever wanted to let this baby go again. But when Clara finally drifted off, becoming heavy with sleep, Tina got up and gingerly lowered the baby into the crib.

She padded to the kitchen, where Harris seemed to be taking an inordinately long time to fix the tea. She could tell by the rigid set of his back that he was aware of every move that she had made since putting Clara down.

"Harris?"

He went completely still. And then, with palpable reluctance, turned to face her. His face was devoid of any expression, but his swollen eyes were a reminder of the heartbroken tears he had shed earlier.

"Wh—" His voice broke, and he scowled before starting again. "What is sudden infant death syndrome?"

She sucked in a pained breath at the unexpected question.

"I'm sorry," he said quickly, seeing her reaction. "I shouldn't have asked. I'll google it or something. I should have known asking would be insensitive."

"No," she replied, shaking her head. "*No*, Harris. It's fine. I was just . . . I suppose I've done so much reading up on it after . . . what happened. And I just expected you to know what it was as well."

"You don't have to talk about it, Tina. I just wanted . . . I want to understand."

"It's exactly what it sounds like," she said, her voice even as she tried to keep the emotion out of it. She had read so many research articles on the syndrome that she hoped she could explain it as scientifically as possible. "That's what they call it when an infant under twelve months of age dies unexpectedly for no apparent reason. They had to . . ." Her voice wobbled, and she shut her eyes as she tried to gloss over the next bit. The police involvement had been confusing and terrifying and had definitely added to her feelings of guilt and inadequacy. "To investigate, of course."

Harris swore violently, and she jumped.

"A *police* investigation?" he asked, the violence still there but restrained.

"Yes. They had to rule out . . . you know?"

"Oh Jesus," he moaned, covering his face with both hands. She watched him uncertainly, not sure if she should continue. His shoulders were shaking—no, his entire body was trembling. He looked up, his face ravaged by stress. "I'm sorry. Just . . . give me a moment, please."

She nodded, her eyes downcast, while she nervously picked at a cuticle on her thumb. When she couldn't tug it off, she lifted her thumb to her lips and chewed nervously. She hissed when she tore the cuticle and tucked her thumb into her palm, folding her fingers protectively around it as she continued to watch Harris. He finally moved, gently taking hold of her elbow to steer her toward the sofa.

She sat down without question, while he took the chair across from her.

"I think we should be sitting down for this discussion," he muttered. "I'm sorry I interrupted you."

"I know it sounds awful, but it's not personal or anything. It's procedure." She tried to keep her voice even. It had felt *very* personal to answer questions about whether she had ever shaken her baby, or hit him, or covered his mouth or face to stop him from crying. She shuddered at the vile memories and shoved them determinedly aside. "But I was cleared of any wrongdoing."

"Oh God, Tina, of course you were," he said unevenly.

"I felt so *violated*," she admitted and then silently reprimanded herself for allowing the personal observation to creep into what should have remained a clinical explanation.

He made a muffled sound, but she averted her eyes to the floor. It was easier to talk about this when she didn't have to deal with his emotions too.

"After that, they did an autopsy." She swallowed back a surge of nausea. Even years later, the thought of them cutting into her baby was intolerable, and she stopped for a moment to control her breathing.

In: nose. Out: mouth.

She could do this. She could. He waited patiently, his own breath sounding a lot less controlled than hers.

"They couldn't find a definitive cause of death," she continued. "I mean, there are possible contributing factors to SIDS. It was a teenage pregnancy. He was premature. And I-I . . ." This was the hardest one to say out loud. It was the one that made her feel like a monster. "I didn't take much in the way of prenatal vitamins. I was in denial for the first five months. I refused to believe what was happening. I kept hoping the symptoms would just go away. I was terrified and just wanted it to be a really bad dream. I wished him away."

She laughed, the sound ugly and devoid of humor.

"I guess in the end I got my wish."

Harris swore again, and this time she lifted her eyes to meet his. He looked devastated and like he had aged ten years in the last few minutes. But the only way Tina could get through this was to bury her emotions, and that meant suppressing her natural instinct to comfort as well.

"Don't say that! You didn't in *any* way cause what happened, Tina," he said, his hoarse voice filled with urgency.

"I know that," she admitted. "Logically I know that. Emotionally? I wouldn't be human if I didn't feel responsible. I was his mother. I should have loved him from the very beginning."

"You were young and frightened. Your initial reaction was perfectly normal. You were alone. God."

"I wanted answers. I *needed* answers. Accepting 'unknown' as a cause of death was a bitter pill to swallow."

"Sweetheart . . ."

"Please don't call me that," she pleaded rawly.

"Tina," he amended, his voice hollow. "Sometimes we don't get the answers we need or the outcome we crave. Sometimes life just fucking *blows*."

"Stick that on a Hallmark card," she joked half-heartedly, wiping the tears from her face.

"I'd make millions," he countered, giving her a sad smile and swiping at his own wet cheeks.

They heard a car crunch up the graveled driveway, and Harris glanced at the wall clock in surprise.

"It's only nine thirty. They're back early."

"Harris," Tina began, not exactly sure what she wanted to say, but she was interrupted by the angry slam of a car door, followed by equally furious footsteps up the porch steps. The door to the house next door opened and then crashed shut seconds later.

"What the fuck?" Harris growled when the sound startled Clara, who began to wail. Tina got up and reached into the crib and picked the crying baby up without hesitation.

She was rocking her gently when the lighter, feminine footsteps reached her front door. Harris swung it open before Libby could knock.

"You're back early." Tina wasn't sure if Harris knew that his words sounded like an accusation. Libby looked exhausted, and her eyes automatically sought and then found her baby. Surprise, followed by pleasure, lit up her expression when she saw Clara being cradled by Tina.

"It wasn't meant to be a late night," she responded absently as she padded to Tina and the still-crying Clara. She reached for her daughter with eager arms, and Tina carefully handed the little one over.

"Oh, sweetie, did you miss me?" Libby crooned to the baby. "I'm so sorry. Mummy's here now." She looked at Tina and smiled warmly. "The evening went well, I take it?"

Tina nearly laughed at that question. So much had been revealed between her and Harris that her irrational fear of looking after Clara seemed like ancient history now. But she knew that that was what her friend was asking about.

"As can be expected. A few hiccups, but we overcame them."

"Harris." Libby shifted her gaze to her brother-in-law, and Tina was distressed to see her expression go cold. "Thank you for helping out."

Harris nodded uncomfortably, avoiding Libby's gaze.

What was *that* about?

"I take it my brother is in a foul mood?" Harris asked, and Libby dropped a kiss on Clara's head before answering.

"I handed him divorce papers tonight," she said. "I gather, from his reaction to them, that he wasn't expecting it."

Harris swore vehemently beneath his breath and smoothed a hand over his face. He looked shattered and at the end of his tether. And like a man who had lost everything he had ever cared about. And it made Tina desperate to reach out and hug him. She wanted to tell him that everything would be okay. That she was here for him. That she *always* wanted to be here for him.

The astonishing urge to comfort him with promises of forever came from so far out of left field that she was momentarily staggered by it. Harris, in the meantime, screwed his eyes shut for a moment before sending them heavenward as if seeking guidance and strength.

"I have to go," he said to no one in particular. He looked at each of them in turn, Tina, Libby, and then Clara. And after a moment of indecision moved forward and kissed only one of the females in the room. The one who was still screeching bloody murder.

He left without another word, and Tina felt immediately and unexpectedly abandoned.

"Greyson?" The house was barely lit when Harris walked through the front door, and once his eyes adjusted to the dimness, he found his brother sitting on the lumpy sofa, facing the broken TV.

God, he didn't know if he had the fortitude for this. Not after everything he had just been through, and part of him was desperate to just turn away and closet himself in his room with only his thoughts for company till morning. But his mind drifted back to the happiness and excitement he had seen on Greyson's face just hours ago, and he couldn't do it. He couldn't leave him there alone in the dark. He rounded the sofa.

"Grey?" He hadn't called his brother that since they were both fourteen, at which time Greyson had stiffly informed him that he would rather be referred to by his full name. The nickname felt right in this moment. His brother needed familiarity rather than formality right now.

"Olivia wants a divorce," Grey said quietly, his voice lacking inflection.

"I just heard, yeah."

Grey dropped his head in his hands and sighed heavily.

"Fuck," he breathed, the word heartfelt and uncharacteristic. "I would kill for a drink right now."

He looked up again, his face shrouded in darkness, so Harris couldn't read his expression. But he could tell, by the sudden tension in the other man's broad shoulders, that something had alarmed him.

"You look like hell," Grey said quietly. The words stunned Harris, who hadn't expected his brother to notice his distress, and it, quite embarrassingly, made his eyes flood with moisture. Grey leaped to his feet and stepped out of the darkness, his expression alarmed.

"What's going on?" he asked, his voice low and almost protective.

"She had a baby," Harris said. The words felt like they were being ripped from some deep private part of him, and it was agonizing. He didn't realize how tight a leash he'd kept on his emotions until he stumbled and braced his hand on the kitchen countertop for support. Those words were bad, the ones that had to follow were excruciating, and he didn't know how the hell Tina had managed to say them. He finally, *truly* understood why she had kept them bottled up for so long. It hurt too much to speak them.

"Oh my God," Grey said, his voice unsteady as he immediately grasped whom Harris was referring to.

"His name was Fletcher," Harris continued, tears flowing freely down his face now, and he couldn't find it in him to care that he was crying in front of his brother. The last time Grey had seen him cry, they had been eight, and Harris had fallen and broken his arm. "Oh God, Grey. He died. And Tina had to go through all of that alone. While I got off scot-free. How can she ever forgive me for something like that? When I'll never be able to forgive myself?"

Grey wrapped an arm around Harris's shoulders and attempted to steer him toward the sofa, but Harris turned in his hold and leaned on his brother for support. Grey hesitated for only a second before his arms went around Harris in a comforting hug. He wrapped his palm around Harris's nape and tugged his head down to his shoulder.

"I'm so sorry, Harris," Grey murmured directly into his brother's ear. "I'm so damned sorry."

Libby was extremely subdued. The two women packed up Clara's things, but conversation was minimal. Tina's eyes kept drifting to her friend in concern; she knew that Libby was going through some pretty powerful stuff right now. But since she felt like she'd just been through an emotional blender herself, Tina didn't mind the silence.

"He didn't take it well," Libby said after another few minutes of quiet, and Tina, who had been digging a stuffed toy out from between the sofa cushions, turned to look at the younger woman. Libby sank down into an armchair, and Tina followed suit. "He thought . . . I don't know. I think he thought our dinner tonight was some kind of date. He took me to this completely inappropriate restaurant. I tried to choose the place, but he said he had reservations somewhere, and . . . *God*, Tina, the place was ridiculous. Stupidly romantic. He and I have never gone anywhere remotely similar before. On the night I plan to tell him I want a divorce, he pulls out all the stops and takes me there."

She buried her face in her hands.

"Stupid man!" Her voice was muffled, but her frustrated words were clear. She shook her head and looked up again. "And when I gave him the papers. He was stunned. Completely stunned, I could tell. And . . . he looked hurt. Mr. Ice Cold, who had never before shown any evidence of emotion at all, looked *hurt*. Why is he doing this to me?"

"Is he going to contest the divorce?" Tina asked, and Libby shrugged.

"He says he doesn't want a divorce, says we should try again for Clara's sake. Says we're compatible and could have a good marriage. He never speaks of emotions, mind you. It's all very clinical. And he thinks that because I let him spend a few nights looking after Clara and that I *foolishly* allowed him to attempt to fix some things around the house—something I agreed to only to prove to him that he couldn't be good at *everything*, by the way—and okay, maybe we kissed a few times. And did some *other* stuff. But I'm only human! And I foolishly allowed him a few freedoms that I shouldn't have. I'm such an idiot. The man hasn't properly apologized for his emotional abandonment during my pregnancy. He seems to think I should be *grateful* that he now believes Clara is his daughter . . . he's . . . oh my God, he's so frustrating and annoying and . . ."

She muffled an exasperated scream behind her hand.

"I just want to break something. Possibly my grandmother's ugly, fake Ming dynasty vase . . . over his stupid, stubborn head!"

"What are you going to do?" Tina asked, and Libby raised her hands and shoulders in another angry shrug.

"Push for the divorce. I need to move on with my life. I'm sorry, Tina. I don't mean to lay this all on you like this."

"That's what friends are for, Libby," Tina said.

"Really, Tina? Because sometimes I feel like I tell you everything, and you tell me nothing." Tina knew Libby was referring to the massive secret she had kept for more than a decade, and she couldn't blame her friend for sounding a little bitter and disillusioned.

"I told Harris about . . . about Fletcher tonight." Saying her baby's name was hard, but she hadn't used it when she told Libby about him the other day, and he deserved to be referred to by name. "It wasn't easy."

"How did he take it?" Libby asked softly.

"I think he was . . . shocked. Devastated. He shed a few tears."

"*Good!* Why should you be the only one to live with that, Tina? He should face up to his accountability as well. I'm so angry with him. I expected more from him." Libby's expression had gone flinty, and Tina inexplicably felt herself wanting to defend Harris from her friend's wrath.

"To be fair," she began, keeping her tone rational. She had never meant to drive a wedge between Libby and Harris. Libby valued his friendship too much, and vice versa. "I told him I was on the pill—I *was* on the pill—but I foolishly thought that it would be effective after only a few hours." The words were coming out slowly, the thoughts forming as she said them. But as she verbalized those thoughts, Tina recognized that these were things she should have told herself years ago. "He had no idea I would get pregnant; he trusted that I wouldn't. Blaming him for something he had zero control over, and no knowledge of, is . . . unfair."

Libby sucked her lips into her mouth, her cute dimple making an appearance as she considered Tina's words.

"He should have used a condom." Her words carried no real heat, and Tina nodded.

"He would probably agree with you."

"Ugh, these Chapman men. Why couldn't we fall for sweet, uncomplicated guys?" Libby asked on a tired exhalation.

"I didn't fall for Harris," Tina denied quickly, even while her conscience called her a big fat Liar. With a capital *L*. "I had a stupid teenage crush on him, and unfortunately there were consequences."

"I didn't fall for Greyson either. Well, not much," Libby said before continuing with a wry grin. "Only a little, really—barely a stumble."

Tina laughed at her friend's self-deprecating wit.

"Only an idiot would fall for a man whose heart is completely encased in ice," Libby finished, her smile fading and the light disappearing from her striking eyes. She cleared her throat self-consciously and got up, smoothing her palms down the front of her skirt.

"We should get going. Thank you for watching Clara tonight." Tina got up as well, stuffing the toy that she had been clutching to her chest throughout their conversation into Clara's baby bag.

"I honestly could not have done it without Harris," Tina admitted. "But tonight has helped, Libby. So much. And finally holding her made me remember so many wonderful things about my baby."

"I'm glad, Tina," Libby said and reached out to hug her. Tina clung to her taller friend for a moment, comforted by her embrace.

Harris couldn't sleep; his thoughts were too chaotic to settle down. And he was concerned that the stress of that night would result in another nightmare for Tina. When hours passed without a sound from the other side of the wall, he wondered if her thoughts were keeping her awake too.

"Tina?" He used his normal voice. His bed, like hers, was flush against the wall, and, bizarrely enough, because of the way the house had been divided, it was easier to hear Tina moving around in her room than it was to hear Greyson, whose room was separated from Harris's by the bathroom.

His phone pinged, and he dragged it out from beneath his pillow.

I refuse to talk to you through a wall.

His lips tilted, and he put his palm against the wall, picturing her on the other side, doing the same.

I was worried you'd have a nightmare.

Hard to have a nightmare when you can't sleep. Her response was immediate. She was typing again, so he refrained from responding, waiting to see what she would add.

Are you okay? The question made him blink repetitively in an attempt to clear the blurriness from his eyes.

I should ask you that.

I've had ten years to come to terms with what happened. You've had two hours.

He stared at those words for a long time, not sure how to respond to them. Ten years, two hours, the loss remained the same, merely a bit blunted by time, in her case.

Would you mind sending me pictures? Of Fletcher?

He stared at the screen fixedly.

Nothing. Not even typing.

Please? Seconds after he sent the word, he received a veritable barrage of pictures.

Ping! Ping! Pingpingping!

About fifty photos in thirty seconds, and they kept coming. By the time the welcome onslaught had stopped, he was already scrolling through the more than a hundred pictures, and a few clips, of Fletcher and Tina that she had sent him.

His phone pinged again while he was watching a sweet little video clip of Fletcher dozing off, his pink mouth blowing bubbles as he drifted off. He could hear Tina's gentle voice singing in the background. Alicia Keys.

Of course.

Do you want to come over?

Because he was scrolling through the pictures, the message appeared at the top of the screen in banner form. He blinked at it, then clicked on it. But in his haste, he missed the banner and enlarged the clip instead. Fumbling with his phone and swearing under his breath, he finally managed to get back into his messages.

I'll be right there.

Tina was waiting for him just inside her front door, barefoot and wearing her fuzzy pajamas. Harris was also barefoot, and dressed in nothing but a T-shirt and his boxer briefs. She turned away silently when he entered the house, and he closed and locked the front door before trailing wordlessly behind her as she padded back to her room.

"This doesn't mean anything," she said when she reached her room. "I thought we could look at the pictures together and I could tell you about them?"

"I'd like that." His voice was husky with gratitude, and she nodded before getting into bed and scooting to the wall. She held the covers up invitingly, and he climbed in next to her.

They took a few moments to get comfortable. Harris was on his back, and she had her head on his chest, while his right arm curled around her shoulders and his hand found its favorite resting place in her hair. She had a hand palm down on his chest. In his left hand, he held his phone, and he brought up the pictures again.

"They're in chronological order," she said. "He was only a few hours old in this one."

"Tiny," Harris observed, his voice rough with emotion as he gazed at the sleeping infant, so fragile and helpless in a terrifying-looking incubator.

"He was. He slept so much. All of that saved energy going into growing bigger and stronger every day. This was the first time they allowed me to hold him . . ."

She detailed every moment, trying her best to describe sounds, smells, movements; for nearly forty minutes she talked, and her voice grew hoarse and her words started slurring. She fell asleep in midsentence, about halfway through Fletcher's sixth week. She went boneless, her head heavy on his shoulder. He placed his phone on the bedside table and turned slowly until he had her completely cradled in his arms. She sighed contentedly in her sleep, nuzzling against his chest. Her arm crept around his waist, and one of her legs happily snuck between his.

Harris sighed, too, breathing in her apple-scented hair, with one of his hands still entangled in her hair while the other was tucked around her waist.

His last thought, before he finally succumbed to sleep, was that this was exactly how he wished he could spend every night of the rest of his life.

Warm.

That's how Tina felt. Warm and comfortable and contented. She opened her eyes. It was still dark. Just before dawn, as far as she could tell. Pretty much the time she usually got up. But she couldn't remember the last time she'd ever been this well rested.

Harris was in bed with her. She was pressed up against his chest and surrounded by his wonderful scent. Memories of the night before—highs, lows, darkness, and light—gently ebbed and flowed through her mind. She inspected each memory carefully, turning it all around in her brain, testing her reaction to each one.

Nothing. No panic, no regret, just serene acceptance of last night's every word, every action, and every emotion. Who knew what she would say, do, or feel today? There were so many capricious external factors that it was hard to predict. All she knew was that her world—for once—felt completely right.

Her hand crept beneath Harris's shirt, stroking his firm, hot flesh, rediscovering the angles and planes of his chest. He awoke almost immediately, and his breath hitched before speeding up. The boxer briefs he wore did nothing to disguise the growing erection against her thigh, and she undulated lazily against him, wanting him to know that she felt it and she wanted it. Her hand continued to languidly explore, finding a hard little masculine nipple, and he groaned. He pressed his own hand—through the thin fabric of his shirt—against her busy one, flattening it against his pec in an attempt to still the movement.

"I should leave," he said, his voice having that attractive morning huskiness to it.

"Why?" she asked, lifting her head to meet his eyes, and she sucked in a sharp breath. There they were: her missing panic and regret, swimming around in his liquid gaze.

"It's a lot, Tina," he said.

"I know," she responded tightly, dragging her hand away. His abdominal muscles jumped beneath her fingertips as she pulled her hand out from beneath his shirt. "I know it's a lot. And sometimes it feels like too much. But you'd be surprised by how very much you can bear."

"I also have to bear the additional burden of having to live with the knowledge that I was a callow, irresponsible idiot who didn't deserve a single moment of your time ten years ago. You should have met someone worthy of you. Instead you had an encounter with me. The fucker who ruined your life. I don't know how to begin making amends for that."

"You don't have to make amends," she said, and he shook his head in vehement denial of her words before sitting up and putting some space between their bodies.

"I fucking *do*. But I can't—everything I did was unforgivable. How can I expect you to forgive me, like me . . . *love* me, when I can't fucking stand to be in my own skin?"

Love him? Why would he mention love? It had no bearing on their situation. Never had and never would. He got out of bed, still magnificently aroused, his shorts merely serving to accentuate his impressive hard-on. Tina tried not to be distracted by the eye-level erection and kept her gaze on his face. He looked torn and tormented.

"Intimacy will complicate everything even more. I know you want to compartmentalize it. Call it just sex or fucking . . . or whatever the hell else. But I can't do that. I never could. Not with you. And especially not now. Not after . . . not after him. After Fletcher."

"But . . ."

"I need some time to think."

"What do you want from me, Harris?" she asked, her voice a whisper, and he paused as he considered her question.

"What are you willing to give?"

"I'm not sure."

"How do you feel about me?"

"I don't know." He covered his eyes with the palm of his right hand; his lips compressed and his nostrils flared as he struggled to keep his breathing even.

"That's the problem, Tina," he said, his voice shaky. "You don't know. How could you? Anything you feel for me will be forever entangled with so much negativity and ambivalence. Any positive emotion will be massively outweighed by pain and grief and absolute horror. For ten years I've been waiting for the chance to tell you I was sorry. To explain what happened, why I did what I did. I've been trying to apologize for a foolish young man's mistakes . . . thinking that if I could only get you to hear what I had to say and see my absolute regret, you'd forgive me, and maybe we could reset. That was a tall-enough order . . . ," he said with a humorless laugh.

"While all along the reality was that I was literally responsible for your worst nightmares—I abandoned you when you most needed me, I fucked up your life by making the most selfish of decisions—and then I have the gall to attempt to weasel my way back into your life, into your routine, like I had a right to be there."

"Harris . . ." Tina chose her words very carefully. She wasn't sure what to say. Did she *want* to offer complete forgiveness? She wasn't sure. She wasn't sure of anything right now. Did she even have the right to arrogantly choose to forgive him for something that hadn't been his fault? "The choices I made were my own. *I* chose to have him. *I* chose to keep him. And *I* chose to not to inform you of these decisions. Neither of us can say how you would have reacted to the news of my pregnancy."

"You're too generous," he said bitterly, and she shook her head.

"I wasn't generous enough. I got to hold him. I got to sing to him, and I got to rock him to sleep at night. You didn't. And I think . . ." She paused for a moment, gathering her thoughts, before continuing slowly. "I think—callow and irresponsible though you may have been—I feel certain you would have wanted to do those things."

"I would have," he whispered, his voice hoarse with repressed emotion. She got up and stood directly in front of him. He towered above her, the height difference between them all the more evident with her in bare feet. "I would have loved him."

His eyes yearningly ran over her face, cataloguing every detail. "You're so beautiful."

He reached out and traced her features with his forefinger: just the barest of touches as he stroked across her cheekbones, down the bridge of her nose, across her jawline where it dipped beneath her chin and tilted her face upward. He kissed her, sweetly and tenderly . . . his lips as featherlight on her mouth as his finger had been on her face.

"You were seventeen when I first looked at you and *saw*," he murmured, and her eyes reopened; his face was so close to hers she could see the tiny freckles on the top of his crooked nose. "Wearing a light-green dress with ties on the shoulders; it made your body look lush, and I wanted to touch you so badly. Touch you and taste you. But you were a kid. I was nearly twenty. I didn't know why I suddenly wanted you; all I knew was that I got embarrassingly turned on every time you were in my general vicinity. I imagine that bet was the perfect justification for me to do a little wish fulfillment. I had the excuse I thought I needed. I was so fucking stupid.

"You were twenty-three when I recognized how brave you were. It was Christmas, and we were having dinner with your family. Your brothers were being assholes about your latest job at that salon. You were convinced that you wanted to be a hairstylist, and they were just laying into you. I was on the verge of intervening when you smiled at Kyle and told him you would be happy to help him disguise his gray hairs at a discounted price. You shut him up with grace, dignity, and good humor, and despite the fact that I could *see* how much their negativity upset you, you didn't get defensive. You let it roll over you. It was the bravest thing I'd ever seen. I admired you so fucking much. That was the first time I tried to invite you out to coffee or lunch with me. You refused, of course. It didn't stop me from trying every time I saw you after that.

"Tina, I don't know when it happened . . . but I love you. *So* fucking much." She gasped at the words, her hands flying up to her mouth. He kept his eyes steadily locked onto hers. The intensity of his stare both unnerving and hypnotic. "And I have to . . . I can't . . ."

He sucked in a deep, frantic breath and tugged his fingers through his hair as he stalled, looking like he was trying to gather his thoughts. Tina, whose entire world had just shifted on its axis, could do nothing but stare at him in absolute disbelief.

"I can't compartmentalize," he continued. "I can't do just the sex without all the messy emotions that go along with it. I won't. And if it can't be all—which I know it can't be, not after everything that's happened—it'll have to be nothing."

Before she could say a word in response to his astonishing confessions, he dropped a quick, hard kiss on her mouth, turned, and walked away.

Her legs turned to rubber, and she sank slowly down onto the bed, feeling wobbly and disoriented. How could he *love* her? Where did that come from? Yes, he had constantly asked her out, had often tried to talk to her, but she had known it was just to offer an apology for his behavior that long-ago night.

And this past week, despite his assertion that he was here to offer support to Libby, he had spent more time with Tina than with the other woman. But how did that translate into love? How could it?

She became aware of movement in the room on the other side of the wall. Thumps, knocks, and Harris's heavy tread on the floor. Then muffled masculine voices. Greyson was up. She couldn't quite hear what they were saying, especially once the voices faded, probably because they had left the room.

She wasn't sure what to do next. She wasn't sure how she felt about Harris. She didn't harbor any antipathy toward him, not anymore. Immediately after learning about the bet, she had been hurt, confused, and angry. After she had discovered her pregnancy, that confusion and pain had festered into blistering resentment and all-consuming rage. But as the years had passed, the resentment and anger had faded into regret and a hollow pang in her heart every time she saw him.

His presence had stopped reminding her of the bet; instead he brought to mind the baby she had loved so dearly and lost. And that soon became the main reason she had continued to avoid him. He reminded her of Fletcher, and too often, remembering her baby gave her nightmares of the horrific moment she had found him lying cold and unmoving in his crib.

She didn't know how long she sat there, caught up in her thoughts, before she became aware of doors opening and shutting next door. Followed by two sets of masculine footsteps on the porch. Tina pushed her hair out of her face and padded to the front door. Wondering what was going on. It was only seven thirty in the morning; where could they be going?

She stood at the front door, her ear shamelessly pressed against the wood. More talking, farther away. She went to her front window and peeked through the lace curtain, feeling like a voyeur.

Both men were standing beside Harris's rented 4X4. They appeared to be having a very intense discussion. Tina couldn't remember the last time she'd seen them in such earnest conversation with each other.

Greyson was wearing sweatpants and a T-shirt—still so weird to see him outfitted like that—and Harris was fully dressed in ripped jeans, a T-shirt, and his fur-collared denim jacket. As she watched, the two men embraced, and her jaw dropped. That was new. She couldn't recall them ever hugging before.

She was still mulling over that unprecedented show of affection between the brothers when Harris swung into the driver's seat of the car and dragged his seat belt over his chest.

Wait. *Was he . . . ?*

He started up the car, and before Tina could so much as blink, he was reversing down the drive. Greyson stood watching and lifted his hand to wave as the car turned, once it had exited the gates, and drove off.

Tina flung the door open as Greyson turned back, and he lifted startled eyes to meet hers.

"Where's he going?" she asked bluntly.

Greyson, who looked haggard and despondent, shrugged helplessly. "Home."

"What?"

But he didn't say goodbye. The ridiculous thought was the first thing that came to mind, and she felt a sharp pang of hurt at the realization.

"Why?"

"I think you're better able to answer that question than I am, Martine," Greyson pointed out gently.

"Will he return?" she asked, not sure why she felt such overwhelming panic at the thought of Harris not coming back.

"Doubtful. He's flying out to Australia on Wednesday."

She swayed, and Greyson grabbed her elbow to steady her.

"Easy there," he crooned. He pushed something into her hand, and Tina stared uncomprehendingly down at the object in her palm.

"He wanted me to give that to you," Greyson explained, and Tina's fist closed tightly around the pendant. She would think about it later. She had more immediate concerns now.

"He told me he loves me." The words emerged before she could stop them. She didn't know why she had said it, just knew that she wanted to see if it sounded as ridiculous out loud as it did in her head. She waited for Greyson to laugh at the words, but he continued to merely stare at her somberly.

"That doesn't surprise me," he said.

"How can he love me? He barely knows me!" She heard the anger seeping into her words and embraced it. She'd rather be pissed off at him for throwing this curveball than confused and frightened.

"He knows you," Greyson said placidly, leading her up the steps to the swing.

"He didn't know about my baby," she said triumphantly, hoping to shock him and quite irrationally feeling like she'd scored a point or something.

"No, he didn't," Greyson admitted. His calm acceptance of her words told her that he had known about Fletcher before she had thrown the words at him. "But I think learning about Fletcher only made him love you, and hate himself, that much more."

"You know about Fletcher," Tina murmured, the wind leaving her sails completely. She sat down on the swing, and Greyson sank down next to her.

"Harris told me."

"How could he say something like that to me and then leave? Before I have a chance to even process the words?"

"I don't think he expects anything in return. I think he just needed you to know."

Natasha Anders

"Well, it was selfish! I was fine without him. I was doing *fine*. I don't need his crazy confessions of love, I don't need his kindness, and his . . . his . . . understanding. I don't want his apologies or his regrets. I'm *fine*!" Her voice wobbled on the last two words, and without any warning whatsoever, she simply burst into tears.

Greyson made a soft sound of distress and gently gathered her into his arms. She accepted the comforting embrace. Clinging fiercely to this man who looked so much like Harris, but who smelled completely wrong and whose arms didn't hold her in remotely the same way.

Chapter Fourteen

Harris couldn't sleep. Jet lag and thoughts of Tina had kept him tossing and turning for hours. His phone pinged at about three thirty in the morning, and he swore violently beneath his breath. He lifted the device, and his breath whooshed from his lungs in one quick exhalation.

Hey! Guess who came to MJ's today?

It was from Tina. He hadn't heard from her since he'd left Riversend on Monday morning. It was now Friday. Well, technically it was Thursday night in South Africa. He was six hours ahead in Perth. He tried his best to keep his focus on business, but whenever he found himself with a quiet moment, which was more often than he'd anticipated, he went through his pictures of Fletcher, playing the clips over and over again. Hearing her singing or talking to the baby making her absence a little more bearable.

It was fast becoming a crutch, and he knew he should limit his viewings, but he missed her so damned much: the sound of her voice, the sight of her hesitant smile. In the years before his week in Riversend, he had coped. She would never be his; he had accepted that. But now, after spending time with her again, laughing with her, *crying* with her . . . making love with her, he felt her absence like a knife wound to his heart. It was piercing, painful, and constant.

Are you awake? Crap. What's the time? I thought you were six hours behind us. There was a pause before the next message flashed onto the screen. Oh man! I see it's ahead of us. Jeez. I hope your phone's on silent.

He grinned at that. He could almost hear her saying the words. Breathless and apologetic. He tapped out a quick response.

I'm awake. He laughed when the smiling poo emoji appeared on his screen an instant later.

I'm sorry. I didn't mean to wake you.

You didn't. Jetlag.

She sent a little wincing emoji in response to that.

Who came to MJ's today?

The hipster who sculpted jaundiced David!!

No shit! Did you tell him he was robbed?!

I told him he should have placed second for sure (after Spongebob). He thanked me. He's quite nice. I think he has a crush on my manager, Ricardo.

Harris stared at her message for a long moment, not sure what to say next.

I should let you get to sleep. Her words floated onto his screen before he could reply to her previous message.

Highly doubt that's possible. Especially not after her messages. He wasn't sure what to make of it. He'd been in contact with both Libby and Greyson all week. The former had harangued him for leaving without saying goodbye to her and Clara, and Harris had taken the messages to mean that she wasn't angry with him anymore. Which had been a relief. Leaving Tina had been fucking awful; losing Libby's friendship in addition to that would have been the shitty icing on an already crappy cake.

And Grey—he had taken to thinking of, and referring to, his brother by the shortened version of his name more and more these days—he called regularly to ask about business. Something he had never done before. Usually he'd leave Harris to do his thing and vice versa; if communication had been essential, they would text or email before actually resorting to speaking. The phone calls always started off about business but inevitably strayed to more personal topics, like how Clara was doing, how Tina was coping with the restaurant, or Grey's frustration with his inability to win Libby back. They also spoke about the town and the people Grey was spending time with. Another surprise—Grey had always preferred being a loner. He had never had close friends, and suddenly he was Mr. Sociable. Sometimes they talked about their parents, who occasionally sent both men a text. They had always had a loose, hands-off style of parenting. Expecting something different now that Grey and Harris were adults would be futile. But mostly the brothers talked about absolutely nothing of any import. Sport, the news, the weather, everyday mundane crap.

And it was pretty damned awesome. Harris felt like he had a brother again. No, not *again* . . . they had never talked just for the sake of it. And he could tell that Grey enjoyed it as much as he did.

He was staring at his phone, waiting for a reply to his last message, and he tried to curtail his excitement when he saw that she was typing something.

Still. You should try. She was right. But he'd rather talk to her and try to figure out why, after four days of silence, she had suddenly decided to text him.

But he knew it would be best not to push it.

Yeah. I should. Goodnight, Tina.

Night, Harris.

And that was it.

Check it out! The text came five days later—this time with a picture attached—while Harris was going through one of the many, *many* forged financial documents the group of six corrupt employees had fabricated to cover their asses over the course of two years. The Sleazy Six, as Harris—and the rest of the investigative team—had dubbed them, included two personal assistants, two financial managers, an accountant, and one of their property managers. They had succeeded in defrauding the company of nearly $10 million over the last two years and were leasing at least three of their Australian properties to groups affiliated with drugs and gunrunning. It was a mess and was taking longer to fix than Harris had imagined.

Not that he minded. He welcomed the distraction. But the distraction wasn't proving at all effective when the person he was hoping to be distracted from had been sending him text messages every day for the last five days.

Tonight, it was a picture of Clara in a tiny "Riversend Rockets" football jersey. Apparently, Spencer Carlisle had decided to make the older-versus-younger monthly football game official and had named the teams and ordered jerseys for all the players.

Team mascot!!

Harris smiled fondly at the picture of his niece in the blue-and-white jersey. He'd already received the same picture from both Libby and Greyson but decided not to mention that.

Cute ☺

Number Nine. Like her daddy.

Another fact that Greyson had bragged about.

Naturally.

He didn't know why she was so determined to stay in contact with him. He thought she'd be happy that he'd left, but while she never mentioned anything of a personal nature, she sent him random pictures every day. Told him how the restaurant was doing, what new marketing strategies she and Daff had cooked up. Yesterday she'd sent him a picture of the sunrise, and his throat had closed up unexpectedly at the familiar view, obviously taken from her swing.

Harris decided not to question this—whatever it was—anymore. He was going to accept it and expect nothing from it. At the same time, he had so many questions. Ones that he knew were best left unasked. How was she? Had she had any more nightmares since he'd left? Did she miss him? Was she happy?

He got up and padded to the hotel window and took a quick, grainy snapshot of the night skyline and sent it to her without any explanation.

Nice view.

It's okay. Your view from the front porch is better.

No reply. Not for several minutes, and he went back to studying the documents, even though his concentration was shot.

Had his statement been too personal? The unspoken rules of this bizarre little text relationship appeared to be: keep it light and frivolous. Maybe his observation hadn't been light enough.

Sorry. Got distracted. Somebody wanted to say "hi"! Eek! Nobody in this town seems to realize that I'm crap at small talk.

He grinned at that. That town was perfect for Tina. She needed to be drawn out of her shell, and the curious, friendly, and kind people of Riversend were just the ones to do it.

I think you'll be an expert at it in no time. You're THE MJ everybody is going to want to know you.

Dear God! NO! She added a screaming emoji to the message, and he chuckled. Crap! Gotta go. One of our new servers just spilled wine all over the mayor!

He was in the process of typing his response when she followed up with:

Ps. THE MAYOR IS HAVING DINNER AT MY RESTAURANT TONIGHT!! THE!! MAYOR!! Later. She followed the message up with a smoochie face, and Harris wondered if she even realized she had done that. He obsessed over that fucking emoji—work forgotten—for the rest of the night, wondering what, if anything, it meant.

The following Friday at about two a.m., his phone pinged, waking him from a sound sleep. He fumbled for it and was surprised to see Tina's name on the screen. After that first night, she had been careful about not texting him after midnight, her messages usually coming after nine in the evening his time.

He clicked on the message and stared blankly at the voice note for a long time, his stomach knotting up nervously, before clicking the play button.

"Hey!" His eyes burned at the welcome sound of her excited voice. God, he had missed just hearing her speak. "Guess what? Your cheese-carver guy? His name is Alistair, and he's in a band . . . a band! I mean, that's a little obvious, right? But remember, I told you I think he has a crush on Ricardo, my manager? Anyway, it looks like that's becoming a thing. But I digress . . . I thought it would be cool to have some live music on Friday nights, and I invited Alistair and his band to play. I know, I know what you're going to say . . . it's a risk. What if they're crap and all that? But they're not. They're really freaking good. They're getting ready to play their next set. Listen to this!"

The band struck up a familiar poppy tune, and Harris smiled when he heard Tina squeal in excitement, sounding for all the world like a giddy teen at a pop concert. If the cheering crowd was any indication, it sounded like she had a full house tonight, and that made him so damned happy for her. She had recorded the entire song, but Harris barely listened to it; he was too distracted by her squeals and her terrible singing when she chimed in with the chorus.

This was so much better than watching those clips of her with Fletcher. This wasn't tinged with sadness. This was sheer, vibrant joy, and he adored it. He played it twice more before responding with a voice note of his own.

"And you had the nerve to criticize *my* singing? I could barely hear the band above your caterwauling, woman!"

He didn't have to wait long for her response.

"Shuddup, Harris! You *wish* you could sing half as good as me!"

"No, seriously, Tina. There are dogs howling on the streets of Perth right now, thanks to you." He knew she could hear the smile in his voice.

She sent him a picture in response to that. A selfie of her with a scrunched-up face, sticking her tongue out at the lens. It was taken in terrible light and had a grainy, orange quality to it, but he couldn't stop staring at it.

"What the hell are you doing to me, Tina?" he moaned to himself, his thumb tracing the lines of her pretty, round face on his screen.

> You sound tired! Sorry I woke you. But I had to share the news. Back to text.

> The band's good. Well done. Glad the evening was a success.

She sent him a thumbs-up emoji, followed by a snoozing one.

He didn't reply but fell asleep still staring at that beautiful picture.

"Hi, MJ! Loved the jam session last night," someone called as Tina walked down Main Road to MJ's. The townspeople had taken to calling her MJ and often went out of their way to greet her or chat with her when they saw her around town. At first it had been a little unnerving to have random people striking up conversations with her, but Tina felt less awkward about it now. She even knew some of them by name.

She was starting to feel a lot more integrated into the town, and after a rocky first month, the restaurant was doing well. They were heading into their eighth week of business now, and MJ's had regained its status as the favorite eating-out spot for locals. People could not stop raving about the new menu.

Libby had been pushing to do the dessert-menu thing for quite some time, and after doing a little market research on some of their competitors in surrounding towns, Tina had decided that it was a unique enough idea to give it a go. That decision had paid off in spades. The dessert-tasting menu was a hit with everybody, and naturally Libby was happy, since it gave her the excuse she needed to continue experimenting with new flavor combinations and cutting-edge techniques. MJ's was acquiring a reputation for outstanding desserts, and people were traveling from other towns just to sample Libby's Wednesday-night dessert-tasting menus.

Tina was also very pleased with her decision to offer live music on Friday nights. It drew in a younger crowd, who traveled from surrounding towns grateful for the opportunity to dance and hang out without having to drive nearly an hour out of their way. Alistair and his band now had a regular Friday-night gig with them, and Tina was trying to find other acts to support them.

It was hard to believe that just a few weeks ago, she would have been petrified to make these bold decisions. She would have considered them and dismissed them as too daring, too out there, and doomed to failure. Now she was eager to try new things, happy to experiment and see what worked. She often talked things through with Libby, and sometimes with Daff. Even though the woman had had her baby—a beautiful little boy named Connor—a few weeks ago and wasn't freely available to help out anymore, she was always happy to have a quick chat. But Tina was becoming more confident in her business acumen and was starting to make a lot of decisions without seeing the need to go to someone else for validation first.

In fact, the band had been all her, and she felt a thrill of excitement and pride whenever she saw the crowd they drew.

Business was booming, life was good, and, despite all the wonderful things happening, Tina was staggeringly lonely. Which was odd, because she was surrounded by so many amazing people. People she liked and who cared about her. Her brothers had started calling more often; Smith had even visited a couple of times to check out the restaurant. Conrad and Kyle were constantly offering unsolicited advice and messaging random ideas for the restaurant, and none of them ever had a negative word to say. Which was a welcome change.

Libby and Greyson appeared to be at an impasse with each other, but it didn't look like Greyson was going anywhere soon. He had become something of a friend to Tina. He was still her next-door neighbor, seeming disinclined to find a better place, and would often invite himself over for breakfast in the mornings, since he was a truly terrible cook. Even worse so than Tina.

Logically, Tina had no reason to be lonely. Only . . . she was. And her loneliness was only alleviated when she was texting Harris. They had graduated to more frequent voice notes, and Tina often wished she were brave enough to actually call him and have a real-time conversation with him. He was still in Perth; he had been there for nearly six weeks, but he had mentioned during their half-text, half-voice-note conversation last night that it looked like he'd be heading home within the week. The news had made her heart race, because she wasn't sure how having him back in the same country would affect their nightly texting ritual.

It hadn't escaped her notice that she was always the one instigating contact. He never texted first, and she knew it was probably because he was uncertain about what the acceptable boundaries of their relationship were. Not that Tina knew. She just liked being in contact with him, sharing her daily little triumphs and failures with him. As much as she liked hearing about his.

"Morning, Tina," Ricardo called from his front-of-house spot, where he was chatting with the waitstaff, who had formed a loose semicircle in front of him.

"Hi, guys. Sorry I missed the meeting," she said. Ricardo usually had a morning meeting with his waitstaff, and while Tina tried to attend most of them, she'd had yoga with Lia this morning and was running half an hour late. "Ricardo, I'm sure you'll let me know if anything came up. And I think it's time, people. Get ready!"

Ricardo tossed her a thumbs-up, and she grinned before making her way into the kitchen, where Libby was having a similar meeting with the kitchen staff.

"Morning!" she said cheerfully. "Am I in time?"

"In time for what?" Libby asked with a confused frown, and Agnes nodded and grinned wickedly before everybody started singing "Happy Birthday." The waitstaff flooded into the kitchen, and Agnes produced a large cake from beneath one of the countertops, with *Happy Birthday, Libby* sloppily iced on top of it.

"Oh my God." Libby's hands flew to her flushed cheeks, and her eyes flooded with tears. She fanned at her face before staring down at the messily frosted, fluorescent pink-and-green two-tier cake they had placed in front of her. She stared at the cake in comically confused horror. "Who made this? Agnes? Did you do this? It's terrible!"

"That would be me," Tina said with a grin. And Libby laughed.

"Seriously? Tina, the last time you baked anything, it was inedible!"

"I know! That's why this cake isn't for eating!"

"What do you mean?"

"It's a smash cake!" Tina informed her with relish.

"*No!* Not in my kitchen!" Libby said, her eyes going wide with dread. "Smash cakes are for toddlers."

"Live a little, Chef!" one of the busboys called, and she sent him a death glare.

"And will you be cleaning up the mess, Vusi?"

"I always do anyway," he retorted cheekily. Libby pursed her lips and kept her gaze focused on him before grabbing a fistful of the cake without warning, and, keeping her eyes fixed on Vusi, squashed it right in Tina's face.

Tina squealed in horror, completely suckered by the move, and stood in disbelief as cake and frosting dripped down her face and onto the front of her green blouse.

"Oh. *Oh!* It's so on now, my friend!"

In the end, the carnage wasn't too bad; they remained mindful of the fact that they'd be opening for service in a couple of hours and kept the mess confined to one spot in the kitchen. Both Tina and Libby and a few other casualties had to change into new clothes, but everybody had pretty much anticipated needing a change of clothes and had planned ahead. Tina had even brought something for Libby. Which hadn't been an easy task. She had been forced to enlist Greyson's aid because, since he was babysitting Clara at Libby's house these days, he had easier access.

The kitchen was cleaned and prepped in time for their morning service, and everybody went into it in awesome spirits and with smiles on their faces. Tina retreated to her office to order inventory, and after finishing that task, she sent Harris some pictures of her and Libby both covered in cake.

That looks like a waste of some perfectly good cake.

I made the cake.

I take it back! Looks like it got exactly the treatment it deserved. She laughed at that brutally frank comeback, but really there was no arguing with the truth.

I'm at the airport. I have a six pm flight home today. The news disturbed her; she wondered if he would have told her if she hadn't texted him first.

Oh. Travel safe. She didn't know what else to say.

Thanks.

"Don't be stupid, Tina," she told herself sternly after she put her phone down. "He doesn't *have* to tell you anything."

She got up and paced the tiny confines of the office for a moment before heading back out into the bustling restaurant. People called out greetings, and she absently waved and returned the smiles and the hellos, but her mind wasn't on what she was doing. She needed to figure out what else she wanted from her life. Because it currently felt like she was stuck in limbo.

"I'm thinking of selling my flat. And I was wondering if you had any advice for me. Some dos and don'ts, maybe?" The achingly familiar voice, coming from so close by, startled Harris. His head jerked up, and there she was. Right there in his office, standing just inside the closed door and staring at him with wide, nervous eyes.

"Tina?" He shoved himself up and rounded his desk, not even aware of what he was going to do until after he'd done it. Before he knew it, he was within a foot of her, crowding her against the door. He swallowed and took a deliberate and extremely reluctant step back to give her some space.

"How did you get in here?" he asked, and she smiled, the parting of her lips beautiful but also a bit strained, as if she, too, wasn't yet sure what she was doing here.

"I called Greyson and made him order your PA to let me in without forewarning you. Apparently, he's a bigger boss than you are," she said, her smile widening tentatively.

"Yeah, he could probably fire my ass if he wanted to," Harris quipped. Only half his brain was on his words; the other half was wholly preoccupied with dealing with the bombardment of his senses. Her scent, her voice, the warmth of her body—his pupils dilated to take in as much of her as he could. She was dressed in another one of those fantastic dresses. This one was aquamarine, strappy—a nod to the warm early-spring weather—with a sweetheart neckline, form-fitting contours, and a flirty little ruffle at the knee. Her long red hair—crackling with good health—tumbled to her pale, freckled shoulders in a mass of vibrant curls.

She was so damned sexy that he was having a *very* hard time keeping his hands to himself. He folded them behind his back and instead leaned toward her like a total creeper and inhaled the fresh scent of her hair.

"You look—" He stopped himself in time. Not sure anything he wanted to say to her would be considered remotely appropriate. He settled on "nice."

"Thank you."

"It's good to see you again." He couldn't stop those words from emerging, and he didn't fucking care what she made of that.

"It's good to see you too," she echoed faintly, and she genuinely looked like she meant the words.

"What can I do for you?" he asked, remembering himself and where they were and taking another step back from her. "And why are you in Cape Town? Who's running the restaurant?"

"I couldn't expect Libby and Ricardo to pick up the slack—they each have a lot on their plates as it is—so I asked Greyson to keep an eye on things while I'm gone."

Grey? That was new. Since when did Tina trust Grey enough to ask him for a favor like that?

"He didn't mention it to me," Harris said, feeling a little betrayed; he and Grey had been sharing a lot more of their everyday lives with each other lately.

Tina cleared her throat uncomfortably, looking strangely guilty.

"I asked him not to. I figured if you knew I was coming, you'd try to avoid me."

He said nothing in response to that. He couldn't deny the truth in her words, and after an awkward pause, she cleared her throat again.

"We should have lunch," she suggested evenly, and he stared at her for a moment, not sure what to say in response to that. Her voice softened and she added, "Please, Harris. Let's have lunch."

It would take a stronger man than he to deny the gentle appeal in that husky voice. He glanced back at his desk; he was still jet lagged after his return from Australia two days ago and wasn't getting much work done anyway.

"Yeah, okay," he acquiesced, patting his jacket pockets absently. "Just let me get my phone and wallet."

He turned away to gather his thoughts and his equilibrium. After a few deep breaths, he faced her again with what he hoped was an insouciant smile.

"Do you have any place in mind? For lunch?" She shook her head. "Right. Uh, let's go."

Twenty minutes later they were facing each other across a tiny table in an equally tiny coffee shop in Sea Point, about ten minutes away from the Chapman Global Property Group's head office on the Foreshore. The coffee shop was alarmingly intimate, and Harris cursed himself for choosing it. He had never noticed the close confines before, usually coming here for quick working lunches because it was quiet.

"I was saying that I wanted to sell my Bantry Bay flat," she repeated after they had placed their orders, and his brow lowered.

"Why? It's a good investment."

"MJ's is doing quite well, and I like Riversend. The town suits me. I feel at home there. Hanging on to the flat seems pointless."

"I'm not a real estate agent, you know?" he said, forcing humor into his voice, when inside he felt scraped raw. She wasn't coming back. That made sense. She was starting a new chapter in her life, but she couldn't do that without closing the old one.

And Harris knew that he could not be part of that new stage of her life. Not if she stood a realistic shot of making a success of that fresh start.

"But you guys deal in rentals, resales, and property development," she pointed out, practically citing their motto. The Chapman Global Property Group dabbled in real estate, but they mainly concentrated on property development. Their primary business focus was the design and building of upmarket housing estates, which they then sold to investment groups or private companies.

"Yes, we do. Pretty damned well too. But you should find a property agent to help you with your flat. I can recommend someone reliable."

"See? You've helped me already," she said, and his eyes narrowed.

"It's not like I'm telling you anything you didn't already know. So, what's the real reason behind this lunch?"

"I needed to give you this. I can't keep it." She picked up her handbag and scratched around a bit before producing a tiny tissue-wrapped object and placing it in the center of the table. Harris knew what it was even before he'd slowly reached for it and unfolded the paper.

His pendant. He swallowed and shook his head, trying to hand it back to her, but she moved her hands out of reach beneath the table.

"I can't take it," he protested, his voice taking on a hoarse, panicked note. "I never had any right to it."

"Why did you keep it?" she asked, and he glared at her, angry that she was pushing this.

"You *know* why!" he snapped.

"Not really."

"Because it reminded me of you. Because it made me feel close to you." The words emerged involuntarily, and it pissed him off that he'd actually spoken them.

"And now you no longer need it?"

What the fuck was she trying to do to him? This was deliberate torture, and he was done with it.

"I have to go," he muttered, pushing himself away from the table.

"We haven't even eaten yet," she pointed out, staring up at him, naked pleading in her vulnerable eyes. "Please, Harris. Sit down."

He blinked repeatedly, bringing a hand up to his nape in a futile attempt to massage the tension from his neck. He had sunk down, unable to resist, when she turned those lethal eyes on him.

"I don't know what you want from me," he said on a helpless whisper. "This is agony, Tina. And maybe I deserve to be punished, but you've never struck me as a deliberately cruel person before."

"I don't think you deserve to be punished, Harris. *You're* the only one who thinks that. I am angry with you, though. But only because you dropped a bombshell on me and then left before I had a chance to process it. That was a crappy move."

"It was the only option open to me," he said. "I couldn't stay there any longer. I should never have been there in the first place. Libby didn't need me; Grey didn't either."

"Turns out that *I* needed you," Tina said, keeping her eyes level and her expression neutral. Her statement confused him completely, and he wasn't sure what to say in response to it.

"I don't understand."

"For ten years I was stuck in the past, Harris. I felt incapable of moving forward with my life. I was trapped by my own incapacity to let go. I suffered from panic attacks, awful nightmares, and a crippling inability to settle in one job for too long. I know I appeared flighty and irresponsible. When in truth I was incapable of digging myself out from beneath a mountain of suffocating self-doubt and fear."

"You had reason to—"

She held up a hand, stopping him in midsentence. "I had reasons, yes. Good ones. But I let them become the biggest part of who I was. I couldn't speak my own child's name for ten years, Harris. But you—"

Tina's eyes flooded, and she shook her head helplessly as she tried to formulate her thoughts.

"When you came to Riversend, you were just there! Constantly. A reminder of everything I had lost, everything I could have become."

"I'm sorry . . ." His voice was absolutely soaked in misery, and she shook her head firmly.

"Stop apologizing, Harris. You've apologized enough. Let me speak, please."

His throat worked, and he looked like he wanted to say something more, but he nodded. She was about to continue, when their food was brought to the table. They both stared at their meals in dismay, neither in the mood to eat. Tina gently pushed hers aside, and Harris did the same before refocusing his attention on her.

"You were inescapable," she continued, absently toying with a salt-shaker. "Just *everywhere*, but I found that I didn't mind. I liked having you around. I liked spending time with you."

"You did?" he asked, a hopeful note creeping into his voice. She nodded and curled her hand into a fist, in an attempt to stop aimlessly pushing the shaker around.

"And the more time I spent with you, the guiltier I felt about the secrets I'd kept from you for so long. But in the end, after telling you . . . that heavy mountain of fear and despair and self-doubt? It lightened considerably. Sharing that with you . . ." There was a tremor in her voice, and she paused for a moment in an attempt to control it. "I felt relieved. And less alone. But I feel like I put all of that on you, Harris. Everything I'd been carrying for the last decade was planted firmly on your shoulders."

"My shoulders are broad," he murmured. "They can carry a lot."

"But it was too much. I put you in that place, that truly awful and lonely place that I'd been occupying for so long. And maybe it was unintentional and inevitable, but it also wasn't fair. It should always have been a shared burden. Not mine or yours to carry alone."

"Tina."

"Harris," she responded, a gently teasing note in her voice when he didn't follow up with anything else.

"Why did you start sending me those texts?" he asked unexpectedly, and she hesitantly reached over to place her palm over the back of his hand, where it rested on the table between them.

"I think because I knew what you were going through. Ten years ago there was no one to help me through the grieving process. And I suppose I wanted you to know you weren't alone. I wanted to be there for you. Even if it was just through silly texts."

"I didn't deserve such consideration."

"Harris, you would have been there for me." She stated it as unequivocal fact, because she knew, in her heart of hearts, that the words were true.

"I'm not so sure," he said doubtfully, and her hand tightened over his.

"I am." He turned his hand over, and her palm was cradled in his. No longer passively receiving comfort but actively returning it.

"How long will you be in town?" he asked after a comfortable moment of quiet.

"Not long—a few days at most. I have to get my flat on the market and spend some quality time with the fam."

He winced.

"Sounds grim."

"Yep, family dinner tonight," she said with a shudder. "The last time I went to one of those, Libby went into labor and saved me from the horror. A true friend, that."

"What a champ," Harris said, his voice so dry it cracked, and she chuckled.

"Wanna come with me? I could use some backup."

His head tilted as he watched her assessingly, as if trying to figure her out.

"Okay. But only if you join me at *my* obligatory parental dinner, tomorrow night."

"Deal!"

"Why, Harrison, how *lovely* to see you." Mercy Jenson greeted them effusively when Tina and Harris walked into the huge family den in the Jenson home that evening.

"Mrs. Jenson." Harris greeted her smoothly and walked over to drop a kiss on the older woman's unnaturally smooth cheek. He turned to pump Tina's father's hand effusively. "Sir, good to see you again."

More handshakes with her brothers and Dumi and a peck on the cheek for Kitty. Smith was going stag that night; apparently things between him and Milla had hit a rocky patch. Tina's youngest brother gave her an effusive hug, lifting her off the floor in the process, and she laughingly commanded him to put her down.

It was nice being home; she had actually missed her brothers, and it was so much easier to converse with them, now that they were no longer starting every second comment with "Do you know what your problem is . . ." Tina knew that Smith had told Conrad and Kyle about her pregnancy, but neither man had asked her about it. She could tell they were still on eggshells around her, but that was okay, if it meant no longer being constantly criticized.

Her parents, on the other hand, did not seem to have noticed the sea change in their sons' attitude toward their daughter. They had all just sat down to dinner when her mother started in on her weight.

"Goodness knows, Martine, you went into the wrong business," she fretted. "I swear you've put on at least ten kilograms. I hope you're not sampling everything Olivia cooks."

Tina refrained from rolling her eyes. She had been so busy in Riversend, and with the constant walking to and from the restaurant, plus regular yoga sessions with Lia, she'd actually *lost* weight. Not that it had been intentional—she had stopped actively dieting years ago. She would probably gain the weight back once she acclimated to life in Riversend. And that was fine too.

"As the owner, it would be a complete dereliction of duty if I didn't know what every item on my menu tasted like," she pointed out nonchalantly, happily picking up a bread roll to dip into her creamy corn soup.

Smith sniggered at her words.

"Don't blame you—Libby's cooking is amazing!" her brother enthused.

"Hmm," Tina said around a mouthful of bread. "Her desserts are the highlight of our menu. We've started a dessert-tasting menu. Wednesday night is dessert night. People travel all the way from Plett for our desserts. It's really boosted business."

"When will you come to your senses about this, Martine? You're not a restaurateur," her mother fussed. "I don't understand *why* you keep doing these things. This is such a waste of money. And this time, you have people depending on you. For heaven's sake, how will it look when this falls through, and all those people find themselves unemployed?"

"Jeez, Mom," Tina said, knowing her mother hated to be called *Mom*. "Thanks for the vote of confidence."

"Martine!" the older woman gasped, casting an awkward glance at Harris, who was watching the exchange with a determinedly neutral expression on his face. But Tina knew him well enough to know his blood was boiling beneath that placid facade. "What has gotten into you? You know your father and I only have your best interests at heart."

"Do you? Dad? You haven't said much tonight. What's your opinion on this matter?" Tina asked, with a challenging tilt to her jaw. Her father, as tall and handsome as his sons, coughed and took a sip of water before self-consciously dabbing his napkin over his lips.

"Well . . . ," he began, casting a nervous glance toward his wife. "You chose to dabble in a challenging business this time, Martine. And if it goes belly up, that's your investment gone. There's no recouping those losses."

"And you're certain it'll go belly up?"

"Very few new restaurants survive their first year."

"It's not a new restaurant," Harris suddenly said, and Tina shot him a warning glare. He acknowledged her look with a raised eyebrow.

"I told you before, don't speak for me, Harris," she reminded him between gritted teeth, and he nodded, leaning back in his chair and folding his arms over his chest. Watching her with a lazy grin. "It's not a new restaurant," Tina repeated, aiming the words at her father. "I bought an existing restaurant in a small town. If you'd shown the slightest bit of interest instead of assuming it was another one of my doomed experiments, you'd have known that."

"That's no way to speak to your father, young lady."

"God, Mother, she's not twelve," Smith pointed out, exasperated.

"Well, sometimes she behaves like she's twelve," her mother shot back, looking annoyed that her sons were not backing her up tonight. "It's just been one disappointment after the other with her for years!"

"Starting with the way I looked, right? Way back at birth?" Tina glared at the older woman angrily and folded her arms over her chest. "And then I was that awkward teen without any real friends, except for the Chapman cook's daughter."

"Martine, that's enough. We won't speak of this in front of our guest." Her mother cast another look at Harris, definitely uncomfortable that their dirty laundry was being aired in front of a Chapman.

"I don't mind," Harris said, his arms still crossed over his chest. Everybody else was staring at the unfolding tableau with a mixture of horror and fascination on their faces. Smith looked downright gleeful.

"I think it's high time we speak of it," Tina said. "High time we speak of *him*. My baby. Fletcher."

"You stop this at once," her mother said, turning an unbecoming shade of red.

"You never forgave me for that, did you?" Tina whispered. "For having him. For wanting him. For loving him. You were relieved when he died. I know you were." She blinked, and tears angry and heartbroken escaped from beneath her eyelids to slide down her face.

Harris, who was sitting next to her, unfolded his arms and slipped a hand beneath the table to squeeze her knee comfortingly, silently reminding her that he was there for her.

"I wasn't relieved, Martine," her mother said in a low voice. "What a terrible thing to say. Of course I wasn't relieved. I still had hope that you'd give him up for adoption, because I did not see how you could have any kind of future with a baby holding you back. When he passed away . . . I admit . . . my first thought—and I'm not proud of myself for this—but my first thought was that we no longer needed to worry about convincing you to give him up."

"Jesus, Mom," Smith said, his voice disgusted, and Tina, without looking up, could sense that her other brothers and in-laws were equally disturbed by her mother's words.

Harris's hand was squeezing her thigh so hard that Tina knew he would leave bruises.

"I would never have given him up," Tina stated vehemently. Harris's other hand appeared in front of her face, this one clutching a white linen handkerchief, which she gratefully took. Wiping her face and then blowing her nose indelicately.

"Harrison, I'm so sorry you had to witness all of this; what must you think of us?" her mother apologized, her voice faint and her eyes still fixed on Tina's face.

"I'm thinking you should appreciate your amazing daughter more," he said, and every eye at the table swiveled to his face.

"Why are you here tonight, Harris?" Smith suddenly asked. "You don't seem surprised by any of our family's dirty laundry. Why is that?"

"I'm . . ."

"Harris. No," Tina said, a warning note entering her voice. Tonight was enough of a train wreck without him exacerbating the situation. He squeezed her thigh and leaned toward her.

"It's not your burden to bear alone," he said, the words meant for her ears only. "Not anymore, Tina."

He lifted his gaze to meet Smith's and took in a deep, bracing breath.

"Fletcher was my son."

Chapter Fifteen

"You foolish man," Tina chastised him two hours later, sitting cross-legged on a sofa in Harris's apartment and holding a steak to his swollen eye. "Tossing a bombshell like that in a roomful of my brothers? What the hell did you think was going to happen? You're lucky only Smith went for you."

"Only because Kitty was physically holding Conrad back—she's quite strong for a woman who had a baby three months ago—and I'm pretty sure Dumi and Kyle were trying to pull Smith off me because they both wanted a turn. In fact, I'm sure I felt Dumi's elbow in my ribs."

Tina snorted, then compressed her lips. She shouldn't laugh; it wasn't a laughing matter. It had been awful. The evening had devolved into chaos seconds after Harris's revelation.

Smith had called him a "motherfucker" and had practically leaped across the table to get to him.

"I-I keep seeing . . ." A snigger escaped, and she clapped a horrified hand over her mouth as she tried to get herself back under control. She attempted to speak again. "I-I keep seeing m-my mother snatching the Lalique candleholders from the table! Never mind that Smith was trying to k-kill you. She needed to get those—" Another chortle. "Those damned . . . oh God. Those damned candleholders to s-safe . . ." She couldn't stop herself; she knew she was borderline hysterical. It had been an extremely trying evening, but she could not stop laughing.

Harris watched her closely, the corners of his lips canting upward as he enjoyed her laughter. He wanted to commit every lovely nuance of that laugh to memory. He reached up to remove the steak from his eye and placed it on a plate on the coffee table. She was still helplessly laughing, her arms folded over her stomach. He knew this was another one of her little coping mechanisms. And understood that if she weren't laughing right now, she'd be crying. It upset him that she was this disturbed by the evening's events, but he could not find it in him to regret his confession at dinner.

His hands moved, and he brought them to cup her jaw, sliding beneath her hair until his fingertips met at the nape of her neck. His thumbs tilted her head up, and the laughter faded from her eyes. Leaving her looking much too vulnerable. Her own hands flattened against his chest and then curled into the fabric of his shirt.

"I'm sorry you had a fight with one of your best friends. I know it's my fault."

"Nah," he dismissed carelessly. "It's *my* fault. I messed with my friend's baby sister. I'd beat the shit out of me, too, if I were him."

"'Messed with me'? Is that what the kids are calling it these days?" she asked, latent laughter still adding a lilt to her voice.

"That's what *I'm* calling it. And I desperately want to mess with you again," he said, his eyes dipping to her lips.

"Desperately, is it?"

"*So* fucking desperately," he reiterated fervently.

"Do you think that's wise?" she asked softly, and he shook his head.

"I know it's not. But I can't resist you, Tina! I never could." He dropped his forehead to hers, and then, before either one of them could think about it any further, he claimed her lips in the sweetest of kisses. His mouth exerted only the slightest pressure, while his tongue delicately flicked along the seam of her lips until she opened for him. Despite his words, there was nothing desperate in his kiss; he kept it patient and undemanding. He took his time exploring her mouth, her lips, her tongue . . . and it was absolutely wonderful.

"Come here, sweetheart." His hands fell to her hips as he encouraged her to crawl into his lap. She happily complied, sitting sideways with her butt against his crotch. She wriggled a bit trying to get comfortable, and he groaned.

"Sorry, but there's no room for my ass with this *thing* taking up practically all the space in your lap," she complained, and he laughed, the sound strained.

"Nothing I can do about that right now," he said, and she wrapped her arms around his neck and kissed him again. He swelled even more beneath her butt, and she lifted her hips and looked at him sternly.

"Stop that—you're making it hard for me to get comfortable," she mock scolded him.

"Not as hard as *you're* making it!" He couldn't resist the lame pun but was rewarded when her eyes lit in amusement.

"That was terrible," she said with a giggle.

"Sorry," he mumbled, kissing her again. Things became serious in very short order after that.

"I love these dresses," he said after trying to wriggle his hand down her bodice, without making any progress. It was very fucking frustrating. "But they're very difficult to work with."

"Hold on," she said and clambered off his lap to stand in front of him. She turned her back to him, brushing her fall of hair to the side. "Unzip me."

He stared at her gorgeous round ass for a moment before sweeping his ravenous gaze upward, past the dip of her waist, her back, to where her off-the-shoulder red dress revealed pale, freckled skin. She was absolute perfection, and he couldn't wait to get the tight dress off her. He leaped to his feet, then grimaced, taking a moment to adjust himself.

"Anybody ever tell you you're built like a sexier, curvier Jessica Rabbit?" he asked reverentially, and she laughed.

"All tits and ass, you mean?"

"Just two of my *favorite* things." His fingers slowly tracked the line where the dress ended and flesh began, shoulder to shoulder, and she shuddered. He traced it halfway back to where the zipper was, and, after taking the time to scatter kisses over a few random freckles, he unzipped her. And, taking his time, he revealed her soft skin, inch by silky inch. Trailing more soft kisses down her spine. She was wearing a strapless bra, and he took a moment to unclasp the lacy red thing before continuing with his appointed task. The zipper ended just below the small of her back, revealing the band of her low-riding lace panties.

Harris slipped his hands beneath the gaping fabric of the dress and moved them around front, cupping her breasts beneath her loosened bra and pulling her back against him, until her naked back was flush against his fully clothed front.

He nuzzled her neck just below her ear, and she gasped, her nipples, already hot little beads beneath his palms, tightened further. She arched voluptuously against him, her own hands coming up to cover his through her dress.

"Harris." Her voice cracked sexily on his name. *"Please."*

"No rush, sweetheart. We have all the time in the world. I'm going to make love with you, and it's going to be slow and thorough. I'm going to make you beg and scream and come. Many, *many* times. And that's a promise."

The man knew how to keep his promises, Tina marveled two hours later. She was limp, sated, and exhausted and had less energy than a sloth. She lay sprawled, facedown, on the bed, with an arm thrown over his hard, naked chest and a leg flung over his thighs. He was running his fingertips lazily up and down her spine.

"Hmth pho moob," she mumbled incoherently into his chest, which rumbled when he laughed.

"Didn't catch that," he said.

And she managed to lift her heavy head enough to form proper words.

"Was so good," she praised, patting his abs in appreciation.

"Happy you enjoyed it. I know I did." He had been incredibly gentle, sweet, considerate . . . *loving*. She had lost count of her orgasms, and she knew he had come a few times as well, which had been revelatory. She hadn't known a man could do that and still continue. He'd merely changed condoms and carried on.

She pushed her hair out of her face and peered up at him, curious about that.

"I didn't know guys could come more than once without taking a breather or something in between," she said, and he shook his head, looking a little awed himself.

"It's never really happened to me before," he said, looking bemused. "Guess I have you to thank for that."

She grinned, feeling a little smug about that. The grin faded when she took a proper look at him.

"Your poor eye is swollen shut," she said in horror, and he lifted his free hand to gingerly probe at the contusion. It was darkening from red to purple.

"Hurts like a son of a bitch," he complained, and she couldn't stop herself from glaring at him.

"I hope this doesn't destroy your friendship with Smith."

"I'll talk to him. Like I said before, it's my fault. He has every right to be pissed off. But I wanted to acknowledge Fletcher as my son. And I wanted you to know that I have your back."

Tina's heart turned into a puddle of goo at those words. The only other person who had ever really had her back was Libby. And because Tina had chosen not to tell her friend about her pregnancy, that support had been absent when she'd needed it most. She once again acknowledged that she should never have isolated herself from people who cared about her. People like her best friend and her brothers.

And now . . . so many years later, she knew she could trust that this man, who had once inadvertently hurt her so badly, truly had her best interests at heart. He had been nothing but kind and supportive. Generous and loving.

"Your mother is way too obsessed with weight," he was saying, still reflecting on their disastrous dinner with her family. "She's bordering on malnourished herself—you guys should stage an intervention or something." His words startled a laugh out of Tina. She could just imagine her mother's reaction to that. The woman was petite but not underweight, yet Harris looked perfectly serious.

"My mother's weight is fine, Harris. She's got a nice little body for someone her age. I reckon a lot of guys would think she's quite the MILF."

He shot her such a truly appalled look that she choked on another laugh. "Dear God! Why would you put such an awful image in my head?" he asked, aghast.

"No, seriously, I've seen guys check her out."

"Jesus! Stop! You're being gross. You don't see me telling you my dad could very well be a stud if he wasn't so devoted to my mom, do you?"

"I wouldn't argue with you. Your dad is pretty good looking. He's like a sexier version of George Clooney or something."

"Why are we talking about this?"

He sounded totally disgusted with her, and she laughed, pushing herself up and straddling him in one smooth motion. "Why don't I do something to get those distasteful images out of your head?" she asked on a seductive purr, and he growled a sexy assent, his big hands stroking down her waist to settle on her hips.

"Yeah, go for it," he said invitingly, and she trailed a finger down his chest, over his rib cage, and then to his side.

Without any warning, she prodded his ribs, and he jumped.

"No!" he gasped, and she grinned before launching into a relentless tickle attack, targeting his ribs and sides in particular. He convulsed into helpless laughter, punctuated with the occasional *No!* while attempting to buck her off. He finally succeeded in flipping her over and pinned her hands above her head.

"That wasn't nice, Tina," he scolded. "Taking advantage of my weakness like that . . . now, how do I punish you?"

Tina smiled trustingly up into his beautiful face.

"I don't know . . . but I'm sure it'll be good." His expression softened, and he kissed her until she was breathless. She couldn't quite believe that either of them was capable of another session of lovemaking after their last marathon.

But they both proved very capable.

It was hard and fast and intense. So very different from before. She lost herself in their mutual passion. Relishing the weight of his body on top of hers, his lean hips pistoning between hers, the thick, hard thrust of him inside of her. It was indescribable, and her fingernails dug into his back when she gasped her way into another amazing orgasm. Her climax triggered his, and he lowered his forehead to her shoulder as he plunged into her a final time.

"Oh God, Tina." His voice was dazed and breathless and a little lost. "I love you. I love you so much."

He went limp and collapsed on top of her for a few seconds before sluggishly removing the condom. He shifted to the side but tugged her close, his arm draped across her stomach and his head resting on her chest. His body slackened and grew heavy with sleep mere seconds later.

While Tina lay there, trapped by his weight and unable to get his final, groaning confession out of her head. She fell asleep with the words still ringing in her ears.

"Whachu doing?" Harris's voice was muffled by a pillow, and he peeled open his good eye to catch Tina's gaze as she dragged on her dress.

"Getting ready to do a walk of shame down to my car." Tina had driven him home the night before. With his eye swelling at an alarming rate, he'd been in no fit state to drive himself.

"Whazza time?" he slurred. He looked shattered, which reminded Tina that he was probably still suffering from jet lag.

"Just after eight."

"Fuuuuuuck!" He pushed himself up reluctantly and blinked sleepily. "I have a meeting at eight thirty."

"Postpone it—you look far from professional right now. You look like a prizefighter. It's kind of sexy but definitely *not* professional. And you have jet lag. Take some time to get acclimated, for heaven's sake."

He cracked his neck and opened his mouth with a jaw-popping yawn. "Where are you off to?"

"Back to my hotel, for a shower and change. I have a meeting with a real estate agent at nine."

"See you tonight?" he asked, his voice deliberately nonchalant.

She sauntered over to the bed and bent at the waist to kiss him.

"What time?" she asked huskily.

"Eight. Meet at my parents' place?"

"Sounds fine. Thank you for coming with me last night and . . . you know? Everything else." She tried to keep the blush at bay but failed miserably, her face heating up at the memory of what "everything else" had entailed.

He grinned wickedly, the smile combined with his swollen blue eye and crooked nose giving him a decidedly roguish appearance.

"Oh, Bean, it was most *definitely* my pleasure."

Harris was in the shower when he first realized it was there. He was so used to its weight that he didn't notice it at first. In fact, his hand must have brushed over it a few times while he was soaping his chest before he registered its presence.

"Damn it, Tina," he swore mildly as his fingers traced the familiar contours of his pendant. She must have slipped it over his head while he was sleeping. Part of him wanted to remove it immediately, but the other, much larger part was relieved to have it back. He had felt incomplete without it. The pendant had always made him feel more connected to Tina. And now that she knew he was wearing it, that attachment felt much stronger.

He left it where it was.

It was a crutch—he knew that—but he also knew that he was going to need something to lean on once he let her go.

After seeing his face, he had agreed with Tina's assessment that he probably wasn't fit to be seen in public and had postponed all his meetings and appointments. But he needed to speak with Smith. He wasn't sure if his friend would be willing to meet with him, but Harris had to at least make the attempt.

When he called, he was stunned when Smith picked up on the first ring.

"What?" The word was loaded with hostility.

"We need to talk."

"You looking to get your ass kicked again?" Smith asked belligerently.

"Look, Smith, Tina would be devastated if we don't at least attempt to mend fences. She'd blame herself."

"Don't you fucking *dare* say her name!" Smith's voice had a dangerous edge to it.

"I didn't know about her pregnancy; she didn't tell me." Harris was
trying to defend the indefensible, and he felt lower than a rat because
of that.

"That's beside the point, Harris! The point is, you got my *eighteen-
year-old* sister pregnant! You seduced her when she was barely out of
school! And then for ten years, you still acted like *we*—you and I—were
friends! Like everything was still the same. When it wasn't. When there
was *this* between us."

Fuck.

"Not that it makes any difference," Harris muttered, feeling sick
to his stomach, "but I'm in love with her. And if it makes you feel better, the feeling is not reciprocated." His hand crept up to his pendant,
clutching it through the cotton of his T-shirt. "So, if you want me to
suffer, I'm suffering."

Smith was quiet for a long time, the silence punctuated by nothing
but the sound of his angry breathing.

"Good." Smith severed the connection after that single, abruptly
spoken word, and Harris screwed his eyes shut, mourning yet another
loss.

Tina's mother had called shortly after her meeting with the real estate
agent and demanded—because the woman was incapable of making
polite requests—that Tina join her for lunch. Tina had been tempted
to tell her mother to stick her invitation where the sun didn't shine, but
curiosity had won out over indignation, and she'd agreed to lunch at
the house with her mother.

Now she cursed herself for acquiescing to this awkward sham.
She couldn't remember the last time she and her mother had shared
a meal without someone else present. Definitely not since before her

pregnancy. And as she sat facing her freshly Botoxed mother, she futilely tried to gauge how the other woman was feeling.

Serene . . . and slightly startled. That was all she was getting from her mother's shiny, smooth face.

Her mother abruptly spoke into the increasingly strained silence. "After three boys, I was desperate for a daughter. And I was so *happy* when you came along. My precious baby girl. I imagined us doing so many things together. But the older you got, the more apparent it became that we had very little in common."

"Not quite the raving beauty you—"

Her mother interrupted her sharply. "You *stop* that! I was never disappointed in the way you look. Although you can stand to lose a few kilograms, Martine! Let's be honest." Tina rolled her eyes at that but kept her own counsel, waiting for her mother to continue. "You're my daughter. I love you! I was disappointed that you never wanted to go shopping with me or experiment with makeup or do all the mother-daughter things I was expecting us to do."

And the prickly, defensive teen Tina had been had always assumed that her mother's attempts to shop with her or teach her about makeup had been the older woman's way of trying to improve her disappointing daughter. It had never occurred to Tina that maybe it had been her mother's idea of bonding. She stared at her impeccably dressed mother—with her perfectly made-up face and her Botox injections and her discreet cosmetic "improvements"—and felt sudden and complete shame at the way she'd always assumed the worst of the other woman.

"I was naturally disappointed when you got pregnant." Her mother continued to speak after taking a delicate sip of tea. "You were always a marvelous student. I was never that good at school, and I was proud of you. Of your ambition. You would have made an excellent doctor. But a baby, that was something else. You couldn't raise a baby. You were only a baby yourself. You were *my* baby." Despite the absolute lack of expression on her mother's face, Tina was shocked to see the tears in her eyes. There was a wobble in the older woman's voice as she uttered the last two words, and Tina's own eyes flooded with tears.

"I felt like you were ruining your life," her mother continued. "I didn't agree with your decision to keep him, and perhaps I should have been more supportive, but all I wanted was for you to get your life back on track. He was a beautiful baby. But I didn't want to bond with him, because I truly believed he was destined to be someone else's grandchild. What happened was terrible. Your father and I weren't sure how to deal with it, how to deal with your grief. I'll be the first to admit that we handled it wrong. But we *were* saddened by his death, Martine. He was a helpless baby. We wanted more for him. We just didn't want that more to come from *our* baby."

It was the second time her mother had referred to Tina as "her baby," and the words created a little lump of emotion in Tina's throat. And she couldn't seem to swallow past it.

"But after he died, it felt like we'd lost you along with him. You just were never the same. Our clever girl who had so much potential. It's like all that potential died with Fletcher." It was the first time Tina had ever heard her mother refer to him by name, and the lump in her throat expanded. "Your father and I were saddened and disappointed by your resulting lack of drive and ambition. We didn't know how to make it better. And I suppose our concern and our attempts to offer advice probably seemed condescending and critical."

Probably? Considering all the other truly moving revelations, Tina was happy to let that understatement slide. She felt like she was meeting her mother for the very first time, and the lump in her throat was starting to choke her.

Her mother was an unapologetic, controlling snob who had never understood Tina's friendship with Libby and who still tried to dictate every aspect of her adult children's lives, but there was absolutely no doubting her sincerity right now.

"I'm sorry our relationship was never what you wanted it to be," Tina said quietly. "I'm rubbish at shopping—I order all my clothes online."

Her mother offered her the tiniest of smiles. Her Botox guy had really gone overboard today.

"I really do like the fashion sense you've developed over the years, Martine. Making the best of your assets, so to speak. Your dresses and those pencil skirts are very attractive."

"Thank you."

"And I've wanted to tell you for years: you have a glowing, flawless complexion, so your decision to only wear eye makeup and lip gloss is inspired."

"Thanks," Tina said with a slight grin. She understood that her mother had said everything she was ever going to say on the subject of Fletcher, and this was her idea of pleasant small talk. And Tina found that she didn't mind that at all. For the first time in years she felt that she actually had a semblance of a relationship with her mother. And if that meant talking about clothing and makeup, then so be it. She now knew that it came from a place of love and concern. And that was enough for her.

"God, you look gorgeous," Harris said that evening when they met outside his parents' front door. "Why don't we ditch this and just head back to my place for some fun?"

His words were lighthearted, but his eyes and smile were strained. Tina tilted her head as she assessed him.

"What's wrong?" she asked, and he thrust his hands into his jacket pockets. He was wearing a business suit, and she wondered if he had gone into the office after all.

"It's nothing," he said, his voice gruff with suppressed emotion.

"It's not nothing at all. Something happened. Tell me!" she demanded, reaching over to grip his forearm urgently. "Is it Greyson? Did you guys have an argument?"

Harris shook his head, looking conflicted.

"Smith."

Ah. Of course. The youngest of her brothers hadn't returned any of her messages or answered her calls today, and she knew he needed time to process. She *had*, however, received separate calls from Kyle, Conrad, and Dumi, all asking if she needed Harris's ass kicked. Touched by their concern though she was, she had kindly declined their offers. She knew her older brothers had been outraged on her behalf, but to Smith, it had also been the betrayal of a friend. Of a man he considered another brother.

"He'll come around," Tina said, her voice riddled with doubt.

"You don't believe that any more than I do, Bean," Harris said with a half-hearted smile. She put a sympathetic hand on his chest and felt the outline of the pendant nestled between his pecs.

"You're wearing it," she said, changing the subject. "Good."

"I shouldn't," he said with a bitter shake of his head. "I don't deserve it."

"Stop that," she remonstrated, her hand traveling up to his clenched jaw. "*Stop.* It's yours. It's back where it belongs."

He tipped his head toward her hand, his eyes shutting tightly as he nuzzled against her palm.

"I wish I knew . . . ," he began, but he was interrupted when the door swung inward. The Chapmans' maid stood blinking at them in shock, her mouth forming an O of surprise.

"Oh. I'm sorry," she said. "Only, Mrs. Chapman heard cars come up the drive a while ago, but when there was no knock she sent me to check if—"

"That's okay, Clementine," Harris said, stepping away from Tina. Her hand hung suspended for a moment before she dropped it self-consciously to her side. "We were just having a conversation. After you, Tina."

He stepped aside and ushered Tina into the house. The maid scampered away without another word. But Tina barely noticed the woman's disappearance, instead stopping to look around the grand entrance hall of the Chapman home. The place hadn't changed much since she had been there last. She hadn't willingly set foot in the house since that long-ago night. Avoiding—to her parents' dismay—any and all events the Chapmans had hosted after that.

Memories of that night bombarded her. The excitement and giddy elation when Harris had finally seemed to notice her. And the sickening aftermath: all that teenage adoration and devotion doused in an awful instant of horror, pain, and devastation.

Harris stared down at her in concern before seeming to register the reason for her hesitation.

"Shit. Tina . . ." His voice was riddled with guilt and regret, and Tina didn't want all those negative emotions to surface again.

"It's okay, Harris," she said, offering him a tight smile. "I just . . . haven't been here in a while, that's all."

"We can leave."

"We're here now; leaving would be rude. Let's go and say hi to your parents." She took a confident step toward the living room, where she knew the Chapmans liked to enjoy a civilized predinner drink.

Harris should have known coming here would be hard on her. He was an insensitive prick. All these years, and Tina had never once come back to this house. After she had returned from Scotland, Libby had visited her at the Jenson home. And Harris had only seen her at her family's events.

Now here she was, her self-assured stride pausing only once, when she stopped and waited for him to catch up with her.

"You look like a man on his way to face a firing squad," she teased, and he forced himself to smile. "It can't get any worse than the messed-up Jenson family dinner last night."

"I think my mother would die if anything that dramatic ever happened at our dinners." Harris chuckled. "Dad would probably enjoy it—I swear he looks bored to death since his retirement."

Constance and Truman Chapman both seemed puzzled to see Tina show up for dinner with Harris, but they hid it well. They also looked disconcerted by Harris's impressive shiner but appeared to accept his explanation that he'd banged his head at the gym.

The older couple was too proper and polite to ever react with anything so vulgar as horror or shock. Tina was always amazed that Harris came from this family. He had a ready smile and a wicked sense of humor. He wasn't afraid to show emotion, good or bad.

The rest of the Chapmans kept all those messy emotions on lockdown. Tina knew she had issues with her parents, but her parents were nowhere near as bloodless as Harris's. The Jensons *felt* like a family. The Chapmans did not interact like a normal family. It was bizarre. Sitting down to dinner with them felt like sitting through the world's most boring boardroom meeting.

There were polite questions about how Tina's restaurant was faring, talk about Harris's recent trip to Perth, and mundane discussions about household affairs. They still had not found a decent chauffeur since Libby's father had retired. Apparently, they had been through three drivers since he'd left.

It was only as dessert was being served that conversation took a more personal turn.

"Martine," Constance Chapman began in her habitually brisk, no-nonsense voice. "I was wondering if you'd mind taking a care package to Olivia for Clara?"

"Oh. No, of course not. I'll be more than happy to do that for you."

"Greyson sent us a picture this afternoon. She's just cut her first tooth. Can you believe that? At only six months old? Harrison and Greyson both cut theirs at a relatively late eight months old."

Tina stared. She knew she was staring, but she couldn't help herself. She was pretty sure her jaw had dropped too. But seriously? Was this the same woman who not five minutes ago had been boringly telling them of her plans to redo the kitchen?

Constance Chapman was *beaming*. And when Tina's eyes shifted to Truman, he was nodding and smiling along with everything his wife said. Looking for all the world like a doting granddad. She half expected both of them to whip out photographs and point out their granddaughter's many charms.

Her stare cut to Harris, who couldn't quite disguise his grin as he watched his parents. Apparently, Greyson had Skyped them last night while he was babysitting Clara and had held the baby up to the laptop so that her grandparents could see her.

"She recognized our voices—I'm quite certain of that and—"

"She tried to touch the screen," Truman interrupted eagerly, and Constance shot him an irritated glare.

"I was getting to that," she said, allowing impatience to creep into her usually emotionless voice. "And she smiled!"

"We couldn't see the tooth," Truman said, looking and sounding extremely disappointed. "But Greyson told us it was there and then sent the photograph this afternoon."

"I thought you were never going to pick your jaw up off the floor," Harris teased in her hotel room an hour later.

"Seriously," Tina hissed urgently. "Who the hell *were* those people?"

"I know, right? It's the most bizarre thing. They're like . . . *real* grandparents. It's as if somebody flipped a switch in their brains after

Clara was born. They're super boring and emotionless one moment but light up like beacons the second anybody mentions Clara."

"I think that's really sweet," Tina said, and Harris nodded.

"Very sweet," he repeated absently, and Tina, who had been pouring them both a glass of wine, looked up to find him staring at her intently. She had invited him to follow her to her hotel after dinner, and he had done so without argument.

"Why am I here?" he asked, and she handed him his glass of red wine before replying.

"You know why."

"I think maybe I do . . ." He grabbed her hand and tugged her down beside him. "But in case I'm mistaken, why don't you show me?"

Hours later, Tina lay curled up against Harris's body, contentedly circling her forefinger around his pendant.

"What is this, Tina?" Harris knew it was probably best not to ask, but he could not seem to help himself. "What's going on between us?"

"I don't know," she said after a long, thoughtful silence. "I just know that I like spending time with you, Harris. I like doing what we do together. I like . . . *you.*"

Harris remained quiet, considering her words. She *liked* him. He had known that her feelings for him were nowhere near as strong as his were for her. And he thought he had resigned himself to that fact. But hearing her say she *liked* him when she was aware of how much he loved her hurt like hell.

"I signed all the necessary documents this morning, Harris," she said into the silence. "Once my tenant's six-month lease is up, the flat is going on sale."

"That's good," he said absently, his thoughts still churning.

Tina couldn't quite get a read on Harris's emotions. He seemed troubled, and she was very reluctant to utter her next words.

"I'm going home in the morning," she whispered, and he tensed, every muscle in his body going instantly taut.

"Home? Already?"

"Yes. I have a business to get back to. Ricardo called me earlier and begged me to come back soon. They fear that Libby and Greyson are going to kill each other. Perhaps not my brightest idea, leaving both of them in charge. The point is, I have responsibilities, and for once, I'm actually keen to get back to them."

"Right." That curt little *right* that he always seemed to utter when he was under emotional strain. He slid out of bed, leaving her feeling abandoned, and hastily donned his clothing.

"Harris?"

"Sweetheart," he said, the absolute tenderness in his voice making her nervous. "When you go back, I think . . . that should be the end of *this*. Before we define it, before it becomes real and even more complicated. This is your new beginning, Tina. Everything that has happened before now has been dictated by the past. I just . . . I feel like having me around would be like dragging a piece of that past with you."

"Harris." She sat up, hugging a sheet to her chest. "That's not what I want."

"I wasn't there for you before, Tina. I couldn't help you, I couldn't . . ." He paused, clearly frustrated as he tried to find the words to explain why he was threatening to abandon her now, when she finally, truly understood just how much she wanted him around. "I couldn't do the right thing. But I can now. Do you understand?"

She shook her head—of course she didn't understand. How could anybody understand this crazy, misguided attempt at nobility?

"Our time together here and in Riversend . . . it meant everything to me. And I'll cherish it forever."

"But . . ." She scooted out of bed, tripping over the sheet she still clutched to her chest. He was leaving. He was really leaving her again.

"I'm just so damned grateful—" His voice cracked on the word, and he cleared his throat self-consciously. "*Grateful* you allowed me to share part of your life for a short while."

He kissed her. And it terrified her, because it truly felt like goodbye.

"*Harris*, wait! Don't do this to—" The word *us* died on her lips when he turned and left.

He actually *left*. How could he just leave?

Tina stared at her closed door in outraged disbelief.

"What the *hell*?"

Harris could barely see through the haze blurring his vision.

He'd thought they would have more time. A little more time together before the inevitable end.

He had been somewhat committed to this course of action since she'd told him she was selling her flat. But hearing her say that she "liked" him had been the incentive he'd needed to solidify his decision. Their past would always be between them, and the best he could ever hope to get from her was *like* and *affection* and *fondness*. None of the stomach-churning, gut-clenching, heart-racing intense emotions he felt for her.

This was a tough decision, but it was the right one. He was sure of that.

Tina needed to move on with her life. Unencumbered by the past. How could she enjoy a truly fresh start by dragging old weighted-down baggage along with her?

He needed to let the dream of *them* go. For Tina's sake. For his own sake. He finally had the chance to do the right thing. And deep down, he knew this was it. She would fly higher and further without him around to constantly remind her of past failures.

All his life, Harris had believed he was a good guy, a decent guy . . . when in reality, he was weak and blind and made stupid decisions.

He hadn't even realized how much he had been hurting his own brother. All those times he had laughed and talked with Libby. They had had their little in-jokes and nostalgic recollections about things they had done, places they had seen without Grey. He had unintentionally excluded his brother and had never even noticed. He had been a selfish asshole. Blind to what was right in front of him.

He should have gone after Tina ten years ago. He should have found her, apologized to her . . . been there for her. Instead he had delayed that confrontation, like the fucking coward he had always been, while she had been left alone, pregnant and terrified.

Harris had always taken the easy way out. The path of least resistance. But not this time. This time he was making the tough choice, the only decision available to him. And he was leaving Tina alone. To flourish and live her life, unencumbered by his past mistakes.

He just thought . . . they'd have a *little* more time.

He made it to his car and slid behind the steering wheel and then sat there, staring straight ahead. He couldn't bring himself to start the engine and drive away. His hand went to his chest and found his pendant—his crutch—and traced the comforting, smooth contours almost obsessively. Grateful to have it back where it belonged, while simultaneously tempted to yank it from his neck and toss it into the street.

He flung his head back against the headrest of his car seat, thumping the back of his skull against the padding. It hurt, so he did it again. He relished the shock of pain; it effectively blunted the persistent throb of anguish that seemed to have taken up residence in his no longer reliable heart.

"I want you to forgive Harris," Tina told Smith when he finally deigned to answer his phone the following morning. She had been crying all night, hating the way things had ended with Harris. She had kept reaching for the phone, tempted to call him and ask him to come back so that they could figure out how to make things work between them. In the end she had decided against that, respecting his decision, even though—in her heart of hearts—she couldn't bring herself to agree with it. Or even understand it. In the meantime, the least she could do was try to fix this one thing for him. "He only recently learned about Fletcher, and it hit him hard. He's still trying to come to terms with that."

Smith was silent for a moment before sighing. "It's not just about the baby, Tina. He used you. My *sister*. There was a blatant lack of respect, of consideration, for both you and the friendship I shared with him."

"I get that, Smith, and I'm sorry you feel that way. But this isn't about *you*. It was never about you. Harris has been a good friend to you."

"He fucking *hasn't*, not when he's known, for the last ten years, what he did to you."

"I was a consenting adult, and I was on the pill. I thought that would be an effective form of protection, but I miscalculated. Harris did nothing wrong." Smith didn't ever have to learn about that damned bet. Especially since Tina now believed Harris had had very little to do with it.

"Morally—"

"God, Smith," she interrupted, exasperated. "Spare me. I can sleep with whomever the hell I want to. Whether he's your best friend or not."

"Fuck, Tina!" She could practically hear the wince in his voice. "Don't say stuff like that. It weirds me out."

"Well, like it or not, you're going to have to listen. Because I'm quite *fed up* with stubborn men acting like spoiled boys. Your friend needs you. You need him. I'm leaving today, and I'd like to leave knowing two of the men I care most about don't hate each other because of me."

"I don't see why you can't let me hang on to my anger just a little bit longer," he said, using his most reasonable voice on a completely unreasonable comment. Her lips twitched.

"I love you, Smith. Take care of Harris for me. I'll speak to you once I'm back home."

He sighed, the sound heavy.

"Love you, too, sis. Drive safely."

Chapter Sixteen

Letting Tina go was so much easier said than done. She texted him often. Nothing that ever required a response. Just pictures and memes and little stories about her life in Riversend. He never replied, but he couldn't stop himself from reading them either.

And whenever he spoke with Grey—even though Harris never asked about her—his brother would volunteer information about Tina. She was doing well, the restaurant was flourishing, everybody liked her. She had framed pictures of Fletcher on her desk and on her walls at home now.

She was sad. She seemed lonely . . . and even when she smiled, it looked like her heart was breaking.

Fucking Grey.

He was doing to Harris what Harris had done to him all those months ago. Deliberately salting the wound in the hopes that Harris would "come to his senses." But Harris believed he *was* being sensible.

"You're a fucking moron," Grey had told him one night, about a month after Harris had let Tina go. "The woman loves you, you love her. Why are you letting something that happened a decade ago keep you apart?"

"It's not that simple, Grey," Harris said. "We never had a choice back then. What happened between us ten years ago had been manipulated by external forces. She could have done so many amazing things, but that one encounter with me held her back. Stunted her emotional growth. I am the worst thing that ever happened to her, and I wanted her to have her life back."

"Did you give her a choice?" Grey said, and Harris's brow furrowed as he tried to make sense of his brother's words.

"What do you mean?"

"Really, Harris?" Grey sounded exasperated and impatient with him. "You need me to break that question down for you? Did you ask her what *she* wanted? Because ten years ago, she willingly went into that room with you. She didn't ask for anything that happened afterward, that's true . . . but *you* were the one who didn't have a choice back then, Harris. You didn't know that they'd spiked your drink, didn't know that they had forced that bet on you . . . didn't even get to choose when or where you finally got to make love with the girl you'd been pining after for a year. And I get that now you're all about trying to reclaim some of what you both lost back then . . . but you're taking *her* choice away. And, in case you need it spelled out even more, that's exactly what Spade and his merry band of dicks did to you."

Harris felt his jaw go slack at his brother's words, and his mind teemed with confusing thoughts as he tried to process everything Grey had just said.

"I-I . . . don't . . ."

"Harris," Grey interrupted his stammering gently. "You were both victims back then. What was done to you was fucking reprehensible, and if I had that asshole Spade in my sights right now, I'd probably beat him to a pulp. But have you ever considered what would have happened that night if you hadn't been doped? If they hadn't interfered, and if there had been no bet?"

Harris swallowed painfully as he considered his brother's words. And, for the first time since it happened, found himself wondering how that night would have ended for him and Tina if not for Jonah Spade.

He disconnected the call, his mind teeming with images of that night. Some so clear it was as if it had happened just yesterday. Others lost forever in a haze of confusion, fear, and regret.

When he had first seen her that night, he had been unable to take his eyes off her. She had been so vibrantly beautiful in her sparkly red dress. He had made a conscious decision to dance with her—he remembered defiantly thinking that he didn't care what the hell Smith or anyone else had to say about that. He liked her, and he wanted to dance with her.

All of that was so clear to him. He had approached her with his heart on his sleeve, and he had felt like he could conquer the world when she agreed to that dance.

And then someone had offered him a birthday drink.

Jonah. He hadn't "offered" so much as thrust it into his hands as Harris was walking Tina to the patio. And Harris had downed it. Wanting to get the guy out of his face and away from Tina as quickly as possible.

Harris buried his face in his hands as the memories of that night continued to bombard him. How right she had felt in his arms, how perfectly her lips had slotted against his . . . all those powerful emotions. The need, the desire, the affection . . . the absolute certainty that he wanted her. That he would have her, and everybody else be damned.

He had been thinking about *more* than that night. He'd been thinking of a future with her. How they would deal with the distance once he went back to college in the States.

And all that potential had been lost forever because of the awful events that had followed.

"Morning, MJ," the librarian, Mrs. Salie, called as Tina walked down the road toward MJ's. She smiled and waved at the woman.

"Morning, Mrs. Salie. Don't forget to collect those doughnuts for the Books Are Fun story-time session this afternoon," Tina called back, and Mrs. Salie sent her a thumbs-up in acknowledgment.

Tina happily made her way to work, feeling energetic after her regular yoga session with Lia and excited about the new dessert they'd be debuting on their dinner menu tonight. Life was almost perfect . . .

Almost.

It had been a month since she'd put her flat on the market, and Harris hadn't returned a single one of her texts or messages since she'd returned home. And it hurt. More than it probably should have. But she missed him. *So* much.

Every novel experience, every new friendship, every victory or achievement at the restaurant . . . her first instinct—without fail—was to tell Harris. She was looking into purchasing an adorable house farther up the hill, but she was reluctant to make the commitment because she wanted Harris's opinion on it first. It was ridiculous and illogical, but she couldn't seem to make that final decision without talking to him.

And so many things reminded her of him. She couldn't enjoy her porch anymore without missing him, and even a simple cup of coffee had the ability to bring him immediately to mind. Specifically, his excitement and appreciation when she had offered him a mug of her brew.

And then there was Greyson. Who, ever since he'd kept an eye on the restaurant for Tina, had returned to his former surly asshole self. But that didn't stop Tina from jumping a little every time she saw him. For the first time in their history together, she looked at Greyson and thought of Harris. The two had always seemed so different, but now the physical likeness between them was almost too much for Tina to bear. It was hard to look at him—so like Harris and yet so completely different.

"Morning." She murmured a muffled greeting to the staff as she stepped into the restaurant, not wanting to disturb Ricardo's meeting.

She loved the comforting routine of running the restaurant. She knew exactly what needed to be done, and when. The previously daunting task had become a lifesaver; it kept her mind occupied and stopped her from thinking too hard about *why* she missed Harris so much.

She skipped the meeting and headed to her office. She immediately dug her phone out of the bag to check her messages. Smith had sent a pic of his new girlfriend, a pretty brunette named Kelly. Kyle and Dumi had both sent adorable pics of their two-month-old daughter, Pippa Jenson-Sechaba. Tina smiled fondly as she stared at the photos of her brand-new niece. It had taken a while for the couple to finalize everything and to finally adopt their gorgeous daughter, shortly after Tina's return to Riversend. Tina was happy for them and couldn't wait to meet her niece.

She sometimes marveled at how much her attitude toward babies had changed. She had loved finally meeting her three-month-old nephew, Edward—Kitty and Conrad's son—on her last visit home. And she was now happy to babysit Clara, even though she was still not confident enough to do it for more than an hour or two. Small steps that to Tina felt like great leaps.

She still slept with her night-light on, but the last nightmare she'd had was on the night she'd returned to Riversend. She scared the bejesus out of poor Greyson. He demanded a spare key to her house after that, so that he could "wake her the hell up" the next time she screamed bloody murder in the middle of the night. Thankfully, he hadn't had to use the key at all since then.

There was a quick knock on her door, and Libby entered the office without waiting for a response from Tina. She sank into the chair across from Tina's and looked at her for a moment. Libby seemed completely stressed out.

"What's up, Libby? You okay?"

"I'm hoping you could give me a week or so off. I'll prep Agnes and the rest of the kitchen staff to handle things in my absence."

"That's fine. I know things will be handled competently while you're away. I'm more concerned about you. Where are you going?"

Libby sighed and buried her face in her hands. Alarmed, Tina rounded her desk to place a comforting arm around her friend's narrow, shaking shoulders. She propped Libby up and led her to the sofa. They both sat down on the small, lumpy piece of furniture, and Tina led Libby's head down to her shoulder.

She was so shocked by her normally unflappable friend's breakdown that she was momentarily incapable of speaking. Instead, she continued to offer her crying friend unconditional love and support.

After the initial storm had passed, Libby sat up self-consciously and patted her swollen, wet face with her palms. Tina got up and retrieved a box of tissues, handing it to her grateful friend before sitting down beside her again.

"Want to talk about it?"

"I just need a break. I thought I'd take Clara to visit my parents and the Chapmans. I came here to get away from him, but he's just always around." Naturally she didn't have to elaborate on who *he* was. "And I've made stupid mistakes. I've allowed . . . *things* to happen." She blushed, and, once again, no elaboration was needed. "And I can't refuse to let him see Clara—he adores her. But it's not just Clara he wants to see. And I can't . . . I *can't* let him into my heart again."

Tina had her doubts as to whether Greyson had ever really left her friend's heart, but she refrained from saying as much.

"Has he spoken about what *he* wants?" Tina asked carefully, and Libby blew her nose before shaking her head.

"You know that man; he's a frickin' closed book. Who the hell knows what's going on in that head of his? I know he loves Clara, I know he wants me, but that's the extent of it. I'm not settling again, Tina. Never again. Why can't relationships and men and . . . I don't know . . . *life* be uncomplicated? Why does it all have to hurt so much?"

Why, indeed?

Tina wished she had the answers to those questions; maybe then she wouldn't go through every day feeling like she had a huge gaping hole in her heart. She was hemorrhaging her hard-earned happiness through that stupid hole and knew only one thing would fix it.

Harris had come to Jonah Spade's office with the intention of confronting the man about what he had done a decade ago. But Jonah had taken one look at Harris and hugged him like they were long-lost friends before steering him toward one of the overstuffed chairs in front of his desk. He sat on the other one and angled himself to face Harris.

"How the hell are you, buddy?" the man was saying. His effusiveness physically nauseating Harris. He wasn't this man's friend. He had never been his friend. Jonah Spade had always been an acquaintance desperate to be more.

Harris's eyes ran over the guy's office. He had done some checking before coming here and had discovered that Jonah Spade held a low-ranking position in his father's shipping company. Apparently, his father was looking for someone outside of the company to take over once he retired. Jonah enjoyed a lavish lifestyle thanks to his trust fund and only rarely set foot in this office. Spending his days playing golf or at the country club, drinking and chatting up pretty waitresses.

"We should hang out together more often," Spade was saying. "Like in the good old days. When we were kids. Fuck, those were the days, am I right? I mean, Schaeffer and I, we still party . . . lots of parties and lots of pussy. You should join us. Booze, babes, and blow. The good life."

Harris hated this guy; he fucking hated him.

He had come here determined to confront Jonah about what he had done to Harris. To Tina. How he had destroyed their lives for the sake of some childish prank . . . but looking at him now, Harris couldn't believe he had almost allowed this pathetic loser to ruin his future as well as his past.

Jonah Spade and his friends had stolen something precious from both Harris and Tina.

A first time that could have led to a beautiful beginning.

Maybe Fletcher would still have been conceived that night, but Tina wouldn't have been alone. Or possibly Harris—completely lucid— would have used a condom. And Fletcher would only have come years later; maybe then he would have been strong enough for this world. Or perhaps he was always destined to be lost to them. There were endless possibilities . . . and they had all been robbed from Tina and Harris by this little toad of a man.

But Harris could see clearly now: depriving himself of a possible future with Tina would be allowing Jonah Spade and his cohorts to wield so much more power than they deserved.

"You're a fucking loser, Spade," he said, his voice dripping with disdain. And he relished the look of utter shock and confusion on the man's face.

"Now, hold on a goddamned—"

"You're a sad and pathetic little bastard who doesn't deserve a moment more of my consideration."

Harris got up and allowed himself one last look at the guy who had unknowingly influenced his life for so long before he walked out.

He was done with the past. He had a future to get to.

Tina's phone rang just after midnight, while she was brewing a cup of chamomile tea, and she fumbled in her robe pocket for the vibrating device. Her eyes widened when she saw the name on the screen, and she answered immediately.

"Harris."

"Hey, Bean. I figured you'd be up."

Of course she was up; dinner service had ended just an hour ago.

"You've been ignoring my messages," she accused, feeling pissed off and weepy and so damned happy to hear his voice.

"I haven't. I read every single one of them," he said, his voice hushed. "And listened to all your voice notes. I've watched every clip of you and Fletcher about a million times."

"Why?" she asked on a whisper.

"Why? Because I've missed you, Tina. I've missed you so much." His voice was quivering, and Tina chewed at her lower lip. Not sure what to say. "I thought it would be better, for both of us, if we maybe . . . ceased contact for a while."

"*Why?*" She could hear the plaintive note in her voice.

"Because this was supposed to be your fresh start, Bean. How could you have a fresh start with me around?"

"How could I not? You're an important part of my life, Harris." *The most important part.* "I wanted to talk, to figure things out. But before I could say a word, you were dressed and spouting so much self-righteous garbage. And then you were gone. And absolutely *nothing* since then."

"What did you want to talk about, Tina?" he asked, his voice brimming with something that sounded like hope. "What did you want to figure out?"

"Well . . . *us.*"

There was a long, long silence on the other end of the line, and when he spoke again, his voice was choked with emotion.

"And is there still an *us* to talk about?"

"Of course there is, Harris. There will always be an us."

"I'm so damned happy to hear that, Tina. I thought . . . I thought I screwed it all up."

"You nearly did." Tina grabbed a dish towel and mopped up her tears.

"We'll talk about it—about *us*—very soon, okay?"

"We can talk about it . . ."

He hung up, and she ripped her phone from her ear and glared at it, resisting the temptation to fling it at the wall. He had hung up on her. How *dare* he? Why wouldn't he just *talk* to her?

Tears were still seeping down her cheeks, and she glared at her cooling tea, wondering if she should call him back. But she was working herself up into a righteous anger right now, and she told herself that *he* had hung up on her. And if he wanted to talk, he could damned well call back!

Tina cried herself to sleep that night and woke the following morning feeling groggy and exhausted. She dragged herself out of bed, pushed her feet into her fuzzy slippers, and padded into the kitchen for her coffee.

The spring mornings were a lot warmer and more fragrant, with the smell of jasmine scenting the air, than those few mornings she had shared on the porch with Harris. But that didn't make her miss him less. Instead she often wished he were there to enjoy the changing temperature and the spring blossoms with her.

For a second, she contemplated not going out after all. Feeling raw after last night's confusing conversation with Harris. But she shook her head, determined not to let his odd behavior spoil this one perfect moment in her day.

Greyson was sitting on the porch steps, his back to her, and she shut her eyes, not in the mood to see the near-exact physical replica of the man she loved.

It had taken a long time for Tina to admit to that love, but she had come home one night after dinner service, lonely and missing him with everything in her. And it had simply been there: a quiet acknowledgment of the undeniable truth.

Of *course* she loved him. Why else would she miss him so much? Why else would she yearn for his company, the touch of his hands on her body, the whisper of his voice in her ear?

She loved him. She had for a long time . . . and she would for the rest of her life.

For so long she had tried to protect herself from strong emotions, from the pain that loving and losing someone could cause. She had cut herself off from those who cared about her and then believed herself inherently flawed and no longer capable of experiencing true depth of feeling.

But what she hadn't recognized was that all those past experiences—the pain and loss, the humiliation and anguish—had forged her into someone strong enough to love with everything in her.

When she thought of the times Harris had told her he loved her, she felt searing regret that she had believed herself incapable of responding in kind. When all along there had been this wealth of love simmering mere inches below the surface.

She stepped out onto the porch and sat down on her swing.

"Morning, Greyson," she said, hoping he would gather, from her subdued tone of voice, that she was not feeling sociable.

"*Greyson?* Has it really been *that* long, Bean?" Her head jerked up at that unmistakable gruff voice, and her grip on the coffee mug slackened enough for it to list to the side.

"Watch the coffee," he warned sharply, and she jerked her hand upright, fortunately not spilling any of the hot liquid. She thumped the mug down onto the seat and surged to her feet all in one motion.

"*Harris!*" She couldn't keep the absolute shock, wonder, and joy out of her voice, and for a moment all she could do was stare at him as he slowly pushed himself upright before turning fully to face her. The rising sun behind him cast his body into silhouette, and she couldn't read his expression.

She couldn't hide her complete confusion at his unexpected presence on her front porch, not sure what this meant. Her arms crept around her torso as she held herself, longing to go to him but uncertain of his reception after their last phone call.

Harris could barely contain his joy at the sight of her. So familiar and adorable in her pajamas and robe. She looked shocked, unsure, and a little fearful as she hugged herself tightly. He recognized the gesture. She'd been doing it since she was a child, and Harris hadn't realized the significance of it until now.

She was self-soothing. Hugging herself because she rarely allowed others close enough to do it for her. He shook his head. And strode toward her.

That was damned well going to end right now.

Tina watched in shock as Harris closed the distance between them in just a few short steps and wrapped his arms around her without hesitation. He enfolded her in his protective embrace while he whispered soft reassurances into her hair. She burst into happy tears, relishing the closeness. She felt loved and protected and so, so relieved to be in his arms again.

"You're here," she sobbed. "You're here. I've missed you."

"I missed you, too, Bean," he muttered, his voice thick. His arms tightened around her, and for a long moment they simply held each other. Content with just this wonderful moment of intimacy for now.

"You hung up on me," she accused after the initial storm had passed, and he circled his hands around her upper arms before gently moving her away from his body so that he could look into her eyes.

"I didn't want to waste a single moment more on that damned phone. Not when I had such a long drive ahead of me. I needed to leave as soon as possible if I was going to make it in time to watch the sunrise with you."

"You drove? Harris," she rebuked, alarmed at how fast he must have been going to make the drive in just under six hours. "Why didn't you take the helicopter? Did you even stop for any breaks?"

"One or two," he said with a dismissive wave of his hand. "The chopper was reserved for the next twenty-four hours. I didn't want to wait for it—I wanted to get here as fast as possible so that we could continue our conversation. Face-to-face."

"You drove six hours just so that we could complete a conversation we were already having?" she asked in disbelief, and he smiled gently.

"Well, you see, ever since I came to this town way back in July, I've been plagued by this annoying . . . I don't know . . . I suppose I could call it an affliction." He appeared to think about that for a moment before nodding decisively. "Yeah, that works. I've been plagued by this annoying affliction."

"You have?" she asked. Curious and a little concerned. He nodded gravely, hooked an arm around her waist, and led her to the swing. He carefully moved the coffee mug she had abandoned there to the floor before sitting down and tugging her down beside him. "What affliction?"

"I've been the helpless victim of a dumb, seemingly indestructible emotion called hope. Every time I think the fucker has died . . . something resurrects it. Last night . . . all it took was one word."

"What word?" she asked breathlessly, and he smiled into her eyes before reaching out to hook a strand of hair behind her ear. His fingertips trailed down her cheek before wandering down to her chin and tilting it up so that her face angled toward his.

"*Us.*" His voice broke on the word, and his eyes shone with the love he had never been afraid to show her. "Two little letters, but they mean the world to me."

His admission choked her up, and she couldn't quite find the words she needed to say, but he didn't seem to mind. He set the swing into motion and tucked her against his side as they watched the horizon, where the sun had once again gifted them with a painter's palette of spectacular colors.

"I don't want you to leave again," she whispered, her quiet words barely registering above the natural early-morning symphony of crickets, soughing leaves, and the happy song of a pair of nearby turtledoves.

"I have no plans to leave anytime soon. I was trying to do the right thing, Tina. I figured you were starting a new chapter in your life, and there was no place for me in it. I thought that I would hold you back, keep you rooted in the past, and I didn't want that for you."

"Making my decisions for me again, were you?" she asked, and he pinched the bridge of his nose tiredly.

"Yeah. I'm working on changing that about myself," he admitted. "I thought I was being so damned noble, until Grey pointed out that I was robbing you of your choice. And that was the last thing I wanted to do. I tried to do this one selfless thing. But it turns out it wasn't selfless at all—it was stupid and selfish. I was an idiot, I know that. And we can get back to my foolishness later, but right now I'd really rather talk about *us*." He seemed to relish the sound of the word on his tongue. "I love that word. So small, but with such huge life-altering ramifications."

"I told you last night . . . and I tried to tell you that night you left me. I can't imagine a fresh start—a life, really—without you in it. A book needs all its chapters to tell a complete story, Harris. You're an integral part of my story, and I want you in every chapter."

"In what capacity?" he asked warily, and she swallowed, taking one of his large, beautifully veined hands in both of hers and stroking a thumb over the back of it.

"Well, we're pretty good in the sack," she started thoughtfully, and his brow lowered.

"I've noticed," he muttered, clearly not happy with the direction the conversation was taking. "But I don't want just that."

"Let me finish," she said with a mildly impatient glower. "I'm kind of making this up as I go along. Like I was saying . . . we're good in bed, so sex—"

"Lovemaking," he interrupted pointedly, and she smiled before rolling her eyes.

"So *lovemaking* has to be on the list."

"What list?"

"The list I'm never going to finish if you keep interrupting me," she retorted smartly.

He didn't look too impressed with her.

"Tina. Please don't toy with me," he implored, and she lifted his hand to kiss his knuckles.

"I'm not. I'm working on the parameters of our new and improved relationship." A big goofy smile lit up his face at the R-word, and she returned it with one of her own before continuing. "Lovemaking is definitely high up on the must-have list. Oh, and we absolutely need to share every sunrise. Or at least as many of them as possible."

"I vote for every single one of them," he said, and she smiled.

"Done. And we have to do more rainy-weekend binge-watching. And sightseeing. And you get to cook. It's essential to our survival."

He laughed at that.

"We need to decide if this is going to be long distance or—"

"*No,*" he interrupted vehemently. "Definitely not long distance. I can't do long distance, Tina. It would fucking kill me. We'll work something out, but since this has become home to you, I'll look into moving as soon as possible."

"Harris," she whispered, moved by his willingness to uproot his entire life, but she feared he might come to regret spur-of-the-moment, life-altering decisions. "That seems like a huge step, and it's a really big ask. I can't expect you to up and move at a moment's notice. I was thinking baby steps. Maybe weekend visits to start off with."

"I'm a grown-ass man, I don't need baby steps. I know what I want and need," he said dismissively. "And *everything* I need, want, and desire is in this town, Tina. That's damned well worth the move."

"Well," she said, at a complete loss for words. "Um, since this is your relationship, too, you have every right to add to the list."

"I'm not looking for anything short term," he asserted. "If that's what this is about, then it's best to tell me now."

She shook her head dazedly.

"No. Not short term," she murmured, even though she had no real idea what she wanted. All she knew was that she wanted *him*. Like she had always wanted him. That didn't seem like a short-term thing.

"I want you to tell me when you're frightened or anxious or concerned or just plain aggravated with me or anyone else. You're too adept at hiding what you're feeling, and it drives me crazy."

"Only if you do the same."

"No more secrets?"

"None," she promised, before hesitating as she remembered one enormous secret she still had to tell him. "Well . . ."

She looked guilty, and Harris's stomach dropped to the soles of his feet. She was hiding something from him. Again. Things were going much better than he'd ever expected, but now, with that furtive little glance, he felt an all-too-familiar surge of dread as he wondered what she was keeping from him.

"I *do* have another secret." Her eyes dropped to his chest and then back up to his face. "Maybe two."

"Jesus, Tina," he began, but she gave him a reassuring smile.

"They won't be secrets for much longer, I promise. I first wanted to make sure we're on the same page, as far as this relationship business goes."

"No short term?" he reiterated.

"No."

"No secrets?"

"Not for long."

"Lovemaking and not sex?"

"Definitely."

"Every sunrise?"

"And possibly every sunset and as many hours in between as humanly possible," she elaborated, and he swallowed past the huge lump that had formed in his throat before nodding.

"Then we're on the same page."

"Good." She unexpectedly put a hand down the neck of his shirt and tugged his pendant out. And then over his head. She held the heavy silver hoop in her hand and peered down at it.

"You kept it."

"Yes. I almost didn't."

"Why not?"

"Because of what you said when you first discovered I was wearing it."

"Remind me?"

"You said it was a keepsake of the worst night of your life. And I couldn't bear to wear it after that. But then I woke up that morning, and you'd sneaked it on me. And I couldn't bear to take it off."

"Why not?"

"Because it reminds me of you. It always has. Not of that night, but of you. My Tina. And when you put it back on, I thought maybe it would be okay, because you clearly *wanted* me to wear it."

"I *do* want you to wear it; I like the thought of you wearing it. You haven't taken it off since I put it on you, have you?"

"No."

"Oh. So, you haven't really looked at it?" Something in her voice caught his attention, and he dipped his head to the side as he tried to catch her downcast eyes. She was looking at the pendant, turning it round and round between her forefinger and thumb. He stilled the movement of her hand with his and gently removed the hoop from her grasp. He inspected the smooth outer surface carefully, then directed his attention to the tiny initials he knew were engraved in there: *MJ*.

He peered closer. Something was different. It was no longer just the two letters. His breath caught, and his crazy, unpredictable heart stuttered and then stalled completely in his chest.

MJ + HC = FJ

His eyes flooded and embarrassingly overflowed as he stared at the complete engraving.

"When did you . . . ?" He couldn't complete the question. He couldn't even complete a single coherent thought. All he could do was peer at that tiny, perfect little engraving. And he could barely do that through the blur of tears in his eyes.

"I know it's not terribly original, but it's apt. I had it done about a week after you left."

"It's wonderful. God, Tina. It's so damned wonderful." She had taken the one perfect thing to come out of that night and put it on the pendant that she had once referred to with such contempt.

"Why did you do this?"

"Because I wanted you to know that you're important to me. That I value our friendship. That I care about you."

"That you *like* me?" he prompted with a smile, wanting to hear those words again. When she had first said them, they had seemed like a death knell to his dreams of a future with her. But now he saw them as a foundation to build upon. You couldn't love someone without liking them first. So he would take that like and nurture it like a flower . . . hoping it would blossom into love someday.

"No, Harris," she said, her beautiful green eyes somber as they gazed levelly up at him. "I didn't know it then. Or maybe I always knew it. But I think I wanted you to know that I *love* you."

The words staggered him. They confused him. He knew he was supposed to feel joy, elation, all of the good things. After all, she was telling him she loved him, and it was everything he thought he'd always wanted. But all he felt was disappointment.

"You don't love me, Tina," he said, confusion and a little bit of outrage in his voice. "You can't. *How* can you?" There was naked pleading in the last three words. He wanted her to explain it in a way that would convince him, beyond a shadow of a doubt, that she meant what she had said. He was desperate to believe her. But realistically he knew there was absolutely no way there was any truth to her words.

She chewed pensively on her lower lip, looking uncertain, clearly not sure how to handle his blatant disbelief. Her pretty brow furrowed as she seemed to gather her thoughts.

"When I was a silly teen, I had a massive crush on you—you know that." He nodded curtly, not sure where she was going with this but happy to hear her out if it meant finding a way to believe her. "And after . . . that night, I thought I loathed you." He flinched but nodded again. This was familiar territory.

"And recently, as you know, I discovered that really I like you. But I do believe that—no, I *know* that—through it all, I loved you. Always, and likely forever. I love you, Harris. I'm completely in love with you."

"No," he denied gently. "You're not, sweetheart. You didn't. You *don't*. You couldn't have. If you grow to love me at some point in the future, I'd consider myself the luckiest man in the world. And I'm happy to wait for that moment. I'm a patient man; I can wait until I've earned your love. Until I deserve it."

"You do deserve it. You *have* earned it. I love you so much. I admit I didn't know it until very, *very* recently, but once I recognized what I was feeling, I understood that I never really hated you. I *did* go through a period of not liking you, Harris. I know you know that. But I never hated you. How could I possibly hate the father of my child? I looked at him and felt so much overwhelming love. There was no room in my heart for hate."

"I think the love you felt for him made you generously want to include me in the emotion," he said logically, keeping that little fucker *hope* squashed firmly beneath his boot.

"Stop telling me how I feel, Harris," she said impatiently. "You really need to work on that. Add it to the list. 'Harrison will *not* speak for Martine, will not make decisions for Martine, and he will never presume to tell her what she's feeling.' Because, while I'm aware of the fact that I've been a hot frickin' mess for years, I do know my mind—for the most part—and I know my heart. I've been in denial, and distracted by so many other emotions. But not anymore, Harris. My love for you is obvious to me now. So clear and untarnished and as bright as the dawning sun."

His lips twitched, and hope tentatively slid out from beneath his boot.

Once upon a time, in the very recent past, Harrison Chapman had been the type of man who had no time for wishes. He had considered them ridiculous and whimsical.

Now he looked at this woman, with her wayward red curls and her milky complexion peppered with cinnamon freckles, and he found himself wishing. The man who had no time to waste dillydallying over wishes closed his eyes and wished, more than anything in the world, for her words to be true. Wished for her to truly love him.

While his eyes were squeezed shut, he felt her lips on his and smiled. Her hands slid up, one to his chest and the other to cup his jaw, and he for damned sure *felt* loved.

He opened his eyes and drew his head back to look at her; his little buddy *hope* crept up to his chest and crawled into his heart, taking up permanent residence next to the newly reawakened *joy*.

"Tell me again," he pleaded, and she smiled. The same hope and joy that were so contentedly snuggling in his heart echoed in that beautiful smile. She leaned forward, her hand curling into the hair at the nape of his neck, and maintained eye contact as she told him what he wanted to hear, the truth shining in her eyes like a beacon.

"I love you, Harris. Then. Now. *Forever.*"

He believed her. She could tell from the way the tension left his body and, of course, from the radiant smile that completely transformed his face from anxious to relieved.

"Then . . ." He began to speak, but his voice was croaky, and he stopped to clear his throat while slipping his precious pendant back over his head. He took her hand, seeming to need some kind of contact between them. "Then you'll marry me?"

She laughed and lovingly traced the veins on the back of his hand.

"You really don't believe in those baby steps, do you?"

"I'm an 'all or everything' kind of guy."

"That's 'all or nothing,'" she corrected, and he lifted her hand to kiss her palm.

"I know what it is, but since *nothing* isn't in the equation, I had to amend the saying. And I can't help but notice that you haven't answered my question."

"Pushy man," she said with a gentle smile. "Why don't we buy a house first? I have a place in mind."

"Hill or beach?"

"Hill. Panoramic views and all that. I didn't want to make a decision until you had seen it."

"*Really?*" He looked ridiculously pleased by that information, and her smile widened.

"Yes. I think I always knew it would be *our* house rather than mine alone."

"Big enough for kids?" The question was wary and emerged on a hesitant breath. He watched her closely, and Tina's smile slipped just a fraction as she shifted her gaze to the sparkling ocean. He cupped her jaw with his free hand, his large thumb stroking across her cheekbone as he patiently waited for her to speak.

"You want children?"

"I'd like a couple. But I'll understand if-if you're unable to make that decision right away. It's not essential. Spending my life with you is most important. Anything else is just bonus content."

She smiled, her eyes still captivated by the ocean, caught up in her memories of Fletcher, the love, the fear, the loss. The absolute elation she had felt whenever she held him close. Harris said nothing further, all patience, even while she felt the tension coming off him in waves.

"Maybe we'll have twins," she breathed. "I think I'd like twins."

When she looked at him again, she saw that his eyes were bright with unshed tears of sheer joy combined with relief, and she leaned forward to kiss him.

"You're sure?" he asked.

"Well, I won't mind if they come in singles either. But . . . maybe I'll need to see someone, a therapist, to help me with any residual anxiety at the thought of being around babies."

He nodded. He reached for one of her hands and gave it a squeeze. "Anything you need, Tina. I'll be there for you."

She smiled, heartened by his unconditional support.

"But first the house," she said.

"Then marriage."

"Eventually," she cautioned, and he huffed impatiently.

"We don't need to rush," she said, finding his pique endearing. "I love you. That's not going to change. I just want to enjoy being with you for a while."

"I think, because I feel like I've loved you forever, finally knowing that you return my feelings makes me want *all* the good stuff. All at once. Right now. I've waited for you for so long, Tina. *So* fucking long, and maybe I'm a little terrified that you'll slip away from me again. So, I guess I want as many ties between us as humanly possible, to make sure that doesn't happen. I want everyone to know about us. I want them to know who has my heart."

God, *this* man! He was truly wonderful, and Tina could not fathom how she had not recognized that sooner.

"We could do that Facebook relationship-status thing?" she suggested lightheartedly, and he shot her a mock glare.

"I'm serious," he chastised, and she bit back a smile.

"Okay. Hold on. *Greyson!*" she shouted, and he winced at the volume in her voice. The front door to Greyson's house opened almost immediately, leading Tina to wonder if the man had been hovering right by the door.

"Yeah?" He sounded disgruntled but looked almost amused.

"So, I'm in love with your brother. And he's in love with me. We're together. We'll probably get married someday. Harris wants the world to know, so I thought we'd start with you."

Greyson's eyes softened and drifted to Harris.

"That's truly fantastic," he said, genuine warmth in his voice. He looked happy, if a little melancholy. "And, if I may say so, about damned time. Be happy."

"Yeah," Harris said, his voice quiet as he dipped his head to kiss Tina's sensitive neck. "I think we will be."

"*Right.* I think . . . I'll head out for a drive," the other man said awkwardly. Neither of them heard him or noticed when he shut the door and made his way down the porch stairs to his car. They were too wrapped up in each other.

"How's that for a start?" Tina asked.

"It'll do for now. But after I make love to you the way I'm aching to, we're doing the Facebook thing."

She laughed at his deadpan expression and crawled into his lap. The swing rocked alarmingly at the sudden movement.

"I absolutely one hundred percent adore you, Harrison Chapman."

His arms wrapped around her waist, and he hugged her close, burying his nose in her hair and inhaling deeply, as if he relished the scent of her.

"I don't know what I did in this world to deserve you, Tina. But I'm so damned grateful for you. I love you."

They kissed, and the pieces that had once felt irreparably broken within Tina shifted gently, like restless butterflies, as they rearranged to shape a new whole. A more beautiful and stronger whole.

With Harris by her side, Tina finally felt complete again.

Five Hours Later, on Facebook:

Martine Jenson
Just now
Got engaged to Harrison Chapman
Today

About the Author

Natasha Anders was born in Cape Town, South Africa. She spent nine years working as an assistant English teacher in Niigata, Japan, where she became a legendary karaoke diva. Now back in Cape Town, she lives with her opinionated budgie, Oliver; her temperamental Chihuahua, Maia; her moody budgie, Baxter; and the latest addition to the family, sweet little Hana the Chihuahua. Readers can connect with her through her Facebook page, on Twitter at @satyne1, or at www.natashaanders.com.